The Tycoon's Pregnant Mistress
by Maya Banks

"Who are you?" she asked.

He was a dominating presence. Tall, lithe, dangerously intent as his amber eyes stared back at her. He wasn't American.

His gaze dropped to the hand she had cupped protectively over her abdomen. "Our baby is fine," he said. "I am Chrysander Anetakis. Your fiancé."

She searched his face for the truth, but he looked back at her, calm, no hint of emotion.

He was someone she had been intimate with. Obviously in love with. They were engaged and she was pregnant with his child. Shouldn't that stir something in her?

"I don't remember," she said, her voice cracking.

"You will," he said, those amber eyes boring into hers.

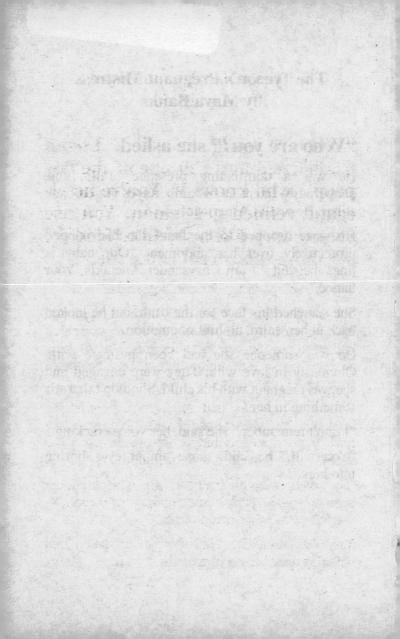

To Tame Her Tycoon Lover
by Ann Major

"You're living a lie, Logan Claiborne, and I'm one of the few people who knows it. You're no elegant, refined gentleman. You use your money like a shield to fend off anything that's real...like me."

"Do the smart thing for once. Just leave."

"Or you'll what?" When she licked her mouth, making her lower lip shine wetly, something that had been wound too tight for nine damn years snapped inside him, unleashing a force he would have denied with every breath in his body.

With a suddenness that startled them both, his hard arms circled her and then crushed her against him. "You shouldn't have come back here. You shouldn't have messed with me again."

"So, you *do* want me...a little," she whispered, her musical voice a husky taunt against his throat. "Is that why you're so afraid of me?"

Yes, she was right. He wanted her naked and writhing underneath him again.

Available in July 2010
from Mills & Boon® Desire™

THE TYCOON'S
PREGNANT
MISTRESS
BY
MAYA BANKS

TO TAME HER
TYCOON LOVER
BY
ANN MAJOR

™ MILLS & BOON®

First published in Great Britain 2010
Harlequin Mills & Boon Limited,
Eton House, 18-24 Paradise Road, Richmond, Surrey TW9 1SR

The publisher acknowledges the copyright holders of the
individual works as follows:

The Tycoon's Pregnant Mistress © Maya Banks 2009
To Tame Her Tycoon Lover © Ann Major 2009

ISBN: 978 0 263 88174 5

51-0710

Harlequin Mills & Boon policy is to use papers that are natural, renewable
and recyclable products and made from wood grown in sustainable forests.
The logging and manufacturing processes conform to the legal environmental
regulations of the country of origin.

Printed and bound in Spain
by Litografia Rosés S.A., Barcelona

THE TYCOON'S PREGNANT MISTRESS

BY
MAYA BANKS

Dear Reader,

The *Tycoon's Pregnant Mistress* launches a trilogy about the Anetakis brothers, Chrysander, Theron and Piers. In this story we meet Marley Jameson, who is struggling to remember a past she had with the handsome and enigmatic CEO of Anetakis International, while Chrysander comes to terms with her supposed betrayal.

As much as Chrysander would like to distance himself from the mother of his unborn child, he finds himself inexorably drawn to Marley. How can he love a woman who tried to destroy him? And what happens when she remembers all that she has forgotten?

These questions form the cornerstone of this emotional story about betrayal, love and ultimate forgiveness. I hope you'll enjoy Marley and Chrysander's road to happily ever after!

Maya Banks

PS Be sure to look for the next THE ANETAKIS TYCOONS book this September.

Maya Banks has loved romance novels from a very (very) early age and, almost from the start, she dreamed of writing them as well. In her teens, she filled countless notebooks with over-dramatic stories of love and passion. Today her stories are only slightly less dramatic, but no less romantic.

She lives in Texas with her husband and three children and wouldn't contemplate living anywhere other than the South. When she's not writing, she's usually hunting, fishing or playing poker. She loves to hear from readers and she can be found online at either www.mayabanks. com or www.writemindedblog.com, or you can e-mail her at maya@mayabanks.com.

To Marty Matthews and Shara Cooper. That bar conversation at RT 2007 was the first kick in the behind to do something about my long-standing dream of writing for Desire™. I still remember that gush-fest fondly.

To Roberta, for saying, "Let's do it" when I outlined my career goals in the summer of 2007. Hey, we did it!

To Amy: You of all people know how much I love category and just how excited I was to be given a chance to write it. Thanks for being just as thrilled as I was.

To Dee, who I think wanted this for me as much as I did and was with me every step of the way. Thank you!

And finally to Steph, who started it all for me. Without you, I wouldn't have written *The Tycoon's Pregnant Mistress* and I wouldn't have submitted. It was that phone call that started everything in motion. I'll always love you for that.

One

Pregnant.

Despite the warmth of the summer day, an uncomfortable chill settled over Marley Jameson's skin as she settled on the bench in the small garden just a few blocks from the apartment she shared with Chrysander Anetakis.

She shivered even as the sun's rays found her tightly clenched fingers, the heat not yet chasing away the goose bumps. Stavros wouldn't be happy over her brief disappearance. Neither would Chrysander when Stavros reported that she hadn't taken proper security measures. But dragging along the imposing guard to her doctor's appointment hadn't been an option. Chrysander would have known of her pregnancy before she could even return home to tell him herself.

How would he react to the news? Despite the fact they'd taken precautions, she was eight weeks pregnant. The best she could surmise, it had happened when he'd returned from an extended business trip overseas. Chrysander had been insatiable. But then so had she.

A bright blush chased the chill from her cheeks as she remembered the night in question. He had made love to her countless times, murmuring to her in Greek—warm, soft words that had made her heart twist.

She checked her watch and grimaced. He was due home in a few short hours, and yet here she sat like a coward, avoiding the confrontation. She still had to change out of the faded jeans and T-shirt, clothes she wore only when he was away.

With reluctance born of uncertainty, she forced herself to her feet and began the short walk to the luxurious building that housed Chrysander's apartment.

"You're being silly," she muttered under her breath as she neared the entry. If the doorman was surprised to see her on foot, he didn't show it, though he did hasten to usher her inside.

She stepped onto the lift and smoothed a hand over her still-flat stomach. Nervousness scuttled through her chest as she rode higher. When it halted smoothly and the doors opened into the spacious foyer of the penthouse, Marley nibbled on her lip and left the elevator.

She walked into the living room, shedding her shoes as she made her way to the couch, where she tossed her bag down. Fatigue niggled at her muscles, and all she really wanted to do was lie down. But she had to determine how to broach the subject of their relationship with Chrysander.

A few days ago, she would have said she was perfectly content, but the results of today's blood tests had her shaken. Had her reflecting on the last six months with Chrysander.

She loved him wholeheartedly, but she wasn't entirely sure where she stood with him. He seemed devoted when he was with her. The sex was fantastic. But now she had a baby to think about. She needed more from the man she loved than hot sex every few weeks as his schedule permitted.

She trudged into the large master suite and started when Chrysander walked from the bathroom, just a towel wrapped around his waist.

A slow smile carved his handsome face. Every time she laid

eyes on him, it was like the first time all over again. Goose bumps raced across her skin, lighting fire to her every nerve-ending.

"Y-you're early," she managed to get out.

"I've been waiting for you, *pedhaki mou,*" he said huskily.

He let the towel drop, and she swallowed as her eyes tracked downward to his straining erection. He paced forward predatorily, closing rapidly in on her. His hands curved over her shoulders, and he bent to ravage her mouth.

A soft moan escaped her as her knees buckled. He was an addiction. One she could never get enough of. He had only to touch her, and she went up in flames.

His mouth traveled down her jawline to her neck, his fingers tugging impatiently at her shirt. Of their own accord, her fingers twisted in his dark hair, pulling him closer.

Hard, lean, muscled. A gleaming predator. He moved gracefully, masterfully playing her body like a finely tuned instrument.

She clutched at his neck as he lowered her to the bed.

"You have entirely too many clothes on," he murmured as he shoved her shirt up and over her head.

She knew they should stop. They needed to talk, but she'd missed him. Ached for him. And maybe a part of her wanted this moment before things changed irrevocably.

He released her bra, and she gasped when his fingers found her highly sensitized nipples. They were darker now, and she wondered if he'd notice.

"Did you miss me?"

"You know I did," she said breathlessly.

"I like to hear you say it."

"I missed you," she said, a smile curving her lips.

It shouldn't have surprised her that he made quick work of her clothing. He tossed her jeans across the room. Her bra went one way, her underwear the other. Then he was over her, on her, deep inside her.

She arched into him as he possessed her, clinging to him as he made love to her, their passion hot and aching. It was always like this. One step from desperation, their need for each other all consuming.

As he gathered her in his arms, he whispered to her in Greek. The words fell against her skin like a caress as they both reached their peaks. She snuggled into his body, content and sated.

She must have slept then, because when she opened her eyes, Chrysander was lying beside her, his arm thrown possessively over her hip. He regarded her lazily, his golden eyes burning with sated contentment.

Now was the time. She needed to broach the subject. There would never be a better occasion. Why did the thought of asking him about their relationship strike terror in her heart?

"Chrysander," she began softly.

"What is it?" he asked, his eyes narrowing. Had he heard the worry in her voice?

"I wanted to talk to you."

He stretched his big body and pulled slightly away so he could see her better. The sheet slid down to his hip and gathered there. She felt vulnerable and exposed and trembled when he slid his hand over the peak of one breast.

"What is it you want to talk about?"

"Us," she said simply.

His eyes grew wary and then became shuttered. His face locked into a mask of indifference, one that frightened her. She could feel him pulling away, mentally withdrawing from her.

A buzz sounded, startling her. Chrysander cursed under his breath and reached over to push the intercom.

"What," he demanded tersely.

"It's Roslyn. Can I come up?"

Marley stiffened at the sound of his personal assistant's voice. It was late in the evening and yet here she was, popping into the apartment she knew he shared with Marley.

"I'm very busy at the moment, Roslyn. Surely it can wait until I come into the office tomorrow."

"I'm sorry, sir, but it can't. I need your signature on a contract that's due by 7:00 a.m."

Again Chrysander swore. "Come then."

He swung his legs over the side of the bed and stood. He strode toward the polished mahogany wardrobe and pulled out slacks and a shirt.

"Why does she show up here so often?" Marley asked quietly.

Chrysander shot her a look of surprise. "She's my assistant. It's her job to keep up with me."

"At your personal residence?"

He shook his head as he buttoned up his shirt. "I'll return in a moment, and we can have our talk."

Marley watched him go, her chest aching all the more. She was tempted to save the discussion for another night, but she had to tell him of her pregnancy, and she couldn't tell him of the baby before she knew how he felt about her. What he thought of their future. So it had to be done tonight.

As the moments grew longer, her anxiety heightened. Not wanting the disadvantage of being nude, she rose from the bed and dragged on her jeans and shirt. So much for looking composed and beautiful. She shook her head ruefully.

Finally she heard his footsteps outside the bedroom suite. He walked in with a distracted frown on his face. His gaze flickered over her, and his lips twitched.

"I much prefer you naked, *pedhaki mou*."

She gave a shaky smile and moved back to the bed. "Is everything all right with work?"

He waved his hand dismissively. "Nothing that shouldn't have already been taken care of. A missing signature." He stalked toward the bed, a lean, hungry glint in his eyes. As he came to a stop a foot away from where she sat, he reached for the buttons on his shirt.

"Chrysander…we must talk."

Annoyance flickered across his face, but then he gave a resigned sigh. He sank down on the bed next to her. "Then speak, Marley. What is it that's bothering you?"

His closeness nearly unhinged her. She scooted down the bed in an effort to put distance between them. "I want to know how you feel about me, how you feel about us," she began nervously. "And if we have a future."

She glanced up to check his reaction. His lips came together in a firm line as he stared back at her. "So it's come to this," he said grimly.

He stood and turned his back to her before finally rotating around to face her.

"Come to w-what? I just need to know how you feel about me. If we have a future. You never speak of us in anything but the present," she finished lamely.

He leaned in close to her and cupped her chin. "We don't have a relationship. I don't do relationships, and you know this. You're my mistress."

Why did she feel as though he'd just slapped her? Her mouth fell open against his hand, and she stared up at him with wide, shocked eyes.

"Mistress?" she croaked. Live-in lover. Girlfriend. Woman he was seeing. These were all terms she might have used. But mistress? A woman he bought? A woman he paid to have sex with?

Nausea welled in her stomach.

She pushed his hand away and stumbled up, backpedaling away from him. Confusion shone on Chrysander's face.

"Is that truly all I am to you?" she choked out, still unable to comprehend his declaration. "A m-mistress?"

He sighed impatiently. "You're distraught. Sit down and let me get you something to drink. I've had a trying week, and you are obviously unwell. It benefits neither of us to have this discussion right now."

Chrysander urged her back to the bed then strode out of the suite toward the kitchen. After a long week of laying traps for the person attempting to sell his company out from under him, the last thing he wanted was a hysterical confrontation with his mistress.

He poured a glass of Marley's favorite juice then prepared himself a liberal dose of brandy. The beginnings of a headache were already plaguing him.

He smiled when he saw Marley's shoes in the middle of the

floor where she'd left them as soon as she'd come off the elevator. He followed the trail of her things to the couch where her bag was thrown haphazardly.

She was a creature of comfort. Never fussy. So this emotional outburst had caught him off guard. It was completely out of character for her. She wasn't clingy, which is why their relationship had lasted so long. Relationship? He'd just denied to her that they had one. She was his mistress.

He should have softened his response. She probably wasn't feeling well and needed tenderness from him. He winced at the idea, but she'd always been there ready to soothe him after weeks of business trips or tedious meetings. It was only fair that he offer something more than sex. Though sex with her was high on his list of priorities.

He turned to go back into the bedroom and try to make amends when the piece of paper sticking out of Marley's bag caught his eye. He stopped and frowned then set the drinks down on the coffee table.

Dread tightened his chest. It couldn't be.

He reached out to snag the papers, yanked them open as anger, hot and volatile, surged in his veins. Marley, *his* Marley, was the traitor within his company?

He wanted to deny it. Wanted to crumple the evidence and throw it away. But it was there, staring him in the face. The false information he'd planted just this morning in hopes of finding the person selling his secrets to his competitor had been taken by Marley. She hadn't wasted any time.

Suddenly everything became clear. His building plans had started disappearing about the time that Marley had moved in to the penthouse. She'd worked for his company, and even after he'd convinced her to quit so that her time would be his alone, she still had unimpeded access to his offices. What a fool he'd been.

Stavros's call to him hours earlier stuck in his mind like a dagger. At the time, it had only registered a mild annoyance with him, a matter he'd planned to take up with Marley when he saw her. He'd lecture her about being careless, about being safe, when in fact, it was him who wasn't safe with her. She'd gone to his office then disappeared for several hours. And now documents from his office had appeared in her purse.

The papers fisted in his hand, he stalked back to the bedroom to see Marley still sitting on the bed. She turned her tear-stained face up to him, and all he could see was how deftly she'd manipulated him.

"I want you out in thirty minutes," he said flatly.

Marley stared at him in shock. Had she heard him correctly? "I don't understand," she choked out.

"You have thirty minutes in which to collect your things before I call security to escort you out."

She shot to her feet. How could things have gone so wrong? She hadn't even told him about her pregnancy yet. "Chrysander, what's wrong? Why are you so angry with me? Is it because I reacted so badly to you calling me your mistress? It came as a great shock to me. I thought somehow I meant more to you than that."

"You now have twenty-eight minutes," he said coldly. He held up a hand with several crumpled sheets of paper in them. "How did you think you'd get away with it, Marley? Do you honestly think I would tolerate you betraying me? I have no tolerance for cheats or liars, and you, my dear, are both."

All the blood left her face. She wavered precariously, but he made no move to aid her. "I don't know what you're talking about. What are those papers?"

His lips curled into a contemptuous sneer. "You stole from me. You're lucky that I'm not phoning the authorities. As it is, if I ever see you again, I'll do just that. Your attempts could have crippled my company. But the joke is on you. These are fakes planted by me in an attempt to ferret out the culprit."

"Stole?" Her voice rose in agitation. She reached out and yanked the papers from his hand. The words, schematics, blurred before her eyes. An internal e-mail, printed out, obviously from his company ISP address, stared back at her. Sensitive information. Detailed building plans for an upcoming bid in a major international city. Photocopies of the drawings. None of it made sense.

She raised her head and stared him in the eye as her world crumbled and shattered around her. "You think I stole these?"

"They were in your bag. Don't insult us both by denying it now. I want you out of here." He made a show of checking his watch. "You now have twenty-five minutes remaining."

The knot in her throat swelled and stuck, rendering her incapable of drawing a breath. She couldn't think, couldn't react. Numbly, she headed for the door with no thought of collecting her things. She only wanted to be away. She paused and put her hand on the frame to steady herself before turning around to look back at Chrysander. His face remained implacable. The lines around his mouth and eyes were hard and unforgiving.

"How could you think I'd do something like that?" she whispered before she turned and walked away.

She stumbled blindly into the elevator, quiet sobs ripping from her throat as she rode it down to the lobby level. The doorman looked at her in concern and offered to get her into a cab. She waved him off and walked unsteadily down the sidewalk and into the night.

The warm evening air blew over her face. The tears on her cheeks chilled her skin, but she paid them no heed. He would listen to her. She would make him. She'd give him the night to calm down, but she would be heard. It was all such a dreadful mistake. There had to be some way to make him see reason.

In her distress, she took no notice of the man following her. When she reached the curb, a hand shot out and grasped her arm. Her cry of alarm was muffled as a cloth sack was yanked over her head.

She struggled wildly, but just as quickly, she found herself stuffed into the backseat of a vehicle. She heard the door slam and the rumble of low voices, and then the vehicle drove away.

Two

Three months later

Chrysander sat in his apartment brooding in silence. He should have some peace of mind now that there was no longer any danger to his company, but the knowledge of why was hardly comforting. He stared at the pile of documents in front of him as the evening news droned in the background.

His stopover in New York was going to be short. Tomorrow he'd fly to London to meet with his brother Theron and have the groundbreaking ceremony for their luxury hotel—a hotel that wouldn't have happened if Marley had gotten her way. A derisive snort nearly rolled from his throat. He, the CEO of Anetakis International, had been manipulated and stolen from by a woman. Because of her, he and his brothers had lost two of their designs to their closest competitor before he'd discovered her betrayal. He should have turned her over to the authorities, but he'd been too stunned, too *weak* to do such a thing.

He hadn't even ridded his apartment of her belongings. He'd assumed she'd return to collect them, and maybe a small part of him had hoped she would so he could confront her again and ask her why. On his next trip back, he'd see to the task. It was time to have her out of his mind completely.

When he heard her name amidst the jumble of his thoughts, he thought he'd merely conjured it from his dark musings, but when he heard Marley Jameson's name yet again, he focused his angry attention on the television.

A news reporter stood outside a local hospital, and it took a few moments for the buzzing in Chrysander's ears to stop long enough for him to comprehend what was being said. The scene changed as they rolled footage taken earlier of a woman being taken out of a rundown apartment building on a stretcher. He leaned forward, his face twisted in disbelief. It was Marley.

He bolted from his desk and fumbled for the remote to turn the volume up. So stunned was he that he only comprehended every fourth word or so, but he heard enough.

Marley had been abducted and now rescued. The details on the who and why were still sketchy, but she'd endured a long period of captivity. He tensed in expectation that somehow his name would be linked to hers, but then why should it? Their relationship had been a highly guarded secret, a necessary one in his world. His wish for privacy was one born of desire and necessity. Only after her betrayal had he been even more relieved by the circumspection he utilized in all his relationships. She'd made a fool of him, and only the knowledge that the rest of the world didn't know soothed him.

As the camera zoomed in on her pale, frightened face, he felt something inside him twist painfully. She looked the same as she had the night he'd confronted her with her deception. Pale, shocked and vulnerable.

But what the reporter said next stopped him cold, even as an uneasy sensation rippled up his spine. He reported mother *and* child being listed in stable condition and that Marley's apparent captivity had not harmed her pregnancy. The reporter offered only the guess that she appeared to be four or five months along. Other details were sketchy. No arrests had been made, as her captors had escaped.

"Theos mou," he murmured even as he struggled to grasp the implications.

He stood and reached for his cellular phone as he strode from his apartment. When he broke from the entrance of the well-secured apartment high-rise, his driver had just pulled around.

Once inside the vehicle, he again flipped open his phone and called the hospital where Marley had been taken.

"Her physical condition is satisfactory," the doctor informed Chrysander. "However, it is her emotional state that concerns me."

He simmered impatiently as he waited for the physician to complete his report. Chrysander had burst into the hospital, demanding answers as soon as he'd walked onto the floor where Marley was being treated. Only the statement that he was her fiancé had finally netted him any results. Then he'd immediately had her transferred to a private room and had insisted that a specialist be called in to see her. Now he had to wade through the doctor's assessment of her condition before he could see her.

"But she hasn't been harmed," Chrysander said.

"I didn't say that," the doctor murmured. "I merely said her physical condition is not serious."

"Then quit beating around the bush and tell me what I need to know."

The doctor studied him for a moment before laying the clipboard down on his desk. "Miss Jameson has endured a great trauma. I cannot know exactly how great, because she cannot remember anything of her captivity."

"What?" Chrysander stared at the doctor in stunned disbelief.

"Worse, she remembers nothing before. She knows her name and little else, I'm afraid. Even her pregnancy has come as a shock to her."

Chrysander ran a hand through his hair and swore in three languages. "She remembers nothing? Nothing at all?"

The doctor shook his head. "I'm afraid not. She's extremely vulnerable. Fragile. Which is why it's so important that you do not upset her. She has a baby to carry for four more months and an ordeal from which to recover."

Chrysander made a sound of impatience. "Of course I would do nothing to upset her. I just find it hard to believe that she remembers nothing."

The doctor shook his head. "The experience has obviously been very traumatic for her. I suspect it's her mind's way of protecting her. It's merely shut down until she can better cope with all that has happened."

"Did they…" Chrysander couldn't even bring himself to complete the question, and yet he had to know. "Did they hurt her?"

The doctor's expression softened. "I found no evidence that she had been mistreated in any way. Physically. There is no way to find out all she has endured until she is able to tell us. And we must be patient and not press her before she is ready. As I said, she is extremely fragile, and if pressed too hard, too fast, the results could be devastating."

Chrysander cursed softly. "I understand. I will see to it that she has the best possible care. Now can I see her?"

The doctor hesitated. "You can see her. However, I would caution you not to be too forthcoming with the details of her abduction."

A frown creased Chrysander's brow as he stared darkly at the physician. "You want me to lie to her?"

"I merely don't want you to upset her. You can give her details of her life. Her day-to-day activities. How you met. The mundane things. It is my suggestion, however, and I've conferred with the hospital psychiatrist on this matter, that you not rush to give her the details of her captivity and how she came to lose her memory. In fact, we know very little, so it would be unwise to speculate or offer her information that could be untrue. She must be kept calm. I don't like to think of what another upset could cause her in her current state."

Chrysander nodded reluctantly. What the doctor said made sense, but his own need to know what had happened to Marley was pressing. But he wouldn't push her if it would cause her or the baby any harm. He checked his watch. He still had to meet with the authorities, but first he wanted to see Marley and said as much to the doctor.

The physician nodded. "I'll have the nurse take you up now."

Marley struggled underneath the layers of fog surrounding her head. She murmured a low protest when she opened her eyes. Awareness was not what she sought. The blanket of dark, of oblivion, was what she wanted.

There was nothing for her in wakefulness. Her life was one black hole of nothingness. Her name was all that lingered in the confusing layers of her mind. Marley.

She searched for more. Answers she needed to questions that swarmed her every time she wakened. Her past lay like a great barren landscape before her. The answers dangled beyond her, taunting her and escaping before she could reach out and take hold.

She turned her head on the thin pillow, fully intending to slip back into the void of sleep when a firm hand grasped hers. Fear scurried up her spine until she remembered that she was safe and in a hospital. Still, she yanked her hand away as her chest rose and fell with her quick breaths.

"You must not go back to sleep, *pedhaki mou*. Not yet."

The man's voice slid across her skin, leaving warmth in its wake. Carefully, she turned to face this stranger—or was he? Was he someone she knew? Who knew her? Could he be the father of the child nestled below her heart?

Her hand automatically felt for her rounded belly as her gaze lighted on the man who'd spoken to her.

He was a dominating presence. Tall, lithe, dangerously intent as his amber eyes stared back at her. He wasn't American. She nearly laughed at the absurdity of her thoughts. She should be demanding to know who he was and why he was here, and yet all she could muster was the knowledge that he wasn't American?

"Our baby is fine," he said as his gaze dropped to the hand she had cupped protectively over her abdomen.

She tensed as she realized that he was indeed staking a claim. Shouldn't she know him? She reached for something, some semblance of recognition, but unease and fear were all she found.

"Who are you?" she finally managed to whisper.

Something flickered in those golden eyes, but he kept his expression neutral. Had she hurt him with the knowledge she didn't know him? She tried to put herself in his position. Tried to imagine how she'd feel if the father of her baby suddenly couldn't remember her.

He pulled a chair to the side of the bed and settled his large frame into it. He reached for her hand, and this time, despite her instinct to do so, she didn't retract it.

"I am Chrysander Anetakis. Your fiancé."

She searched his face for the truth of his words, but he looked back at her calmly, with no hint of emotion.

"I'm sorry," she said and swallowed when her voice cracked. "I don't remember...."

"I know. I've spoken to the doctor. What you remember isn't important right now. What is important is that you rest and recover so that I can take you home."

She licked her lips, panic threatening to overtake her. "Home?"

He nodded. "Yes, home."

"Where is that?" She hated having to ask. Hated that she was lying here conversing with a complete stranger. Only apparently he wasn't. He was someone she had been intimate with. Obviously in love with. They were engaged, and she was pregnant with his child. Shouldn't that stir something inside her?

"You're trying too hard, *pedhaki mou*," he said softly. "I can see the strain on your face. You mustn't rush things. The doctor said that it will all come back in time."

She clutched his hand then looked down at their linked fingers. "Will it? What if it doesn't?" Fear rose in her chest, tightening her throat uncomfortably. She struggled to breathe.

Chrysander reached out a hand to touch her face. "Calm yourself, Marley. Your distress does you and the baby no good."

Hearing her name on his lips did odd things. It felt as

though he was speaking of a stranger even though she did remember her name. But maybe in the madness of her memory loss, she'd been afraid that she'd gotten that part wrong, and that along with everything else, her name was a forgotten piece of her life.

"Can you tell me something about me? Anything?"

She was precariously close to begging, and tears knotted her throat and stung her eyes.

"There will be plenty of time for us to talk later," Chrysander soothed. He stroked her forehead, pushing back her hair. "For now, rest. I'm making preparations to take you home."

It was the second time he'd mentioned home, and she realized that he still hadn't told her where that was.

"Where is home?" she asked again.

His lips thinned for just a moment, and then his expression eased. "Home for us has been here in the city. My business takes me away often, but we had an apartment together here. My plan is to take you to my island as soon as you are well enough to travel."

Her brows furrowed as she sought to comprehend the oddity of his statement. It sounded so…impersonal. There was no emotion, no hint of joy, just a sterile recitation of fact.

As if sensing she was about to ask more questions, he bent over and pressed his lips to her forehead. "Rest, *pedhaki mou*. I have arrangements to make. The doctor says you can be released in a few days' time if all goes well."

She closed her eyes wearily and nodded. He stood there a moment, and then she heard his footsteps retreating. When her door closed, she opened her eyes again, only to feel the damp trail of tears against her cheeks.

She should feel relief that she wasn't alone. Somehow, though, Chrysander Anetakis's presence hadn't reassured her as it should. She felt more apprehensive than ever, and she couldn't say why.

She pulled the thin sheet higher around her body and closed her eyes, willing the peaceful numbness of sleep to take over once more.

When she woke again, a nurse was standing by her bedside placing a cuff around her arm to take her blood pressure.

"Oh, good, you're awake," she said cheerfully as she removed the cuff. "I have your dinner tray. Do you feel up to eating?"

Marley shook her head. The thought of food made her faintly nauseous.

"Leave the tray. I'll see to it she eats."

Marley looked up in surprise to see Chrysander looming behind the nurse, a determined look on his face. The nurse turned and smiled at him then reached back and patted Marley's arm.

"You're very lucky to have such a devoted fiancé," she said as she turned to go.

"Yes, lucky," Marley murmured, and she wondered why she suddenly felt the urge to weep.

When the door shut behind the nurse, Chrysander pulled the chair closer to her bed again. Then he settled the tray in front of her.

"You should eat."

She eyed him nervously. "I don't feel much like eating."

"Do you find my presence unsettling?" he queried as his gaze slid over her rumpled form.

"I—" She opened her mouth to say no, but found she couldn't entirely deny it. How to tell this man she found him intimidating? This was supposed to be someone she loved. Had made love with. Just the thought sent a blush up her neck and over her cheeks.

"What are you thinking?" His fingers found her hand and stroked absently.

She turned her face away, hoping to find relief from his scrutiny. "N-nothing."

"You are frightened. That's understandable."

She turned back to look at him. "It doesn't make you angry that I'm frightened of you? Quite frankly, I'm terrified. I don't remember you or anything else in my life. I'm pregnant with your child and cannot for the life of me remember how I got this way!" Her fists gripped the sheet and held it protectively against her.

His lips pressed to a firm line. *Was* he angry? Was he putting on a front so as not to upset her further?

"It is as you said. You don't remember me, therefore I am a stranger to you. It will be up to me to earn your…trust." He said the last word as if he found it distasteful, and yet his expression remained controlled.

"Chrysander…" She said his name experimentally, letting it roll off her tongue. It didn't feel foreign, but neither did it spark any remembrance. Frustration took firm hold when her mind remained frightfully blank.

"Yes, *pedhaki mou?*"

She blinked as she realized he was waiting for her to continue.

"What happened to me?" she asked. "How did I get here? How did I lose my memory?"

Once again he took her hand in his, and she found the gesture comforting. He leaned forward and touched his other hand to her cheek. "You shouldn't rush things. The doctor is quite adamant in this. Right now the most important thing for you and our child is to take things slowly. Everything will come back in its own time."

She sighed, realizing he wasn't going to budge.

"Get some rest." He stood and leaned over to brush his lips across her forehead. "Soon we will leave this place."

Marley wished the words gave her more reassurance than they did. Instead of comfort, confusion and uncertainty rose sharply in her chest until she feared smothering with the anxiety.

Sweat broke out on her forehead, and the food she'd picked at just moments ago rolled in her stomach. Chrysander looked sharply at her, and without saying a word, he rang for the nurse.

Moments later, the nurse bustled in. At the sight of her, sympathy crowded her features. She placed a cool hand on Marley's forehead even as she administered an injection with the other.

"You mustn't panic," the nurse soothed. "You're safe now."

But her words failed to ease the tightness in Marley's chest. How could they when soon she was going to be thrust into an unknown world with a man who was a complete stranger to her?

Chrysander stood by her bed, staring down at her, his hand covering hers. The medication dulled her senses, and she could feel herself floating away, the fear evaporating like mist. His words were the last thing she heard.

"Sleep, *pedhaki mou*. I will watch over you."

Oddly, she did find comfort in the quiet vow.

Chrysander stood in the darkened room and watched as Marley slept. The strain of the frown he was wearing inserted a dull ache in his temples.

Her chest rose and fell with her slight breaths, and even in sleep, tension furrowed her brow. He moved closer and touched his fingers to her forehead, smoothing them across the pale skin.

She was as lovely as ever, even in her weakened state. Raven curls lay haphazardly against the pillow. He took one between his fingers and moved it from her forehead. It was longer now, no longer the shorter cap of curls that had flown about her head as she laughed or smiled.

Her skin had lost its previous glow, but he knew restoring her health would bring it back. Her eyes had been dull, frightened, but he remembered well the brilliant blue sparkle, how enchanting she looked when she was happy.

He cursed and moved away from the bed. It had all been a ruse. She hadn't ever been happy. Truly happy. It seemed he'd been incapable of making her so. All the time they were together, she'd plotted against him, stolen from him and his brothers.

Though he'd considered her his mistress, he'd never placed her in the same category as his others. What he'd shared with her hadn't been mercenary, or so he'd thought. In the end, it had boiled down to money and betrayal. Something he was well used to with women.

Yet he still wanted her. She still burned in his veins, an addiction he wasn't equipped to fight. He shook his head grimly. She was pregnant with his child, and that must take precedence above all else. They would be forced together by the child, their futures irrevocably intertwined. But he didn't have to like it, and he didn't have to surrender anything more than his protection and his body.

If she would once again be placed under his protection, then he'd do all he could to ensure she had the best care, her and their baby, but he'd never trust her. She would warm his bed, and he wouldn't lie and say that prospect wasn't appealing. But she would get nothing more from him.

Three

Two days later, Marley sat nervously in a wheelchair, her fingers clutched tightly around the blanket the nurse had draped over her lap. Chrysander stood to the side, listening intently as the nurse gave him the aftercare instructions. Marley fingered the maternity top that one of the nurses had kindly provided for her and smoothed the wrinkles over the bump of her abdomen. They'd all been exceedingly kind to her, and she feared leaving their kindness to venture into the unknown.

When the nurse was finished, Chrysander grasped the handles of the wheelchair and began pushing Marley down the hallway toward the entrance. She blinked as the bright sunshine speared her vision. A sleek limousine was parked a few feet away, and Chrysander walked briskly toward it. The driver stepped around to open the door just as Chrysander effortlessly plucked her from the wheelchair and ushered her inside the heated interior. In a matter of seconds, they were gliding away from the hospital.

Marley stared out the window as they navigated the busy New

York streets. The city itself was familiar. She could remember certain shops and landmarks. She possessed a knowledge of the city, but what was missing was the idea that this was home, that she belonged here. Hadn't Chrysander said they'd lived here? She felt like an artist staring at an empty canvas without the skills to paint the portrait.

When they pulled to a stop in front of a stylish, modern building, Chrysander bolted from the limousine while the doorman opened the door on her side. Chrysander reached inside and carefully drew her from the vehicle. She stepped to the sidewalk on shaky feet, and he tucked her to his side, a strong arm around her waist as they walked through the entrance.

A wave of déjà vu swept over her as the lift opened and he helped her inside. For the briefest of moments, her memory stirred, and she struggled to part the veils of darkness.

"What is it?" Chrysander demanded.

"I've done this before," she murmured.

"You remember?"

She shook her head. "No. It just feels…familiar. I know I've been here."

His fingers curled tighter around her arm. "This is where we lived…for many months. It's only natural that it should register something."

The lift opened, and she cocked her head as he started forward. His phrasing had been odd. Had they not lived here just a short time ago? Before whatever accident had befallen her?

He stopped and held out his hand to her. "Come, Marley. We're home."

She slid her fingers into his as he pulled her forward into the lavish foyer. To her surprise, a woman met them as they started for the large living room. Marley faltered as the tall blond young woman put a hand on Chrysander's arm and smiled.

"Welcome home, Mr. Anetakis. I've laid out all contracts requiring your signature on your desk as well as ordered your phone messages by priority. I also took the liberty of having dinner delivered." She swept an assessing look over Marley, one that had Marley feeling obscure and insignificant. "I didn't imagine you'd be up for going out after a trying few days."

Marley frowned as she realized the woman was implying that Chrysander had been through the ordeal and not Marley.

"Thank you, Roslyn," Chrysander said. "You shouldn't have gone to the trouble." He turned to Marley and pulled her closer to him. "Marley, this is Roslyn Chambers, my personal assistant."

Marley gave a faltering smile.

"Delighted to see you again, Miss Jameson," Roslyn said sweetly. "It's been ages since I last saw you. Months, I believe."

"Roslyn," Chrysander said in a warning voice. Her smile never slipped as she looked innocently at Chrysander.

Marley glanced warily between them, her confusion mounting. The ease with which the woman moved around the apartment that Chrysander called home to both of them was clear, and yet Roslyn hadn't seen Marley in months? The proprietary way his assistant looked at him was the only thing currently clear to Marley.

"I'll leave you two," Roslyn said with a gracious smile. "I'm sure you have a lot of catching up to do." She turned to Chrysander and put a delicate hand on his arm once more. "Call me if you need anything. I'll come straight over."

"Thank you," Chrysander murmured.

The tall blonde clicked across the polished Italian marble in her elegant heels and entered the lift. She smiled at Chrysander as the doors closed.

Marley licked her suddenly dry lips and looked away. Chrysander was stiff at her side as though he expected Marley to react in some way. She wasn't stupid enough to do so now. Not when he was so on guard. Later, she would ask him the million questions whirling around her tired mind.

"Come, you should be in bed," Chrysander said as he curled an arm around her.

"I've had quite enough of bed," she said firmly.

"Then you should at least get comfortable on the sofa. I'll bring you a tray so you can eat."

Eat. Rest. Eat some more. Those dictates seemed to compose Chrysander's sole aim when it came to her. She sighed and allowed him to lead her into the living area. He settled her on the soft leather couch and retrieved a blanket to cover her with.

There was a stiffness about him that puzzled her, but then she supposed if the roles were reversed and he'd forgotten her, she wouldn't be very sure of herself, either. He left the room, and several minutes later returned with a tray that he set before her on the coffee table. Steam rose from the bowl of soup, but she wasn't tempted by the offering. She was too unsettled.

He sat in a chair diagonally to her, but after a few moments, he rose and paced the room like a restless predator. His fingers tugged at his tie as he loosened it and then unbuttoned the cuffs of his silk shirt.

"Your assistant…Roslyn…said she left work for you?"

He turned to face her, his eyebrows wrinkling as he frowned. "Work can wait."

She sighed. "Do you plan to watch me nap then? I'll be fine, Chrysander. You can't hover over me every moment of the day. If there are things that require your attention, then by all means see to them."

Indecision flickered across his handsome face. "I do have things to do before we leave New York."

A surge of panic hit her unaware. She swallowed and worked to keep her expression bland. "We'll be leaving soon then?"

He nodded. "I thought to give you a few days to rest and more fully recover before we go. I've arranged for my jet to fly us to Greece, and then we'll take a helicopter out to the island. My staff is preparing for our arrival as we speak."

She stared uneasily at him. "Just how wealthy are you?"

He looked surprised by the question. "My family owns a chain of hotels."

The Anetakis name floated in her memory, what little of it there was. Images of the opulent hotel in the heart of the city came to mind. Celebrities, royalty, some of the world's wealthiest people stayed at Imperial Park. But he couldn't be *that* Anetakis, could he?

She paled and clenched her fingers to control the shaking. They were only the richest hotel family in the world. "How... how on earth did you and I..." She couldn't even bring herself to complete the thought. Then she frowned. Had she come from such a family?

Fatigue swamped her, and she dug her fingers into her temples as she fought the tiredness. Chrysander was beside her in an instant. He picked her up as though she weighed nothing and carried her into the bedroom. He carefully laid her on the bed, his eyes bright with concern. "Rest now, *pedhaki mou*."

She nodded and curled into the comfortable bed, her eyes already closing with exhaustion. Thinking hurt. Trying to remember sapped every ounce of her strength.

Chrysander slumped in his chair and ran a hand through his hair. He fingered the list of phone messages as his gaze lighted on the one from his brother Theron. There was a message from his other brother, Piers, as well.

He shifted uncomfortably and knew he wouldn't be able to put them off for long. They would have gotten his messages by now and be curious. How he was going to explain this mess to them and also explain why he was taking the woman who had tried to damage their business home to Greece was beyond him.

With a grimace, he picked up the phone and dialed Theron's number.

He spoke rapidly in Greek when his brother answered. "How did the groundbreaking go?"

"Chrysander, finally," Theron said dryly. "I wondered if I was going to have to fly over to beat answers from you."

Chrysander sighed and grunted in response.

"Do hold while I get Piers on the phone. It'll save you another call. I know he's as interested in your explanation as I am."

"Since when do I answer to my *younger* brothers?" Chrysander growled.

Theron chuckled and a moment later Piers's voice bled through the line. He didn't bandy words.

"Chrysander, what the hell is going on? I got your message, and judging by the fact you never showed up in London, I can only assume that you're otherwise occupied in New York."

Chrysander pinched the bridge of his nose between his fingers and closed his eyes. "It would appear that the two of you are going to be uncles."

Silence greeted his statement.

"You're sure it's yours?" Theron finally asked.

Chrysander grimaced. "She's five months pregnant, and five months ago, I was the only man in her bed. This I know."

"Like you knew she was stealing from us?" Piers retorted.

"Shut up, Piers," Theron said mildly. "The important question is, what are you going to do? She obviously can't be trusted. What does she have to say for herself?"

Chrysander's head pounded a bit harder. "There is a complication," he muttered. "She doesn't remember anything."

Both brothers made a sound of disbelief. "Quite convenient, wouldn't you say?" Piers interjected.

"She's leading you around by the balls," Theron said in disgust.

"I found it hard to believe myself," Chrysander admitted. "But I've seen her. She's here…in our—my apartment. Her memory loss is real." There was no way she could fake the abject vulnerability, the confusion and pain that clouded her once-vibrant blue eyes. The knowledge of her pain bothered him when it shouldn't. She deserved to suffer as she'd made him suffer.

Piers made a rude noise.

"What do you plan to do?" Theron asked.

Chrysander braced himself for their objections. "We're flying out to the island as soon as I feel she's well enough. It's a more suitable place for her recovery, and it's out of the public eye."

"Can't you install her somewhere until the baby comes and then get rid of her?" Piers demanded. "We lost two multimillion dollar deals because of her, and now our designs are going up under our competitor's name."

What he didn't say but Chrysander heard as loudly as if his

brother had spoken the words was that they had lost those deals because Chrysander had been blinded by a woman he was sleeping with. It was as much his fault as it was Marley's. He'd let his brothers down in the worst way. Risked what they'd spent years working to achieve.

"I cannot leave her right now," Chrysander said carefully. "She has no family. No one who could care for her. She carries my child, and to that end, I will do whatever it takes to ensure the baby's health and safety. The doctor feels her memory loss is only temporary, merely a coping mechanism for the trauma she has endured."

"What do the authorities have to say about her abduction?" Piers asked. "Do you know why yet, and who was responsible?"

"I spoke briefly with them at the hospital, and I have a meeting with the detective in charge of the investigation tomorrow," Chrysander said grimly. "I hope to find out more then. I'll also tell them of my plans to take her out of the country. I have to think of her safety, and that of the baby."

"I can see you're already decided in this," Theron said quietly. "Yes."

Piers made a sound as though he'd protest but was cut off when Theron spoke once more. "Do what you have to do, Chrysander. Piers and I can handle things. And for what it's worth, congratulations on becoming a father."

"Thanks," Chrysander murmured as he pressed the button to end the call.

He set the phone aside. Instead of making him feel any better about the situation, his discussion with his brothers had only reinforced how impossible things were. He didn't doubt that Marley didn't remember him or the fact that she'd stolen from him. Her confusion couldn't possibly be that feigned.

Which left him with the only choice he had, one he'd made the instant he'd known she was pregnant with his child. He would keep her close to him, take care of her, ensure she had the best care possible. He'd hire someone to stay with her when he couldn't be there and to provide the more intimate details of her care. It would enable him to keep her at arm's length while still keeping a close watch on her progress. And he would set aside, for now, the anger over her betrayal.

Four

The next morning, Marley sat across from Chrysander as he watched her eat breakfast. He nodded approvingly when she managed to finish the omelet he'd prepared, and he urged her to drink the glass of juice in front of her.

Despite her anxiety and uncertainty, it felt good to be taken care of by this man. Even if she wasn't entirely sure of her place in his world. He was solicitous of her, but at the same time he seemed distant. She wasn't sure if it was out of deference to her memory loss, and he had no wish to frighten her, or if this was simply the normal course of their relationship.

She caught her bottom lip between her teeth and nibbled absently. The idea that this could be ordinary bothered her. Surely she hadn't desired marriage with someone who treated her so politely, as though she were a stranger.

And yet, for all intents and purposes, they were strangers. At least he was to her. A flood of sympathy rolled through her. How awful it had to be for him to have his fiancée, a woman he loved and planned to marry, just forget him, as though he never existed. She couldn't imagine being in his shoes.

He'd watched her closely through breakfast, and she knew she must be broadcasting her unease, but he said nothing until he'd cleared their dishes away and taken her into the living room. He settled her on the couch and then sat next to her, his stare probing.

"What is concerning you this morning, Marley?" Chrysander asked.

His gaze passed over her face, and his expression left her faintly breathless.

"I was just thinking how perfectly rotten this whole thing must be for you."

One eyebrow rose, and he tilted his head questioningly. He looked surprised, as though it were the last thing he'd expected her to say.

"What do you mean?"

She looked down, suddenly shy and even more uncertain. He reached over and touched his fingers to her chin. He slid them further underneath and tugged until she met his gaze.

"Tell me why things are so horrible for me."

When put like that, it sounded ridiculous. Here was a man who could have, and probably did have, anything he wanted. Power, wealth, respect. And yet she presumed to think it was so terrible that his mousy fiancée couldn't remember him. It would have been enough to make her laugh if she hadn't felt so forlorn.

"I was trying to imagine myself in your place," she said sadly. "What it feels like when someone you love forgets you." His thumb rubbed over her lips, and a peculiar tingling raced down her spine. "I think I would feel…rejected."

"You're worried that I feel rejected?" Faint amusement flickered in his eyes, and a smile hovered near the corners of his mouth.

"You don't?" she asked. And did it matter? She hated this lack of confidence. Not only was her memory of this man stolen, but any faith she had in who she was to him had been erased, as well. She hated the idea that she couldn't speak of their relationship frankly because she worried that she might make errant assumptions and look a fool.

Embarrassment crept over her cheeks, leaving them tight and heated as he continued to stare at her.

"You cannot help what happened to you, Marley. I don't blame you, and neither do I harbor resentment. It would be petty of me."

No, she couldn't see him as petty. Dangerous. A little frightening. But not petty. Was she afraid of him? She shivered lightly. No, it wasn't him she was afraid of. It was the idea that she could have been so intimate with a man such as him and not remember it. She couldn't imagine ever forgetting such an experience.

"What happened to me, Chrysander?" A note of pleading crept into her voice. Her hands shook, and she clenched them together to disguise her unease.

He sighed. "You had…an accident, *pedhaki mou*. The doctor assures me your memory loss is only temporary and that it's imperative for you not to overtax yourself."

"Was I in a car accident?" Even as she asked, she glanced down, searching for signs of injury, bruising. But she had no muscle soreness, no stiffness. Just an overwhelming fatigue and a wariness she couldn't explain.

His eyes flickered away for the briefest of moments. "Yes."

"Oh. Was it very serious?" She raised a hand to her head, feeling for a wound.

He gently took her hand and lowered it to her lap, but he didn't relinquish his hold. "No. Not serious."

"Then why…how did I lose my memory? Did I suffer a concussion? My head doesn't hurt that way."

"I'm very glad your head doesn't pain you, but a head injury isn't what causes memory loss."

She cocked her head to the side and stared at him in puzzlement. "Then how?"

"The physician explained that this is your way of coping with the trauma of your accident. It's a protective instinct. One meant to shield you from harmful memories."

Her forehead wrinkled as her eyebrows came together. She

pressed, trying to struggle through the thick cloak of black in her mind. Surely there had to be something, some spark of a memory.

"Yet I wasn't harmed," she said in disbelief.

"A fact I'm very grateful for," Chrysander said. "Still, it must have been very frightening."

A sudden thought came to her, and her hand flew from his in alarm. "Was anyone else hurt?"

Again his gaze flickered away from her for just a second. He reached up and recaptured her hand then brought it to his lips. A soft gasp escaped her when he pressed a kiss to her palm. "No."

She sagged in relief. "I wish I could remember. I keep thinking if I just try a little harder, it will come, but when I try to focus on the past, my head starts to pound."

Chrysander frowned. "This is precisely why I do not like to discuss the accident with you. The doctor warned against causing you any upset or stress. You must put the incident from your mind and focus on regaining your strength." He placed his other hand over her abdomen and cupped the bulge there protectively. "Such upset cannot be good for our baby. You've already gone through too much for my liking."

She tugged her hand free and placed both of hers lightly over his hand that was still cupping her belly. Beneath his fingers, the baby rolled. He snatched his hand back, a stunned expression lighting his face.

Her brows furrowed as she gazed curiously at him. His hand shook slightly as he returned it to her stomach. His fingers splayed out, and once again her belly rippled underneath his palm.

"That's amazing," he whispered.

He looked so completely befuddled that she had to smile. But on the heels of that smile came confusion. He acted as though he'd never experienced their baby kicking.

She licked her lips and cursed the fact that she couldn't remember. "Surely you've felt it before, Chrysander."

He continued his gentle exploration of her stomach. It was a long moment before he spoke. "I was often away on business," he said with a note of discomfort. "I had only just returned when I learned of your accident. It had been…a while since we'd been together."

She let her breath out, relief sliding over her and lightening her worry. If they had been separated for a time, it would explain a lot.

"I don't suppose it was the homecoming you expected," she said ruefully. "You left a woman who knew you, who was pregnant with your child and planned to marry you. When you came back, you faced a woman who treats you like a stranger."

She glanced down at her finger automatically as she spoke. No ring adorned it. She frowned at it before she quickly looked back up, trying to make the uneasiness disappear once more.

"I was only happy that you and our baby were unharmed," he said simply. He eased away from her, shifting his body until more space separated them. His gaze still drifted back to her belly as though he was fascinated with the tiny life making itself known there.

A buzz sounded, and Chrysander stood and strode to the call box on the wall. Marley strained to hear who he was speaking to, but she only heard his command to come up.

He returned to her and sat down, collecting her hands in his. "That was the nurse I hired to look after you. I have a meeting that I can't miss in an hour's time."

Her eyes widened. "But Chrysander, I don't need a nurse. I'm perfectly capable of remaining here while you attend to your business."

His grip on her hands tightened. "Humor me, *pedhaki mou*. It makes me feel better knowing I'm leaving you in capable hands. I don't like to think of you having need of anything in my absence."

A smile curved her lips at his insistence. "How long will you be gone?" She hated the hopeful, almost mournful quality to her voice. She sounded pathetic.

He stood as the sound of the elevator opening filtered into the living room. "Stay here. I'll return with the nurse."

Marley relaxed against the back of the couch and waited for Chrysander to return. His attentiveness was endearing, even if unnecessary.

A moment later, he walked back in with a smiling woman dressed in slacks and a sweater. She beamed at Marley as she stopped a few feet away from the sofa.

"You must be Marley. I'm so pleased to meet you. I'm Mrs. Cahill, but please do call me Patrice."

Marley couldn't help but return the older woman's smile.

"Mr. Anetakis has discussed his wishes with me, and I'll do my utmost to make sure you're taken care of."

Marley pinned Chrysander with a stare. "Oh, he did, did he? May I ask what his instructions were?"

Chrysander made a show of checking his watch. "Her instructions are to make sure you rest. Now, I'm sorry, but I must go out for a while. I'll return in time for us to have lunch together."

"I'd like that," she softly returned.

He leaned down and stiffly brushed a kiss across her forehead before turning to walk away. Her gaze followed him across the room, and she realized how clingy she must look.

With effort, she dragged her stare from his retreating back and looked up at Patrice. "I'm really quite fit," she explained. "Chrysander makes it sound like I'm a complete invalid."

Patrice smiled and winked. "He's a man. They're famous for that sort of thing. Still, there's no harm in a little rest, now is there? I'll see you to bed, and then I'll see about making us a nice cup of tea for when you wake."

Before Marley even realized what was happening, the other woman was effectively shuttling her toward the bedroom. She blinked when Patrice tucked her solidly into bed and arranged the covers around her.

"You're quite good at this," Marley said faintly.

Patrice chuckled. "Getting my patients to do what they don't want to is part of my job. Now get some rest so that man of yours is happy with me and with you when he returns."

Marley heard the light sounds of Patrice's shoes as she walked from the bedroom. When the sound faded away, Marley glanced to the fireplace on the wall opposing the foot of her bed. Chrysander had started the flame the evening before, more for coziness than actual warmth, because the apartment suffered no chill. Even the floors were heated, which she loved, because she hated to wear shoes indoors.

The thought hit her even as a burst of excitement swept over her. What else could she remember about herself? She concentrated hard, but the effort caused her head to ache again.

The baby moved, and she slid her hand down to rest over her swollen abdomen. The movement eased the discomfort in her head, and she smiled. Despite the temporary loss of her past, she had a future to look forward to. Marriage and a child. She just wished she could remember how she'd gotten to this point.

With a sigh, she resigned herself to living in the moment. Hopefully her memories would return and fill in the gaps.

She dozed, and when she awoke, she looked at the clock by her bed and saw that an hour had elapsed. She felt refreshed and drew away the covers, wanting to get up and move around. The constant rest was starting to make her restless.

Though she was dressed in soft pajamas, she nevertheless reached for the silk dressing robe lying at the foot of her bed. Tying it around her body, she walked out of the bedroom and into the living room, where she found Patrice.

She smiled at the other woman and assured her she was feeling well when Patrice prompted her. Patrice nodded approvingly, and as if sensing Marley's need to be alone, excused herself.

Marley took the opportunity to explore the spacious penthouse. She walked from room to room, acquainting herself with her home. Only it didn't *feel* like home. She could see Chrysander in the style and makeup of the decorations and furnishings, but she couldn't see anything that made her feel as though she'd made any mark on the apartment. For some reason, that discomfited her. She felt like a guest intruding where she didn't belong.

When she entered the master suite, her frown grew. Chrysander had placed her in what apparently was one of the guest rooms. She hadn't given any thought when he'd put her to bed and seen to her comfort in the extra bedroom. She'd been too overwhelmed, too focused on trying to process everything.

She retreated, unable to shake the thought that she was somehow trespassing. Next to the master suite was a large office. It was obviously Chrysander's work space. The furnishings were dark and masculine. Bookcases adorned the back wall, and a large mahogany desk sat a few feet in front of them. Her feet brushed across a plush rug as she walked farther into the middle of the room.

A laptop rested on the desk, and she sat down in the leather executive chair in anticipation of browsing the Internet. She only hoped he had a wireless connection since she could see no evidence of a cable line connected to the computer.

She touched the keypad, and the monitor lit up. At least she wasn't a useless vegetable and had retained knowledge of the basics. As frustrating as her memory loss was, she was relieved to know it was confined to her personal history and not to the world around her.

She shook her head, plagued by the sheer absurdity of it all.

For the first half hour, she did countless searches on memory loss, but wading through the mass of conflicting opinions only gave her a vile headache. So she turned her attention to looking up information on Chrysander.

It was a bit frightening to see just how powerful and wealthy Chrysander was. He and his two brothers were a formidable presence in the hotel industry. There wasn't much personal information, though, and that was what she craved.

She sat back, irritated with her cowardice. What she needed was to ask Chrysander for the information she wanted. For goodness' sake, he was her fiancé, her *lover*. They'd created a child together, and he'd asked her to marry him. If only she could remember those events, she would feel more sure of herself.

"What are you doing?"

Chrysander's whiplike voice lashed over her, and she jerked in surprise and fright. She stared up to see him standing in the doorway, anger and suspicion glittering in his eyes. His mouth was drawn into a tight line. He strode toward her before she could even formulate a response.

"Chrysander, you scared me." Her hand went to her chest to try and calm the erratic jumping of her pulse.

"I asked you what you were doing," he said coldly as he walked around the desk to stand beside her.

Hurt and confusion settled over her. "I was just surfing the Internet. I didn't think you'd object to me using your laptop."

"I prefer if you leave the things in my office alone," he said curtly, even as he reached out and closed the computer.

She slid out of the chair and stood staring at him in shock. Tears burned the corners of her eyes. He looked at her with such…loathing. A shiver took over her body, and she desired nothing more than to be as far away from him as possible.

"I'm sorry," she managed to choke out. "I was just trying to discover something about me…you…this horrid memory loss. I won't bother you or your things again."

She turned and fled the room before she embarrassed herself and broke into sobs.

Chrysander watched her go and cursed under his breath. He dragged a hand through his hair before he sat down and reopened the laptop. A quick check of the browsing history showed she'd done nothing more than research memory loss and a few articles about his company. Another check of his files indicated none of his business documents had been accessed.

He cursed again. He'd reacted badly, but seeing her using his computer had immediately put him on guard. In that moment, he'd wondered if her memory loss was all a ruse and she was plotting again to betray him.

He propped his elbows on the desk and held his head in his hands. His meeting with the detective in charge of the investigation into Marley's abduction had been an exercise in frustration. They had little to no information to go on, and the one person who could supply it couldn't remember.

Marley hadn't been rescued as the news had led viewers to believe; rather, she'd been abandoned by her kidnappers, and an anonymous caller had alerted police to her presence in the rundown apartment building. When they'd arrived, they'd found a frightened pregnant woman obviously in shock. When she'd awoken in the hospital, she'd remembered nothing. Her life, in essence, began on that day.

So many questions, so much unknown.

What had been made clear to him, though, was that he couldn't take chances with her safety. Whatever threat there was to her was still out there, and he'd be damned if he let anyone get close enough to hurt Marley or his child again. He'd expected the authorities to balk when he said he was taking Marley out of the country, not that he cared, because her well-being was his top priority and he would do whatever it took to ensure it.

Instead, they'd agreed that it was the best choice and advised him to step up his security. They wanted to be notified the moment her memory returned, so they could question her. Chrysander supplied them with his contact information and told them he would be leaving with her the next day.

There was much to do to prepare for their departure. He'd already alerted his security team both here and on the island. Preparations were under way, but he still had many phone calls to make. Yet the sight of Marley's tears and the hurt in her voice gave him pause. He should shove it aside and continue with his plans. Her safety was important. Whether she was upset was not.

Even as he thought it, he was on his feet and going after her.

Marley stood in the closet of the bedroom Chrysander had given her, staring blindly at the row of clothing hanging in front of her. She wiped the tears with the back of her hand and concentrated on what to wear.

She rummaged through the many outfits, but none of them felt like her. With an unhappy frown she turned to the row of shelves that lined the right side of her closet and saw a stack of faded jeans next to several neatly folded T-shirts.

She reached for the jeans, knowing that this was what she felt comfortable in. But when she unfolded the first pair, she saw that they weren't maternity pants. A quick search of the rest yielded the same results.

She turned back around and flipped through outfit after outfit on the hangers and saw that they, too, were not suitable clothing for a woman in the more advanced stages of pregnancy. Why did she have nothing to wear? She glanced down at the bulge of her stomach. While she wasn't huge, the waistlines of the clothing in her closet were too confining for a woman five months along.

She felt his presence before he ever made a sound. Slowly, she turned to see Chrysander standing in the doorway of her closet. His expression softened when she swiped at her face and turned quickly away.

He stepped forward and captured her wrist in his hand. "Marley, I'm sorry."

She stiffened and raised her chin until she met his gaze. "I shouldn't have meddled in *your* belongings." She raised her hand to gesture at the closet full of clothes. "We obviously keep a very separate lifestyle. You'll pardon me while I relearn the ropes."

He frowned darkly and stared at her in confusion. "What are you talking about? There will be no separation of our lifestyles."

She shrugged indifferently. "The evidence is here. It doesn't take an idiot to figure it out. You've put me in my own room. My clothes are separate. Our things are separate. Our beds are separate. It's a wonder I ever got pregnant," she added wryly. She swallowed and then pressed on with the question burning uppermost in her mind. "Why are you marrying me, Chrysander? Was my pregnancy an accident? Was I some lascivious bitch who trapped you into a relationship?"

She knew she sounded hysterical even as the words tumbled out, but the hurt was eating away at her insides. She needed reassurance, some sign that the life he claimed was hers was a happy place and not one filled with dark gaps like the holes in her memory.

"*Theos!* Come with me."

Before she could protest, he was dragging her from the closet. He ushered her over to the bed and sat her down before settling beside her.

She glanced uncomfortably around. "Where is Patrice?" She had no wish to have a disagreement in front of anyone else.

"I dismissed her when I arrived," he said impatiently. "She is only here when I cannot be until we leave for Greece. She'll remain on the island with us for as long as you have need of her."

Marley couldn't keep the disappointment from her expression. "But Chrysander, I don't need her at all, and I thought we would be alone once we reached the island."

His look told her that he wanted anything but, and hurt crashed in again at his seeming rejection.

"You may think she isn't needed, but I won't take chances with your recovery. Your health is too important to me." His voice became softer, and his eyes lost some of their hardness. "You're pregnant, and you've undergone a great deal of stress. It's only natural that I would want the best care possible for you."

She swallowed and slowly nodded.

He stared intently at her. "Now, as for my earlier rudeness…I apologize. I had no right to speak to you that way."

She snorted, which caused his eyebrows to rise. "I don't think rude adequately covers it. You were a first-class jerk."

Color rose in his cheeks, and he swallowed. "Yes, I was, and for that I apologize. I have no excuse. I've been busy making arrangements for our travel, and I took my frustrations out on you. It's unforgivable, but I ask for your forgiveness nonetheless."

"I accept your apology," she said coolly.

"And as for your other assertions." He took one of his hands away from hers and dragged it carelessly through his dark hair. "We do not lead separate lives. Nor will we. You did not trap me into a proposal, and I won't have you say it again." He paused and sighed. "I put you in this room out of deference to your condition. I didn't think it fair of me to expect you to share a room and a bed with a man who is a stranger to you. I had no wish to put such pressure on you."

In that light, her worry seemed silly. What she'd perceived as a slight had in fact been an act of caring on his part. Her shoulders sagged as her breath escaped in a sigh.

"I thought…"

"What did you think, *pedhaki mou?*"

"I thought you didn't want me," she said lamely.

He let out a curse and cupped her face in his palm. For a long moment, he stared at her. Light blazed in his golden eyes, and then he lowered his head to hers. Her breath caught in her throat and hung there as his lips hovered over hers.

A fierce longing ignited within her, and suddenly she wanted nothing more than his mouth on hers. When their lips met, a bolt of electricity shot down her spine and rebounded, spreading through her body like wildfire.

Instinctively, she arched into him, working her body into the shelter of his as his fingers fanned across her cheek and he deepened the kiss. Her breasts tightened as desire hummed through her belly. His chest brushed across her taut nipples, and she flinched in reaction.

Her arms snaked around him, and her fingers dug into the hair at his nape. Peace enveloped her. A sense of rightness she hadn't experienced since waking in the hospital bed lodged in her mind.

A low groan worked its way from his throat as he pulled away. His breath came in ragged spurts, and his eyes shimmered with liquid heat.

"Your body remembers me, *pedhaki mou,* even if your mind does not." Pure male satisfaction accentuated his statement. It sounded arrogant, self-assured, but it gave her flagging confidence a much-needed boost. He sounded very pleased at the idea that she recognized him, if only on a physical level.

"I don't have any suitable clothing," she blurted, then blushed at the absurdity of her statement. Her brain had gone to mush as soon as he'd kissed her, and now she scrambled to cover the awkwardness.

One brow went up again.

"Why don't I have any maternity clothes?" she asked. "Did I not buy any?" She reached for any plausible explanation as to why she wouldn't have appropriate clothing among the closet-ful of outfits she owned.

Chrysander frowned. "I am sorry, *pedhaki mou.* I did not think of this. Of course you cannot go around in your jeans." He smiled a slow, sensual smile. "Even if I do love to see you in them."

She cocked her head to one side.

He chuckled, and the sound, sexy and low, vibrated over her hypersensitive body. "You do not like to wear them around me. Something about looking nice when we are together, but I assure you, you would look beautiful in a sackcloth if you chose to wear one."

Heat bloomed in her cheeks, and she smiled at the compliment.

He shook his head ruefully. "I am not doing a good job of taking care of you since your release from the hospital. I've upset you and not seen to your needs. This is something I must remedy at once. I admit, though, that your safety and well-being, not your clothing, was uppermost on my mind."

"Don't say that," she protested. "You've been wonderful. Well, except the brief stint as a big jerk." She smiled teasingly at him as she spoke. "This can't have been easy for you, and yet you've been incredibly patient. I'm sorry for being such a shrew."

He touched her face again, and for a moment, she thought he'd kiss her once more. "I won't let you apologize, Marley. You keep worrying about how hard this is for me, when you are the one who has suffered." He took his hand away and stood. "Now I must make some phone calls so I can have more appropriate clothing arranged for you."

She blinked in surprise. "Couldn't we just go shopping?"

He frowned. "You are not up for a shopping trip. I want you to rest. We're leaving for the island tomorrow morning, as soon as you have seen the doctor and he gives his approval for you to travel."

"Tomorrow?" she parroted. "So soon?"

He nodded. "Now you know why I must hurry if I am to have your clothing delivered on time."

She put her hands up helplessly. He said it as though he had much experience in making things happen in accordance with his wishes. If he could have clothes delivered to her on such short notice, then who was she to argue?

"Now—"

She held up a hand to silence him. She knew enough about

the look on his face and the tone of his voice to know that an order to rest was about to follow.

"If you tell me to rest again, I may well scream."

His gaze narrowed, and he was about to protest.

"Please, Chrysander. I feel well. I napped while you were gone. Now, you promised me lunch when you returned from your meeting, and I find myself starving. Can we go eat?"

He cursed again and clenched his fingers into fists. "Of course. Apparently, I strive to be thoughtless in all things. Come and sit down at our table. I'll get us something to eat."

Five

The next morning, Marley dressed in one of the chic outfits that had been delivered straight to their penthouse by a local boutique specializing in maternity wear. Chrysander had insisted she see an obstetrician before they departed for his island, and so, accompanied by Chrysander and flanked by several members of his security team, they entered the medical building where the doctor's offices were housed.

She felt conspicuous and faintly embarrassed, but she also glowed under Chrysander's constant attention and his apparent concern for her well-being.

To her surprise, there was no waiting once Chrysander announced their arrival to the receptionist. His security detail remained in the lobby, and Marley smiled at the image of the big, burly men standing amidst a dozen pregnant women.

She and Chrysander were ushered to an exam room by a young nurse who assured them that the doctor would attend them shortly.

When the nurse retreated, Chrysander lifted Marley and

settled her on the exam table. Instead of sitting in the chair to the side, he stood in front of her and rubbed his hands up and down her arms in a comforting manner.

She leaned into his arms, unable to resist the pull between them. She rested her cheek on his broad chest and closed her eyes as his hands slipped around to caress her back.

The door opened, and Marley quickly pulled away. But Chrysander seemed in no hurry to relinquish her. He slipped an arm around her shoulders and pulled her against him as the doctor introduced himself.

After a few preliminaries and a discussion of her condition, the doctor looked over his clipboard and said, "I'd like to perform an ultrasound just to make sure everything is as it should be."

Chrysander frowned. "Do you have cause for concern?"

The doctor shook his head. "It's purely precautionary. Given the fact that you're traveling out of the country, and that Miss Jameson has recently suffered a trauma, I'd just like to take a look at the baby and make sure everything is well."

Chrysander nodded and took Marley's hand. As the doctor left the room, he turned to her. "I will be with you, *pedhaki mou*. There is nothing to fear."

She smiled and squeezed his hand. "I'm not worried. I wasn't even injured in the accident, so there's no reason anything should be wrong with the baby."

His expression became unreadable, but his hand remained tight around hers.

A few moments later, the doctor returned and instructed Marley to recline on the table. When he asked her to tug her pants below her waistline and to raise her shirt, Chrysander frowned fiercely.

"Her belly must be exposed in order to perform the scan," the doctor said, amusement twinkling in his eyes.

Chrysander himself arranged her clothing, only baring the minimal amount of flesh, and he hovered close, his hand resting above the swell of her stomach.

When the probe slid over her belly and the screen lit up with a blurry image that resembled a blob, Marley reached a shaking hand for Chrysander's. Chrysander bent over her, his face close to her ear as he strained to see the monitor.

"Would you like to know what you're having?" the doctor asked with a broad smile.

Chrysander looked at Marley, and she held her breath for a moment, excitement making her pulse race. "I do," she whispered to Chrysander. "Do you?"

He smiled and brought her hand to his lips. "If that is what you wish, *pedhaki mou*. I, too, would like to know whether we're having a son or a daughter."

Marley turned her head to look at the doctor. "Yes, please. Tell us."

She watched as the screen changed, blurring in and out as the probe moved over her belly. A few seconds later, the image slowed and then became clearer.

"Congratulations, you're having a boy."

Marley's breath caught in her throat. "Is that him?" she whispered as she viewed what appeared to be two legs and round buttocks.

"Indeed it is. Handsome devil, isn't he?"

"He's beautiful," Chrysander said huskily. He bent and brushed his lips across Marley's cheek. "Thank you, *pedhaki mou*."

She twisted to look up at him. "Why are you thanking me?"

"For my son." His gaze was riveted to the screen, and delight shone deeply in his eyes. He was clearly enthralled with the tiny baby, and her heart squeezed with emotion.

"We're finished here," the doctor said.

Chrysander gently arranged Marley's clothing and then put an arm behind her back to help her sit forward again.

"Was everything all right?" Chrysander asked the doctor.

"Quite so. Make sure she checks in with an obstetrician when you arrive in Greece. I don't anticipate any problems. She and the baby appear perfectly healthy, but it's a good idea if she has regular care during her pregnancy."

"I've arranged for a private physician as well as a nurse to remain on the island as long as we do," Chrysander said. "She will be well looked after."

The doctor nodded his approval and then smiled at Marley. "Take care, young lady, and best wishes on your pregnancy."

Marley returned his smile then took Chrysander's hand as he helped her from the table. He ushered her out moments later and helped her into the waiting limousine.

"Are you feeling all right?" Chrysander asked as they pulled away. "The plane is waiting at the airport, but if you're tired from your appointment we can take the flight after you've rested."

"Are our bags already there?" she asked in surprise.

He nodded. "I had them brought over while you were at your appointment."

"We can leave now. I can rest on the plane."

He leaned forward to tell the driver to take them to the airport, and then he closed the privacy glass between them.

She gazed at him, suddenly a little shy. "Are you happy about our son, Chrysander?"

He looked startled by her question. Then he pulled her closer to him, until she was nearly in his lap. He cupped his hand to her belly and rubbed tenderly over the swell.

"Have I given you reason to think I am not happy about our child?"

She shook her head. "No, I just wondered. I mean, now that I know what I'm having, it suddenly seems so *real*."

"I couldn't be happier about our son. I would have loved a daughter just as well. As long as our child is healthy and safe, I am very content."

"Yes, me, too." She sighed. "Now if only I could remember, things would be so perfect. It's been such a good day."

He put a finger over her lips. "Don't spoil it by lamenting over things that are out of your control. It will come. Don't rush it."

She grimaced. "You're right. I just wish…"

"What do you wish, *pedhaki mou?*"

"I wish I could remember loving you," she said quietly.

His eyes darkened, and for a moment, what she saw sent a

shiver down her spine. There was such conflicted emotion in the golden orbs.

"Maybe you can learn to love me again," he finally said.

She smiled. "You're making it easy." She settled against him, content. But then an uneasy thought assailed her. She'd spoken of loving him, something she couldn't remember, but felt that she had, but there had been nothing said of his love for her. Not once had he voiced words of love, and shouldn't they have come? When she was in the hospital. Weren't reaffirmations of love common after a scare? Wouldn't he seek to reassure her that he loved her when she couldn't remember their life together?

She raised her head to ask him, to seek confirmation of that fact, but the question died on her lips when she saw his attention was already focused on the small television screen in the corner of the large compartment of the limousine.

She let the question die and contented herself with remaining snuggled into his body. The next thing she knew, they were arriving at the airport.

"We are here," Chrysander said.

She nodded, and Chrysander stepped from the limousine. He reached in and helped her out, and she blinked as the bright sunshine hit her eyes. The wind blew, and she shivered against the slight chill.

Chrysander wrapped an arm around her and hurried her toward the waiting plane. The inside was warm and looked extremely comfortable.

As he guided her toward a seat, he said, "There is a bed in the back. Once we've taken off, you can go lie down."

"That sounds lovely," she said with a smile as he settled into the seat next to her. She turned and looked out the window and then glanced toward the front of the plane as she saw several of Chrysander's security detail file into the cabin.

"Chrysander, why do you have so many security people?"

He stiffened beside her. "I am a very wealthy man. There are those who might seek to harm me...or those important to me."

"Oh. Is the danger very high?" she asked as she turned her gaze on him.

"It is the job of my men to ensure there is no danger. Do not worry, Marley. I will see to the safety of you and our child."

She frowned. "I didn't mean to imply that you wouldn't. I'm merely trying to understand your world."

"Our world." He stared pointedly at her. "It's our world, Marley. One that you are very much a part of."

A blush colored her cheeks. "I'm trying, Chrysander. I'm trying very hard. It's difficult when I'm in a place but can't remember any part of it. Please be patient with me."

"If I spoke too harshly, then I apologize," he said soothingly. He reached across her lap to pull her seat belt over her waist. With a click, he secured it then pulled it snug. "We'll be taking off soon."

A few minutes later, the plane began to move, and she settled back in her seat, trying not to think too hard about the uncertainty that lay ahead.

They landed at a small airstrip in Corinth several long hours later, and Chrysander helped her down the few steps onto the concrete runway. He urged her toward a waiting helicopter several feet away. When she looked questioningly at him, he leaned in close and said, "The island is a fifteen-minute ride by helicopter."

She glanced appreciatively out the window of the helicopter as it rose over Corinth and headed out to sea. In the distance, she saw ancient ruins and turned to question Chrysander about them. When she had no luck making him hear over the noise of the rotors, he slid a pair of earphones with an attached microphone over her head and suddenly she could hear him clearly.

"The Temple of Apollo," he explained. "If you like, we can fly back and tour the ruins when you've recovered from your journey."

"I'd like that."

She turned her attention to the brilliant blue expanse of sparkling water, but already in the distance she could make out a small dot of land. "Is that it?" she asked, pointing.

He nodded.

"Does it have a name?"

"Anetakis," he responded.

She laughed. "I should have known." She shook her head. It

seemed unreal that he'd own an entire island. But his naming the island Anetakis didn't surprise her in the least. He wore arrogance like most people wore clothing.

As the island loomed larger on the horizon, she curled her fingers into tight balls. Her anxiety must have been evident to Chrysander, because he reached over and took one of her hands in his. "There's nothing to worry over, *pedhaki mou*. You'll like it on the island, and it will be good for you to have time to relax and concentrate on regaining your strength."

She didn't argue with him over her condition, knowing full well it was a useless expenditure of energy. But she had no intention of spending her time on the island "resting."

They landed on a small concrete helipad situated at the rear of a palatial house. Chrysander curled a protective arm around her as they ducked and walked away from the helicopter.

He touched her shoulder and indicated that she wait while he spoke to the pilot. She stood, staring up at the sprawling house, waiting for some flicker of recognition. A cool breeze blew off the water, and a chill raced up her arms. Still, she remained, staring, hoping, but she was convinced she'd never been here.

"Come," Chrysander said as he took her hand. "You're getting cold."

As the helicopter droned away, she took a step to follow Chrysander and then paused again. He turned and looked inquisitively at her. "What is wrong?"

She swallowed as she continued to gaze over the grounds. There was a sense of wonder, as though she'd stepped into some wild paradise, but no feeling of home, that this was a place she had any knowledge of. It terrified her.

Chrysander closed the distance between them and touched her face in concern. He cursed when she trembled.

"I've never been here," she said in a low voice. She looked to him for confirmation.

He nodded. "This is so. This is your first visit to the island."

"I don't understand," she said faintly. "We're engaged, and I've never been to the place you call home?"

His lips pressed together. "We made our home in New York, Marley. I told you this."

The cloud of confusion grew around her. Would they not have visited? Even once? She allowed him to take her hand, and they walked up the long, winding path toward the house. As they neared the gate, Marley could see the sparkling waters of a swimming pool.

A large patio extended from the back of the house, and the pool was carved in the middle. To her surprise, the pool entered the house under an elaborate archway.

"It's heated," Chrysander explained as he drew her inside the house. "It's too cool this time of year for outdoor swimming, but you can enjoy a light swim indoors if the doctor gives his permission."

She rolled her eyes and allowed him to tug her along with him. They entered a huge room that looked to be in actuality three separate areas. They stood in the living room but the floor plan into the kitchen and dining area was open, and they flowed seamlessly into one another.

Marley's gaze wandered to the glass doors leading onto a patio where yet another pool was situated with a view of the ocean in the distance. To her shock, a woman in a skimpy bikini appeared at the entrance and stepped inside the house.

She recognized her as Chrysander's personal assistant, but why would she be here? And it was certainly too cold to be out sunbathing in such a suit.

Roslyn looked up, and it was apparent to Marley that she feigned surprise at seeing them. Though she had a wrap draped over one arm, she made no move to put it on as she hurriedly crossed the floor toward Chrysander.

"Mr. Anetakis, I didn't expect you until tomorrow!"

Her long blond hair trailed seductively down her back, and Marley gaped as she saw the bottom of Roslyn's bikini was actually a thong.

"I hope you don't mind that I took advantage of the facilities," Roslyn rushed to say as she put well-manicured fingers to Chrysander's arm.

"Of course not," Chrysander said smoothly. "I did tell you to avail yourself of whatever you liked. Did you set up my office as I requested?"

"Of course. I do hope it won't be a problem for me to remain one more night? I didn't arrange for the helicopter to fetch me until tomorrow morning."

Roslyn's wide, innocent eyes didn't fool Marley, and she felt the beginnings of a headache drumming in her temples. She pulled her hand from Chrysander's and merely walked away, having no desire to listen to the mewings of his assistant any longer.

"You are welcome to stay, Roslyn. I do hope you'll have dinner with us tonight," Chrysander said politely as Marley mounted the stairs.

She really had no idea where she was going, but upstairs seemed as good a place as any, and it would put her solidly away from the source of her irritation. She was nearly to the top when Chrysander overtook her.

"You should have waited for me," he reproached. "I don't like you navigating the stairs by yourself. What if you were to fall? In the future, someone will escort you up or down."

Her mouth fell open. "You're not serious!"

He frowned, clearly not liking her tone of disbelief. "I'm very serious when it comes to your well-being and that of our child."

She blew out her breath in frustration as Chrysander escorted her from the landing of the stairs down the hall to a spacious bedroom. Clearly this was the master suite. She set aside the protests forming on her tongue and stared at Chrysander in question.

"Is this to be my room?"

"It is *our* room."

Heat rose in her cheeks. Her throat suddenly went dry as she imagined sharing the big bed with Chrysander. Satisfaction gleamed in his eyes as he observed her reaction.

"Do you have any objections?" he asked softly.

She shook her head. "N-no. None."

A slow smiled curved his sensual mouth. A predatory gleam entered his eyes. "That is good. We are in agreement then."

"I—w-well, not exactly," she stammered.

He cocked one imperious brow. "We are not?"

She shook herself from the intimate spell he was weaving over her. The one that had her reduced to a mass of writhing stupidity. She lifted her chin and stared challengingly at him. "I don't need an escort to get up and down the stairs, Chrysander. I'm not an invalid, and I don't wish to be treated like one."

"And I would prefer you had someone with you." His voice became steely and determination creased his brow.

"I will not spend our time here as a prisoner, only allowed out whenever someone can make the time to fetch me back and forth." She crossed her arms over her chest and glared mutinously at him.

To her surprise, his shoulders relaxed and laughter escaped him.

"What's so funny?" she demanded.

"You are, *pedhaki mou*. You sound just like you always have. Always arguing with me. You've always accused me of being too set on having things my way." He gave a shrug that said he accepted as much.

"Well, since we're arguing, what is that woman doing here parading around in next to nothing?"

She hadn't meant it to come out quite like that. She'd wanted to sound more casual and less like a jealous shrew, but she'd failed miserably.

Chrysander's expression hardened. "You never liked her, but I would appreciate it if you weren't rude."

Marley raised a brow. "Never? And you don't wonder why?" She turned her back to Chrysander and walked to the window that overlooked the pool and the garden to the left that separated the two swimming areas. "Why is it she is here and seems so comfortable, and yet this is my first visit?"

She tensed when Chrysander's hands cupped her shoulders. "Roslyn often travels with me. This time I arranged for her to stay in Corinth so she is available if I need her, but her presence won't be an issue for you." His lips brushed across her temple. "As to why you've never been here, I can only say that it has never come up. When I would return to New York after being away for weeks at a time, I was more interested in spending that time with you, not wasting it traveling."

Marley turned around and without thinking wrapped her arms around Chrysander and buried her face in his chest. "I'm just so frustrated. I won't apologize, however, for not liking the fact that my fiancé's personal assistant is cavorting around with barely a string covering her assets, or that she seems perfectly at home in a place that I should, but don't."

"If it makes you feel better, I did not notice her assets." There was a tone of amusement in his voice, and it only served to irritate her further.

When she tried to wrench away from Chrysander's arms, he gripped her shoulders and held her fast. His eyes glistened with a need that made her stomach do odd flips. Nervously, she wet her lips, and he groaned just before he slanted his mouth over hers.

She felt as though someone had lit a match as she went up in flames. Oh, yes, her body recognized, craved his touch. His tongue swept over her lips, demanding she open to him. Her mouth parted on a sigh, and his tongue laved hers, hot, electrifying.

She went weak and sagged against him, but he caught her, holding her tightly against him. A low moan worked from her throat, and he swallowed it as it escaped. Her hands scraped across his shoulders, clutching and seeking his strength.

Her nipples beaded and tingled when his fingers skimmed underneath the waist of her shirt, feathering across her belly and up to where the lacy bra cupped her breasts. Before she could fully process what his intentions were, her bra fell loose, and his thumb rolled across one taut point.

Uncontrollable shudders wracked her small frame as his mouth slid down her throat and lower. He blazed a molten trail to the curve of one breast, and when he took the sensitive nipple in his mouth, she nearly shattered in his arms.

"Please," she begged.

His head came up at her plea, and shock was reflected in his golden eyes. "*Theos mou!* I would have ravaged you on the floor," he said in disgust. He quickly rearranged her bra and settled her shirt back over her body.

Her hand shook as she raised it to her swollen lips. Every nerve-ending in her body screamed in want. Her reaction to Chrysander frightened her. It was intense. Volatile. How easily she'd gotten carried away as soon as he'd touched her.

"Do not look at me that way," he said in a near growl.

"How?" she asked, her voice shaking.

"Like you want nothing more than for me to carry you to our bed and make love to you all night. I only have so much control."

She laughed, a hoarse and needy sound. She attempted to calm her response to his words by smoothing her hands down her sides. "And if that was what I wanted?"

He reached out to cup her chin. "The doctor will arrive in a few moments. I want him to examine you and make sure you haven't overexerted yourself with our travel. Your health is my first priority."

"I do believe I've been shot down," she murmured ruefully.

He moved so quickly she barely had time to blink. One minute they were a foot apart, and the next she was hauled against his chest, his eyes burning into her.

"Don't mistake my hesitation for disinterest," he said in a soft, dangerous tone. "I assure you, as soon as the doctor has given his approval on the state of your health, you *will* be in my bed."

He slowly let go of her, and she stepped back on faltering feet. "I believe I hear the helicopter now. That will be the physician and Mrs. Cahill. Why don't you freshen up and make yourself comfortable. I'll send the doctor up to see you."

Marley nodded like a dolt then watched as he strode away. As soon as he disappeared, she sagged onto the bed and clenched her trembling fingers together in her lap. How could she react so strongly to a man who was, for all practical purposes, a stranger? It was as he said, though. Her body recognized him even when her mind did not. She should find comfort in that, but the intensity of her attraction to him frightened her. In just a few moments, she'd so easily lost herself to his touch.

Remembering that the doctor would be up in a few moments, and not wanting to give him any excuse to send her straight to bed, she hastened to the bathroom, where she splashed cool water on her face in an effort to rid herself of the flush that still suffused her cheeks.

She dragged a hand through her curls and frowned at her reflection in the mirror. Her hair didn't look right. A brief image flashed across her mind. It was her, laughing, but with shorter hair. Hair that curled riotously around her head in an unruly cap. Even with such a brief glance into her memories, she knew she preferred her hair short. So why had she let it grow long? She shook her head and vowed to get it trimmed as soon as she was able.

A knock sounded at her door, and she rushed out of the bathroom. Chrysander walked in, an older man following closely behind him. Patrice entered after them and smiled at Marley across the room.

"Marley, this is Dr. Karounis. He is a leading obstetrician in Athens, and he has graciously agreed to see to your care while we are here on the island," Chrysander said as he curled one arm around her waist.

"Miss Jameson, it is my pleasure to provide what assistance I may," the doctor said formally.

She smiled a little nervously. "Thank you. Chrysander fusses a bit much. I'm sure it wasn't necessary for you to come all this way."

"He wants the best for you and his child," Dr. Karounis said with an easy smile. "I can hardly fault him for that."

She smiled ruefully. "No, I suppose you can't. Do whatever it is you need to do to persuade him I'm quite all right." She aimed a glare at Chrysander. "And that I'm perfectly capable of navigating the stairs by myself."

Chrysander's expression never wavered. "You will do this for me, *pedhaki mou*. It is a small thing I ask. Having someone assist you up and down the stairs will take no longer than if you were to go by yourself, and I would feel more at ease."

Oh, he knew just how to make her feel about an inch tall. She sighed. "Very well." She looked pointedly at the doctor and then made shooing gestures at Chrysander and Patrice.

Chrysander pulled her hand to his lips and kissed her palm. "After the doctor has finished, why don't you take a long bath and rest before dinner. I'll come up for you when it's time to go down."

She nodded, and Chrysander's eyes gleamed in triumph. He turned and walked out of the room, shutting the door behind him.

Six

Somehow, between the visit with the physician and a very long, relaxing bath, Marley had managed to forget all about Roslyn's presence at the house. When Chrysander walked into their bedroom to escort her down the stairs, she smiled welcomingly.

He stopped in front of her and studied her for a moment. Then he brushed his lips across hers and folded her hand in his. "You look beautiful. Your color is much better, and you look rested."

"The good doctor has proclaimed me fit as a fiddle. So there's no cause for concern."

"That is good, *pedhaki mou*. Your health is important to me."

He tucked her arm underneath his, and they headed out of the bedroom and down the stairs. As they neared the bottom, Marley looked up and saw Roslyn standing in the entrance to the formal dining room.

Marley stiffened. The woman was immaculately turned out in a designer dress that molded to every single one of her curves. She looked down self-consciously at her own very casual slacks and maternity blouse. She felt a sudden desire to race back up the stairs and change.

Not willing to allow the woman to know how much she had rattled her, Marley tightened her grip on Chrysander's arm and plastered a smile on her face.

"If I had known we wouldn't be dressing for dinner, I would have chosen different apparel," Roslyn said. She made a gesture at her outfit that drew attention to the plunging bodice. "You usually like a formal dinner." She made her last remark directly to Chrysander and cut her eyes toward Marley as if gauging her reaction to the fact that she knew more about Chrysander's likes than Marley did.

Chrysander ushered Marley forward, curling his arm around her waist in a casual manner. "Marley's comfort is what is most important, and since we intend to enjoy a great deal of privacy while we're here, it makes no sense to be so formal."

Marley relaxed and wanted to throw her arms around Chrysander. Roslyn didn't seem to be too affected by his statement, however.

"Come, *pedhaki mou*. Mrs. Cahill and Dr. Karounis are waiting on us to begin dining."

They walked past Roslyn, leaving her to follow. Marley could feel the other woman's malevolent stare boring into her back.

The food, she imagined, was delicious, but she didn't register the taste for all the attention she paid it. She smiled until her jaw ached and nodded appropriately when Patrice or Dr. Karounis spoke, but her focus was on the quiet conversation between Chrysander and Roslyn.

Chrysander's head was bent and his expression intent as the two spoke in low tones. When dessert was served and Chrysander showed no signs of turning his attention from the woman who sat a little too close, Marley scooted back in her chair, tossed her napkin down and rose.

Chrysander jerked his gaze to her. "Is everything all right?"

"Just fine," she said tightly. "Don't let me disturb you. I'm going upstairs." Before he could respond, she turned and walked away as calmly as she could.

When she reached the foot of the stairs, Patrice caught up to her. "Mr. Anetakis doesn't want you to go up the stairs alone," she said as she took Marley's elbow in her gentle grip.

Marley turned but saw no sign of Chrysander. He wasn't so worried that he'd see to the task himself. Obviously Roslyn's company was a little more important than his posturing over Marley's safety.

Fatigue beat at her as she entered the master suite and Patrice returned downstairs. The long, hot bath she'd taken before dinner had relaxed her, and she could have gone to bed then. Dinner had just brought back the tension she'd managed to rid herself of, and she knew she wouldn't sleep now.

She gazed down at the pool and gardens from the large window. The entire area shimmered under bright moonlight. It glowed with a magical quality, one that called to her. Maybe a walk in the garden would soothe her irritation.

She pulled a sweater from the closet and tugged it over her shoulders as she left the bedroom and headed for the stairs.

Not sparing one iota of guilt over the fact that her *doting* fiancé wouldn't be pleased that she was ignoring his dictate, Marley eased down the stairs. She held tightly to the banister, cursing the fact he'd made her paranoid with his concern.

She could still hear the murmur of voices filtering in from the dining room as she stepped down into the living room. She turned left and hurriedly crossed the floor to reach the French doors leading to the patio.

When she opened the door and slipped out, a chill blew over her face and raised goose bumps on her neck. Still, it was a lovely evening, and the moon shone high overhead.

She followed the stone pathway that led beside the pool and then veered right into the winding walkway of the garden. In the distance, the faint sound of the ocean soothed her ears. As she walked farther into the garden, the sound of running water overrode the distant waves. To her delight, as she rounded the corner of a thick row of hedges, she found a fountain, illuminated by spotlights angled from the ground.

Marley moved closer and inhaled the brisk night air. The salty breeze tasted tangy on her lips, and her fingers crept higher to pull the sweater more firmly around her body. She shivered with the cold but was reluctant to depart the scenic spot so soon.

"You should not be out here."

Chrysander's voice startled her even as his hands closed around her shoulders, spinning her around to face him. Anger glinted in his eyes, and displeasure tightened his jaw.

"How did you find me so quickly?" she asked, refusing to apologize for her flight.

"I've known where you were as soon as you left the house," he said calmly. At her confused expression, he said, "I have security posted all over the island. I was notified the moment you stepped onto the patio. You've been closely watched ever since."

Her mouth turned down into a frown even as she looked around, trying to ferret out the security he mentioned.

"You were not to navigate the stairs alone, and you should not come outside in the darkness unless I am with you."

"You could hardly accompany me anywhere, glued as you were to your personal assistant," she said dryly. She wanted to be flip and sound like she couldn't care less, but hurt registered in her voice, and she clenched her fingers together.

"I neglected you at dinner. For this, I am sorry. I had several things I needed to go over with Roslyn before she leaves in the morning. I will be away from my offices during our stay, and while I can work from here, I'd rather devote the time to you."

He drew her closer as he spoke, and she felt herself go weak. She hated jealousy and would like to believe she wasn't a jealous person, but how was she to know? Did she always feel such burning insecurity when it came to Chrysander? She hoped not. It had to be a miserable existence.

She leaned her forehead on his chest and closed her eyes. His spicy scent surrounded her, blocking out the salt in the air and the fragrance of the garden. Warmth enveloped her and bled into her body. "I'm sorry," she whispered.

He pulled her away and tilted her chin up with one finger. "Promise me you won't go off like this again. I cannot protect you and our child if you won't heed my precautions."

She stared up at him, watched slow desire burn its way through his eyes. Her breath caught in her throat, and all she could do was nod. She wanted him to kiss her again, touch her.

"I have spoken with Dr. Karounis," he said huskily. His finger trailed up her jaw and then over her cheek and back to her lips.

"What did he say?" she asked breathlessly.

He reached down and swept her into his arms. She let out a startled gasp as she landed against his hard chest.

"He saw no reason I could not make love to you."

"You asked him that?" she squeaked. Mortification tightened her cheeks, and she buried her face in his neck.

His low chuckle vibrated against her mouth. "I would not endanger you or our child, so I had to be sure I would not hurt you by taking you to my bed."

He strode back up the path toward the patio, bearing her weight without the slightest difficulty.

"Chrysander," she protested. "If there are all these security men around who see everything we do, then you shouldn't be carrying me off like this. They'll know what you're doing!"

He laughed but continued on. "You are cute when you're embarrassed, *pedhaki mou*. They are all men. They understand very well what it is I do."

She groaned and kept her face firmly planted, unable to bear the thought of looking up and seeing one of the security men milling about.

He nudged the French doors open with his foot then shouldered them aside as he ducked inside with her. As he climbed the stairs, Marley's nervousness grew. She wanted what was about to happen, but she also feared it. How could she retain any amount of control when he shattered it with one touch?

Her physical reaction to him made her feel vulnerable, as though she couldn't shelter any part of herself from him. She wasn't even entirely sure she wanted to, but until she could fully remember the scope of their relationship, she needed to be able to protect her emotions.

Chrysander laid her on the bed and stared down at her with glittering eyes. He touched her cheek and then let his hand trail down her body and over the swell of her stomach.

He bent and tugged her shirt up then touched his lips to her belly. There was a tenderness to the gesture that made her heart ache. He placed his hands on either side of her head and held his body over hers.

"Is this what you want?"

"Yes, oh yes," she breathed. She twisted restlessly, wanting him to fulfill the promise in his eyes.

"In many ways this is our first time together," he said huskily. "I don't want to frighten you."

She reached for him, pulling him down to meet her kiss. Her uncertainties evaporated under the heat of his lips. He took command of her mouth, leaving her to clutch desperately at his shoulders.

"I want you," she whispered when he pulled away from her, his chest heaving.

He stood to his full height, and she stared up at him from her position on the bed. Her lips were full and trembling. Her pulse ratcheted up, and excitement raced through her veins as he reached for the buttons at his neck.

Slowly, with exacting precision, he divested himself of his shirt. It fell to the floor, and he began to undo his pants. Her breath caught in her throat at the familiarity of his actions. He'd done this for her before. Teased her. Taunted her until she was crazy for him.

"You've done this before," she murmured.

A predatory smile curved his lips as the pants fell down his legs. "It is something you enjoy, or so you've told me. I like to please my woman."

Finally the silk boxers inched down his thighs, and she swallowed as his erection bobbed into view. He was simply beautiful. All powerful male. Strength rippled through the muscles in his body as he leaned forward once again.

"And now to rid you of your clothes, *pedhaki mou.*"

She curved her arms over her chest in a moment of panic. Would he find her beautiful? Would he react to her as she'd reacted to him? She strained to remember more of their lovemaking, seeking more familiarity than the fact that he'd undressed for her before.

He gently took her wrists in his hands and pulled them away until they were over her head, pressed against the mattress.

"Don't hide from me. You're beautiful. I want to see all of you."

She licked her lips as little goose bumps raced across her skin. Her nipples tightened against the confines of her bra, and suddenly she ached to be skin to skin with him, without the impediment of her clothing or her doubts.

Chrysander lowered one hand and began to pull at her shirt. His mouth found the soft skin of her neck, and he began nibbling a path to her ear. The room went a little fuzzy around her, and she struggled to keep up with the need for oxygen. She simply couldn't breathe.

Amazingly, he'd removed every stitch of her clothing. Her mouth rounded in shock, and he smiled arrogantly at her as he tossed the last of her undergarments over his shoulder.

He lifted her and positioned her on the pillows in the middle of the bed then followed her down, pressing his hard body to hers. He cupped her belly protectively then slid his hand lower, finding her most sensitive flesh.

"Chrysander!" she gasped as she arched into him.

Hot, breathless and aching, her body tightened as his mouth closed around one hard nipple. A sob escaped her as his fingers brushed across the tiny bundle of nerves at her center.

"I want you so much," he whispered. "I've missed this. We're so good together. Give yourself to me. Give me your pleasure."

He covered her, his skin pressed to hers. He inserted one thigh between her legs and positioned himself. She wrapped her arms around him as he slowly entered her body.

Even as he possessed her, he cradled her tenderly against him, taking care not to put too much of his weight on the swell that rested below her heart.

He took her to paradise, and in that moment, for the first time, she felt like she was truly home. That she belonged and wasn't living someone else's life. Tears streamed down her cheeks, and only when she found completion in his arms did he shudder above her and slowly come to rest on her body.

When he tried to move, she uttered a weak protest.

"I'm too heavy," he murmured as he settled beside her. He drew her into his arms and tucked her head underneath his chin. He ran a hand down her side and came to a rest over the curve of her hip. His fingers tightened possessively as she snuggled further into his chest.

For a long moment, they breathed in silence. Warm lethargy stole over Marley, and sleepy contentment weighed on her eyelids.

"Chrysander?"

"Yes?"

"Was it always like this?" she asked softly.

He went still against her. "No, *pedhaki mou*. This…this was much better."

A smile curved her lips as she drifted off, the smell and feel of Chrysander surrounding her.

Seven

Morning sun streamed into the bedroom and cast a warm glow on the bed where Marley lay. She opened her eyes and promptly burrowed more deeply underneath the covers. Her hand sought Chrysander, but she found only an empty spot.

She frowned and sat up, looking around the bedroom, but he was nowhere to be found. The unmistakable whir of the helicopter caught her attention, and she got out of bed and walked to the window.

Chrysander stood with Roslyn a short distance from the helicopter, his hand on her arm. She nodded and ducked down to hurry into the helicopter. A few seconds later, it lifted and headed toward the mainland. Marley couldn't help but breathe a sigh of relief.

She stood watching a moment longer before she turned and hurried toward the bathroom. After a quick shower, she pulled on her robe and walked back into the bedroom to dress. Chrysander was waiting for her.

She eyed him nervously and pulled her robe tighter around her.

"I'll leave you to dress," he said shortly. "I'll send Mrs. Cahill up to escort you down in half an hour."

Without another word, he turned and walked out of the bedroom, leaving Marley to gape after him. Hurt trickled up her spine. He'd acted as though he couldn't wait to be away from her, and after last night, his behavior certainly wasn't what she'd expected.

And sending Patrice to collect her? If he was so bent on her not navigating the stairs alone, then he could at least see to the task himself rather than foist her off on the hired help like she was some undesirable chore.

She drew her shoulders up and went to the closet to choose an outfit. There were enough concerns she had to deal with without adding a surly, moody man to the equation. Whatever the reason for his fit of temper, he could damn well get over it.

All warm and floaty feelings from the night's lovemaking evaporated as she walked out of the bedroom. She wasn't going to stand around like a lapdog and wait to be summoned. It was ridiculous that he insisted on having her helped up and down the stairs like a child.

She was halfway down when she saw Chrysander standing at the bottom, his jaw set and anger flashing in his eyes. She faltered for a moment but gripped the railing and continued downward. It made her feel childish and a little petty to defy him over such an insignificant matter, but at the moment she didn't mind irritating him in the least.

She met his gaze challengingly as she navigated the final step. His lips thinned, but he said nothing. He put a hand to her elbow to guide her to the breakfast table, but she firmly moved her arm forward and walked ahead of him.

They ate in silence, although she couldn't really say she ate anything. She pushed the fruit around on her plate and sipped mechanically at her tea, but the stony silence emanating from Chrysander had her wanting to flee.

Several times she opened her mouth to ask him what was the matter, but each time, something in his expression kept her silent. Finally, she gave up any pretense of eating and shoved her plate away.

Chrysander looked up and gave a disapproving frown when he noted the food still on her plate. "You need to eat."

"It's rather difficult to eat when a black cloud resides at your breakfast table," she said tightly.

His lips thinned, and his eyes flickered. He looked as though he would respond, but then she heard the sound of a helicopter approaching.

"It's a regular airport this morning," she murmured.

Chrysander stood and tossed down his napkin. "That will be the jeweler. I'll return in a moment."

Jeweler? She watched him go, confusion running circles through her head. What the devil did he need a jeweler for? She sat back with a sigh and wondered where Patrice or Dr. Karounis was. At least with them present, she wouldn't have to face Chrysander's stormy silence.

She stood and looked around for a moment before finally deciding to venture outdoors. The sun looked warm and inviting, and she had yet to see any of the island in daylight.

She stepped out onto the terrace and immediately closed her eyes in appreciation as the sea breeze blew over her face. It was cool but not uncomfortably so, and sunshine left a warm trail over her skin as she sought out the stone path leading to the beach.

The farther she walked from the house, the sandier the pathway became. She stopped on the walkway and shed her sandals, wondering how the warm sand would feel sliding over her feet.

At the end of the pathway, there was a short drop off to the beach. When she stepped down, her toes sank into the loose grains, and she smiled.

The waves beckoned, and so she ventured toward the frothy foam spreading across the damp sand at the water's edge. The sea was so blue it took her breath away. Paradise. It was simply paradise. And Chrysander owned it.

The wind picked up the curls at her neck and blew them

around her face. After several attempts to tuck the wayward strands behind her ears, she laughingly gave up and let them fly.

She glanced back toward the house, but seeing no one coming, she continued to walk down the beach, paralleling the water. The sounds of the incoming waves soothed her, and soon the tension in her shoulders began to unravel. She felt at peace here, but more than that, she felt safe.

The word startled her, and she stopped where she was, her forehead wrinkling in consternation. Why wouldn't she feel safe? Chrysander had a veritable mountain of security that he insisted on taking everywhere with them. If anyone was safe, she was. And yet, until they'd landed on the island, she'd felt uneasy, panic just a heartbeat away.

"You're losing your mind," she muttered. "Well, you've already lost that. Maybe the sanity isn't far behind."

Marley spied a large piece of driftwood wedged against a mound of sand, and she walked toward it. There was a place on the end that was relatively smooth, so she dusted off the sand and settled down to sit.

She sighed contentedly. She could sit here for hours watching the waves roll in and listening to the soothing sounds of the ocean. If it was warm enough to swim, she'd be tempted to shed her clothing and wade in. But then she had no idea where all the lurking security men were, and she had no desire to give them a free show.

Movement out of the corner of her eye caught her attention, and she turned her head to see Chrysander striding down the beach.

She grumbled under her breath even as he approached. Stopping in front of her, he fixed her with a frown. He pursed his lips then shook his head before moving to sit down beside her on the log.

"I can see you're going to keep my security team very busy, *pedhaki mou.*"

She shrugged but didn't say anything.

"What are you doing out here?" he asked mildly.

"Enjoying the beach. It's very beautiful."

"If I promise to bring you out again, will you come back to

the house with me? The jeweler is waiting for us, and he must return to the mainland soon."

She glanced sideways at him. "Why is a jeweler here, and why must we meet with him? Doesn't one usually visit a jeweler in his shop?"

Chrysander stood and gave her an arrogant look that suggested everyone came to him, not the other way around. He held out his hand to her, and she extended hers in resignation.

"You're really no fun," she muttered as he pulled her up to stand beside him.

"I can see I will have to change your opinion of me."

She tried to pull her hand away as they started back toward the house, but he held it fast. Hot then cold. At this rate, she'd never figure out the man. Memory loss or not, she couldn't imagine not wanting to tear her hair out around him.

They walked into the library, where an older man was arranging velvet-covered trays on Chrysander's desk. When they entered, he looked up and beamed.

"Sit, sit," he encouraged as he walked around the desk to grasp Marley's hand. He raised it to his lips and brushed a polite kiss over her skin.

When Chrysander had settled her into a chair, he took the one beside her, and the jeweler hastened around the desk.

Marley took in the stunning rings, the dazzling array of diamonds, in front of her, and gasped. She turned a questioning gaze to Chrysander.

"He is here so we can choose your ring," Chrysander said matter-of-factly. As if having a jeweler personally come out was an everyday occurrence.

"I don't understand," she began lamely.

Chrysander picked up her left hand and raised her fingers to his lips. "It is important to me that you wear my ring, *pedhaki mou*. We had not gotten around to choosing one when you had your…accident. I want to rectify that matter now."

"Oh." As responses went, hers wasn't terribly brilliant, but it was all she could manage.

Chrysander urged her to turn her attention to the rings, and she did so a little nervously. They were so huge. And expensive! She didn't even want to know how much they cost. After trying several on, she spotted one that she loved, but then wondered if he'd be offended by her choice.

Her gaze kept wandering to it even as she continued to try on the rings the jeweler pressed on her.

"That one," Chrysander said, pointing to a ring to the far right.

To her surprise, the jeweler plucked the one she'd been staring at and handed it to Chrysander. Chrysander slid it onto her finger, and it fit perfectly. It was smaller than the others, and simple, but it suited her. A single sapphire-cut solitaire sparkled on her finger, and suddenly she had no wish to take it off.

"You like it," Chrysander said.

"I love it," she whispered, then looked quickly up at Chrysander. "But if you'd prefer another, I don't mind."

"We'll take this one," Chrysander told the jeweler.

If the jeweler was disappointed, he didn't show it as he smiled broadly at the couple. He efficiently boxed the jewelry back up and stored it in a briefcase that he locked. A few minutes later, Chrysander walked the jeweler out to the waiting helicopter but not before issuing Marley a stern order not to move from her spot.

She giggled as he left. He looked so exasperated, but then he was probably used to people obeying his every command and staying where they were put. A sudden thought horrified her. Had she been one of those people? Surely not. She may have lost her memory, but she hadn't had a personality transplant.

With that in mind, she left the library and went in search of something to eat. Her nonbreakfast was now a regret as her stomach protested.

Before she could open the refrigerator, she heard Chrysander enter the kitchen.

"How did I know you would not be where I left you?" he said.

She turned around and smiled sweetly. "Because you didn't ask nicely?"

He let out a low laugh, a sexy sound that vibrated right up

her spine. "I've asked the helicopter to return in an hour's time. If you are feeling well enough, I thought we could go visit the ruins you were interested in and maybe take in some of the other sights."

"Oh, I'd love to!" Forgotten was food or anything else as she hurried across and threw herself into Chrysander's arms. She hugged him tightly in her excitement.

Chrysander chuckled again. "Am I forgiven then for being no fun?"

She pulled back and made a face. "Trust you to throw my words back at me. But yes, you are forgiven. Let me just go change."

"Bring a sweater," he cautioned. "It will grow cooler toward evening."

She started to hurry off, but he caught her hand and pulled her back to him. She landed against his chest and looked up to see his mouth just inches from her own.

"Surely I deserve a reward?" he murmured.

She licked her lips, and he groaned. "I suppose a little one wouldn't be remiss," she said huskily.

His mouth closed over hers, and she melted into his arms. She trembled as he deepened his kiss, and a small moan escaped her lips.

He pulled away, his eyes blazing. "I better take you upstairs to change, or we will not be going anywhere but to bed."

She grinned impishly then pulled away and headed for the stairs. Not that she thought she'd get far, and she didn't. He caught up with her before her foot hit the first step.

She gave him an exasperated look as they climbed the stairs. "I am perfectly capable of navigating the stairs on my own, Chrysander. I'm not completely helpless."

"I can be a reasonable man. Just not in this matter," he said arrogantly. "I'm sorry, but you'll have to live with the fact that I intend to take care of you."

She rolled her eyes, but a smile twitched at the corners of her mouth. She could tell she strained his patience, and for some reason that amused her.

He waited while she changed and handed her a sweater when she was finished. She laid it over her arm, and once again he took her down the stairs and out to the helipad, where the helicopter waited.

Soon they were flying over the water and a while later landed in Corinth. A car was waiting, and to her surprise, Chrysander put her into the passenger seat of the Mercedes then slid into the driver's seat himself.

"I do know how to drive," he said dryly when she looked at him questioningly.

She laughed. "It's just that I've never seen you do so." She frowned as she realized what she'd said. "What I mean is, I haven't seen you drive since…"

He laid a hand over hers. "I know what you meant, Marley. True, I don't drive very often. I'm usually occupied with business matters, but I have a car both here and in New York."

She settled into the soft leather seat as he drove away from the airport.

They spent much of the morning walking among the ruins. He explained the history, but she was more focused on the fact that it was a beautiful autumn day and they were together. No annoying personal assistants, no doctors or nurses, no business calls or faxes. It was, in a word, perfect.

"You're not paying a bit of attention, *pedhaki mou.*" Chrysander's amused voice filtered through her haze of contentment.

She blushed and turned to look at him. "I'm sorry. I'm enjoying it, truly."

"Are you ready to return to the island?" he asked. "I'm not overtiring you, am I?" The amusement had turned to concern, and if she didn't dissuade him of the notion that she was not well, she'd find herself bundled back on the helicopter and her perfect day would be at its end.

"Tell me about your family. You've said nothing about them. I realize the information may be redundant, but since I can't remember any of it, perhaps you could humor me."

"What would you like to know?" he asked.

"Anything. Everything. Are your parents still living? You don't talk about them."

A flash of pain showed in his eyes, and she immediately regretted the question.

"They died some years back in a yachting accident," he said.

She slipped her hand into his and squeezed comfortingly. "I'm sorry. I didn't mean to bring up such a painful subject."

"It's been a long time," he said with a shrug. But she could tell speaking of them bothered him.

She opened her mouth to change the topic when he suddenly frowned and lowered his other hand to his pocket. He pulled out his cell phone and studied it for a moment before opening it and putting it to his ear.

"Roslyn," he said shortly, after a quick glance at Marley.

Marley stiffened and pulled her hand away from Chrysander's. Trust his assistant to know just when to call. She must have radar.

She could see the tension rise in Chrysander, and when he looked in her direction, it was as though he stared right through her.

"Everything is fine here," Chrysander said. "Find out from Piers how things are going for the Rio de Janeiro hotel and report back." There was a long pause. "No, I don't know when we'll return to New York." He glanced again at Marley, and she got the distinct impression Roslyn was talking about her. "No, of course not," he said in a soothing voice. "I appreciate your diligence, Roslyn. You'll be the first to know when I plan to leave the island."

Marley looked away in disgust, no longer able to listen to his part of the conversation. A few moments later, he snapped the phone shut and put it into his pocket. As expected, when she turned back to him, his entire demeanor had changed for the worse. He looked at her almost suspiciously, though she couldn't imagine why. But she wasn't imagining it. There was a distinct change in his mood.

"I'm sorry for the interruption," he said almost formally. "What were we talking about?"

"Tell me about your hotels," she said impulsively, wanting to steer him away from his concerns.

His expression froze and wariness stole over his face. "What would you like to know?"

She found a place to sit that overlooked the tall pillars and tugged him down beside her.

"I don't know. Anything. Where do you have hotels? Imperial Park in New York is one of yours, isn't it?"

He nodded.

"Where else do you have hotels? Are you very international? I heard you say something about Rio de Janeiro. Do you have a hotel there?"

He'd gone completely stiff, and she puzzled over why. Did he not like to discuss his business? In truth, she craved whatever details about him she could get. He hadn't been very forthcoming about his work life, a fact she found odd.

"We have hotels in most major international cities. Our largest are in New York, Tokyo, London and Madrid. We have several others, slightly smaller, across Europe. We're currently working on plans for one in Rio de Janeiro."

"But not in Paris? I think I'd like for you to have one in Paris so we could visit." She grinned teasingly at him.

Her smile faded when his eyes went cold and hard. A shiver worked its way up her spine, and a knot formed in her stomach. He looked angry. No, he looked *furious*.

"No, we do not have one in Paris."

His clipped tone had her backing away. She slid several inches down the bench. "I'm sorry…." She didn't even know what she was apologizing for. His mood had gone black in an instant, and she had no idea why. She seemed to have a penchant for dredging up the wrong subjects. First his parents and now his business. Was there any safe topic for them to discuss?

She stood and clenched her fingers into tight balls. "Perhaps you're right. Maybe we should go back now." She turned swiftly, her intention to walk back toward the car, but she moved too fast and the world spun dizzyingly around her.

She thought briefly of her missed breakfast before her knees buckled and she blacked out.

When Marley regained consciousness, the first thing she heard was a furious voice rapidly firing in Greek. As her eyes opened and her gaze flickered around her surroundings, she realized she was on an exam table in what appeared to be a clinic.

Chrysander's back was to her, and he was interrogating the doctor standing in front of him.

"Chrysander," she murmured weakly.

He spun around immediately and hurried over to where she lay. "Are you all right?" His hands swept over her body even as his eyes bored intensely into hers. "Are you in pain?"

She tried to smile, but she felt shaky. The doctor moved in front of Chrysander and held a cup toward her.

"Drink this, Miss Jameson. Your blood sugar is too low, but I think some juice will set you to rights."

Chrysander took the juice then curled an arm underneath her neck to help her sit up. He held the cup to her lips as she cautiously sipped at the sweet liquid.

"When was the last time you ate, Miss Jameson?"

The doctor pinned her with an inquiring stare, and she felt her cheeks warm with embarrassment. She ducked her head. "I didn't eat breakfast," she admitted.

Chrysander bit out a curse. "Nor did you eat much dinner last night. *Theos,* but I should not have brought you here today. I knew you hadn't eaten properly, and yet I didn't think to remedy the situation."

She gave him a wan smile. "It isn't your fault, Chrysander. It was foolish of me. I didn't give it much thought in my excitement over our trip to the ruins."

"It is my job to take care of you and our child," he said stubbornly.

The doctor cleared his throat and smiled at them. "Yes, well, no harm was done. A proper meal, and she'll feel like a new woman. I'd suggest being off your feet for the rest of the day. No sense in chancing things."

"I'll personally see to it," Chrysander said stiffly.

Marley sighed. He was taking her fainting spell personally. He fairly bristled with guilt, and she knew there'd be no swaying him from his course. She might as well resign herself to the rest of the day in bed.

"Can I take her home now?" Chrysander asked the doctor.

The doctor nodded. "Just make sure she eats promptly and that she rests."

"You can be certain I will," Chrysander said grimly.

Marley made to slide off the exam table, but Chrysander put out a hand to prevent her movement. Then he simply plucked her up into his arms and strode out the door.

When they got outside, a dark car pulled immediately in front of them, and a man jumped out to open the door for Chrysander. He ducked in, still holding Marley close to him.

"So much for you driving," she muttered as they were whisked away toward the airport.

"I cannot drive and hold you at the same time," Chrysander said patiently.

"I wasn't aware of the need to be held."

"I *will* take care of you."

It was said with ironclad resoluteness, his voice solemn, and she knew he took his vow very seriously. Realizing she wouldn't win any arguments with him today, she relaxed against his chest and curled her arms around his body.

He stroked her head and murmured softly in Greek. She was nearly asleep when the car came to a halt. Soon after the door opened, and a shaft of sunlight speared her eyes as she looked up.

Chrysander threw his arm up to shield her then gently turned her head back into his chest. He got out of the car still holding her and walked rapidly toward the helicopter.

"Go back to sleep if you can, *pedhaki mou*," he murmured as he climbed in.

But when the whir of the blades started, the fog of sleep disappeared. She contented herself instead with snuggling into the curve of his neck as they lifted off toward the island.

He'd obviously called ahead and issued a montage of orders, because when he walked into the house with her, Patrice had a meal waiting, and Dr. Karounis stood by to monitor Marley's condition. After an initial fuss, Patrice and the doctor, once they'd assured Chrysander that Marley was well, excused themselves, leaving the two alone.

Marley dug into the bowl of soup first and sighed as it coated her empty stomach.

"You will not skip any more meals," Chrysander said reproachfully as he watched her from across the table.

"I didn't intend to skip any," she said. "I just got sidetracked."

"I'll make sure that doesn't happen again."

She raised an eyebrow then grinned mischievously. "So it's back to being no fun then?"

He glowered at her.

That glower reminded her of what had transpired right before she'd fainted. She sobered and looked pensively at him.

"What is the matter?" Chrysander asked.

She fiddled with her spoon then set it down. "Before, when we were at the ruins. Why did you become so angry?"

His expression remained neutral, but she could tell he had no liking for the question. "It was nothing. I was just thinking about work," he said dismissively.

She stared doubtfully at him but didn't pursue the matter. When she had finished eating, Chrysander once again swept her into his arms and carried her up the stairs to the bedroom.

He settled her onto the mattress and methodically removed her clothing. By the time he'd pulled away her pants, she lay in only her bra and filmy panties. She heard the catch in his breath just as he turned away.

"Chrysander," she whispered.

He turned back, the muscles rippling through his body as if he were under a great strain.

"Stay with me. Could we take a nap together? I find I'm very tired after all."

If he didn't look so tortured, she'd laugh. She worked to keep her expression neutral as he grappled with her request. Finally he began working the buttons to his shirt. In silence he undressed to his boxers then crawled onto the bed with her.

Then he cursed. She looked inquiringly at him as he stared down at her.

"Would you like something to sleep in? You cannot stay in your bra. It doesn't look comfortable."

She blushed but nodded. "A nightshirt will do."

He got up and returned with one of his shirts. He helped her sit up and unclasped her bra. His hands shook slightly as he pulled the shirt over her head and let it fall to her swollen belly.

With gentle hands, he urged her back down and knelt above her. "Better?"

"Much," she said huskily.

He settled down beside her and tucked her into his arms. She twisted about, trying to find just the right spot. When she scooted her behind into his groin, she froze, feeling his arousal there against her skin. She started to move away, when Chrysander growled in her ear.

"Be still."

He clamped his arms around her, rendering her immobile. Her cheeks flaming, she tried to relax. The moment he'd touched her, her fatigue had fled. Now she faced trying to sleep with him wrapped around every inch of her body.

His warmth bled into her. He stroked her hair and murmured in her ear. Greek words she couldn't understand, though the comfort they intended was well recognized. She sighed in contentment as his hand glided down her arm, to her hip, coming to rest on her thigh.

She felt a wave of such utter rightness, and she was stunned to realize the nameless emotion she'd been grappling with was love. Her eyes fluttered open even as she heard Chrysander's even breathing signal his slumber.

She loved him. It shouldn't surprise her, but now that she'd acknowledged it, she realized that she hadn't immediately recognized it after her memory loss. Shouldn't she have known on some level that she loved this man?

He was complicated, there was no disputing that. Complex, hard and reserved. Well, if she'd broken down his barriers once, then surely she could do so again.

She settled down to sleep, purpose beating a steady rhythm in her mind.

Eight

Warm lips kissed a line from her shoulder down her arm. Marley stirred and opened her eyes to see Chrysander's dark head move sensuously down her body.

"That's a very nice way to wake up," she murmured.

His head came up, and she met the liquid gold of his eyes. "How are you feeling, *pedhaki mou?*"

She rolled onto her back and lifted her hand to thread it through his short hair. "Much better. I'm full and had a nap. What more could a pregnant woman want?"

"Our child did not sleep much," Chrysander said as he slid his hand over her rippling abdomen.

She smiled. "No, he's been very active lately. The obstetrician said they do the most moving in the second trimester."

He stared intently at her rounded belly, fascination lighting his eyes. "They don't move in the last trimester?"

"Yes, just not as much. There isn't as much room. In the last month, they do very little as their environment gets even more cramped."

"I would think it would be easier for you to rest then."

She yawned then covered her mouth with her hand as her jaw nearly cracked with the effort.

"You're still tired," he said reproachfully.

"I'm pregnant. I expect I'll be tired for the next eighteen years. I feel much better though. Truly, Chrysander. Let's get up."

He straddled her body, putting one knee on either side of her hips. He looked down at her, his eyes gleaming with a predatory light. "You're so eager to rise. Why is this?"

She blushed and smacked his chest with her fist. He leaned down and tugged her lips into a kiss. He nipped at the fullness of her bottom lip until it was swollen and aching.

"I have half a mind to keep you in bed until tomorrow morning," he murmured.

Putty. She was complete putty in his hands. If he so much as breathed on her, she went to mush. She twined her arms around his neck and returned his kiss hungrily. She could feel his erection straining against her, knew he wanted her as badly as she wanted him.

With obvious reluctance he pulled away and climbed off the bed. She looked at him in confusion. Why was he withdrawing?

He reached down and touched her hair, smoothing the tendrils away from her cheek. "You've been through an ordeal today, *agape mou.* I don't want to tire you any more."

He seemed as surprised as she was when the endearment slipped out of his mouth. Her eyes widened, and he tensed. Then he turned around and strode to the closet.

She watched him dress and then disappear from the bedroom. He'd called her my love, and while it had given her an indescribable thrill, it was obvious that it wasn't something he meant to say.

But he had said it. She held tight to that truth as she got out of bed to dress. Not knowing how he felt about her and why he took such pains to hold himself distant had puzzled her from the beginning. Was it because of her memory loss? Did he fear that her feelings for him couldn't possibly be considered valid while he was still a stranger to her?

She'd focused so much on her own problems that arose from the gaping hole in her past, but it was obvious that he, too, had difficulties with the situation.

If only she could remember. If only she could reassure him that she loved him whether or not she could remember loving him in the past.

All she could do was show him. And hope that her memory was restored before too much longer.

Chrysander sat in his office, staring out the window that overlooked the beach. Marley stood close to the water, her feet bare and the maternity dress she wore rippling in the breeze. He kept careful watch over her and had instructed his security team to do the same. He wouldn't take any chances after her fainting spell of the day before.

Just moments earlier, he'd hung up after speaking to the lead investigator on Marley's case. There had been no arrests made yet. No leads. The men who had abducted her were still out there. Still a danger to her and their child. It was unacceptable.

The detective had promised to stay in touch and to inform him the moment there was a break in the case, but Chrysander still wasn't satisfied. He wanted results. He wanted to make the men who'd dared to touch Marley pay.

He focused his attention back on Marley, who was still staring out to sea. Every once in a while she raised her hand to shove the curls from her face, only for them to blow back. She lifted her chin and laughed, and Chrysander could feel the impact from where he sat.

She was beautiful and carefree. Unguarded in the moment. He searched his memory for the times when they had been together. Happy. He hadn't appreciated it at the time, but their relationship—he now admitted to himself that they'd had a relationship—had been open and undemanding.

So what had driven her to betray his trust? He'd almost have preferred she'd betrayed him with another man; but no, she'd gone after his family, his brothers. And that he couldn't forgive...could he?

Indecision wracked his brain. A large part of him was still conflicted and angry. But another, smaller part was ready to move on. To forget what she had done and embrace a new beginning. Maybe she'd never remember, and if he was honest, it would make things easier if she never did.

He continued to watch her, and his gaze moved beyond her to where one of his security detail stood on guard at a distance. She continued to defy him, and he pretended annoyance, but all he did was make sure his men shadowed her at every turn. Her determination to go against his wishes amused him because he didn't sense any real irritation on her part. She liked goading him.

And he knew he was being overprotective, but the fact that her kidnappers were still out there, that they still posed a threat to her and their child, sent dark fear through his veins. She was his. He'd failed her once. No matter that she had betrayed him. He'd sent her and his child unprotected into the hands of her kidnappers because he'd allowed emotion to cloud his judgment.

He turned in annoyance when his phone rang. Tearing his gaze from Marley, he put the phone to his ear.

"Mr. Anetakis." Roslyn's voice broke clear over the line.

"Roslyn, have you spoken to Piers about the status of the Rio de Janeiro deal?"

"Yes, sir, and he said to tell you that if you'd answer your phone he'd let you know how things were going himself."

Chrysander chuckled. "I will deal with my younger brother."

"If at all possible, you need to attend a conference call tomorrow evening, seven our time. I'll send out an e-mail with the details. Theron and Piers will both be on hand, but Mr. Diego specifically wished to speak personally with you."

"I'll make it," he said.

"And how are things with you?" Roslyn asked hesitantly.

Chrysander frowned and glanced back to the beach, where Marley stood watching the waves roll in.

"Has she regained her memory yet?" she continued.

"No," he said shortly.

There was a moment of silence, and he could hear Roslyn's

soft breathing as though she battled over whether to say what was on her mind.

"If that's all," he said in an effort to end the call.

"Have you considered that she's faking her memory loss?" Roslyn said in a rush.

"What?"

"Think about it," she said impatiently. "What better way to circumvent your anger than to pretend to have forgotten it all? You can't even be sure the child is yours. She was in captivity for months. Who's to say what went on during that time?"

Ice trickled down Chrysander's spine. "That's enough," he said tersely.

"But—"

"I said enough."

"As you wish. I'll phone you if anything changes."

Chrysander hung up and yanked his gaze back to the beach, but Marley was gone. Could Roslyn be right? Could Marley be faking her amnesia? The thought had crossed his mind when they'd still been in New York and Marley was fresh from the hospital. His instincts said no, but then he'd already been so wrong about her in every way. If someone had told him six months ago that she was capable of betraying him as she had, he would have cut them down to size.

Anger and confusion took turns battering his head. He rubbed a weary hand across his face and closed his eyes. It didn't really matter what he thought at this point. She was pregnant with his child and that took precedence above all else. He could overlook a lot for his son.

A sound at the door made him look up. Marley stood just inside his office, a sparkling smile on her face. Her eyes glowed with…happiness.

He found himself relaxing, the turmoil of a few minutes ago dissipating.

"You grew tired of your walk on the beach?"

Her lips twisted ruefully as she walked forward. "I should have known you knew exactly where I was."

He gestured toward the window. "I had a prime view. You looked to have enjoyed yourself. Are you feeling well today? You haven't overdone it?"

She stopped at his desk, and he nearly gestured her around to settle on his lap, but he refrained, needing to maintain a distance while he felt so volatile, so uncertain. He didn't want to think of her as a deceiver, nothing more than a practiced actress bent on escaping retribution.

"I'm fine, Chrysander. You worry far too much. I don't need to be coddled. You would think I was the first woman to ever be pregnant."

"You are the first woman to bear my child," he pointed out.

She laughed. "And so I am. I'll make allowances for your overbearing ways because this is your first child. When we have our next, I expect you to act sanely."

Every muscle in his body stiffened, and he fought the darkness that spread across his face. Another child. It suggested permanence. A lasting relationship. Yes, he planned to ask—no, insist—she marry him, but he hadn't given thought to what it would mean. A permanent place in his life for her. More children.

Were his brothers right? Should he have installed her in an apartment, hired suitable staff to look after her until the baby was born and then removed her from his life?

"Chrysander? Is something wrong?"

He glanced up to see her staring at him with worried eyes. There, again, as it had so many times before when she looked at him, was a flash of uncertainty. Of fear almost. He cursed under his breath. He had not intended to frighten her, nor did he want to upset her.

He reached for her. "No, *pedhaki mou*. Nothing is wrong."

She hesitated the briefest of seconds before she finally walked around and into his arms. She settled on his knee, and he watched as she worked her lower lip between her teeth.

"Don't you want more children?" she asked.

He cocked his head to the side, trying to adopt a casual air. "I don't suppose I'd considered it yet. Our first son is still to be born."

She nodded. "I know. I suppose I just assumed since you have brothers that you'd want more than one child. Have we discussed it before? Did I want more than one? I look ahead now and feel like I'd love several more. Maybe four total. But I don't know if I've always wanted that many."

Unable to resist her worried brow, he pressed a kiss to her forehead. "Let's not worry about it now. We have plenty of time. First you have to marry me," he said teasingly. "Let's wait until our son is born to think about adding more to our family."

A beautiful, captivating smile lit up her face and knocked the breath from him all in one moment.

"That sounds so lovely when you say it," she breathed.

"What's that?"

"Family. I don't have family, or so I was told. To know that you and I will have a family of our own means so much. Sometimes I feel so lonely, like I've been lonely forever."

She shivered lightly against his chest as the haunting words left her lips.

"You aren't alone," he said softly. "You have me, and we have our son."

It was a vow. One that he felt only passing discomfort over making. Part of him wondered at the ease with which he committed himself to a woman who'd done so much damage, but the other part could no sooner turn away than he could cut off his arm.

"You should go rest," he said firmly, more because of his need to distance himself from her before he totally succumbed to the pull between them than a real concern over her health. The doctor had assured him she was fit and well, that her fainting spell had been nothing more than a product of missed meals. "I'll summon Mrs. Cahill to help you up the stairs."

Her lips turned down into a frown. She struggled up from his lap even as he put a hand to her arm. "I'm perfectly rested, Chrysander. The walk on the beach was very refreshing."

"Still, a short repose wouldn't be unreasonable," he said. "I have some work to finish. I'll come for you when I'm done, and we can have dinner together."

Disappointment dulled her eyes before she looked away. She nodded but said nothing as she left the room.

Marley closed Chrysander's door quietly and glanced up as Patrice approached. She tried to look welcoming, because after all she did like Patrice. She was just doing her job.

"Are you ready to go up?" Patrice asked with a smile.

Marley sighed. "Honestly? I'd like to smother Chrysander with the pillow he insists I rest on."

Patrice tried to stifle her laughter, but a chuckle escaped. "Could I interest you in a cup of tea on the terrace instead?"

Marley immediately brightened. "That sounds wonderful."

She fell into step beside Patrice as the two headed toward the glass doors. A cool breeze, scented by the ocean, blew over Marley's face when she stepped outside.

"I hope you don't mind if Dr. Karounis joins us." Marley noticed the way Patrice's cheeks turned pink as she spoke. "He and I take tea here every afternoon."

"Of course not," Marley replied as she settled into one of the chairs surrounding the small table overlooking the gardens.

When Patrice ducked back inside to prepare the tea, Marley was left alone. She leaned back and stared out over the grounds. Even with the constant company that Patrice and Dr. Karounis afforded, loneliness surrounded her like a cloak. That and frustration.

Every time Chrysander relaxed around her and they shared any sort of intimacy, he immediately backed away, as if he became aware of what was happening and rushed to correct it.

She was convinced that Patrice and Dr. Karounis were here more as a barrier between her and Chrysander than they were here over any worry he had of her health. Not that he didn't care. She wasn't petty enough to think he wasn't genuinely concerned for her and their child. But at the same time, she couldn't discount the convenience of him pawning her off on Patrice whenever things got too personal.

It seemed that when she actually started to relax, he only grew more uptight. Nothing about her supposed relationship with this man made any sense to her. If only she could remember.

If only she knew someone she could ask. Had she truly been so closed off from the rest of the world during her relationship with Chrysander?

"Surely things aren't that bad," Patrice said as she set a tray down on the table in front of Marley. "You look as though you have the weight of the world on your shoulders."

Marley managed a faltering smile. "Oh, nothing so serious. Just thinking."

Dr. Karounis walked up behind Patrice and nodded a greeting to Marley. Patrice smiled broadly and urged the doctor to sit down while she poured tea.

Despite her own inner turmoil, Marley couldn't help but smile at the older couple. They were obviously enjoying a mild flirtation. It was good to see someone happy and content. She'd give anything to enjoy a moment's peace.

With another sigh, she collected her cup and brought it to her lips as she looked out again over the beautiful garden. Maybe she was expecting too much in too short a time. Maybe she was pushing too hard, which precipitated Chrysander pushing her away. So much would be solved if she could only remember.

At any rate, she couldn't expect an overnight miracle. There had to be a way to break through Chrysander's defenses. She just had to find it.

Nine

Their days slowly began to settle into a routine much as their nights did. Once he was assured of her health, Chrysander made love to Marley every night, possessing her with passion that left her breathless. But in the mornings, he was always gone before she woke up.

She'd made it a habit to seek him out, bothered by the fact that he left their bed so early. More often than not, she'd find him in the library, either on the phone, on his computer or poring over contracts and faxes. He'd look up when she entered, and for a brief moment, she'd see fire flare in his eyes before his expression became more controlled, and after murmuring a polite good-morning, he'd return to his work. And she was summarily dismissed.

So she spent most mornings alone or in the company of Patrice and Dr. Karounis who seemed quite content to spend their time together. At lunch, Chrysander would make his appearance as if he hadn't just spent hours sequestered in work. To his credit, he devoted the afternoons to Marley.

She'd cajoled him into taking walks with her on the beach,

though he grumbled about the chill and her tiring herself. She looked forward to these times because she had Chrysander all to herself, and at least in those few short hours, he seemed to lose his cautious reserve with her.

It was during one of those walks that Chrysander pulled her down to sit on the log she often sat on to watch the ocean. He stared out over the water for a moment then turned to her, his expression serious.

"We should get married soon."

She twisted the engagement ring around her finger with her thumb and wondered why this wasn't a happier conversation.

"I wanted to give you time to recover and regain your strength. The doctor feels you are strong and healthy now."

She relaxed a little under his intent gaze. "When were you thinking of?"

"As soon as I can arrange it. I don't want to wait any longer. I don't want our child born a bastard."

She frowned and twisted her neck to gaze up at him. It was hardly a romantic declaration of love and devotion. But then she didn't want her child to be born out of wedlock, either. She suddenly felt selfish for wanting a more flowery reason for the hastiness of their marriage.

"Will you marry me, *pedhaki mou?* I'll take care of you and our child. You'll want for nothing, I swear it."

She worked to keep another frown from her face. The more he talked, the less desirous she was for marriage. He made it sound like a bargain. She didn't want their marriage to be cold and clinical.

He tipped her chin up with his finger and stared down into her eyes. "What are you thinking about so hard?"

She didn't want to tell him the truth. So instead, she slowly nodded.

One of his eyebrows lifted in question. "Is that a yes?"

"Yes," she whispered. "I'll marry you as soon as you can arrange it."

Satisfaction glinted in his eyes. He leaned down to brush his lips across hers. "You won't regret this, *pedhaki mou.*"

Such an odd choice of words. Why would she have reason to believe she'd regret marrying the man she loved, the father of her child? She wondered if he'd always been so cryptic and that she'd learned to love him in spite of it. Obviously she had.

As they walked back to the house, she slid her hand into his. There was a need for comfort in her action. After only a slight hesitation, he curled his fingers around hers and squeezed. Bolstered by the small gesture, she shrugged away the doubts tugging at her.

That night, Marley was dressing for bed when Chrysander came up behind her and curled his arms around her waist. His hands rested over the swell of her stomach as he nuzzled a line from the top of her shoulder to the sensitive region just below her ear. Goose bumps danced and scattered along her skin, and she trembled against his chest.

"I much prefer you naked, *pedhaki mou*," he said as he slid one hand up to pluck at the string of the gown she'd just slipped on.

His words speared through her mind, sparking a distant remembrance. For a moment, she had an image of him standing before her, staring at her with glowing eyes, saying those exact words. She struggled to remember more, but it slipped away as fast as it had slipped in.

She closed her eyes in frustration even as she gave way to the pleasure of his touch.

He slid the strap over her shoulder, following it with his lips until it tumbled down her arm. Then he turned his attention to the other side, giving it the same thorough attention. He thumbed the thin string down her arm until the satin material spilled from her body and landed in a pool on the floor.

Uncertainty and vulnerability washed over her as she stood naked save for the lacy panties she wore. She jumped when he placed his hands over her belly again and then did a slow walk up and over her curves. His palms smoothed up her sides and then curved around to her breasts, where he cupped both soft mounds. His lips found her neck again, and she shivered uncontrollably as his thumbs caressed her taut nipples while he landed light nips with his teeth.

"I want you," he said in a guttural voice. "You're so beautiful, *agape mou*. Come to bed with me."

It was so easy to forget her doubts and insecurities in the shelter of his arms. When they made love, they truly connected. There were no barriers, no stiffness and no reluctance. She lived for these moments, when he made her his, when he showed her far better than words what she meant to him.

She turned, allowing his hands to slide over her skin. When she was facing him, she leaned up on tip toe and linked her arms around his neck. "Kiss me," she whispered.

With a low growl, he swooped in and captured her lips with barely controlled restraint. His movements were impatient tonight, as though he couldn't get enough of her, as if he couldn't wait to possess her.

She allowed him to urge her toward the bed, his body pressed tightly to hers. He eased her onto the mattress, his lips never leaving hers. He lifted himself off her, his eyes blazing in the dim light. With jerky motions, he stripped out of his clothing before lowering himself once more.

"Make love to me, Chrysander," she said as she reached up to touch his face.

He bent, and his lips moved heatedly down her jaw to her neck and then lower to her breasts. He tugged one taut nipple with his mouth before going to the other. Lightly, his tongue rolled over the crest, sending shock waves to her throbbing center.

His dark head bobbed as he continued a path downward to the rise of her belly. Scooting his body down, he framed the mound between his hands with a reverence that brought tears to her eyes. Then he pressed his mouth to her stomach in a gentle kiss.

Emotion knotted in her throat until it became hard to breathe around it. If only they could stay this way. Here, where there were no words, no defenses, she felt loved and cherished. No walls, no barriers, no secrets.

His mouth moved lower, and she gasped when he nudged her thighs apart and touched his mouth to her pulsing core.

"Chrysander!" she cried out as he licked over her sensitive bundle of nerves.

"You taste so sweet, *agape mou,*" he said as he moved up her body again.

He fit himself against her damp heat and then slowly slid inside her body. She closed her eyes and reached for him with a sigh of pleasure. Her hand threaded through the short hair at the back of his head and down to his nape where she caressed as he moved back and forth with exquisite gentleness.

Then his lips found hers again, and he swallowed her abrupt cry as he sank deeper than before.

"Give me your pleasure," he said against her mouth. "Only to me."

She arched against him, her body tightening as the first stirrings of her release began deep and rushed in a thousand different directions. Her soft cry split the night, and he gathered her tightly to him. His hand smoothed down her side to her hip and then to the curve of her belly.

"I can never get enough of you," he admitted in a voice that sounded strangely vulnerable.

She opened her eyes to see him staring down at her, his expression fierce and haunted. And then he began to move harder, more demanding. Wordlessly he took her to indescribable heights. She floated freely, her body cocooned in bliss.

So began the night. She'd barely come down from the peaks he'd driven her to when he began making love to her all over again. He possessed her tirelessly, commanding her body with a practiced ease that left her gasping. Throughout the night he was insatiable, and just before dawn, they both fell into an exhausted sleep.

Even as Marley hovered in the euphoric aftermath, her sleep was troubled. There was a familiarity to Chrysander's demanding lovemaking, as if for the first time he'd shown her part of her past life with him.

In her dreams, she struggled to open a firmly shut door,

knowing that on the other side lay her life, her memories, everything that had happened to her in her lifetime. She pulled at it then beat on it, sobbing for it to open and show her.

She clawed at it, and finally, she managed to pry it open the barest amount. Light poured from the crack, and then, as suddenly as it had shone, brilliant and white, it was doused by an overwhelming feeling of fear and despair. She knew without a doubt that she didn't want to see what was on the other side.

In her shock, she loosened her grip and the door slammed shut, leaving her kneeling and shaking against the cold wood. No! She needed to know. She had to know. Who was she and what had happened to her?

"Marley. Marley!" Chrysander's urgent tones intruded on her dream. "You must wake up, *pedhaki mou*. It's just a dream. You're safe. You're here with me."

She opened her eyes to see Chrysander over her, his eyes bright with concern. He'd turned the lamp on beside the bed, and for that she was grateful. She felt suffocated by the darkness of her dream.

She felt wetness on her cheeks and realized she'd been crying in her sleep. Her heart still raced with panic, and she couldn't dispel the awful feeling of foreboding that had gripped her.

She tried to speak, to tell Chrysander she was all right, but a cry wrenched from her throat. He gathered her tightly in his arms and held her close as her body shook with sobs.

"You're going to make yourself ill, Marley. You must stop."

For a long time she gripped his arms, not wanting him to pull away from her. When she finally managed to regain control of herself, he gently eased her back onto the pillows.

"What has frightened you so badly, *agape mou?*"

The images from her dream came roaring back, but she was hard-pressed to make sense of them. Thankfully, the awful panic had receded so that she could breathe normally again.

"I was at a door," she said, her speech faltering. "And I knew that on the other side of the door were my memories. But I couldn't open it no matter how hard I tried. Finally, I managed to crack it but then…"

"Then what?" he asked gently.

"Fear," she whispered. "So much fear. I was afraid. I let go of the door, and it slammed shut."

He lay back down beside her and curled his arms around her. "It was just a dream, *pedhaki mou*. Just a dream. It can't hurt you. You fear the unknown. This is natural."

She slowly began to relax against him. He stroked her back, his palm gliding up and down her spine.

"Are you all right now? Do you want me to call for Dr. Karounis?"

She shook her head against his chest. "No. I'm fine. Really. I feel so silly now."

"You're not silly. Try and go back to sleep. I fear I kept you awake far too long tonight."

His voice had deepened to a husky timbre, and her body tightened all over as she remembered the ways he'd kept her up.

With a yawn, she burrowed as tightly as she could against his hard body and let herself fall into what was this time a dreamless sleep.

Chrysander rose at dawn the next morning. He hadn't slept since Marley had awakened with her nightmare. After he'd soothed her, and she had fallen into a more peaceful rest, he'd lain awake, staring at the ceiling as he realized the impossibility of their situation.

Careful not to wake Marley, he showered and dressed. After checking to make sure she hadn't been disturbed, he went quietly down the stairs. He bypassed his office, though it was his custom to begin the day with business matters.

This morning something drove him to the beach where Marley so often visited. The air was chilly blowing off the water, but he took no notice as he stood watching the waves break and slide into shore.

Marley's past, *their* past, threatened her in sleep. Her memories waged war at her most unguarded moments, and what would he do when it all came back?

The terrible conflict that ate at him was wearing him down. He should be angry, and at times he was. But it was also easy to forget. Here on the island, safeguarded from the rest of the world, it was easy to pretend that it was just him and Marley and their unborn child. No past betrayals, no lies, no deceit.

He shoved his hands into his pockets and bowed his head in resignation. Never before in his business or personal life had he felt so out of control, so indecisive. Could he forgive her for trying to destroy him and his brothers? That was the million-dollar question, because if he couldn't, they had no future. When she remembered, things would irrevocably change, and he could either hold on to the acid taste of betrayal, or he could forge ahead and offer his forgiveness.

Theos mou, but he didn't have the answer. He didn't know if he had it in him to be so generous. He wanted her, no question. He was drawn to her, even knowing her sins. She was pregnant with his son, but could he honestly say that if she weren't pregnant, he could so easily cast her aside?

Small arms circled his waist, and a warm body burrowed against his back. He looked down to see Marley's hands clasped around his middle, and he brought his up to cover hers automatically.

She hugged him tightly, and he could feel her cheek pressed against his spine. She felt…right.

Slowly he eased her hands away so that he could turn in her arms. She looked up at him with warm and welcoming eyes before she dove into his arms and nuzzled against his chest.

"Good morning," he said, unable to prevent the surge of desire from racing through his body.

"I stopped by your office but didn't find you. I was worried," she said as she pulled away.

He cocked his head. "Worried?"

"You're never not in your office," she said lightly. "And then I couldn't find you anywhere in the house. I thought…I thought you might have left."

He ran his hands up to her shoulders and squeezed reassuringly. "I wouldn't leave without telling you, *pedhaki mou.*" Was he so distant, so caught up in his efforts to avoid her that this was what she thought of him? If she did think so, he could hardly blame her. Between Mrs. Cahill and Dr. Karounis, he'd erected a veritable arsenal of people to put between them.

"Would you like to take a walk with me?" she asked. "I always walk on the beach in the mornings when you're working. That is, if you aren't too busy?"

He caught her hand and brought it to his lips. "I'm not too busy for you and our child. But should you be resting?"

An exasperated shriek left her lips, startling him with her ferocity. She yanked her hand from him and parked both of her fists on her hips.

"Do I look like I need to be resting?" Anger and disappointment burned in her eyes. "Look, Chrysander, if you don't want to spend time with me, just say so, but stop throwing out your pat 'You need to be resting' line."

She turned and stalked farther down the beach, leaving him there feeling like she'd punched him in the stomach. He ran a hand through his hair as he watched her hurry away, and then he strode after her, his feet kicking up sand as he closed the distance between them.

"Marley! Marley, wait," he called as he caught her elbow.

When he turned her around, he was gutted by the tears streaking down her cheeks. She turned her face away and swiped blindly at her eyes with her other hand.

"Please, just go away," she choked out. "Go do whatever it is you do with your time. I'll wait for my *appointment* with you in the afternoon."

It came out bitter and full of hurt, and he realized that he hadn't fooled her at all with the distance he put between them.

He reached for her chin and gently tugged until she faced him. With his thumb, he wiped at a tear that slipped over her cheekbone.

"You aren't an appointment, Marley."

"No?" She yanked away from his touch and retreated a few feet until there was a respectable distance between them. "I've tried to be patient and understanding even though I don't understand any of it. Us. You or even me. I can't figure you out, Chrysander, and I'm tired of trying. I've tried to be strong and undemanding, but I can't do it anymore. I'm scared to death. I don't know who I am. I wake up one day to find myself pregnant, and there's a stranger by my bed who says he's my fiancé and the father of my child. One would think this would tell me that at least I was loved and cherished, but nothing you've done has made me feel anything but confusion. You run hot and cold, and I never know which one to expect. I can't do this."

Coldness wrapped around Chrysander's chest, squeezing until he couldn't draw a breath. "What are you saying?" he demanded.

She looked at him tiredly. "Why are you marrying me? Is it just because of the baby?"

He frowned, not liking the corner she was backing him into. "You're tired and overwrought. We should go back in and continue this conversation where it's warm—"

She cut him off with a furious hand. "I am *not* tired. I am not overwrought, and I want you to stop with the overprotective hovering. I don't even buy that you're that concerned, only that it's a convenient barrier you can hide behind when I start asking questions."

He opened his mouth to refute her words but then paused. He couldn't very well deny it when it was true. Still, he had no desire for her to become distraught. Surely *that* couldn't be good for the baby.

"What in my past am I so afraid of?" she whispered. "Last night terrified me. I woke this morning with a feeling of such fear, and not because I can't remember, but because I'm afraid to remember."

She stared earnestly at him, her eyes pleading.

"Tell me, Chrysander. I need to know. What were we like before? How did we meet? Were we very in love?"

He turned toward the water and shoved his hands back into his pockets. "You worked for me," he said gruffly.

She moved beside him, not touching him. But she was close enough that he could feel the soft hiccups of her breaths.

"I did? At your hotel?"

He shook his head. "In the corporate offices. You were my assistant."

She looked at him in shock. "But Roslyn is your assistant, and she seems awfully comfortable in that role. Like she's been there for years."

He offered a small smile. "You weren't my assistant for long. I was too intent on having you in my bed. I convinced you to quit and move in with me. You were too much of a distraction for me at work."

She didn't look pleased by his statement. A worried frown worked over her face, and her lips turned down into a dissatisfied moue.

"So you've made it a practice to put me where it's most convenient for you," she murmured.

He cursed softly under his breath, but again, he couldn't very well deny that he'd been intent on having his way when it came to her.

"And I allowed this?" she asked. "I just quit my job and moved in with you?"

He shrugged. "You seemed as happy to be with me as I was with you."

She frowned harder and curled her hands protectively over her waist. "Was our baby planned?"

He drew in his breath. Here was an area he had to tread lightly. "I wouldn't say planned, but your pregnancy certainly wasn't unwelcome."

If possible, she looked more miserable. She hunched her shoulders forward and turned away, but not before he saw the reemergence of tears.

He sighed and reached for her, pulling her into his arms. "Why are you so sad this morning, *pedhaki mou?* What can I do or say to make you feel better?"

She glanced up at him, her eyes shining with moisture. "You can stop avoiding me. You can stop using concerns over my health and that of the baby as an excuse to treat me as an invalid. You can stop treating my past like it's something I have no right to know."

He pressed his lips tightly together. "I will try to be less conscientious of your…health, though I reserve the right to be concerned."

She smiled then, and the relief that hit him almost caused him to stumble. He hadn't realized just how much her happiness was important to him. Was he crazy to be so concerned when she'd had no regard for his happiness in the past?

She leaned up to kiss him, and he caught her against him, holding her possessively as he devoured her lips.

"Thank you," she said as she pulled back. "I just want…" She stopped, and longing flooded her eyes before she look away.

"What do you want, *pedhaki mou?*"

Her gaze flickered back to his. "I want us to be happy," she said huskily. "I want to be sure of my place in your life. I want to remember, but more than that, I want to feel like I have more than just a small piece of you and your time."

He regarded her thoughtfully. She'd never been so direct before her memory loss. She'd been shy and hesitant about voicing her wants and desires. But had she felt like this before? Had she resented his prolonged absences? The way he fit her into his life at his convenience? Was that why she'd lashed out? Had it been a bid to gain his attention?

"I want you to be happy, too, Marley. I want this very much. And while I can't convince you of your place in my life with mere words, hopefully I can prove it to you over time."

Her smile warmed him to his toes. It was like watching the sun break over the horizon. She reached for his hands and slid her palms into his grip.

"Come walk with me," she invited.

Unable to deny her anything in that moment, he gathered her close and began walking down the beach.

Ten

Marley knelt in the cool soil of the garden and plucked the few weeds from around the flowers and greenery. With Chrysander's morning ritual of working, she'd found other ways to occupy her time, much to the dismay of the gardener who flew out twice a week to tend the grounds.

Ever since her outburst on the beach, Chrysander had ceased to push Patrice and Dr. Karounis at her for every little health concern. Instead, they stayed firmly in the background on an as-needed basis, and Chrysander had relented on her traveling the stairs alone.

Despite the fact that he continued to work in the mornings, he came out to have breakfast with her before returning to his office. Then the fun began for Marley. Each day she found a new method of driving him insane. He'd come looking for her when work was finished, and invariably she tried the restraint he'd promised to exercise when it came to demanding that she rest.

When Chrysander had found her in the garden on her hands and knees, she thought he was going to burst a blood vessel. He'd promptly carried her inside and up the stairs, stripped her down and put her into the bathtub.

She'd giggled at his ferocious scowl, listened with pretended solemnity to his decree that she not endanger herself in that manner anymore and promptly plotted to return as soon as he was caught up in work again.

It began a fun game between them, although the amusement was entirely hers because Chrysander failed to see the hilarity in her continued disobedience.

So here she sat, waiting with amused delight for his arrival.

She heard his sigh behind her and grinned even as she found herself lifted into the air. She tumbled against Chrysander's hard chest and smiled serenely up at his dark expression.

He strode for the house, grumbling the entire way.

"I promised to ease up on my *overprotective tendencies.* I stopped insisting you rest and even allowed you to walk unaided up and down the stairs."

Marley rolled her eyes.

"But you would try the patience of a saint," he growled.

As he had done before, and as she was counting on, he stripped her down and deposited her into an already drawn bath. He glared balefully at her, and she giggled as she sank lower into the water. He watched intently as she slowly washed herself, hunger glittering in his eyes.

Relishing the fact that she had his full attention, she took advantage as she worked the cloth over every inch of her body. When she was finished, she glanced innocently up at him as he towered over her. She flashed him her best smile, but he continued to glower at her.

"Your cuteness is not going to get you out of trouble, *pedhaki mou,*" he said.

"Well, at least I'm cute," she said pertly.

"Why do you insist on provoking me? My hair is turning gray, and it is solely your fault."

She glanced up at his dark hair, not marred by a single gray strand, and raised an eyebrow. "You poor baby. Are you too old to keep up with one little pregnant woman?"

"I'll show you old," he growled as he plucked her from the bathtub.

He barely took the time to dry her before he strode into the bedroom and deposited her on the bed. Her eyes widened appreciatively as he began stripping his clothing from his muscled body.

"Clearly I need to be bad more often," she murmured. "I could learn to live with the punishment."

"Little minx," he said as he lowered himself into her waiting arms.

He was always in control in their lovemaking, and she knew this was the way it had always been, but now she had a sudden desire to turn the tables. To make him as crazy as he made her.

She pushed at him, and he withdrew with a frown. She followed him up and placed her hands on his shoulders, forcing him to lie on his back. She straddled his legs and stared at his shocked expression, a mischievous grin working at her lips.

"I want to touch you, Chrysander," she said softly. She placed her palms on the tops of his thick legs and smoothed them slowly upward.

His eyes smoldered and sparked. "Then by all means, touch me, *agape mou.*"

With a little nervousness, she touched his male flesh, and he jerked in reaction. Feeling a little bolder, she wrapped her fingers around the turgid length and stroked lightly.

A groan worked from his throat, and she could see sweat beading on his brow. He was beautiful. Hard, male, his strength rippled through his every muscle.

She leaned down and pressed a kiss to his taut abdomen and then worked her way up to his flat nipples. A thin line of hair dusted his midline, and she ran her fingers over it, liking the feel of it on her skin.

She knew what she wanted to do but was unsure of exactly how she would accomplish it. He must have sensed her uncertainty and her hesitation, because he reached down with his strong hands and grasped her hips.

He lifted her then eased her down over the length of his erection. She closed her eyes as he slid inside her.

"You're killing me, *pedhaki mou*," he rasped. "God, it's so good. You're so sweet."

Encouraged by the satisfaction and approval in his voice, she made love to him, raining kisses over his chest as his hands helped guide the movements of her hips.

Her body trembled, and she knew she was nearing her release, but she wouldn't succumb until he went with her. He tensed beneath her, and suddenly his hands tightened around her hips. He arched into her, and with a cry, the world exploded around her.

She fell forward, but he caught her with gentle hands. He lowered her to his heaving chest and stroked her hair as they struggled to catch their breaths.

He turned so that he could position her beside him, and he eased out of her body, eliciting another soft moan from her. She cuddled against him, warm and replete.

"Was I any good?" she asked, her words muffled by his chest.

He shook with laughter then turned her face up so she could see him. "If you were any better, you really would make me an old man before my time."

"But did you like it?" she asked softly. "Or do you think I'm a brazen hussy now?"

He tweaked her on the nose then kissed the same spot. "I liked it very much. I liked it so much that I might consider letting you go play in your garden again tomorrow."

She rolled her eyes and yawned sleepily. He drew his finger down her cheek. "Sleep now. I'll wake you for dinner."

"I don't need a nap," she grumbled, but she was already drifting off.

Not wanting to be entirely predictable, Marley forewent the garden the next day and opted instead for the heated pool. She'd been eyeing it with longing since they'd arrived, and thanks to boutiques only too willing to deliver to the island, she had a simply decadent swimsuit she was dying to try out.

As she pulled the skimpy suit on, she realized that in essence she was trying to seduce Chrysander. Not that she hadn't already, but she was attempting to make him fall in love with her.

She frowned back at herself in the mirror. Wasn't this backward? He was the one with the memory. Shouldn't he be trying to make her fall in love with him? She knew she loved him but hadn't said the words. Something had held her back, and now she pondered what it was that made her unwilling to take that jump.

There was a hesitation about him that niggled at her, as though he wanted to keep a certain amount of distance between them. She didn't want that. She wanted him to love her as she loved him.

She sighed. If only she could remember.

She wiggled a bit and readjusted the bikini until she was satisfied with the result. The top cupped her small breasts and did a remarkable job of making them seem more impressive than they actually were. The bottom… She smiled as she turned at an angle to view the back of the bikini. It wasn't a thong…exactly, but it did draw attention to her gently rounded bottom.

Straightening again, she smoothed a hand over the swell of her belly. Chrysander seemed to enjoy her pregnancy. He touched and kissed her belly frequently and seemed entranced by the mound. She hoped he'd find the suit, and her, sexy.

Recognizing that she was stalling, she reached for the silk robe and tugged it on. She wanted no chance that someone else would see her in such a scandalous suit. This was for Chrysander's eyes only.

She slipped down the stairs and made it through the living room unseen. She walked into the smaller room that housed the indoor portion of the pool and eyed the rippling water with anticipation. Chrysander or no Chrysander, she was looking forward to a swim.

Shedding the wrap, she tossed it over one of the loungers and walked to the edge of the pool to dip her toe in. It was wonderfully warm. She moved to the steps and carefully descended into the water.

Oh, it was marvelous. She swam toward the back glass enclosure that overlooked the outdoor portion of the pool. She was tempted to duck under the divider and swim outside, but the breeze would be cold on her damp skin.

She floated lazily on her back for a while then did a few laps, gliding underneath the water for as long as she could hold her breath. She came up with a gasp and grabbed on to the side of the pool. And then she saw a pair of leather loafers.

She glanced up to see Chrysander watching her, arms folded across his chest, a mock scowl on his face. Even she could see that his lips were twitching suspiciously.

With an innocent blink, she smiled and offered a hello. He squatted down and put a finger underneath her chin, nudging it upward.

"Enjoying yourself, *pedhaki mou?*"

"Very much," she returned.

"And to think I was looking forward to hauling you out of your garden today," he murmured.

Her face heated as she recalled all that had happened yesterday when he'd done just that. She extended her hand. "Help me out?"

He grasped her hand, and she reached to grip his wrist with her other hand at the same time she planted her feet against the side of the pool and pulled with all her might. He gave a shout of surprise as he toppled over and hit the water with a gigantic splash.

He came up sputtering, and for a moment, she worried that he was truly angry. He scowled ferociously at her before glancing down at his soaked clothing. Then he started laughing.

Before he could think retaliation, and since she still wanted him to see her suit, she swam over to the steps and exited the pool in slow, deliberate movements. She glanced over her shoulder to see his mouth drop open as he viewed the back of her suit.

When Marley reached the top, she turned so he could see her profile, and she heard him suck in his breath. She turned away again and began walking toward where her wrap was laying.

"Oh no you don't, you little tease," he growled.

She blinked at how quickly he got out of the pool. She gave a shriek of surprise when he closed in on her then laughed when he gathered her into his arms and headed back toward the pool.

"Chrysander, your clothes!"

"As if they matter now. You've quite ruined them."

"I'm sorry."

He laughed. "No, you're not." He bent down at the side of the pool and gently eased her back into the water. Then he stood and fixed her with a glare. "You stay right there."

She giggled. Her laughter died in her throat, though, when he began peeling his clothing off his body. First his shirt came off, revealing his muscular chest. Then he kicked off his shoes and yanked off the soaked socks. When he reached for the fly of his trousers, she blushed but couldn't look away to save her life.

The discernible bulge in his boxers as he stepped out of his pants told her that she'd certainly been successful in her quest to make him a little crazy. But now she wondered what exactly he'd do about it.

He hopped over the side, landing next to her with a minimal splash. Then he hauled her against him, kissing her hungrily.

"That suit should be illegal," he said as he worked his mouth down her neck.

"You don't like it?" she asked innocently. "I could always get rid of it."

"Oh, I like it," he murmured. "I'm going to like taking it off of you even better."

She broke loose and dove beneath the water, swimming away from him as fast as she could. She surfaced after a short distance but didn't immediately see him. She looked down, too late, to see his glimmering body. He grabbed her legs and yanked her underneath.

His lips closed over hers, and he propelled them both above

the water. She wrapped her arms around his neck and smiled up at him. "I suppose I'm going to have to take back what I said about you being no fun."

"It would seem so."

"I wouldn't object to you hauling me out of the pool and taking me upstairs," she said with pretended innocence.

He kissed her again, hot, breathless. His hands slid around her waist to cup her bottom. He lifted her upward, and she latched her legs around his waist.

"Hold on to me, *pedhaki mou*," he murmured. "I'm hauling you out of the pool right now."

He mounted the steps and carefully climbed out of the pool. As he neared one of the loungers, she noticed that he'd brought two towels with him. Apparently he had planned to come in all the while. She grinned impishly at him. He wasn't so serious all the time.

He put her down in one of the loungers then reached for a towel. He dried her hair and her body, allowing his hands to linger in some of her most sensitive areas. He touched and caressed until she was squirming in the chair.

"Now who's teasing?" she said breathlessly.

He straddled the lounger and lowered his body to hers.

"Mmmm, you're warm."

"Are you cold?" he asked huskily. "I wonder what I can do to warm you."

She pulled him closer, wrapping her arms around him. She threaded her fingers into his wet hair and kissed him. A sound of contentment purred from her throat as he returned her kiss with equal ardor.

His erection strained against her belly, hot, like steel. Warmth shot through her body, leaving her flushed and aching. She wanted him. Wanted him so badly.

"Take me upstairs," she whispered as his lips scorched down her neck and to the swell of her breasts.

The sound of a door closing startled them both. Chrysander let out an oath as he rolled away from Marley and yanked up a towel to cover her. Marley stiffened when she saw Roslyn over Chrysander's shoulder.

Her surprise turned to anger. The woman had barged in, intruded on their privacy without so much as a call to let them know she was coming out to the island. They hadn't even heard the helicopter land, but then they'd been occupied with other matters.

"What are you doing here?" Chrysander said icily.

"I'm sorry to interrupt, Mr. Anetakis," Roslyn said, though her expression said she was anything but. Her gaze skimmed Marley in triumph, but the look was gone when she turned her attention back to Chrysander. "There were several things that needed your attention, and I thought it best to see to them personally rather than rely on the phone or e-mail."

"They certainly haven't failed in the past," Chrysander said stiffly. "If you'll excuse us, I think perhaps it would be better for you to wait in my office."

"Yes, of course, Mr. Anetakis. Again, my apologies for the disturbance."

Marley shivered, this time the chill setting in deep. The woman had impeccable timing.

"I'm sorry," Chrysander said as he helped her from the lounger. He wrapped the towel around her shivering body and tucked her against his side. "I'll take you upstairs so you can change into something warmer. This shouldn't take but a moment, and then I'll return."

Marley nodded, but for her, the moment was ruined. Gone was Chrysander's fun-loving mood. The passion that had sizzled between them just minutes ago was now a cold blanket thrown by his trusty assistant.

He took her upstairs and ushered her into the shower. When she stepped out, he'd already dressed and gone back downstairs. With an unhappy sigh, she gathered the towel around her and sat down on the edge of the bed.

Chrysander entered his office, irritation replacing his earlier good mood. He stared hard at Roslyn, who stood to the side. "I do not appreciate this intrusion," he said crisply. "There was no call, no warning, no *permission* asked to come out to the island."

Roslyn paled and her eyes widened.

"This is my private living area, and as such, you do not have free rein as you do in my business settings. Are we understood?"

"Yes, sir," she said stiffly.

"Now, what was so important that it didn't warrant a phone call?" he demanded.

"I've discovered that another design was stolen," she said softly.

"What?" Curses spilled from his lips, and it took a moment for him to realize he was speaking in Greek, and Roslyn didn't understand a word of it. He shook his head and put both hands down on his desk. "What design? Tell me everything."

Roslyn's expression hardened. "It's an older one, a design you discarded. It was the original plan for the Rio de Janeiro hotel. But still, she must have sold it to Marcelli with the others, because his hotel going up in Rome bears a remarkable likeness. I saw the proofs myself just two days ago."

Rage burned like acid in Chrysander's veins. "Do my brothers know of this yet?"

Roslyn shook her head. "I thought you would want to tell them."

He nodded and closed his eyes as he turned to look out the window to the beach. Every time he thought he had come to terms with Marley's betrayal, the past came back to haunt him. As much as he wanted to forget, to move on, to put the past behind them, it always came back, insidious and unrelenting.

He struggled to remember how Marley could have gotten access to the hotel plans. He certainly hadn't guarded himself at home. As careful as he was in the office and in all other aspects of his life, he'd been relaxed and free with her, never thinking to protect his interests from her.

How could he build a life with her when he could never trust her? Was he a fool for building a temporary relationship when it would all come tumbling down the minute she remembered? When she'd have to face the sins she'd committed and reap the consequences of her betrayal?

Through it all, he could only remember one thing. The way she'd looked the night he'd confronted her in their apartment. The absolute shock and horror on her face. Could anyone fake such a reaction that well?

For the first time, he took a long, hard look at the woman she'd been during their time together before her abduction and the woman she'd been since. There was no marked difference. The only inconsistency was her betrayal.

"Chrysander." Roslyn spoke up in a soft voice.

His eyes narrowed at her use of his name. It was not something he ever tolerated from his employees, though he wasn't sure why it bothered him coming from someone he had worked closely with for some time.

"You won't allow her to do it again, will you?"

He turned around to face her. "No, it won't happen again," he said tightly, anger creeping up his spine. His anger wasn't totally at Marley. For some reason, it rankled that Roslyn would think to warn him away from Marley.

Roslyn looked uncomfortable. "I just hope she doesn't ruin things for you with this hotel deal. Not again. It's too important."

"I don't think that's any of your concern. I will handle Marley."

She flinched at his tone. "I apologize. This company, this job, is very important to me. I've worked hard for you, sir. I worked hard on the Paris deal."

Chrysander let go of some of his anger and blew out a sigh. She had worked hard, and he could see why she would harbor some anger toward Marley even if he wouldn't tolerate it. Even if he didn't feel she was justified in that anger. That thought struck him hard, because it meant on some level he didn't believe Marley capable of her crime.

"I appreciate your concern, Roslyn. However, it is not your business. If that is all you wanted, then I'll call for the helicopter to return you to the mainland."

She looked as though she would protest, but then she nodded. Thirty minutes later, Chrysander escorted her out to the helipad, and as soon as the helicopter lifted off, he turned and strode back into the house.

His anger and uncertainty evaporated when he entered the bedroom and found Marley sitting on the bed, wrapped only in a towel, her expression sad and distant.

He knelt in front of her and touched her cheek. "What is it, *agape mou?* Are you all right?"

She smiled, though it didn't reach her eyes. Her beautiful blue eyes that had sparkled just a short time ago with laughter. He wanted them to sparkle again. He wanted that stolen moment at the pool back. Before Roslyn had arrived and given him news that could very well change everything between him and Marley. Again.

"I'm in an impossible situation," she confessed.

His brow wrinkled in confusion. He didn't like the sadness in her tone. The resignation.

"What do you mean?" he asked softly as he trailed a finger down the silken curve of her cheek.

She looked into his eyes. "I don't like the way she has free rein in our lives. This is our home. We should be able to make love, have fun together, without fear of being caught in a compromising situation by a stranger. But if I voice this, if I say I don't like her and I don't want her here, it makes me a catty bitch. There is no way for me to come out the winner and every way for me to be the loser in this."

She looked down for a moment then stared back up at him, emotion shimmering in her eyes. "I don't like the way you back away from me every time she appears. She sweeps in on some pretext of business, then she leaves and you become distant. The last weeks have been so utterly wonderful, and now she barges in and I can already feel you pulling away from me. I don't know that I can bear it."

Tears pooled in her eyes, and he was struck speechless, for what she said, all of it, was completely true. He hadn't realized how it would look to her, had thought he'd hidden the conflicting emotions he experienced when reminded of the fact she'd stolen from him, lied to him, betrayed him.

He raised one of her hands to his mouth and pressed it firmly to his lips. "I'm sorry, *agape mou*. I'm sorry her presence has bothered you and that I've ignored it. It won't happen again. I've already informed her that under no condition is she to just arrive here without at least phoning."

"I could stand her presence. I won't lie and say I like the woman, but I could tolerate her. What I cannot bear is the way you pull away from me every time she appears. Without any memories to bolster my confidence, I have nothing to point to and say, Marley, you're being ridiculous. Of course there's nothing going on between him and his assistant."

His mouth fell open in surprise. "You think I'm having an affair with her?" He couldn't control the shudder of distaste that rolled down his spine.

She shook her head emphatically. "Oh, I've made a mess of this. I'm only trying to say that for me, this is all new. Our relationship is new. I can't remember our time together before, so in essence, we're building new, starting all over. I can't help the insecurity I feel when I look at her and know she's trying to undermine our relationship."

He gathered her in his arms, having no idea what to say to her. He couldn't very well deny that Roslyn probably did want to keep him from Marley. She knew Marley had stolen from the company, a company that Roslyn was devoted to and had put in a lot of long hours for in preparing the deal that had disappeared along with the plans for the Paris hotel. And now he'd learned that yet another of the Anetakis designs would be going up under the Marcelli name. No matter it was one he'd discarded. Marley couldn't have known that at the time.

What an impossible situation. Surprising to him was the anger that Roslyn's words had caused. His first reaction had been to defend Marley and to chastise Roslyn for speaking out against Marley. But how could he when Roslyn was right?

All he knew was that he didn't want Marley to hurt. As stupid as that sounded given the hurt she'd caused him, he wanted to wipe away the sadness in her eyes. While he couldn't do anything to erase the past, what he could do was make sure that Roslyn wasn't a source of contention between them. He would honor Marley's wishes in this, for they mirrored his own. He didn't want anything to come between them here on the island. Roslyn wouldn't return.

Eleven

Chrysander hung up the phone with a grimace and leaned back in his leather chair. He put his hands behind his head and stared up at the ceiling.

He had to return to New York. Piers had called him with the news just moments ago, and Chrysander greeted the fact with a discomfort that was alien to him. Worse, he'd had to inform Piers and Theron that another of their designs had been stolen. They were understandably furious. With Marley. How would they react when they learned he had every intention of marrying her as soon as possible?

He was torn between wanting Marley to go with him and wanting to keep her sheltered here on the island. Away from any chance she might remember. Away from the judgment and animosity of his brothers.

The beginnings of a headache plagued him as he considered the selfishness of that particular thought. He knew, though, that when she remembered, and the doctors had assured him she would, things would irrevocably change between them.

He should still be furious with her, and he should be working to maintain distance between them, but she'd chipped away his resistance during their time on the island. As much as it shamed him, it no longer mattered to him that she'd lied, that she'd stolen from him and his brothers. He wanted things to remain as they were, and if she remembered, then they would be forced to face the events of the past.

And he'd likely lose her.

It bothered him more than it should. She was pregnant with his child, he told himself, and that should be reason enough not to want things to sour between them.

His time here with Marley had brought him back to the times they'd spent together before the night he'd discovered her betrayal. He hadn't really appreciated her before. He'd taken her and her presence in his life for granted, but now he knew how much he'd liked having her there when he returned from business.

She was fun and carefree. Gentle and loving. All the things he'd wish for in the mother of his child.

But she'd betrayed him. It always came back to that even as he wanted to forget it.

"Chrysander?"

He looked up on hearing his softly spoken name to see Marley standing in the doorway, her hand resting on the frame as she peered in. He shook himself from his grim thoughts and hoped his expression wasn't as brooding as he felt. Things had been strained and tense between them since Roslyn had come to the island. A fact he regretted but was unable to fully remedy when he still carried his own doubts and uncertainties where Marley was concerned.

"What is it, *pedhaki mou?*"

"Are you all right?" She let her hand fall and started forward, her steps hesitant.

He guessed he did look brooding.

"Come here," he said, holding out his hand to her as she neared. He pulled her down onto his lap, suddenly wanting her close. "I have to return to New York."

A shadow crossed over her face. "When?"

"In the morning. My brother called, and a dignitary we are courting for a hotel project is going to be at a reception at our New York hotel. Piers and Theron thought to handle it, but the man wished to meet with all three of us. It's something I cannot miss, I'm afraid."

She looked disappointed, and even as the uneasiness over her going back to New York lingered in his mind, he found himself saying, "You could go with me."

Her eyes lightened. "I wouldn't be in the way?"

He frowned. "You are never in the way, *agape mou*. This would be good, I think. We could announce our wedding plans. My brothers will want to meet you," he said, warming to the subject. "We could even be married in New York with my family around us and then return here."

In his mind, the sooner they married, the better.

"I'll arrange for Dr. Karounis to return to Athens. I don't think we need him any longer."

Her smile broadened. "And Patrice? Not that I don't love her, but she and Dr. Karounis seem to have gotten along extremely well. Maybe she'd like to take a trip to Athens."

"I'll extend the offer," he said with a smile.

"Then yes, I'd love to go." She threw her arms around him and kissed him exuberantly on the lips. Before he could deepen the kiss, she scrambled off his lap. "I have to go pack!"

He chuckled and caught her hand. "You have plenty of time."

But still she hurried away, and he stared after her, long after she'd disappeared through the doorway. He should feel relieved that soon they'd be married, and she'd be bound to him, but he couldn't dispel the uneasy feeling that gripped him.

Chrysander's jet touched down in New York in the late afternoon, and a limousine was waiting for them when they stepped off the plane. A tall, formidable-looking man stood by the car, and as they drew closer, Marley could see a strong resemblance between him and Chrysander.

"Theron," Chrysander called out. "I did not expect you to meet us. This is a surprise."

Theron gave a half smile. "Can I not greet my brother?"

Chrysander put an arm around Marley's waist and drew her forward. "Theron, this is Marley. Marley, this is my younger brother Theron."

She smiled. "I'm very glad to meet you."

His gaze flickered impassively over her, and he didn't return her smile. Slowly hers faded as she read the unwelcoming look on his face. Instinctively, she shrank into Chrysander.

Then Theron's gaze dropped to the hand on which she wore the engagement ring, and he outright frowned. He stared back up at Chrysander, his jaw tight.

"You will be courteous," Chrysander said in a very low tone. Even so, she could hear the bite in his voice.

"I'm pleased to meet you," Theron said stiffly, though his body language said just the opposite. He turned on his heel and walked toward another car parked a short distance away.

Marley looked up at Chrysander in bewilderment. "What was that all about?"

"It is nothing, *pedhaki mou*. I am sorry he was rude. It won't happen again."

"But *why* was he rude?" His behavior baffled Marley. And then another thought occurred to her. "Have we met before? Of course we would have. He's your brother. Did I do something to offend him in the past? Has he always disliked me?"

Chrysander ushered her into the car and slid in beside her. "No, you haven't met before. You needn't worry that you've done anything. It's just Theron's way." He sounded a bit strangled, and her gaze narrowed at what she thought must be a lie.

When his cell phone rang, he lunged for it in his haste to answer. She put her lips together and seethed in silence. Something didn't add up. Why would his brother dislike her so intensely on sight? And for that matter, why had she never met him before? It couldn't be normal for her not to have met the family of the man she was going to marry, the father of her child.

She leaned back against the seat and blew out her breath in frustration. While in New York, she fully intended to seek answers and maybe try to dislodge the block that seemed permanently embedded in her mind. There had to be some way to break her memories free. And if there was, she was going to find it. Preferably before she got married.

Yet more was in store when they reached the penthouse. She very nearly growled her frustration when the lift opened and she caught sight of Roslyn. Was she doomed to find this woman in her home at every turn?

Roslyn smiled warmly in greeting, and Marley did not miss that it extended only to Chrysander. She stood beside him while his assistant outlined the schedule of meetings, phone calls he needed to return and contracts that needed his attention. She wouldn't retreat this time and allow Roslyn any victory, implied or otherwise.

Roslyn spoke in low, sultry tones and touched Chrysander's arm frequently. She laughed huskily at something he said, all the while overtly ignoring Marley's presence. The woman had brass. Marley had to admit that. If she weren't pregnant, she'd give serious consideration to throwing the woman out of the penthouse on her ear.

It was good as fantasies went, but Chrysander would be horrified. She sighed even as the image of the beautifully coiffed woman banned from the apartment cheered her considerably.

Finally, Roslyn made to leave, and Marley's shoulders sagged in relief. But as the elevator opened to admit her, another man, also bearing a strong resemblance to Chrysander strode off.

She wanted to ask Chrysander just how many people had access to their private quarters but bit her lip.

"It would seem our apartment is a revolving door today," Chrysander said dryly, and Marley wondered if he'd read her mind.

While Theron's disapproval of her might have been more subtle, there was nothing left to imagine about this man's opinion of her. He scowled openly even as Chrysander introduced him to her as his brother Piers.

"A word if you don't mind, Chrysander," Piers said, his jaw clenched tight.

"Don't let me interrupt," Marley said. She turned and walked toward the bedroom, having had enough of the chilly reception she'd received.

Even as she closed the door, she could hear raised voices and Chrysander's angry tone. She hesitated a moment, wondering if she should listen to their conversation. Would she want to hear what they were saying? With a sigh, she turned to survey the room that Chrysander had given her upon her release from the hospital.

Not knowing what else to do, she slipped out of her shoes and sat down on the bed. The trip hadn't been tiring, but sliding under the covers and hiding appealed to her. Her head was beginning to ache from tension, and if she could just get away for a few minutes, she might feel better. And maybe when she woke, there wouldn't be anyone in their apartment anymore.

When she did wake, she was in a different bed. She blinked the sleep-induced fog away and realized that she was in Chrysander's bedroom. She stretched and was glad not to feel the pressure in her head any longer.

She sat up and saw Chrysander standing across the room looking at her. For some reason, she felt unsure of herself in that moment.

"I must have been more tired than I realized," she said lightly. "I didn't even wake when you moved me."

"You will sleep in our room, in our bed."

She blinked. "Well, okay. I just didn't think. That was the room I had before."

He closed the distance between them and sat down on the bed next to her. "Your place is here. With me."

She cocked her head. She had the distinct impression he wasn't just speaking to the fact that she'd gone to bed in another room. It was almost as though he was convincing himself, and others, that she belonged with him.

"Your brothers don't approve of me," she said quietly.

His face became a stone. "My brothers have no say in our relationship. I will announce our forthcoming marriage at the reception two nights from now, and we'll marry in a week."

And that was that, she thought. The law laid down by Chrysander Anetakis.

He leaned down to kiss her. "Why don't you dress? We'll go out for a nice dinner."

"Lobster?" she asked hopefully then realized what she'd said. Her eyes widened in excitement. "Lobster! Chrysander, I remember that lobster is my favorite."

He smiled tightly and kissed her again. "So it is, *pedhaki mou*. I used to have it delivered here, and we'd sit naked on the bed to eat it."

She flushed to the roots of her hair but had to admit the image was appealing. Chrysander helped her up, and she went into the bathroom to shower and change. Thirty minutes later, Chrysander escorted her down the elevator and out to the waiting car.

He took her to an elegant restaurant, and they sat in an intimate corner set away from the main dining area. The lighting was low, and it reminded her of Christmas. A warm feeling of nostalgia took hold as she recalled how very much she loved the holiday season.

In another month, decorations would be going up, and many of the shops and restaurants would twinkle with lights and holly. She smiled dreamily as she imagined spending Christmas with Chrysander.

"You look lost in thought, *agape mou*. With such a sweet smile on your face, I can only hope that I am what is occupying your thoughts."

She looked across the table to see Chrysander studying her, his bronze skin illuminated by soft candlelight. "I was imagining spending Christmas with you. I was remembering how much I love the holidays."

"Your memories seem to be coming back," he said, though there was no joy in his tone.

Her lips twisted into a rueful smile. "Not very quickly, I'm afraid. Just a snippet here and there, and it's more of an awareness, not a true memory."

"It will come. You must be patient."

She nodded, but she could feel the frustration creeping over her. Determined not to let the evening go the way the rest of the day had, she forced herself to relax and enjoy the wonderful meal and being with Chrysander. With no interruptions from family members or personal assistants.

"Would you like to go shopping tomorrow?" Chrysander asked.

She blinked in surprise at the sudden change in topic.

"I have a meeting first thing, but then we could eat lunch together and shop for the things you will need for the reception we will be attending. You could also look for a wedding dress."

She couldn't wrap her brain around the image of Chrysander shopping, and she was sure no amount of searching her memory would find one. He simply wasn't a man to do such a thing.

"Are you sure you want me there?"

He cocked one eyebrow. "As I plan to announce our upcoming wedding, it would be strange if you weren't. Unless you have no wish to go."

"No, that isn't it at all. I'd love to go. I just wasn't sure…." She trailed off, determined not to dig her hole any deeper.

"Then it is settled. We'll go out shopping tomorrow after I've fed you properly."

She grinned. "You make me sound like a pet."

A slow, sexy smile curved his mouth. "I like the sound of you being my pet. My own personal, pampered pet," he purred.

Heat sizzled through her body like an electric current. She swallowed and took a sip of her water in an attempt to assuage the tingling warmth.

Then he laughed, and the sound sent a flutter of awareness over her nerves. "You like the idea, too, I see."

She blushed and ducked her head. "I like the idea of being your anything," she said honestly.

He reached across the table and tugged her fingers into his hand. "You are mine, *agape mou*. That is what you are."

"Then take me home and make love to me," she whispered.

Twelve

The next morning, Chrysander left their bed early. He kissed her softly on the brow and told her he would come for her at noon. Marley yawned sleepily, murmured her goodbye and turned over to go back to sleep. His soft chuckle echoed in her ears as she drifted off.

When she woke again, she squinted against the sunlight and glanced over at the clock. She still had hours until her lunch date with Chrysander, and she had no desire to spend them sitting around the apartment.

With so many of Chrysander's security men milling about, surely one of them would have access to transportation. She could commandeer one of them and go out on her own a bit, though she had no idea where she'd go exactly.

And then another thought occurred to her. With Chrysander being such a stickler for tight security, she doubted she'd gone anywhere without it in the time they were together. If that was the case, then surely one of them would have an idea of the places she'd visited and the things she liked to do.

Considerably cheered by that realization, she hurried into the shower. Thirty minutes later, she rode the elevator down to the lobby and got off. She could see a burly-looking man standing by the door and recognized him as the man Chrysander called Stavros.

He snapped to attention when he saw her walking toward him.

"Miss Jameson," he said in a heavy Greek accent. "Is there something I can do for you?"

She noticed the way he subtly moved to bar the door so she could not exit and nearly laughed.

"I'm sure Chrysander has told you that I…that I've lost my memory."

He nodded, and his expression softened.

"What I was wondering is if you could tell me whether or not I had security assigned to me before my accident."

"I personally saw to your protection," Stavros said.

"Oh, good! Then maybe you can help me. I'd like to go out, but I don't really know where. I mean, I don't know what places I liked to go, and since you no doubt followed me everywhere I went, maybe you could take me to some of those places today."

He paused for a moment as if considering her request. Then he dug out a cell phone from his pocket, punched a button and stuck the phone to his ear. He spoke rapidly in Greek, nodded a few times then extended the receiver to her.

"Mr. Anetakis would like to speak to you."

"Oh, for heaven's sake," she huffed as she took it. "You didn't waste any time ratting me out, did you?" She stared accusingly at Stavros, who didn't look the least bit apologetic.

Chrysander laughed in her ear. "What sort of trouble are you causing, *agape mou?*"

She sighed a little ridiculously. After that first awkward time he'd murmured the endearment, he'd used it with increasing frequency. It turned her to mush every time it slid over her ears, warm and vibrant.

"I wanted to go out for a while. I'll be back in time for our lunch, I promise."

"Enjoy your morning, but be careful and don't overexert

yourself. If you find you're running late, have Stavros call me, and I can meet you for lunch so you don't have to return to the apartment."

She smiled and murmured her agreement. They rang off, and she handed the phone back to Stavros. "You and I need to have a conversation about tattling."

He didn't bat an eyelash. "I assure you, Miss Jameson, we've had such conversations in the past."

She grinned and then watched as Stavros put a hand to the small earpiece he wore and barked out several orders in Greek.

Within moments a car rolled around the front, and yet another security man got out to open the door for her. Stavros ushered her out of the building and settled her comfortably in the vehicle before he and the other man took seats in the front.

The privacy glass between the front and backseats lowered, and Stavros turned to look at her over his shoulder.

"Where would you like to go, Miss Jameson?"

"I don't know," she said with a laugh. "Can you give me a tour of some of the places I used to go?"

He nodded, and they drove onto the busy New York streets.

Their first stop was a small coffee shop a few blocks away from the apartment. It was clear that Stavros hadn't expected her to want to get out, because when she made the intention known, his lips drew into a disapproving line. Still, he and the other man with him escorted her inside the small café.

It was cozy and brimming with conversation and laughter. It felt inviting, and she could well see herself in a place like this. But it didn't spark any memories. With a sigh, she turned and told Stavros she was ready to leave.

Next they pulled up to a small market, and she looked at Stavros in surprise.

"You liked to cook for Mr. Anetakis, particularly when he'd been out of the country for an extended period of time. We would come here to shop for the necessary ingredients. Then you'd make me carry back all the sacks," he added with a small smile.

"Was I so very trying?" she teased.

"It was my pleasure to accompany you on your outings," Stavros said.

"Why, it sounds like you like me." She grinned up at the burly man, trying to gain any sort of recognition, some flicker that maybe they'd bantered like this in the past. "Where to next?"

They visited a library and a small art shop, and while she could see herself in those places, she recalled nothing. When the car rolled to a stop in front of a park, for a moment panic quivered in her stomach.

"Are you all right?" Stavros demanded.

She looked up to see him standing at the open door, waiting for her to climb out.

"Maybe we should return now. It's nearly time for your lunch with Mr. Anetakis."

"No," she said as she hastened out of the car. No, she wanted to be here. Needed to be here. Something about this place had caused a tremor in her mind even if it was uncomfortable.

She walked down the pathway and gathered her coat tighter around her. In truth, it wasn't that cold. The afternoon sun shone warmly, but she felt a chill, one that reached far inside her.

Behind her, Stavros and his second flanked her, and she had the brief thought that she appeared far more important than she was. Her gaze locked on to a stone bench that overlooked a statue, and she moved toward it, not sure why she was so drawn by it.

Marley sat down and spread her hands over the cool stone. She stared ahead and felt a glimmer of sadness. It made no sense, but she knew she had sat here before, and she knew that she had felt fear. Uncertainty.

She raised her hands to cup her face and leaned over, huddled on the bench. It was there, just out of reach, so close she could feel the heavy weight of sadness, of indecision.

A hand touched her shoulder, and Stavros's concerned voice reached her. "Are you all right? Do I need to call Mr. Anetakis? Perhaps I should take you to the hospital."

She shook her head and looked up. "No. I'm fine. It's just that I've been here before. I can feel it."

Stavros nodded, though the concern didn't leave his eyes. "You often said this was your thinking spot."

"It would appear I had a lot to think about," she murmured.

He checked his watch. "Let me call Mr. Anetakis and tell him to meet us at the restaurant. By the time we return to the apartment, you could already be eating."

She didn't object when he gently helped her up, and instead of walking just behind her, he held her elbow as they walked back to the car.

"Stavros, please don't concern Chrysander," she said as he put her into the car. "He'll have me back at the apartment in bed."

"Which is perhaps where you should be," Stavros said.

She made a face. "You're seriously no fun. I'm supposed to go shopping. For a wedding dress no less. I can't very well do that if I'm in bed."

Stavros looked to be fighting a smile as he closed the door. A moment later, the privacy glass slid down and Stavros turned to look at her. "If Mr. Anetakis asks, I'll simply say we had a quiet day on the town."

"I knew there was a reason I liked you," she said cheekily, her good spirits restored.

When they arrived at the restaurant, Chrysander met them at the car and promptly dismissed Stavros, saying he would have his driver take him and Marley home when they were through shopping.

Over lunch, Chrysander asked how her morning had gone, and she explained about all the places Stavros had taken her. But when she asked him about his morning, he grew silent and vague.

Not wanting to cast a pall over the day, she swiftly changed the topic to their shopping.

"Exactly how fancy is this reception we're attending?" she asked as she savored another bite of the rich pasta.

He quirked one eyebrow. "That depends on your definition of fancy."

"Oh, then I can wear my blue jeans and maternity top," she said sweetly.

He laughed. "While I certainly would not object to you

wearing your blue jeans, I do not want others seeing you in something that cups your bottom so lovingly."

"Am I supposed to dress up then?" she asked with a sigh.

"Don't concern yourself with it, *pedhaki mou*. I will choose the perfect dress for you."

"I won't wear high heels," she said resolutely. "There is no way I'm waddling around on toothpicks."

"Of course not," he said in a tone that suggested she was crazy for even mentioning it. "I'm certain it's not advisable for a pregnant woman to put herself through such torture. What if you fell?"

"Maybe I could go barefooted," she said mischievously.

He laughed. "And maybe I should stick to a plan of keeping you at home solidly under lock and key."

She swallowed the last bite of her pasta and reluctantly pushed the plate away. "That was so wonderful, and I ate far too much."

"You need to gain some weight. You are too slight as it is. It is good that you ate well."

"And if I eat any more, I won't fit into whatever dress you plan on buying me." She glanced down at her rounded belly. "Do they make ultra-chic wear for pregnant women?"

Chrysander gave her a patient look. "Trust me, Marley. We will find you something suitable."

"Just how do you know so darn much about buying dresses anyway?" she grumbled as he took her out to his waiting car.

"Surely you don't expect me to answer that?" he said with barely suppressed amusement.

She shot him a withering look and settled into the car.

As it turned out, he did indeed have a skill for choosing the perfect dress. He nailed it with the second one she tried on. White silk in a very simple design. It had spaghetti straps with a conservative bodice, and the material hugged her belly, drawing attention to the soft mound.

"It makes me look...well, very pregnant," she said as she turned to allow Chrysander to look.

"You look absolutely exquisite," he murmured. "I think every pregnant woman should like to look as you do right now."

The appreciation in his eyes sold her on the dress. She had no desire to look any further. It was carefully wrapped and set aside along with the low-heeled shoes that she had chosen.

"Tell me, *agape mou,* do you want a traditional wedding dress?"

She pursed her lips then shook her head. "No, I'd prefer something simpler, I think."

The saleslady set several really gorgeous selections in front of them, and Marley watched Chrysander closely for his reaction.

She fell in love with a peach-colored gown that scraped the floor and fell in soft waves from her waist. It accentuated her pregnancy in such a way that she truly felt beautiful and feminine. It was clear by the look on his face that Chrysander agreed.

To her surprise, instead of returning to the car, he walked her next door to a jeweler and proceeded to choose a stunning set of diamond earrings and a matching necklace to go with her wedding dress. Already speechless, she was reduced to a mere croak when he next selected a sapphire necklace and earrings that he suggested she wear with the white silk dress to the reception.

"They will look beautiful with your eyes, *agape mou,*" he murmured next to her ear. "And later, I'd love nothing more than to see you in these jewels and nothing else."

Her face exploded in heat, and she looked around to make sure no one could see her furious blushing.

"You spoil me, Chrysander," she said as they left the jewelry store.

"It is my right to spoil my woman," he said with a shrug.

"I find I quite like it," she said with a smile.

"That is good, because it would be a shame for you not to enjoy something I intend to be doing a lot of."

Impulsively, she scooted against him in the seat and kissed him full on the lips. A staggered breath escaped him as his hands went out to grip her arms. Her cheek slid down his until she nuzzled against his neck and she hugged him tightly.

"Thank you for today. I had so much fun."

His hand went to her hair and stroked softly as he hugged her back with his other arm. "You are quite welcome."

She raised her head and started to move away, but Chrysander held her fast against him.

"Am I a good cook?" she asked, cocking her head at him.

His face registered surprise. "I'm sorry?"

"Cook. Stavros informed me that I liked to cook for you and frequently went to the market for ingredients. I wondered if I was any good at it."

A peculiar expression lit his face. "That's right. You did. I hadn't thought about it in a while, but yes, you did often cook a meal for me on my first night home."

"Were you gone very often?" she asked.

He paused for a moment then slowly nodded. "I'm afraid I was. I was often out of the country on business. Sometimes we went weeks without seeing each other."

"I can't imagine it," she said softly. "I missed you in just the few hours we were apart this morning."

He kissed her again. "And I missed you, *pedhaki mou.*"

She settled against his side as they continued the ride home. She was a bit tired, but there was no way she'd tell him that. The day had been nearly perfect, and they still had the evening together.

Thirteen

Marley fidgeted and tugged at her dress as she surveyed her appearance in the mirror. Sapphires glinted from both ears, and the matching necklace lay against the skin of her neck.

"You look beautiful, *agape mou*."

She turned to see Chrysander behind her. She sucked in her breath as she took in his appearance. The excellently tailored black suit fit him to perfection, drawing attention to his muscular build. The white shirt contrasted with his bronze skin, dark hair and golden eyes, and quite frankly, she felt like drooling.

"So do you," she finally managed.

He chuckled and walked toward her. "Beautiful? Surely you can do better than that."

"Gorgeous? Devastatingly handsome? So good-looking that I'm tempted to fall on you and tear your clothes off?"

"I like the way you think."

"I wasn't joking," she muttered.

"Are you ready? The car is waiting for us below."

She took a deep breath and twisted her engagement ring around her finger with the pad of her thumb. "As ready as I'll ever be."

He reached for her hand and tugged her into his arms. "It won't be so bad. I will be with you the whole night."

She reached up on tiptoe to kiss him. "I'm a coward. I fully admit it."

He took his time exploring her lips, moving with a sensual thoroughness that left her weak and breathless. When they drew apart, she could see he was as affected as she was.

"I think we should leave now," he said hoarsely. "Otherwise we won't be going anywhere for a very long time."

They rode to the hotel, and Marley could see several limousines lining the circular drive outside the main entrance as they pulled up. She swallowed nervously as she saw the glitz and glamour of the people stepping from the cars and entering the hotel. She suddenly felt underdressed and unprepared.

When they reached the front entrance, the doors were opened and Chrysander stepped out, extending his hand to help her from the car. He tucked her arm securely underneath his, and they walked inside the hotel.

Butterflies performed a rendition of the River Dance in her stomach as they entered the large ballroom. A jazz band played softly from a small stage at the back of the room. Waiters circled with trays of wine and champagne while others offered a selection of hors d'oeuvres.

Chrysander murmured to one of the waiters as he took a glass of wine from the tray, and a few moments later, he returned with a glass of mineral water for Marley.

As she scanned the room, glass in hand, she mentally groaned as she saw Theron and Piers and then Roslyn. While she knew they'd be in attendance, she'd truly hoped to avoid them as much as possible. That wasn't going to happen, she mused as she saw Theron start across the room toward Chrysander.

Her first reaction was to excuse herself to the ladies' room, but Chrysander's grip tightened on her fingers as though he knew of her impending flight.

"Chrysander," Theron said by way of greeting. His gaze skimmed quickly over Marley, and he offered the briefest of nods. At least it wasn't a full-blown snub, nor did he scowl at her.

She listened as the two exchanged pleasantries, and then Theron gestured toward Piers and a distinguished older gentleman who was standing beside him. She hung back as Chrysander started toward his brother, but he tugged her along with him, and her dread increased.

Piers frowned when she and Chrysander approached. The older gentleman smiled broadly and uttered a polite greeting to Chrysander. A woman Marley assumed was his wife also offered an enthusiastic hello from his side.

Chrysander urged her forward. "Senhor and Senhora Vasquez, I'd like you both to meet Marley Jameson. Marley, this is Senhor Vasquez and his wife. They're here from Brazil on business."

Marley smiled and exchanged pleasantries with the older couple then relaxed against Chrysander. Piers was being polite, and Theron had joined the group minus the complete indifference he'd shown in her presence a moment earlier. Maybe she could endure the evening after all.

Chrysander reached down and squeezed her hand, and then he faced the others, odd tension on his face. "Marley has agreed to be my wife. We plan to marry while we're here in New York. We'd be honored if you all could attend."

A gasp sounded behind Chrysander, and Marley whirled around to see Roslyn standing a few feet away, shock reflected on her face. She recovered quickly, but not quick enough for Marley to wonder what she could possibly have found so shocking about the announcement. As she turned and looked at the others, only the Vasquezes looked congratulatory over the news.

Piers's and Theron's expressions both mirrored Roslyn's shock. Then their surprise turned to outright distaste. Chrysander shot them warning looks, but Marley was at a complete loss. She trembled against Chrysander, and his grip tightened on her hand as if he understood her desire to flee.

How could their engagement possibly be news? They were

engaged before her accident, and yet everyone acted as though it was a recent development. An unpleasant one at that.

After the obligatory well wishes from the Vasquezes and more from a few people nearby who'd overheard, the conversation switched to more mundane topics. Marley remained silent, numb to the talk around her. Chrysander loosened his hold on her hand, but he slid his arm around her waist and anchored her firmly against him. There was no escaping, no matter how much she might wish it.

The conversation turned to the possible building of a hotel in Rio de Janeiro, and while Marley remained silent, only observing the others, Chrysander's arm never strayed from around her waist.

As the evening wore on, more people offered their congratulations on the upcoming wedding, and soon the room buzzed with the news. The constant smile Marley wore was starting to wear on her. As if sensing her strain, Chrysander whirled her onto the dance floor as a slow jazz song floated melodiously in the air.

She sighed as she melted into his arms. "Thanks. I needed that."

He smiled and leaned down to nibble at the corner of her mouth. "You are the most beautiful woman in the room. The men all look at you with lust in their eyes, and it's enough to make me want to pound them into the ground."

"Mmm, as much as I like the macho act, I'd much prefer if you took me home and worked off some of that male arrogance in another way."

"You tempt me."

She smiled up at him. "I was very serious."

He sighed. "As much as I would like to do just that, I'm afraid I am stuck here for the evening. If it becomes too much for you, I can have Stavros take you back to the apartment."

As if she'd leave him here with Roslyn, Miss Super Assistant.

Despite the fact that Chrysander's brothers and Roslyn seemed determined to treat her as a pariah, there were many others who went out of their way to be gracious to Marley and include her in conversation. She actually found herself enjoying the festive atmosphere despite the evening's inauspicious start.

It was growing late when Chrysander leaned in close to her ear and murmured, "I need to speak with my brothers. Will you be all right for a few moments?"

"Of course, silly," she said with a smile. "I'm going to visit the ladies' room. You go on."

He kissed her then strode toward his brothers. Marley took her time in the bathroom. It was a nice reprieve from the endless chatter and the dark glances thrown her way by the Anetakis contingent.

"You can't hide in here forever," she said to herself. Squaring her shoulders, she exited the bathroom and walked back toward the ballroom. As she passed one of the smaller meeting rooms, she heard Chrysander's voice through the open door. She faltered and came to a stop, debating whether to continue or stay and wait for him.

The next words she heard made her decision for her.

"Damn it, Chrysander, there is no need to marry her. Put her up in an apartment somewhere until the child comes. Don't tie yourself to her and give her access to everything you own."

Her mouth rounded in shock at Piers's angry words.

"She is pregnant with my child," Chrysander said icily. "That I choose to marry her is none of your concern."

She moved closer to the door, not caring whether they saw her. What right did Piers have to talk to Chrysander so?

"You can't mean to marry her!" Roslyn's shrill voice rose. "Do you forget how she stole from you? That she tried to ruin your company? If you need any reminders, just look at the new hotels going up in Paris and Rome. Your hotels, Chrysander. Only they're going up under your competitor's name."

A haze blew through Marley's mind. Red hot. Like a swarm of angry bees, tidbits of information began buzzing in her head. And suddenly it was as if a dam broke. The locked door in her mind that she'd tried so hard to budge simply opened, and the past came roaring through with vicious velocity.

She swayed and gripped the door frame tighter. Nausea boiled in her stomach as each and every moment flashed like a movie in fast-forward.

Chrysander's angry accusation of thievery. His ordering her from their apartment, his life. Her abduction and the months she'd spent in hopeless fear, waiting for Chrysander to answer the ransom demands. Demands he'd ignored.

Oh God, she was going to be sick.

He'd left her. Discarded her like a piece of rubbish. The half million dollars, a paltry sum to a man of Chrysander's means, was an amount he'd been unwilling to part with to ensure her return.

Everything had been a lie. He'd lied to her nonstop since she'd awoken in the hospital. He didn't love her or want her. He *despised* her.

She hadn't been worth half a million dollars to him.

Pain splintered through her chest as she shattered. As everything she'd known as true suddenly turned black. Her heart withered and cracked, falling in pieces around her.

He hadn't tried to save her.

The tortured cry that ripped from her mouth echoed through the room. She clamped a hand over her lips, but it was too late. Everyone looked her way. Theron flinched, and an odd discomfort settled over Piers's face. She met Chrysander's gaze, and she could see the truth in his eyes as he realized that she remembered.

As he started across the room toward her, she backed away, stumbling as she did. Oh God, she couldn't face this. Tears blurred her vision. The image of his pale face only spurred her on.

Marley fled down the hallway toward the lobby. Chrysander called her name, but she didn't stop. Sobs bubbled from her chest and exploded outward. She stumbled but regained her footing and pushed herself forward. Behind her, Chrysander cursed and called out to her again.

She was running for the exit, no clear destination in mind. She was nearly there when she met with a mountain. Stavros stepped in front of her and held her, and she exploded in fury, kicking and shoving. Her only thought was to get away, as far away from this place as she could.

She broke free but stumbled backward and fell to the floor. Stavros was down beside her, asking her if she was all right, and she knew she was trapped.

Pain cycled through her body, an unending stream of agony. She closed her eyes as Chrysander's strong hands slid over her body. In an urgent voice, he demanded to know if she was hurt, but she was incapable of answering him. She curled into a ball, uncaring that she was in the middle of the hotel lobby.

Chrysander picked her up, and she could hear him saying her name. Curses fell from his lips, and then he barked orders for someone to summon a doctor. He strode away from the noise of the lobby, and a few moments later, he entered an empty hotel room.

As soon as he lowered her to the bed, she curled herself into a tight ball again and turned away from him. She flinched when he put his hand on her, his touch light and concerned.

"You must stop crying, *agape mou*. You're going to make yourself ill."

She was already sick, she thought dully. Utterly sick at heart. She closed her eyes, but still hot tears streamed down her cheeks, even as Chrysander wiped them away with his fingers.

She wanted to escape. Go some place where it didn't hurt so much. Through the fog, she heard Chrysander conversing with the doctor. A moment later, she felt a prick in her arm, but she didn't react. She didn't care. And then she floated away, so grateful that the pain had receded. Her mind grew fuzzy as the veil of sleep descended over her. Oblivion. She reached for it. Embraced it and wrapped it around her as she slipped away to a place where there was no hurt and no betrayal.

Chrysander paced back and forth at the foot of Marley's bed while the hotel physician administered the sedative. She was beyond distraught, and the doctor had moved immediately to prevent further upset.

As the doctor stood and backed away from the bed, he looked at Chrysander, a grim expression on his face.

Fear tightened Chrysander's chest. "Is she all right? Is the baby all right?"

The doctor motioned him across the room and away from where Marley now quietly lay. "Her injuries are not physical. If they were, perhaps I would be of use. Her distress is mental. If it is as you said, and she has regained her memory, it is that which has caused her immeasurable pain."

Chrysander stirred impatiently. "What can be done? She cannot be left as she is. There must be something we can do." The sight of her pale face and her eyes, so huge with devastation, twisted his gut painfully.

"You should return her to your home, to a place that is more familiar. She needs a doctor, not for her physical well-being, but one who can help her mentally."

"A therapist you mean?" Chrysander asked grimly.

"This is a very delicate time," the doctor warned. "She is extremely fragile, and remembering such traumatic events could cause an emotional breakdown."

His face twisted in sympathy, and he reached out to grasp Chrysander's shoulder. "This will be hard, but perhaps it is for the best. It is good that her memory returned, even if it causes her such distress."

Chrysander wasn't so sure of that. With her memory regained, she also knew that he'd tossed her out of their apartment, basically put her into the hands of her kidnappers. She would also recall the cruel words he'd thrown at her. And she would remember her own part in the whole mess.

He ran a hand wearily through his hair. Part of him wished she would have never regained those memories. They had started fresh, without past deceptions and betrayals. Something niggled at him even as those thoughts passed through his mind.

Wouldn't she have greeted her memory's return with guilt? All he'd seen in her eyes was hurt. Deep and horrific hurt. There was no guilt, no embarrassment over the fact she'd stolen from him. Just distress so keen that he still felt the knife deep in his chest from the tortured sound of her cry and the memory of her stumbling away from him.

An uneasy sensation took hold of him. He couldn't help but think that there were things buried in Marley's memories that he wasn't going to like.

Fourteen

Marley was only vaguely aware of the things going on around her. After that first pass into oblivion, she registered being carried into a car. She heard Chrysander's worried voice as he murmured to her, but she closed herself off from him, folding inward.

When she next awoke, she knew she was in a bed. As she looked around the room, recognition sparked, and with it, a surge of fresh agony, hot and raw, seared through her body and robbed her of breath.

He wouldn't do this. Surely even he could not be so cruel as to bring her back to the place they'd shared and the place he'd brutally shoved her from.

She reached for the tears, expecting them to come, but curiously all she felt was an odd detachment, a void of nothingness coupled with the need to get out of this place.

When she sat up, her gaze flickered to a chair by the window occupied by Chrysander's sleeping form. He was slouched against the arm, his clothing rumpled and the stubble of over a day's beard shadowing his jaw.

She waited for the rush of anger, of fury, but again, she felt nothing but overwhelming numbness and a need to escape.

She got out of bed, not paying attention to her own rumpled clothing. It occurred to her that maybe she should change, but she couldn't risk waking Chrysander. No, she needed to be away. She couldn't look him in the eye knowing that he'd made such horrible accusations and then left her to the mercy of her kidnappers.

Her thumb brushed across the thin band of her engagement ring, and she wrenched it off. It felt cold in her hand. She gently laid it on the nightstand beside the bed then turned and walked away.

On bare feet, she walked out of the bedroom and to the elevator. Her stomach churned as she relived the night she'd gotten on this elevator as her world crumbled around her, Chrysander's accusation ringing in her ears. How could he? It was the only thought that played over and over in her mind until she wanted to scream at it to stop.

When she reached the lobby, she paused, realizing that not only would Chrysander's security people likely be manning the front entrance but that also the doorman would never let her walk out as she was.

She turned and hurried for the back entrance. To her dismay, one of the men she recognized from Chrysander's detail was standing at the door. She quickly ducked into a service entrance and made her way down the hallway that housed rooms for laundry and building maintenance. A few minutes later, she opened the door and walked out into the pale, predawn light.

Chrysander woke with a monster catch in his neck and shifted in the too-small chair to alleviate his discomfort. He'd wanted to spend the night with Marley tucked into his arms, but she'd resisted his touch at every turn, becoming so distraught that he'd had no choice but to retreat.

He'd taken the doctor's advice and phoned a therapist as soon as he'd returned to the apartment with Marley. The therapist was due to arrive this morning to speak with her. Chrysander just hoped she would be able to.

His gaze moved to the bed, and when he saw it empty, he shot to his feet. He started to bolt from the room, but a glimmer of something on the nightstand caught his eye. When he saw her engagement ring lying there, dread tightened his chest. He ran from the room in search of her. As he went from room to room, his panic grew. She wasn't anywhere to be found.

Even as he hurled himself into the elevator, he dug out his cellular phone. As soon as the doors opened in the lobby, he ran out and nearly collided with Stavros.

He grasped the man's shirt in his hands and pulled him up close. "Where is she?"

Stavros blinked in surprise. "We haven't seen her, sir. No one has. She was with you."

Chrysander pushed him away with a violent curse. "She's gone. Call your men in. I want her found immediately."

He strode to the entrance to question the doorman, but he seemed as baffled as the security man. He turned around to see several of his detail gather in the lobby as they were questioned by an angry Stavros.

Theos! Where could she have gone? She was in no state to be wandering around New York, and the people who had abducted her were still at large.

Worry settled hard into his chest. He turned to go out the door in search of her himself when he saw Theron walk in.

"Chrysander," he said in greeting. "I was on my way up to see you. How is Marley?"

"She's gone," he said grimly.

Theron raised one brow. "Gone? But how?"

"I don't know," he said in frustration. "She's disappeared. I have to find her."

Theron put a firm hand on Chrysander's shoulder. "We'll find her, Chrysander."

"There is something about this situation," Chrysander said in a hollow voice. "Something that doesn't add up. I saw no guilt in her face when she remembered everything. All I saw was complete devastation, as if she were the one who was betrayed. She was so distraught that she had to be sedated, and she becomes extremely upset when I get close to her. She isn't herself right now. I fear where she may have gone. Her frame of mind is not good."

"I will help you, Chrysander," Theron said quietly. "Do not worry. We will find her."

Marley shivered as she eased down onto the cold stone bench and clutched her arms around her trembling body. She glanced down at her feet but couldn't summon any rebuke for having gone out in the chill without shoes or a coat. The only thought she'd had was to get away as quickly as possible. She couldn't face Chrysander now.

Now she knew why she'd been drawn to this place. Her thinking spot, indeed. Just hours before that last night, she'd sat here, afraid of how Chrysander would react to her pregnancy. She'd been right to be afraid. He didn't trust her. He didn't love her. And he'd left her to her fate with the kidnappers.

She refused to allow the memories to roll back in her mind. They simply hurt too much. At least now she realized why she'd chosen to forget. All those weeks of living in fear as her kidnappers waited for their demands to be met had paled next to the betrayal Chrysander had handed her when he'd refused.

How could anyone be so cold? Wouldn't he have been willing to pay such a meager amount of money to free anyone? Even a complete stranger? She'd never imagined him to be so heartless. But he'd cast her aside with little regard for her. She'd been his mistress, someone to slake his lust and nothing more. The fool was her for falling in love with him, not once, but twice.

A small moan escaped her lips, and she closed her eyes as the ache built within her once more. Never had she felt so hurt, so utterly lost.

Her hands closed around the bulge of her stomach, and the tears that she'd thought locked under the ice began to well to the surface.

How could he be capable of such a despicable deception? He had to know she'd remember eventually, and yet he'd spent weeks wooing her, making her love him all over again. Pretending affection for her. And passion. The question was, why?

Was it all an elaborate ruse to punish her? To make her suffer more than she already had? She'd never imagine Chrysander to be so cruel, but it just proved how little she'd known about the man she'd given herself to.

She sat there, rocking back and forth, her arms wrapped protectively around her abdomen. The wind picked up, chasing a chill down her spine, but she ignored the discomfort.

"Marley?"

Her name came out cautiously and sounded distant, yet when she looked up, the man was standing just a few feet away, concern lighting his eyes. She recognized him. Theron. No wonder he'd been so resistant to Chrysander marrying her. He thought her the thief that Chrysander did. It was more than she could bear.

She hugged herself tighter and looked down, determined that he not see her tears.

He squatted down in front of her and put a hand on her wrist. "I need to take you back, *pedhaki mou*. It's not safe for you to be out here," he said gently.

She flinched at the endearment. It was Chrysander's pet name for her, and she wanted no part of it. She shook her head and pulled her hand up in a protective manner.

He glanced down at her feet and swore under his breath. "It's cold, and you shouldn't be out here in your bare feet. Let me take you back home."

She recoiled violently. "No." She shook her head vehemently. "I won't go back there." She slid to the end of the bench, the rough stone scratching against her clothing.

Theron put a hand out to prevent her flight. "Marley, think of your baby. Let me take you back. You're cold."

"I won't go back to that apartment," she said desperately. She stood, prepared to bolt.

Theron look at her with regret. "I cannot allow you to run. You're clearly upset and are not dressed for the weather."

Tears filled her eyes. "Why do you care? I stole from you,

remember? I'm just the harlot who snared your brother and tried to ruin his company," she said bitterly.

Theron's eyes softened. "If I promise not to return you to the apartment, will you come with me? I won't leave you like this, Marley."

She swayed, and he caught her as her knees gave out. He picked her up and began striding away.

She stiffened in his arms. "Please, just leave me alone," she begged.

"I cannot do that, little sister."

"I'm just your brother's whore," she said, allowing more of the anguish in.

His grip tightened around her. "*Theos!* Never say that again."

She turned her face into his shoulder, and hot tears flooded her eyes. "It's true," she whispered.

She closed her eyes and allowed herself to drift away once again. It was easy to flee from reality when it represented so much she wanted to escape. She cursed that she'd ever regained her memory. Doing so had destroyed her.

Fifteen

Chrysander strode into the Imperial Park Hotel, waving off members of the staff as they hastened to greet him. The elevator was being held open for him, and he got in and rode it to the top floor.

A few moments later, he walked into the luxury suite usually reserved for VIP guests. His brother met him in the sitting area, and Chrysander scowled furiously at him.

"Why didn't you bring her back to the apartment?" he demanded.

"She became hysterical at the mere mention of it," Theron said. "She was set to run as far and as fast as she could. I had to promise I wouldn't take her back to the penthouse."

Chrysander swore and closed his eyes. He brought his hand to his face and pinched the bridge of his nose between his fingers in a weary gesture.

"She's about to break," Theron said quietly. "Bring your therapist here to talk to her. Maybe she can help."

Chrysander looked sharply at his younger brother. "You seem concerned about her."

"She carries my nephew." His lips pressed together in a grim line. "It is as you said. There is no guilt in her expression, her actions. She acts as though she has suffered the deepest of hurts. It was uncomfortable for me to see. I suddenly wanted to do all I could to shield her from such pain."

"Where is she now?" Chrysander demanded.

"Asleep," Theron replied. "She fell asleep on the way here and never stirred when I carried her up the elevator and put her into bed."

Chrysander headed for the bedroom, determined to see for himself that she was safe. He made his way through the dimly lit room and stopped at the head of the bed. Even in sleep, her brow was creased in an expression of despair.

He reached down and touched her cheek, tucking a curl behind her ear. She didn't stir. Her pale face lay against the pillow, framed by her dark curls. Deep shadows smudged her eyes, and he could tell from the redness that she had been crying. His chest twisted painfully at the signs of her distress.

As he walked back into the sitting room, he pulled out his cellular phone to call the therapist and have her come to the hotel. When he was done, he closed his phone and turned to Theron.

"Where did you find her?"

Theron handed him a drink. "She was in a garden a few blocks from your apartment." He winced as he looked at Chrysander. "She was barefoot, with no coat or sweater. She looked lost and unaware of her surroundings."

Chrysander swore. "It has been so since she regained her memory. *Theos mou,* but I don't know what to do." He'd never felt so helpless.

"Do you still believe she is guilty?" Theron asked quietly.

"I don't know," Chrysander admitted. "I think sometimes that it doesn't matter." He looked bleakly up at his brother, expecting to see condemnation. Instead, Theron looked at him with understanding.

"When I saw her on the bench, it did not matter to me, either," Theron said softly.

The therapist arrived a few minutes later, and Chrysander filled her in on everything that had happened since arriving in New York.

Despite the discomfort he felt over providing such personal details to the woman, he wanted her to know whatever she needed in order to help Marley. So he told her everything. From the confrontation he'd had with Marley so many months before, to the present.

To her credit, the woman did not react. She took the information in stride and asked to see Marley.

"She is resting, but you can go in and wait for her to awaken. I don't want her to grow upset and try to leave."

The therapist nodded and followed Chrysander to the bedroom. As they entered, Marley stirred. Chrysander automatically stepped forward, but the therapist held up her hand to halt him.

"Leave me to speak to her," she said softly.

Chrysander weighed his desire to be near her with the therapist's request. Finally, he nodded curtly and turned to leave. He didn't go far, though. He stepped from the bedroom and closed the door, but left it slightly ajar so he could hear what was being said within.

There was a long period of silence, and then the slight murmur of voices filtered from the room. The therapist did most of the talking at first as she soothed Marley. After a long while, he could hear Marley's trembling voice, and he strained closer to hear what she said.

"I went to the doctor the day Chrysander was due back from overseas. When I discovered I was pregnant, I was shocked. I worried how Chrysander would react. I wanted to ask him about our relationship…how he felt about me."

"Go on," the therapist encouraged.

Marley's questions that night now made sense to Chrysander. And then he flinched at her next words.

"He told me we had no relationship. That I was his mistress. A woman he paid to have sex with," she said hollowly.

He wanted to protest. He wanted to march into the bedroom and tell her that he'd never considered her someone he paid to have sex with.

"Then he accused me of…" Her voice trailed off, and he could hear a quiet sob rise from the room.

"It's all right, Marley," the therapist soothed.

"He said I had stolen from him. He said I took plans for one of his hotels and gave them to his competitor. He told me to get out."

"And did you steal them?"

"You're the first person to actually ask," Marley said wanly.

Chrysander flinched. She was right. He hadn't asked. He'd judged and condemned her.

"I was stunned. I still don't understand. I'd never even seen the papers he threw at me. I don't know why he thought I took them or how he could even think such a horrible thing."

The tears he heard in her voice felt like little daggers to his chest. The tension grew until he felt he would explode. Dread skated up his spine. What had he done?

"And then…" She broke off as sobs took over.

There was another long period of silence as the therapist murmured words of comfort to Marley.

"Tell me what happened next, Marley."

"I left the apartment, but I knew I had to come back the next day after he'd calmed down so I could make him see reason and tell him I was pregnant. I felt if I could just have the chance to talk to him that he would see what a mistake it was."

"And what happened?" the therapist asked gently.

Chrysander pushed against the door, his body tense with anticipation.

"A man pulled a bag over my head and forced me into a car. I was taken to another place in the city and told that I was being held for ransom. I was terrified. I was pregnant and was so scared that they would hurt me or my baby."

Chrysander's hands curled into fists as he fought the rising rage within him.

"They sent two ransom demands," Marley whispered. "He refused both. He left me there. Oh God, he left me to those men. I wasn't even worth half a million dollars to him!"

Sobs ripped from her throat as she dissolved into tears. Chrysander stood in stunned disbelief. Mother of God. He'd never received a ransom demand. He hadn't! His stomach boiled as acid rose in his throat. He turned and laid his forehead against the wall and brought his clenched fist to rest a few inches away. He felt wetness on his cheeks but made no move to wipe it away.

A few moments later, the therapist eased out of the bedroom and looked at Chrysander. He expected condemnation in her eyes but saw only a faint sympathy.

"I've sedated her. She was nearly hysterical. She needs rest above all else. Her reality is very painful, so she retreats. That same self-preservation is what prompted her amnesia. Now that she no longer has that protective buffer, she struggles to cope in the best way she knows how. Be gentle and understanding with her. Don't push her too hard."

She patted him on the arm as she walked past.

"Call me if you need me. I'll come at once."

"Thank you," Chrysander said hoarsely.

When she left, Chrysander turned and shuffled farther into the sitting room and sagged onto the couch.

"Dear God," he said bleakly.

"I heard," Theron said with a grimace.

"She never stole anything." Chrysander closed his eyes and dragged a hand through his hair. "*Theos.* I never got a ransom demand. She thinks…she thinks I left her to those animals, that I didn't care enough to pay half a million dollars for her return."

Theron put a comforting hand on Chrysander's shoulder. "There is much we need to investigate."

Chrysander nodded. His thoughts hardened as he turned from the anguish over Marley's revelation and forced himself to play back the events of that night.

The realization, when it came, was so startlingly clear that he cursed himself for not having pieced it together before. He'd been too angry, too wounded by what he perceived as a betrayal by Marley.

"Roslyn," he said tersely.

Theron raised a brow. "Your assistant?"

"She was there. Just before I found the papers in Marley's bag. She must have planted them."

Another thought occurred to him, one that sickened him and made him want to empty his stomach. Any ransom demand would have gone to his office. His residences were highly guarded secrets. Marley had said that he'd ignored ransom demands, but now he realized they could have been delivered and intercepted. By Roslyn.

He stood and whirled around to face his brother. "You will stay here with Marley. Make sure she goes nowhere and that she is well cared for. I'll send a physician over to monitor her condition."

Theron also stood. "Where are you going, brother?"

"I'm going to find out if what I suspect is true," he said in a dangerously low voice.

"Chrysander, wait."

Chrysander paused and stared back at his brother.

"You should call the authorities. If you confront her and gain a confession, it won't do any good. Only you will know."

Chrysander clenched his fists in frustration, but he knew his brother was right. He didn't want Roslyn to get away with what she'd done. He could make her life miserable, but she would still be free. He wanted justice.

Chrysander paced the confines of his New York office as he waited for Roslyn to arrive. He didn't want to be here. He wanted to be with Marley. Theron had stayed with her, and Chrysander simmered with impatience. Her condition hadn't changed. Even when she'd awakened, she'd been distant, unfocused, there but not there. It was as if she'd gone to a place where he couldn't hurt her anymore.

He closed his eyes and tried to focus on the task at hand. When he heard Roslyn enter, he stiffened. It was all he could do not to rage at her, not to break her skinny neck. It took everything he had to smile and act as though nothing was wrong, as though he didn't loathe the very ground she walked on.

"You wanted to see me?" Roslyn said breathlessly.

"I did," Chrysander murmured. He let his gaze run suggestively over her body even as his flesh crawled.

Her eyes brightened, and her stance immediately became suggestive.

"I've only just become aware of the lengths to which you went to try and get my attention," he said with a chuckle. "Men can be thick, so you women say, but I think maybe I was thicker than most."

Confusion rippled across her face, and she struggled to retain a look of innocence. She couldn't be sure what he was talking about yet, but it would soon be clear. He watched her body language, her eyes, the windows into the soulless bitch that she was.

"Why did you not just say you wanted me?" he purred. "It would have saved us a lot of trouble. Instead, I was trapped in a relationship I didn't want, though I appreciate the efforts you made to rid me of that problem."

Roslyn relaxed, and a cold smile flashed across her face. It was strange, but Chrysander had never realized just how ugly she was.

"How did you arrange it?" he asked silkily.

He listened in horror as she outlined what she'd done to make it appear as though Marley had stolen the plans. The kidnapping had been an added bonus, but when she'd received the ransom demand at his office, she'd seen her opportunity to be rid of Marley once and for all.

So anxious was she to prove her devotion to Chrysander, that she didn't realize she'd admitted to selling his plans to his competitor.

"So you stole the plans and gave them to Marcelli." His voice was like ice, and she flinched at his tone. Her face whitened as she realized just what she'd confessed to.

"You then framed Marley, thinking not only would you have the proceeds from selling me out to my competitor, but then you would have Marley out of the way so you could move into her place."

Her mouth opened and closed, and he could see the realization settle in that he'd duped her and was furious.

"And then when the ransom demands were delivered to my office, you destroyed them, hoping what, Roslyn, that they would kill her? Permanently remove her from the picture?"

He was shaking he was so angry. She simmered before him in a red haze. All he could see was Marley alone and frightened. Pregnant with his child and vulnerable. Thinking that not only did he hate her but that he'd simply left her to her fate. He wanted to weep.

Roslyn seemed to recover her composure, and she looked scornfully at him. "You'll never prove it."

"I don't have to," he said softly. He pressed the small intercom button on his desk. "You may come in now, Detective."

Roslyn swayed as three policemen entered the room, their expressions grim.

"You can't do this!" she shrieked. "I love you, Chrysander. I would have done anything for you."

He shook his head and turned away from her rantings as she was escorted away in handcuffs. He had no desire to listen to her. He wanted to return to Marley.

"Forgive me, *agape mou*," he whispered.

Marley was dimly aware that she was being carried yet again. It wasn't Chrysander. She was intimately familiar with his touch. For a moment she panicked, and then she heard comforting words being spoken in Greek and then in English.

"Rest easy, little sister. You are safe."

"Where are we going?" she asked weakly.

"Someplace safe," he soothed. "Chrysander won't allow anything to happen to you."

She wanted to protest that Chrysander wouldn't do anything for her, but she couldn't muster the energy. At some point, she heard Chrysander, and she cursed the fact that she immediately felt safer and that some of the panic abated.

She felt the brush of lips against her forehead and then firm hands tucking her into bed. Fingers stroked through her hair, and warmth enveloped her.

"You are safe, *agape mou*. I'll never allow anyone to hurt you again."

"Don't call me that," she cried. "Never again." But she held to Chrysander's promise even as her heart screamed in protest. He'd lied to her. She couldn't believe anything he said. And yet she relaxed and settled into a dreamless sleep.

When Marley next awoke, there was a crispness to her mind that had been absent since the day she'd regained her memory. No longer did fog shroud her memories. She both welcomed and cursed the new awareness. Gone was any confusion, but with that new clarity came inevitable heartbreak.

She felt alert, as though she'd slept a week. And maybe she had. She had no idea how much time had passed, and while her past was no longer a mystery, the events of the last few days were hazy and fractured.

With a reluctant sigh, she pushed back the covers and eased her legs over the side of the bed. As she glanced around, she realized she had no idea where she was. The room was spacious and cheerful, with several windows to allow natural lighting.

She pushed herself up and walked into the adjoining bathroom, her eyes widening at the size and luxury. She eyed the Jacuzzi tub with longing. While she might not know how many days had passed—they'd all been a blur—she did know that she hadn't had a bath in a while, and she couldn't wait to feel clean and refreshed again.

Bracing her foot on the step to the tub, she leaned over and turned the handle to start the water. When she looked up, she saw Chrysander standing in the doorway. A startled gasp escaped her.

He started forward immediately and grasped her arm to steady her. "I'm sorry for frightening you, *pedhaki mou*. It was not my intention. I worried when I came in to check on you and you were not in bed."

"I just wanted a bath," she said in a low voice.

"I do not want you to be in here alone," he said. "I'll

summon Mrs. Cahill so that if you have need of anything, you can just call out."

She closed her eyes for a moment and drew in a steadying breath. Then she met his gaze. "Please, Chrysander, let's not have any further lies between us. There's no need for you to pretend that I'm important to you...that I matter."

Bleakness entered his eyes, and his face grayed underneath the olive tone of his skin. "You matter very much to me, *agape mou.*"

Before she could respond, he retreated from the bathroom, and a moment later, Patrice bustled in. In a matter of minutes, Marley found herself stripped and settled into a warm bath. Not too hot, Patrice assured, since overly hot baths were not good for a pregnant woman.

As Marley settled into the fragrant bubbles, she leaned her head back against the rim of the tub and glanced over at Patrice. "Where are we? And how did you get here? I thought you were in Athens with Dr. Karounis."

"Mr. Anetakis asked me to fly back so I could be with you," she said soothingly. "He was quite desperate. The idea of returning to the apartment upset you so badly that he brought you here."

"And where is here?" Marley asked.

"His house," she explained patiently. "We're about an hour from the city. It's quieter here, more peaceful. He thought you'd prefer it."

Tears blurred Marley's vision. And she thought she hadn't any more tears to shed. She hadn't known he owned a house outside of the city, and like the island, it was one more place she'd never visited in all the time she'd been with Chrysander. Further proof that she'd never occupied an important place in his life.

"He's been very worried about you," Patrice said, her face softening in sympathy. "We all have been."

Marley shook her head in denial. Chrysander hated her. He'd never loved her, and she'd been too stupid to realize it.

"What am I going to do?" she whispered to no one in particular. She'd been an idiot to give up her apartment, her job, every means she had of taking care of herself when she moved in with

Chrysander. She'd been too blinded by her love and convinced that she had a future with him.

"Come out of the tub," Patrice said gently. "You need to get dried off so you can go down to eat."

Marley allowed Patrice to mother her. She was dried off and pampered then clothed in comfortable slacks and a maternity shirt. She rubbed a hand over her belly and whispered an apology to her unborn son.

She couldn't afford to fall apart. Her child was depending on her.

Chrysander was waiting for her when she exited the bedroom. He said nothing, but he cupped her elbow and helped her down the stairs, and she let him, too numb to protest. Marley also remained silent, her emotions too much in turmoil to try and have a reasonable conversation.

They sat at a small table that overlooked a beautifully manicured garden. Bright morning sun shone through the glass doors, and she felt warmed by the sun's rays.

Chrysander set a plate piled high with food in front of her then settled into a seat across from her. She piddled with her fork and toyed with the food, pushing it around the plate as she avoided his gaze.

He sighed, and she looked up to see him staring at her. His expression was somber, as though he was enduring the worst sort of hell. She nearly laughed at the absurdity. To her horror, she felt the prick of tears, and his face swam in her vision.

"We must talk, Marley. There is much I need to say to you." His voice sounded oddly strangled. "But first you must eat so you can regain your strength. Your health and that of our child must come first."

She bowed her head again, refusing to meet his stare any longer. She concentrated on eating, and once she started realized she was actually quite hungry.

As she was finishing the last of her juice, she heard a door slam in the distance, and then she heard the determined stride of someone walking across the floor. She turned to see Theron enter the room, a grim look on his face.

Before he could speak, Chrysander locked his gaze onto his brother and said in a steely voice, "Whatever it is, I'm sure it can wait until Marley has finished eating."

Theron cast a concerned glance her way and nodded his understanding to Chrysander. Anger tightened her throat and made swallowing difficult. Whatever it was they wished to speak about, it was obvious they didn't want to do so in front of her. But then why would they? She was someone they believed had stolen from them.

She stood abruptly and tossed down her napkin. Without a word to either man, she stalked away.

"Marley, don't go," Chrysander protested.

She turned and pinned him with the force of her glare. "By all means, have your conversation. I'd hate to intrude. After all, someone who has stolen from you and betrayed your trust isn't someone you want around when you're talking."

"*Theos,* that is not the issue here. Marley? Wait, damn it!"

But she ignored him and continued walking.

Chrysander watched her leave and cursed. He felt strangled by helplessness. How could he ever hope to make things right between them? She hated him, and she had every right to.

He turned to Theron, who had also watched Marley go, a frown etched on his face. "What brought you here in such a hurry?" Chrysander demanded.

Theron reached into the jacket of his suit and pulled out a folded newspaper. He tossed it onto the table in front of Chrysander. "This did."

Chrysander opened it and immediately cursed in four languages. On the front page was a picture of Marley being carried by Theron on the day she'd run from the apartment. Underneath were pictures of himself and of Roslyn with a story outlining the soap-opera saga that highlighted every single facet of his relationship with Marley.

He threw the paper across the room with vicious force. "It had to be Roslyn. None of my men would have spoken to the press."

Theron nodded his agreement. "Since you had her arrested for her theft and her duplicity in keeping the ransom demands from you, she likely thought she had nothing to lose and everything to gain by giving the public her spin on your supposed relationship with her."

Chrysander sank into the chair and rested his elbows on the table. "I curse the day I ever hired that woman. Marley could have died because of my stupidity."

"You love her."

It wasn't a question, and Chrysander didn't treat is as such. It was simply a statement of fact. He did love her. But he'd managed to kill her love for him not once, but twice.

He nodded and buried his face in his hands. "I wouldn't blame her if she never forgave me. How can she when I cannot forgive myself?"

"Go to her, Chrysander. Make this right between you."

Chrysander stood. Yes, it was time to try and make things right with Marley. If he could.

Sixteen

Marley stood in the bedroom, staring out the window with unseeing eyes. Nothing Chrysander did at this point should hurt her, but he still had that power over her, much to her dismay.

"Marley."

She swung around to see Chrysander standing in the doorway. He looked tired, his features drawn and his eyes worried. There was something else in his expression. Sadness and…fear?

He started forward, a little hesitantly. "We need to talk."

She tensed then braced herself for what she knew would come. His repudiation of her. She turned her face away but nodded. Yes, they needed to talk and get it done with.

His fingers curled around her chin, and he gently turned her to face him. "Don't look like that, *agape mou*. I do not like to see you so sad."

"Please," she begged. "Just say what it is you want to say. Don't draw it out."

He lowered his hand to capture her wrist. His thumb brushed across her pulse, which jumped and sped up at his touch.

"Come, sit down."

She let him lead her over to the bed. He eased down beside her and sat stiffly, his posture screaming discomfort. Suddenly she couldn't wait for what he would say. Her anger bubbled like an inferno within her.

"You lied to me," she seethed. "Every single thing you've said to me since that day in the hospital has been one lie after another. You don't care about me. All those things you said, everything was a *lie*. When you took me to bed, you despised me, and yet you made love to me and made me believe you cared. Who does that sort of thing?"

She shuddered in revulsion and put her hands to her face.

"You are wrong," he said softly. He pulled her hands away from her face and lifted one to his lips to kiss her upturned palm. "I care a great deal about you. I didn't despise you when I made love to you. Yes, I lied to you about details. I was told not to do or say anything to upset you and to let your memory come back on its own. I lied, Marley, but about the little things. Not the important things. Like how much I care about you. *S'agapo, pedhaki mou.*"

She bowed her head. Her nose stung, and tears burned her eyelids. How she wanted to believe him. But he'd done nothing to earn her trust.

"I have wronged you greatly, Marley."

She raised her head to stare at him in shock. Chrysander admitting that he was wrong?

Shame dragged at his eyes, and deep sorrow had pasted shadows under them.

"There are things you must know. I never received any ransom demands. I would have moved heaven and earth to free you. No price would have been too high. I did not know that you had been abducted."

Her mouth fell open. "How could you not know?"

His eyes grew stormy. "Roslyn destroyed the ransom notes. You were right to dislike her, and because I ignored your feelings about her, I placed you in terrible danger."

Marley's mind reeled with all he had told her. She raised a shaking hand to her mouth. He hadn't gotten the ransom demands? "I thought—" She broke off and shook her head, emotion overwhelming her.

"What did you think, *agape mou?*" he asked softly.

"That you hated me," she whispered. "That you wouldn't pay to free me because you thought I had stolen from you. That I wasn't even worth half a million dollars to you."

He groaned and pulled her into his arms. His hands trembled against her back as he stroked up and down. "I am a fool. I was wrong to accuse you as I did. I have no defense."

She pulled away and gazed up at him. "You don't believe I stole from you?"

He shook his head sharply. "No. It was Roslyn. She planted the papers in your bag to make me think it was you." He paused and swiped a hand through his hair. "Even though I thought you had stolen from me, it no longer seemed to matter after your abduction. All that mattered to me was that you were back where you belonged. With me." His mouth twisted. "That night when you asked me about our relationship...I was frightened."

She raised one eyebrow. The idea of anything frightening Chrysander was laughable.

"I thought you were unhappy, that you wanted more than I was giving you," he admitted. "And then I was angry because it scared me. I was determined that you not be the one to decide our relationship, so I pushed you away by telling you that we had no relationship, that you were my mistress."

Her heart sped up as she viewed the vulnerability on his face. Her chest tightened, and it became harder to breathe as her pulse raced. "What are you saying?" she whispered.

"That I love you, *pedhaki mou. S'agapo.*"

Her eyes widened as she realized what the words he'd said a few minutes ago meant. She couldn't even formulate a response, so she stared at him in shock.

Self-derision crawled across his face. "I have a terrible way of showing it. I was proud, too proud to just tell you how I felt. I didn't even know it then. I just knew I didn't want you to leave and was angry that I thought you were unhappy in our current relationship. And then when I saw those papers in your bag, I was shocked and furious. I couldn't believe that you would steal from me."

"But you did," she said painfully.

He looked away, sorrow creasing his features. "I was angry. I've never been so angry. I thought you had used me so you could help our competitor. So I sent you away."

He ran a hand around to clasp the back of his neck. "And God help me, I sent you straight into the kidnappers' hands."

She closed her eyes, not wanting to remember the fear and despair she'd experienced during her captivity. Even though her memory had returned, that part was still very much a blur. Maybe she'd forever block it out.

"You *love* me?" She was still back on those words. The rest of the conversation seemed a muddle, and she was fixated on those three words.

He gathered her in his arms again and held her as delicately as a piece of hand-blown glass. "I've not done a good job of showing you, but I do love you. I want the chance to prove it to you. I want you to marry me. Please."

She shook her head in confusion at his humble plea. "You still want me to marry you?"

He tugged her closer to him until his lips pressed against the top of her head. "I don't expect you to answer now. I know I have said much to shock you. But give me a chance, Marley. You won't regret it, I swear. I'll make you love me again. I'll never abuse your precious gift as I have done."

She'd gone mad. She'd finally lost her mind. Chrysander was holding her in his arms, declaring his love for her and wanting her to marry him. For real this time. No pretense. No lies or half-truths between them.

Gently, he pulled her away and pressed a light kiss to her lips. "Think about it, *agape mou*. I'll wait as long as it takes for your answer."

He stood as if sensing her desire to be alone. He walked to

the door but turned to look at her one last time before disappearing from view.

Marley sat there for a long time simply staring at the now-empty doorway. Her hands shook and her stomach rolled. He loved her? Roslyn had planted the papers in her bag and then destroyed the ransom demands?

She shivered. Had Roslyn hated her so much? Or had she just wanted Chrysander that badly? Maybe both. Or maybe Roslyn had just been working for Chrysander's competition all along.

The events of the last few days still weighed heavily on her. She couldn't just forget everything because he apologized and offered her love and marriage, could she? She couldn't even return that declaration because he'd never believe it if it came now.

She sighed and lay on her side, curling her knees to her swollen belly. She was so tired. So very worn out, both physically and emotionally. She rubbed her stomach, smiling when her son rolled and kicked beneath her fingers.

"What should I do?" she whispered. She was so afraid to trust Chrysander with her love again. She was also afraid to be without him. As much damage as he'd done to her heart, she ached at the thought of leaving him.

She closed her eyes for just a moment. Exhaustion permeated every pore. She couldn't make such a monumental decision in a few minutes' time. Too much was at stake. She had a child to consider. She had herself to consider.

Over the next few days, Chrysander saw to her every need. He coddled her, pampered her and fussed endlessly over her. He told her often that he loved her, though he was careful to keep a respectable distance between them.

It would seem he went to great pains not to pressure her in any way. He wouldn't use the passion that sparked between them as a means to sway her, and for that she was grateful.

Two days after Chrysander had asked her to marry him again, his brothers came to visit. Marley tried to excuse herself, thinking that they'd want to discuss business with

Chrysander, and to be honest, she still felt awkward and shamed in their presence even though she'd done nothing to deserve their censure.

But it was her they asked to speak to, and she stared at them in bewilderment as they looked gravely at her.

"We have acted unforgivably toward you, little sister," Theron said.

Piers nodded in agreement. "It is understandable if you never forgive us. We were harsh. There is no defense for our treating you, especially since you are pregnant with our nephew, as we have."

Guilt was etched heavily into their faces, and they looked so uncomfortable, but she had no idea what to do or say to ease the situation.

Theron moved forward and put his hands gently on her shoulders. He kissed her on both cheeks then stepped back as Piers did the same.

She glanced toward Chrysander, who watched her with solemn eyes. His face was drawn and seemed thinner as though he'd lost weight. He looked…unhappy. It wasn't guilt, though there was a lot of that floating around the room. He genuinely looked as though he'd lost the one thing that mattered most to him.

Her?

The thought nearly paralyzed her. She smiled shakily at Theron and Piers and then excused herself, nearly running from the room in her haste to get away.

She threw open the door to the patio and welcomed the chilly air. She stepped outside taking deep breaths and trying to settle her rioting emotions.

Her mind skated back over everything she'd felt for the last several days. Betrayal. She'd been lied to. She stopped there, because now she wondered if Chrysander really had lied to her about his feelings.

He looked like she felt. Lost. They were both obviously hurting. If he hated her, truly hated her, then why would he enact such an elaborate charade when she lost her memory? Why would he feel obligated to someone who had stolen from him?

"You're pregnant with his child," she murmured. And yes, she could see how a fair amount of care would be due the mother of his child, but why wouldn't he have done as Theron suggested and merely set her up in an apartment somewhere? Why would he woo her, make love to her, act as though she mattered to him?

Did he love her? The declaration couldn't have been easy for him to make. Chrysander wasn't a man prone to sharing his emotions. In all the time they were together before her kidnapping, he'd never spoken to her of his feelings. But he'd shown her in a dozen ways that she had mattered to him.

Could she trust him again? The thought frightened her, and at the same time it offered her a measure of peace. The choice was hers. Her future would be of her own making.

Even as her options rolled over and over in her mind, she knew what she would do. She knew what she wanted, even knowing it might not be the best choice for her. The heart didn't always choose wisely, she thought with a grimace.

Still, she found herself returning inside and going in search of Chrysander. Worry knotted her belly, but she knew she was making the right decision, even if it didn't feel quite right at this very moment.

She found him in the room she'd left him in, staring out the window, a drink in his hand. His brothers were gone and heavy silence lay over the room. She paused for a moment, gathering her courage. He looked as though he hadn't slept in days. His slacks were wrinkled and his shirt sleeves were unbuttoned and rolled partway up his arms. A shadow of a beard covered his jaw, and his hair was rumpled.

And still, he looked so desirable to her. She wanted to cross the room and melt into his arms. She wanted him to hold her and coax away her fears and doubts. The knot in her throat grew bigger, and she knew she had to speak now or risk being unable to.

"Chrysander," she called softly.

He whirled around. He set his drink down and hurried toward her. "Are you all right, *agape mou?* Is there anything I can get you? I'm sorry if my brothers upset you."

She tried to laugh, but it ended in a small sob. She drew in a deep breath and worked to compose herself.

"I'll marry you," she said.

A dark fire sparked in his eyes, making the amber glow more golden. He grasped her shoulders in his hands and stared down at her. "Yes?" he asked in a hoarse voice.

She nodded.

He closed his eyes and then crushed her to him. For a long moment, he just held her, and then he stepped back to stare intently at her.

"You mean it? You'll marry me?"

She licked her lips nervously. "I want a small ceremony. No fuss. As quiet as we can make it."

He nodded and cupped her chin in his hand. "Whatever you'd like."

"And I want…" She looked away and drew her bottom lip between her teeth.

"What do you want, *agape mou?* Tell me. There's nothing I won't do for you. You have only to ask."

"I don't want to stay here," she said quietly. "I'd like to go back to the island." She gripped her fingers together until the tips shone white.

His expression softened, and he dropped his hands to hers and gently uncurled her fingers until they were twined with his.

"We'll fly there as soon as we're married."

Relief surged through her veins. "You mean it? You don't mind?"

"Your happiness is everything to me. You ask such a small thing. How could I not grant it? We'll make the island our home if that is your wish."

She nodded. "I'd like that."

"Then I'll make the arrangements at once."

Chrysander wasted no time in finalizing plans for their wedding and preparing for them to travel to the island. He single-handedly rearranged his business schedule, made sure everything Marley could possibly need was purchased, though they'd already shopped for her wedding gown. She stood in awe of all he could accomplish in such a short time.

The authorities questioned her now that she'd regained her memory, and she spent several exhausting hours providing them with the few details she could remember. The kidnappers hadn't harmed her and had actually shown her consideration when her pregnancy became obvious. They had watched her, knowing she was close to Chrysander, and had struck when the opportunity arose. They'd asked for a small ransom, certain they would get it with no fuss. When no ransom had been forthcoming, they abandoned the kidnapping and arranged for Marley to be found.

It was the realization that Chrysander had ignored the ransom that had pushed Marley beyond her limits. It was that moment in the kidnapping that she blocked out her past, so devastated was she over his betrayal. Overwhelming emotion had crippled her— fear of being abandoned by the kidnappers, the terror of being left alone and having nowhere to go, no one to turn to.

Marley became distraught during the retelling, and Chrysander suffered the agony of being confronted by all she'd gone through. Because of him. He hovered protectively throughout, and finally called a halt when it was clear she was past all endurance.

The police were given their contact information so that Marley could be reached if arrests were made or there was a need for her to testify.

Two days later, they were married. Theron and Piers both attended, and Patrice was the only other witness to the ceremony. Afterward, Piers gave her a somewhat reserved welcome to the family while Theron's was more warm and enthusiastic.

"You've made him very happy, little sister," Theron murmured as he gathered her in his arms for a hug.

She offered a small smile, but she knew Theron wasn't fooled by it.

Soon after, Piers and Theron left, Theron to return to London and Piers to fly to Rio de Janeiro to oversee plans for the new hotel. Patrice returned to Athens, where she'd be met by Dr. Karounis. While Chrysander wanted to wait a day for their own departure, Marley was adamant that they leave as soon as the ceremony was done. She wanted to return to the island, a place she'd been happy even if only for a short time. New York held too many unhappy memories, and she just wanted to be away.

Chrysander bundled her on the plane and insisted she sleep for the duration of the flight. It was late when they landed and later still by the time the helicopter touched down on the island. But Marley felt relieved that she was home.

Chrysander carried her into the house and didn't relinquish her until they were upstairs in the bedroom. He set her down on the bed and then busied himself undressing her and tucking her underneath the covers.

When he crawled in beside her and merely held her lightly against him, as though he was afraid of touching her, she frowned in the darkness. She rose up and reached across him to turn on the light he'd extinguished a moment earlier.

"Marley, what is wrong?" he asked as she stared down at him.

She studied him, the lines around his mouth, the worry in his eyes. In that moment, she understood. He was afraid.

"Make love to me," she whispered.

His eyes darkened and turned to liquid. A ragged breath tore from his mouth.

"I need you to make love to me."

"You have to be sure about this, *agape mou.* I don't want to pressure you into doing anything you aren't ready for."

"I'm sure."

With a tortured groan, he rolled her beneath him. Every kiss, every touch was so exquisitely tender. He touched and stroked her with infinite care.

Her gown was removed, and he slid out of his boxers. His body, hot and straining, covered hers. Pleasure streaked through her body in waves when he closed his mouth over her nipple. He sucked lightly, tonguing the small bud, then he turned his attention to her other breast.

His hand cupped her belly protectively, cradling her against him as he kissed his way up her neck and finally to her lips.

"*S'agapo, pedhaki mou. S'agapo,*" he murmured in a voice so husky, so emotional, that it brought tears to her eyes.

She cried out as he moved over her. "Please," she begged. "I need you."

He entered her slowly, his movements careful and measured. But she didn't want him to treat her so carefully. She wanted all of him. She arched into him and wrapped her legs around his hips.

Sobs of need, of pleasure, ripped from her throat, and for once, pain had diminished to a distant memory. There was only here and now and the man who loved her.

She raced up a mountain slope and hurtled into a free fall of ecstasy. Chrysander was there to catch her, gathering her close against him as he murmured words of love against her lips.

She snuggled into his embrace, melding herself as close to him as she could. She needed this. Needed him.

"Don't let me go," she whispered.

"Never, *agape mou*," he vowed. He stroked her hair, her back, the swollen mound of her belly as she drifted off to sleep. The last thing she was aware of was him telling her he loved her.

Marley slipped out of bed and pulled on her robe to cover her nakedness. Chrysander was still firmly asleep, his arm stretched out as though reaching for her.

He'd made love to her throughout the night, the two of them falling into an exhausted sleep just before dawn. Her body still tingled from his touch, his lips, his gentle caresses. As she stared at him, she knew that she couldn't hold off any longer. She couldn't torture them both. Her uncertainty was gone. Her fears would follow in time.

She padded down the stairs, smiling ruefully at the thought of how Chrysander would fuss that she hadn't waited for him. After a stop in the kitchen, where she nibbled at a bagel and drank a glass of juice, she ventured into the living room to enjoy the view of the ocean.

It was there that Chrysander found her. He slid his arms

around her, cupping her belly with his hands as he kissed the curve of her neck.

"You're up early, *agape mou*."

"I was thinking," she murmured. She swiveled in his arms and met his worried gaze.

They both stared for a long moment, and then finally Chrysander said in a hoarse voice, "Do I ever have a chance of you loving me, Marley? Have I ruined that chance forever?"

Her gaze softened, and her heart turned over again with the love that swelled within her. Love and forgiveness.

"I already do," she said softly.

Surprise flickered across his face, and then doubt crept in.

"I've always loved you, Chrysander. From the moment I met you there has never been another man for me. There never will be."

"You love me?" he said in wonder, hope flaring in his eyes.

"I couldn't tell you before," she explained. "Not in New York when things were so messed up. You wouldn't have believed it if I had said it on the heels of your declaration. I wanted to return here, where we were happy. I wanted our life to begin here."

He gathered her in his arms and held her against his trembling body. His voice shook with emotion as he murmured to her in Greek. He switched back and forth between Greek and English as he told her how much he loved her and how sorry he was for the pain he'd caused her.

Then he swept her in his arms and carried her up the stairs and back to their bed, where he made sweet, passionate love to her again. Later he tucked her against his body and stroked a hand through her hair.

"I love you so much, *yineka mou*. I don't deserve your love, but I am so very grateful for it. I'll spend the rest of my life cherishing it, I swear."

She hugged him to her. "I love you, too, Chrysander. So much. We'll be so happy together. I'll make you happy."

And she did.

Epilogue

Ironically enough, Marley discovered she was in labor halfway down the stairs. Alone. She gripped the banister and doubled over as a contraction rippled across her abdomen. Wasn't labor supposed to start out slow?

She wanted to laugh at the fact that fate was obviously cursing her for trying to sneak down the stairs without Chrysander knowing. While he'd relented about her taking the stairs in the earlier stages of her pregnancy, now that she was so close to her due date he'd once again insisted she not walk the stairs alone. He'd go insane now that she was nine months pregnant and, if the pain ripping out her insides was any clue, about to deliver.

She stood on the step, holding on to the railing and taking deep breaths. She'd have called out if she weren't so busy sucking air through her nose. Besides, Chrysander was busy with endless calls as he and Theron worked out Theron's relocation to the New York offices. Theron was taking over operations there so Chrysander could remain in Europe. They had been tied up for hours discussing security measures since her kidnappers were still at large.

When she heard footsteps above her, she straightened and tried her best to look as though nothing was wrong. She glanced guiltily up to see Chrysander standing at the top of the stairs, a disapproving expression marring his face.

He started down, grumbling in Greek all the way. "What am I to do with you, *agape mou?*" he asked when he got close.

"Take me to the hospital?" she asked weakly. She doubled over again as another contraction hit.

"Marley! *Pedhaki mou,* are you in labor?" He didn't even wait for a response, not that he needed one. He scooped her into his arms and hurtled down the stairs, shouting for the helicopter pilot, who had remained on the island for the last two weeks for just such an event.

"Do not worry, my darling," he said in uncharacteristic English. "We'll have you to the hospital in no time."

"Darling?" She laughed and then ended it in a moan. "It hurts, Chrysander."

He paled as he climbed into the helicopter with her.

"You aren't allowed to use English endearments," she panted. "Greek sounds so much sexier."

"*Pedhaki mou, yineka mou, agape mou,*" he whispered in her ear. My little one, my woman, my love.

"Much better," she sighed. She smiled then winced again as they lifted into the air. Chrysander was a basket case the entire way to the hospital. The pilot set down on the roof, and a medical team was waiting to usher her inside.

A mere hour later, with Chrysander hovering and holding her hand, Dimitri Anetakis squirmed his way into the world to the delight of his father and mother.

"He is beautiful, *agape mou,*" Chrysander murmured as he leaned in close to mother and child. Dimitri was nursing contentedly at Marley's breast, and Chrysander watched in fascination.

"He's perfect," she said in wonder. "Oh, Chrysander, everything's so perfect."

He kissed her tenderly, his love for her overflowing his heart. "*S'agapo, yineka mou.*"

She cupped his face and smiled up at him. "*S'agapo,* Chrysander. Always."

* * * * *

Don't miss Maya Banks's next book in
THE ANETAKIS TYCOONS *series, available
in September from Mills & Boon® Desire™.*

TO TAME HER
TYCOON LOVER

BY
ANN MAJOR

Dear Reader,

For me, there is something romantic about Louisiana. When I lived on the Sabine River, I loved to drive over from Texas to visit that state. I fell in love with its past; with its French culture and Southern traditions; with its slow-moving bayous and fauna; with the Cajuns' fun-loving spirit; with the African-Americans' jazz and swamp pop. My husband is still sad that he can't really hear swamp pop played in south Texas where we now reside. Oh, and Louisiana has great food!

I have enjoyed visiting the old plantation homes along the River Road and reading the diaries of the families who lived there. It always distresses me that in the fast-paced modern world, it is so difficult to preserve these windows into the past. When Katrina struck Louisiana, much was lost.

With my long-time fascination for this state and its stories, I suppose it's only natural that I was inspired to set my latest series in Louisiana.

Vicariously, as I write this series, I will get to return to this lovely place that will always haunt me.

All my best,

Ann Major

I dedicate this book to Krista Stroever, my editor.
I loved writing this book because the characters
and their story were so keenly alive for me.
That said, her editing made this novel far better than it
would have been without her. Many thanks, Krista.

One

Some women are impossible to forget no matter how a man tries.

Logan Claiborne was frowning, and not because the sun was in his eyes as he sped down the narrow, twisting road that led to the antebellum mansion where he'd grown up.

He should be concentrating on Mitchell Butler and the merger of Butler Shipyards and Claiborne Energy, or on how he was going to deal compassionately with Grandpère once he arrived at Belle Rose.

Instead, his grip tightened on the steering wheel as he remembered the open, trusting, dark eyes of the voluptuously proportioned swamp brat he'd seduced and then jilted nine years ago to save his twin brother, Jake.

Until this morning, Logan had told himself that his grandfather had been right, that Cici Bellefleur didn't belong in their world; that he'd had to save Jake from the same sort of disastrous marriage their father had made to a poor girl, *their* mother, whose extravagant dreams of grandeur as well as her need to impress had nearly wrecked the family fortune. He'd continued to tell himself that he'd been right to do what he'd done even after he'd secured the family empire, even after Cici had made a name for herself with her camera and had proved herself a woman of talent and worth.

Then his grandfather had called him this morning and had stunned him by acting as thrilled as an infatuated kid when he'd mentioned Cici had come home again and they were giving tours of the house together.

Why had she, a famous photographer and writer, really come home? What did she want?

"Nine years ago you were dead set against her because of her uncle," Logan had reminded him. Grand-père had always distrusted Cici's uncle.

"In a long life, a man makes a few mistakes. Remember that. I made more than a few. Someday you may have a stroke that leaves you with too much time to dwell on the past. You may regret some of the things you've done. Well, I regret blaming Cici for her uncle Bos. It wasn't her fault he fought cocks, ran with a wild bunch and operated a bar."

"Do you remember that nine years ago you didn't want her anywhere near Jake or me, *especially* Jake, who was running pretty wild back then?"

"Well, I'm sorry for that, if I did."

"If you did?" It was still difficult to reconcile the grandfather he had now with the domineering individual who had raised him.

"Okay, I was wrong about her. I was wrong to be so tough on you, too. It's my fault you're so hard."

A pang of guilt had hit Logan as he'd run his hand through his rumpled, chocolate-brown hair.

"I was too hard on Jake, too."

"Maybe you're being too difficult on yourself."

"I'd like to see Jake again before I die."

"You're not going to die…not anytime soon."

"Cici says the same thing. She thinks I'm getting better every day. She thinks maybe I could stay here instead of…" His voice trailed away.

The mention of Cici and the hope in his grandfather's voice had convinced Logan he had to check on his grandfather at once. Since his stroke, his grandfather had gone from being a strong, commanding man to a clingy, depressed person Logan barely knew. This was why Logan had decided his grandfather couldn't live independently at Belle Rose any longer and needed to be moved to New Orleans near him. The old man needed looking after.

Unfortunately, the dense forest with its vines and wild vegetation was so thick beneath the brooding sky,

Logan was almost past the familiar turn to his childhood home before he saw the gatepost. At the last moment, he spun the wheel of his Lexus to the right too fast and skidded. No sooner had he righted the car than he saw the pillared mansion at the end of the oak alley. As always, the ancient home with its graceful columns and galleries aglow in the slanting sunlight seemed to him the most beautiful of houses, claiming his heart as no other place could.

How could he blame Grandpère, who'd become more childlike and emotional since his debilitating illness, for wanting to stay here? Logan remembered the first time he had mentioned the possibility of moving him to the city. Grandpère had given him a scare by disappearing for several hours.

Cici has no business convincing the old man he's getting better so he'll think he doesn't have to move.

But was that really her motivation?

The mere thought of his grandfather's worsening condition was upsetting. Logan, not Cici, had Grandpère's best interests at heart. The last thing he needed was Cici meddling and making him feel guilty about a decision he'd been forced to make. He didn't want to make Grandpère unhappy, but he couldn't run Claiborne Energy and be down here with his grandfather at the same time.

His thoughts in a snarl, Logan braked too sharply. His tires spun in the damp gravel as he stopped in the deep shade beneath the wide alley of the spreading oaks some anonymous Frenchman had planted a hundred years before the antebellum house had even been dreamed of. Beyond the house, fields stretched to a line of brooding cypress trees draped with moss that edged the wilderness of the swamp.

Logan flung the gleaming door of his late-model Lexus hybrid open and stepped out of the luxury sedan. After having his tall frame jammed behind the wheel for the two hour drive over bad roads from New Orleans, it felt good to stand up and stretch.

Despite the huge live oak trees, the heat was unbearably steamy for this early in March. He inhaled the thick, syrupy air, which to him smelled of home.

Little green frogs croaked. Bees hummed in azalea blossoms. Wood ducks made music. Did he only imagine lusty bull alligators roaring for their mates?

He smiled. How Cici used to love the dark, moss-hung wilderness that bordered the plantation when she'd been a kid. Whenever he'd been home and had put a foot outside, she'd followed him everywhere as eagerly as a devoted puppy. Their relationship had been so simple then. She'd been eight years younger than he and Jake, so Logan hadn't taken her crush on his brother seriously until the summer he'd returned home from law school and discovered that his grandfather was right about Cici not being a child any longer.

Shutting his mind against those pleasant memories that included Cici, he began to regret he was out of the air-conditioned car.

Maybe because he dreaded seeing Cici so much, Logan took the time to rip his tie off and unbutton his collar. Shedding his custom-made suit jacket, he opened the door and tossed his jacket and tie onto his plush, leather seat.

He wished Alicia Butler, his girlfriend of the past four months, had been able to come with him. Maybe then he wouldn't feel so haunted by the past. Or so tempted to remember Cici.

Unlike Cici, Alicia was sleek and elegant. He'd met her because they'd been thrown together due to his ambition to merge his company with her father's. A brunette, her shoulder-length, straight hair made her slim face seem even more regal. She knew how to dress, how to carry herself. Heads turned at fundraisers whenever she was at his side, and not only because of her beauty and stylish attire, but because of her fortune.

Other men, ambitious men, envied him. Not that that was the only reason he felt such a sense of pride that she would soon be his.

Poised, she approached life deliberately, as he did. She was civilized, polished and, therefore, as appropriate for him as his wife, Noelle, had been before her untimely death.

Alicia spoke French and Italian. She set a beautiful table. She never ate too much or drank too much or wore an inappropriate outfit.

Not even when she was angry did she raise her voice. She was equally controlled in bed, too.

As Cici had not been, sprang the wayward thought. For an instant his blood pounded as he remembered Cici wild with pleasure, writhing beneath him.

But Alicia would warm up after they were married. He would be patient. He understood not trusting enough to ever let go. Together he and Alicia would build a life together as he and Noelle, his recently departed wife, had, a life that everyone would envy. They wouldn't quarrel horribly and tear each other to pieces because their passions got in the way.

Briefly he remembered Noelle's sad eyes in that last week before she'd died. Then, quickly as always, he ruthlessly checked the forbidden image. He *would* make Alicia happy. History would not repeat itself.

"I'm sorry I can't come with you and meet your grandfather, darling," Alicia had said when he'd called her this morning. "But Daddy needs me at the office."

"Okay. I understand."

Mitchell Butler, Alicia's father, was a domineering shark, at least in business, but since Logan and he had this huge merger between their businesses pending, Logan didn't want to cross him over something as minor as a personal issue. He would see Alicia tonight.

"Darling, I'm sure you'll know exactly what to say and do to make your grandfather understand why he may not be able to stay at Belle Rose," Alicia had said. "After all, it's *your* family. He's your grandfather. You love him and want only the best for him."

If she only knew what a mess he'd made of things,

Logan thought grimly. He'd made everybody unhappy. His family remained divided, as a result.

He didn't want to dwell on his mistakes, especially not on his brutal handling of Cici the first time around or his nine-year estrangement from his twin. His thoughts on damage control and what was best for his grandfather, Logan had rushed down here today despite his heavy schedule. He was determined to deal with Cici before she got creative and made his grandfather believe he could have the impossible.

He remembered how small and lost Cici had looked standing on the dock after he'd told her he didn't love her. He'd lied to protect her and him. Strangely, his lie had made him feel equally sad.

Don't think about the past. Or how you felt. Just deal with Cici now.

Despite his best intentions not to revisit the past, he remembered young, vivacious Cici trying to pretend she was strong and tough and as good as the rich and powerful Claibornes. He'd hurt her. Hurt Jake. Hurt everybody, including himself. And told himself it was collateral damage because the family was richer and stronger than ever.

After locking the car, Logan turned and strode up the gravel drive toward the softly glowing house. But at the base of the stairs that led to the lower gallery and massive front door, he paused.

Slowly his gaze drifted over the mansion and lawn. A newly built wooden wheelchair ramp that avoided the stairs snaked back and forth from the ground to the front door.

Logan's eyes roved over the familiar grounds, out to the *garçonnière* where he and Jake had lived as teenagers before their quarrel over Cici, and he wondered who owned the two-seater Miata parked at such a jaunty angle beside the building.

Frowning, he made for the stairs, but just as he was about to turn the knob and push at the front door, it was opened by someone inside the house.

"Why, hello there, Mister Logan," said the soft, familiar, French-accented voice of his childhood nanny.

Noonoon, his grandfather's housekeeper now, stood just inside the big door. At the sight of him, her dark face lit up as brightly as a birthday cake.

An answering warmth filled him. This generous-hearted woman had always loved him, loved Jake, too. Ever since their mother's death, she'd practically run Belle Rose single-handedly.

"Lordy, it shore is a hot day."

He nodded, gave her a quick hug, then released her.

"Come on in out of the heat before you melt. If it's this hot now, what'll it be like in August?"

"Don't get me started about August." Because of the gulf heating up in the summer, August was a prime month for hurricanes.

"Can I fix you something? A drink maybe? Iced tea with a sprig of mint?"

He shook his head. "I'm fine."

"You shore are. At thirty-five, you're as tall and handsome as ever."

"Why do you remind me of my age every chance you get?"

"Maybe because it's time you stopped grieving so hard for your pretty Miss Noelle."

He tensed.

She stopped, realizing he wasn't the sort to encourage sympathy. "Life is short," she said.

"I have someone new in my life." He stepped into the welcoming cool of the wide central hall. "Her name's Alicia Butler. You'll meet her soon. She's a real lady. Someone the family will be proud of."

Noonoon shut the door behind him. "I'm real glad. So, what brings you all the way down here from New Orleans?"

"My grandfather. He's so deaf he's hard to talk to over the phone. I thought we had things settled, but this morning he was saying he was better and wanted to stay here on his own." Deliberately Logan refrained from mentioning Cici.

"Mr. Pierre, he be napping upstairs. But he'll be mighty pleased, he will…that you're here…since we don't see much of you these days, you bein' such a busy, important man and all and living in New Orleans."

"Napping? Where is *she,* then?" Logan asked.

"Miss Cici?" Noonoon inquired a little too innocently. Logan nodded. "Who else?"

"I knew it wouldn't take you long…as soon as you heard about Miss Cici. There shore isn't nothing like a rich older man taking an interest in a beautiful, younger woman for getting the rest of his family's hackles up, now is there?"

"That's not why…"

Her intelligent, black eyes regarding him intently, Noonoon placed her hands on her wide hips. So, Cici had already won Noonoon over.

"When you heard about Miss Cici, you come down here faster than that lazy hare sprinting at the last second to catch that tortoise in that story I used to read to you two boys. Why, I'll never forget that last summer she was here. Miss Cici, I mean. She was eighteen and just the prettiest little thing I ever saw."

Logan wished to hell he couldn't remember the way slanting sunlight had washed Cici's breasts with light and shadow as she'd stood in her pirogue the first day he'd come home. When she'd seen him, she'd jumped out of the boat and had run into the woods, her long legs flying gracefully. When he'd followed her, she'd said hi and her dark eyes had sparkled with such joy, she'd bewitched him. After that, she'd been too shy to say more, and, hell, so had he.

Logan's eyes narrowed, and Noonoon changed tack.

"She only be here a week, Miss Cici, and Mr. Pierre, he already plum crazy about her."

"He told me," Logan said coldly, imagining Cici preying on the vulnerable old man.

"He been doing real good. I know you wants him to move to New Orleans and all…"

"To a fabulous assisted living arrangement near my house that I can personally supervise."

"But places like that aren't home, and we all know how busy you be. How often could you get yourself over to see him? Mr. Pierre, he be happy here. Old people at those homes just sit and stare."

"You can't take care of him day and night. You have your own family."

Since the house was open to the public, Noonoon's main job was as a housekeeper, not a caregiver to his grandfather. She'd agreed to help with him temporarily.

"Well, now that Miss Cici is here…"

"She's not staying."

"Well, she sing and play the piano for him every day. She talk to him. Most nights they eat dinner together. She cooks. You remember how she loves to cook."

"The way she runs around all over the world, she won't be here that long."

"You sure about that? She shore is settlin' in. Says she's tired of all that running, that she's had enough pain to last her a lifetime. And she have her book to write."

"Not another book. I hope she's focusing on something that has nothing to do with me this time."

"She hasn't mentioned you."

He wasn't reassured. Cici's book on the oil industry in Louisiana after Katrina had made Claiborne Energy look bad. Had she mentioned even once how many people had jobs because of Claiborne Oil? No, her book had been full of pictures of rusting pipelines and oil-covered wildlife and shots of boats on water that used to be land with captions blaming companies like Claiborne Energy for the state's vanishing marshlands.

"And she wants to see about her uncle Bos and all," Noonoon was saying. "He's not too strong, you know, after his treatments. Stubborn cuss, though. She calls and calls him, but he still won't speak to her. You'd think after all these years, he'd forgive her. All she ever did was be friends with you and Jake."

Guilt made a muscle in his jaw pull. So, she was still estranged from her uncle. Just like he and Jake were estranged from each other…because of that summer. Not that most decent people in these parts thought Bos was worth knowing. Still, he was her uncle. He'd taken her in when she was orphaned.

Bos and Grandpère's enmity had sharpened over the issue of Bos's cockfighting. Once fighting cocks had become illegal, the two had had fewer issues to quarrel over.

"Cici said she wants to live somewhere quiet, and you of all people know the *garçonnière* is mighty quiet."

"You gave her the *garçonnière?* My old rooms?" He was shouting, and he never shouted. Not even when someone as hard as Mitchell Butler tried to screw Claiborne Energy for millions.

"Mr. Pierre, he be the one who rent it to her," she defended herself softly.

Remembering the cute red Miata parked by the two-story octagonal building, Logan's pulse began to thud. So, the dangerous, flashy sports car was hers. Why was that a surprise? Cici had a reckless streak. And no wonder…with that trapper cockfighting, swamp-rat of an uncle who'd raised her, mainly by neglecting her.

If his grandfather had been himself he would know that Cici couldn't be dedicated to him in any real way. No, she probably had some secret agenda.

"Sorry I raised my voice," Logan whispered, straining for control. "This isn't your fault. Or hers. It's mine— for not moving Grandpère sooner. I'll deal with her now."

"Oh, Miss Cici, she don't like anybody bothering her in the afternoon. Not unless it's an emergency. You see, she writes when Mr. Pierre naps. Then at four she and Mr. Pierre, they give the last tour together. I reckon she be free to talk around five."

"How can he manage walking so far in his condition?"

Noonoon's sharp look made him wince as he remembered he hadn't seen his grandfather in a month.

"Miss Cici got him off his walker. Gave him a cane and bought him a new, lightweight wheelchair. She hired Mr. Buzz to build ramps everywhere. She pushes Pierre when he be tired. With the ramps he can get up to all the slave cabins now."

More ramps? Logan's pulse in his temple had speeded up. He didn't believe Cici had come home to care for his grandfather. She had never known how to take proper care of herself. No way could she take care of Pierre. Not for the long haul.

His grandfather needed dedicated nurses and the latest, modern, long-term care, and he was going to have them.

More to the point: his grandfather was his responsibility.

The sooner he dealt with Cici and sent her packing, the better.

Two

Cici turned off the hot water and sighed. For the first time in a long time, she felt good, surprisingly good. Almost at peace with herself.

Maybe taking a break from her cameras and all the death she'd seen in war zones and coming home had been the right decision after all.

She stepped out of the shower, grabbed a towel from the rack and flung it on the floor. Planting her bare feet with their hot pink nails on the thick terry cloth, she sucked in a breath and savored the sensual feel of warm water rushing down her breasts and belly and thighs onto the towel.

Her toes curled into the soft terry in sheer delight. She,

who'd lived for months in tents with no running water, appreciated a hot shower in a safe, familiar locale as the luxuries they truly were. Whipping a second towel free, she wound it around her curly, wet hair and began to rub.

The windows were open. The sweetness of the faint breeze that brought the scents of magnolia and crepe myrtle and pine through the second-story windows caused her to shiver.

Frogs sang. No, they roared in chorus right along with the bull alligators after the rain last night when she'd taken Pierre's pirogue and had paddled it out into the brooding swamp to watch the herons and egrets and buzzards flying home to their nests.

She squeezed her eyes shut and listened. She could almost hear the stirring of moss in the cypress trees.

"Aah," she murmured, sighing heavily and yet very happily. She knew she was procrastinating, that she should be at the computer writing, but she couldn't resist taking a moment to appreciate fully the bliss of being home after years of exile.

Writers had so many excuses for not writing. Life versus work was a biggie. How could you write if you did not let yourself experience life?

Content to procrastinate, she took in a deep breath and then another. Until this particular, miraculous moment, for such moments of true awareness were small miracles, she'd never let herself admit how much she'd longed to come home and see Belle Rose again. For always, always Belle Rose, ever since she'd been orphaned at eight and brought to live in her Uncle Bos's shack on marshy land that bordered the Claibornes' superior property Belle Rose had stood like a vision of paradise in her imagination.

There was no place for her at Belle Rose, yet she'd always wanted to belong. The closest she'd ever come to that had been when Uncle Bos had worked briefly as a part-time gardener for the Claibornes, and she'd had free run of the place. That's when she'd formed the habit of following Logan everywhere any time he was home.

"What the hell?" the deep, too-familiar voice of the present master of Belle Rose roared as lustily as any bull alligator.

For a second or two she felt the same rush of adrenaline in her stomach she'd known when that bullet in Afghanistan had whizzed by her face, missing her by mere inches.

You had to get close to death to film it.

She opened her eyes, and when they fastened on the tall, broad-shouldered man, who was in her bedroom, she screamed.

For nine years she'd imagined what clever thing she'd say or do if she ever saw Logan Claiborne again. She'd give him a piece of her mind, for one thing. But in this long, nightmarish moment, she just stood where she was like a dumbstruck idiot. Vaguely she noted that his eyes were as wide with conflicting emotions as hers probably were.

If he'd taken a single step toward her or said something clever and belittling, she would have screamed again. But since he was as paralyzed as she, she did nothing. Absolutely nothing.

She just stood there without a stitch on and let him gape at her. For the record, and she being a journalist kept minute records, a whirlwind of thoughts and feelings and visual images did storm through her. At first, they flew so fast and hard she couldn't focus on any particular memory. Still, for a second or two she felt keenly in touch with her younger, more vulnerable self—that naive, innocent eighteen-year-old girl who'd loved him, trusted him and had been shattered by his callous treatment.

How could he have misused her so? They'd grown up together. She'd always had a crush on Jake, his wilder twin. Logan had been more like a brother to her, the brother who'd mainly ignored her but with whom she'd felt safe and comfortable around because no powerful childish crush got in the way and had made her shy around him.

He'd played in the swamp with her when she'd been a child. He'd taught her to tease alligators, collect egret feathers, trap crawfish. Then they'd grown up, and she'd given up her infatuation for Jake and had fallen in love with Logan. Hadn't he really, always been her hero? Then he'd made his move, and soon after, her fantasy world had come crashing down around her.

In this very room, or at least the bedroom where he stood, she'd lain naked beneath Logan, warmed by his larger body, never guessing he'd made love to her to save his brother. For an instant those fleeting, pulsing moments of cherished togetherness after he'd taken her virginity became too vividly real, stinging her with raw pain and fresh heartbreak all over again. All through those long summer nights, he'd made love to her again and again.

Every night she'd waited for Bos to go to his bar. Then she'd run through the woods to the *garçonnière*. She'd felt so piercingly alive in Logan's arms. And every night their passion had built.

She'd believed he'd loved her—until that last night when Jake had found them together and Logan had told her why he'd really slept with her—to save Jake from making a misalliance. Then Logan had walked out on her, and her fairy tale had ended.

For days she'd believed he'd come back and tell her he was sorry, tell her he loved her. How little she'd known back then of men.

When she'd called him two months later in the fall to talk, before she could tell him her news, he'd silenced her by coldly informing her he'd married Noelle.

She'd needed to talk to him. She'd felt so alone when she'd hung up the phone knowing she had to face a difficult situation by herself. So abandoned. Because of him, for years she'd hated all men, especially him.

At some point, she'd quit blaming men in general for his crimes, but she'd clung to her intense dislike of him.

But the shock of seeing him like this, with his cold, blue, too-adult eyes burning every part of her body, from her pert nipples to the soft, damp brush of gold between her legs, was so powerful, even her hatred could not compare.

Finally, she regained enough presence of mind to remember her towel. Scowling at him, she leaned down to get it and wrapped it around her with jerky, big movements, making sure she covered the moon-shaped scar on her abdomen first.

Even so, when she looked up, guiltily, warily, she found his male eyes still blazing too hotly with the unwanted memory of her naked body, and his gaze made her own nerves buzz. But covering herself only seemed to intensify the raw, unwanted intimacy between them.

Blushing while fighting not to remember those hot summer nights they'd shared in this very bedroom, she swallowed and tried to make her voice fierce and defiant. "You should have knocked, damn you."

"I did."

"Then you should have waited until I answered."

"Yes," he agreed, finally having the decency to look away. His gaze drifted over her desk that was littered with papers and index cards and photographs, some of him. "I should have."

A flush of dark color climbed his cheeks when he saw the newspaper clippings of his own ravaged face. The shot, which he couldn't stop staring at, had been taken shortly after Noelle's death.

Why, oh why did I leave that particular picture out?

"I didn't think," he said. "I never thought you'd be…"

"Nude?"

His angry blue gaze snapped back to her face. "Why didn't you lock the door? And how could you just stand there…flaunting yourself, like you liked me seeing you."

"Stop right there!" Heat engulfed her and not the good, soothing kind. This fire was a fury that devoured her.

"Damn you! This is not my fault! Nothing is my fault! You barged in here! And because you did, you found me stepping out of my shower, as I have every right to do…"

"Yes, I'm sorry. You're right!"

"I'm not finished. For your information, I've been taking showers these nine years since I last saw you! And nobody else, not even in a war zone, has ever barged in on me! You're in the wrong—not me."

"Okay. So you said…repeatedly. Enough already."

"No. It's not enough. You were horrible to me in the past. You're horrible now. You always act high and mighty because as far as you're concerned, I'll be poor white trash till the day I die. I wasn't good enough for Jake or you…and nothing I ever do will change that."

He swallowed. The muscle that moved in his jawline when he was upset jumped violently. "All right. I hear you. You made your point."

She most certainly had, but since he still hadn't bothered to apologize, she felt consumed by smoldering heat and indignation…and by other awful emotions she didn't want to name. How could he still affect her like this?"

Despite her discomfiture, his changed appearance registered. Not that she hadn't seen pictures of him in magazines and newspapers and on the Internet from time to time. He was a rich, important man. His wife's tragic accident and funeral alone had received a vast amount of coverage last year, all of which Cici had hungrily devoured.

Still, it was different, seeing him this close, knowing his anger was partly due to the fact that he wanted to be done with her, just as she wanted to be done with him.

She assessed him coldly. No longer was he the wiry boy she'd loved or even the gray-faced man in the photograph on her desks whose obvious grief had almost made her feel sorry for him. He'd filled out. And he'd grown, as men often do, even more virile and attractive than ever.

He was close-shaven. He wore an expensive white shirt that was so damp from the heat that it clung to his muscular body in such a way that she couldn't help admiring that he'd kept himself in shape.

He'd rolled up the sleeves, revealing strong, tanned forearms. His chocolate-brown hair might be shorter, but it still looked as thick and sexily tousled as ever.

To all who didn't know better, Logan appeared a respectable, wealthy businessman. But she, who wished she didn't know better, knew the wildness and the dangerous darkness that lurked beneath that suave, too-handsome exterior. Like herself, Logan didn't mind the edgy thrill of risk.

With an effort she reminded herself that Logan Claiborne was utterly self-serving and ruthless, and a smart woman would avoid him.

Still, he looked good. Too good. And not just because she hadn't dated anybody for a while.

Uncle Bos had been right about a few things. He'd said rich people could be crueler and colder than anybody, that she'd best stay away from the Claibornes and their like. "You're swamp trash to them. You're nothing more than a toy to play with. They throw girls like you to the sharks when they're through."

"Get out," she said quietly and yet forcefully.

He crossed his arms across his broad chest and spread his legs in a masculine, stubborn stance.

"Not till we talk," he said.

"If you think I'm going to stand here wearing only a towel and converse with you like nothing happened… after…after the way you barged in here, after the way you looked at me and accused me, you're crazy."

"Get dressed, then." He turned his broad shoulders to her. When she didn't move, he said calmly, "I won't watch. I promise."

"*As if!* As if I'd ever trust the likes of you again!"

He whirled, his blue eyes stormy when he faced her again. "Trust doesn't even enter into it. You're not staying at Belle Rose. Not one more night. You're going to leave my grandfather alone. He's vulnerable and old, easy prey…"

"Stop right there! For your information, I have a three-month lease and a publishing deadline to meet. And *your* grandfather, whom you claim to care so much about, was starving for affection. Starving. And I think I know something about how that condition feels—especially where you're concerned." She paused. "So, his needing me and befriending me when I came home feeling lonely and vulnerable and a bit alienated from my roots is a big part of why I have no intention of moving."

"You're just using him."

"And you know that, how, you who could write a book on that subject?" She took a deep breath. "Get out of my apartment, or I'm calling the law."

"This is Louisiana. I own the law. And since I didn't sign your lease, it isn't worth the paper it's written on. Now get dressed, so we can settle this once and for all. I'll wait downstairs."

"I'm not the same foolish girl I was nine years ago. You can't stomp in here and intimidate me."

"I will reimburse you every penny you've paid my grandfather and then some."

"Money. You think you can buy your way out of any problem."

"That's unfair, and you know it."

"Who just said, 'This is Louisiana. I own the law?'"

His dark face turned a mottled shade of purple that wasn't nearly so lovely on him as it was on the purple water hyacinths that choked the bayou at the edge of the lush grass behind Belle Rose.

"I'll wait for you on the gallery of Belle Rose," he managed, his posture stiff, his deep tone icy.

"I won't be allowed inside the house then?"

"You're the one putting yourself down," he said. "Not me."

"I own the law," she mocked.

When he stalked out without bothering to reply, she resisted the very strong impulse to slam the door. After letting it shut softly, she leaned against it for a long moment and tried to catch her breath.

She couldn't believe she'd been so rude. Even to him.

Did he ask for it, or what? Why did women with a drop of Southern blood always think they were supposed to be nice? Even to total jerks, which he was, even if he was rich and handsome and had a home like Belle Rose that was architectural poetry?

She moved away from the door toward her desk. Slowly she lifted the photograph of him where he looked so lost and sad. She'd taken so many pictures of people in pain, she recognized real suffering when she saw it.

Not wanting to think about that or to feel sorry for him, she slipped his picture inside a drawer.

Suddenly it dawned on her that she hadn't heard him stomp down the stairs. Was he standing on the other side of the door?

Or was he as upset and confused as she was after seeing her again?

Was he human after all?

When she considered the possibility that she might have hurt him, even just a little, she felt a strange catch in her heart just like she had when she'd first seen that picture of him after Noelle's death.

Closing her eyes, she saw his dark, pain-ravaged face after he'd told her making love to her had meant nothing…that he'd never loved her, that he'd only done it to save his twin. She'd never known which to believe: his brutal words or his heartbroken eyes.

She took a breath and told herself his jilting her was all that mattered. Like photographs, actions told the deepest truths.

When she removed her towel to dress, she caught sight of her reflection in the tall mirror on the wall.

Turning on the light, she studied the crescent-shaped scar on her stomach for a long moment. And as always, whenever she let herself remember that terrible night when she'd had an emergency C-section, the night she'd lost their baby son, fathered by a man who'd refused to even listen to her when she'd tried to tell him she was pregnant, she froze.

Under no circumstances could she allow herself to soften toward Logan Claiborne.

Grabbing a blouse, she turned away from the mirror. The last thing she needed was any reminder of how deeply involved she'd once been with the angry man who'd just left.

She was through with him forever.

Three

Logan was furious at himself for storming into the *garçonnière* after becoming impatient when Cici hadn't opened the door the minute he'd knocked.

Furious at her, too. How could she have just stood in her bathroom naked like that, smelling so sweetly of jasmine, her fine-boned face looking so startled and golden and glorious; her glistening, wet lips and body tempting him as she'd towel-dried her glossy ringlets.

She'd had every right to be there as she'd aptly pointed out.

At the sight of those sparkling droplets of water clinging to the grapelike tips of her dusky nipples, his groin had hardened. His blood had coursed like lava.

He'd felt like a beast. Even now he wanted to rush her, to jam her against the wall and take her then and there. He wanted to taste those lips again, to lick those nipples, to lick other secret places until she moaned in ecstasy, to run his hands through her thick, springy curls. Yes, he'd wanted to drown himself in Cici Bellefleur.

How could he still want her with every cell in his being, despite their past? Why did he keep remembering how her golden curls had spread across his pillow like a Southern belle's fan every night after they'd made love? Or how he'd liked to trace her soft, swollen lips with his fingertip, regretting more with every night that passed that his obsession for her had grown with every kiss, with every touch until he'd wanted her for himself far more than Jake had ever wanted her. Then he'd begun to agonize about how painful it would be to give up something so beautiful and infinitely precious to him.

But Grandpère's view had been that Cici was just like his mother—a poor girl out to better herself at their expense—that she would lead him around by the nose as his mother had led his father, that she would spend every last cent of their money until they were completely ruined.

Grandpère kept repeating that he'd had to be tough on him because he'd been too soft on his father and Jake. And as a result of his earlier failure to be firm, the family business was on the verge of bankruptcy, and Jake was wild and out of control. Everything, his grandfather warned, depended upon Logan making a prudent marriage and then settling down to save Claiborne Energy.

Grandpère's opinion about Logan's parents' marriage and the decline in the family fortune had been too true. Their once-proud family and company were on the brink of ruin. Sacrifices had to be made, his grandfather had said, and there was no one else to make them except Logan.

"Don't disappoint me, too, the way your father and brother have always disappointed me," his grandfather said when Logan had been reluctant to come between Jake and Cici. The next night Logan had seduced her to save his brother, and Jake had caught them in bed together. Jake had quit the family in disgust without ever knowing why Logan had acted as he had or that Logan had been cruelly caught in his own trap.

Maybe initially Logan had obeyed his grandfather and slept with Cici to save his brother and his family from ruin, but no sooner had he started making love to her than other forces had him taken over and he'd realized he'd always wanted her for himself.

Still, he soon knew he had to break up with Cici, too, that she was no better as a mate for him than she'd been for Jake. He hadn't wanted to hurt her by caring for her and making her care. He'd hoped that in time he'd forget her and that she'd forget him, too.

When he'd married Noelle, he'd told himself the man who'd loved Cici was dead. But today all the longings of that younger self had clamored inside the man he was now. She was more appealing to him than ever.

Why had Cici saved the picture of him that had been

taken at one of the lowest moments in his life, the day of Noelle's funeral, when he'd come to terms with what a bastard he'd been, and not just to Cici?

He'd been devastated at Noelle's death, but for all the wrong reasons. He'd known then he'd never loved her. That he'd only ever wanted her half as much as he'd always wanted Cici, and he hated himself for that.

Nine years ago he'd believed he'd done the right thing in jilting Cici and marrying Noelle. But his marriage to Noelle was what hadn't worked. Nothing in his personal life had succeeded since Cici.

Deliberately Logan forced his big hand to loosen its crushing grip on his second tall glass of iced tea with a sprig of mint and a slice of lemon. If only the heat in his blood for Cici would lessen.

Alicia would be waiting for him tonight in New Orleans. A sane, mature man would stop lusting after Cici's lush, naked body. But he wasn't sane. And the memory of how she'd looked wetly aglow and achingly vulnerable in the rosy sunlight wouldn't quit.

Maybe Cici's grammar was better—she was a damned good writer, if an annoying one—but was she any more suited to him now than she had been then? She'd always been antiestablishment; a rebel, and an adventuress, while he was conservative to the core. Hell, her uncle was very little short of being an outlaw.

Did those differences really matter in the twenty-first century? Or did the raw, true, primal desire he felt for Cici matter more?

No. He'd been carefully taught that money and breeding and power and the willingness to accept responsibilities that came with position separated people like him from her. He made rules and followed them; she and her uncle stomped over every rule in the book. Nothing was sacred to her. Not even death. Her books and photos proved that.

For money she'd taken a picture of a child being stalked by vultures to horrify her audience of human vultures avid for such shots of lurid misery. At odd moments the picture still haunted him. How could he feel any sympathy for a woman who had lived off the suffering of others?

His feelings for her were driven solely by lust. He'd been obsessed by her in the past. He wasn't about to let his animal urges take over and ruin his life or hers again.

But, oh, God, why did she have to be as lovely as ever—hell, maybe even lovelier? Why did one glimpse of her make his heart open wide and throb with regret? Make him feel as if crucial years of their lives had been cruelly stolen from them?

He was wondering what the cure for such a severe case of lust was—a speedy marriage to the refined Alicia or taking Cici one more time to get her out of his system?—when the front door opened and his grandfather came out holding onto Noonoon's arm.

At the sight of his much stronger and more vigorous grandfather, he did a double take. Gone was the frail, ghostly shadow who had lain in his bed in Baton Rouge less than a month ago and had weepily confided in Logan that he wished he was dead. That's when Logan had left no stone unturned to find the perfect situation in New Orleans for his ailing grandfather.

Logan slugged his iced tea and set his glass down and shot to his feet eagerly. "Grandpère! Where's your walker?"

"Kept tripping over the damn nuisance," Pierre said, sounding gruff, almost angry, almost his old authoritative self. "Cici got me this quad cane." He let go of Noonoon and shook it.

Cici. Glad as Logan was that his grandfather was so much better, he resented that her name alone was enough to make him flush with heat. Would Noonoon and Grandpère see and understand?

The old man lifted his cane in a commanding fashion. "Cici suggested I use a wheelchair when we give our afternoon tour, though. Don't like to, 'cause it makes me look old."

Our tour.

"You're nearly eighty."

"Cici says age is just an attitude."

"She should have seen you in the hospital."

"I'm glad she didn't!"

"Okay. Look, I don't want to quarrel or remind you of unhappier times." Logan went to him, and they embraced fondly. "I'm glad you're better," he said. "You feel solid…so much stronger…heavier."

"He's had the appetite of a horse ever since Cici

started cooking him gumbo and making his favorite spicy boudin with red beans for him. Cici does love to cook. She always did!"

The old man's blue eyes flashed at her name, and a tinge of brilliant color dotted his plumper cheeks. "Cici's been great. She's given me a whole new lease on life. I'm almost glad I had the damn stroke. Don't think she'd be fussin' over me if I hadn't."

The sparkle in his eyes and the intensity of his smile made him look ten years younger. "By the way, did you get our invitation?"

"*Our* invitation?"

"For my eightieth birthday party next Saturday. You didn't R.S.V.P. Cici thought you'd probably be too busy to come. Well, are you?" His grandfather's eyes reproached him.

"I didn't receive any invitation, so I didn't know anything about it. And I don't have my calendar," Logan replied, his voice even.

"Your invitation must have gotten lost in the mail," Cici said with false gaiety behind him.

Lost, my ass. The sexy witch had no doubt cleverly excluded him.

Logan whirled and felt another rush of unwelcome heat as they locked eyes for the length of several, thudding heartbeats. Unable to resist dragging his gaze lower, he noted a pink T-shirt stretching across her ample breasts that read T-Bos's Bar under a stenciled biker's face. Her skintight jeans had holes in the knees.

T-Bos's was a successful biker bar of unsavory reputation that her uncle Bos defied the Claibornes by running on his property next door to Belle Rose.

There should be a law against shirts like that, at least on bodies like hers. The jersey knit hugged her breasts and waist even more snugly than her jeans cupped her ass. Not that he was surprised at her getup. It was sexy as hell, just like the woman who wore it. Conservative, she wasn't.

"Jake is coming," she taunted softly. Or did he only imagine the challenge in her husky voice?

"You invited Jake? And not me?"

"Still competitive?"

"Damn it, no!" His feelings for his alienated twin were more complicated than that single word could possibly describe. "How could I be? Because of you, I haven't talked to him in nine years."

"Only…because of *me?* How easily we forget."

"I've called him, but he refuses my calls," Logan said.

"Do you really blame him?"

Her question reminded him of all he'd done to come between Jake and her once again.

"I'm sorry." She paused. "I don't want to quarrel. I hadn't talked to him either until a few weeks ago. He's been living in Orlando, although I expect you know that…just like I expect you know that he set up a branch of his business in New Orleans after Katrina."

He knew. Jake, a successful architect and builder in Florida, had pledged his support to help rebuild New Orleans after two major hurricanes had nearly destroyed it. Not that Jake ever bothered to look him up when he'd breezed into the city to check his operations. And he didn't blame him.

"I thought it was a shame we'd never talked since that last summer," she said, "so one day I just picked up the phone and called him."

"And he answered?"

She nodded. "Why wouldn't he? I guess my name showed up on his Caller ID. He had no reason to be mad at me. We must have talked for at least half an hour."

"About what?"

"If you come to the party, you can ask him yourself."

"Again, I'll have to check my calendar."

"You will come, won't you?" Grandpère said, his voice weaker, maybe because he'd been up too long.

At his grandfather's question, Logan felt trapped. *Damn.*

"He had so much fun planning his party, and Cici's worked so hard on it," Noonoon pleaded softly. "I'll go inside and get you an invitation."

"A hundred people have already accepted," Cici added. "Lots of them are your friends. I let them think the party was your idea."

"Me? Why how generous of you."

The three of them were all staring at him, waiting, their eyes begging him to say he'd attend. Funny how he could go for the jugular in business, and in a family situation that involved upsetting Grandpère, he was ready to cave in an instant.

"All right. All right. I know when I'm beaten. I'll give the party top priority." After a pause, he continued. "Cici, I need to get back to New Orleans. Tonight. I have a date."

"With Alicia Butler?" Cici's eyebrows arched. "Of Butler Shipyards?"

"And just how in the hell do you know that?" He stopped himself, when he saw her smile.

"I'm a journalist. I read the gossip columns."

He ignored her answer. "You and I need to discuss your lease. Did you bring it with you?"

"Sorry." Cici, who cupped her hands over her mouth, didn't look the least bit sorry. "Forgot."

Like hell.

A woman sharp enough to know what was going on in his personal life better than he did had deliberately refused to bring it just to provoke him.

"Well, go get it!" he thundered.

"All right," Cici purred, smiling at an alarmed Noonoon and Pierre. But just as she turned to go, her gaze darted toward the back of the house and then to her watch. "Oh, dear…. Bad timing. Looks like our tour has assembled. "Noonoon," she said. "I know this is a lot to ask, with all you have to do, but if you wouldn't mind wheeling Pierre around back—you and he could start our last tour of the day. You won't have to say anything…if you'd just be kind enough to push him. I'd do it, but Mr. Claiborne insists he wants to discuss my lease. Maybe by the time the tour is over, he and I will be finished with each other, and he can be on his way."

Cici's sweet smile made Logan wish he had a nail or two to chew. "After all he has a very important date with Alicia Butler. Butler Shipyards."

Feeling like he was about to explode again, Logan nodded curtly toward Noonoon. When Noonoon walked over to Pierre, Cici ran back to the *garçonnière* to fetch the document she should have brought with her in the first place. Fuming, he watched her retreating bottom in those skintight jeans with way too much interest.

Not for the first time today, he told himself to calm down, reminding himself that he was firmly in control, that when she returned, he would be so utterly ruthless she would soon be packing her bags.

"I said I'll double the money you paid my naive grandfather, if you'll be so kind as to rip up this worthless piece of garbage and leave tomorrow morning."

Logan relaxed a little when Cici, who was sitting on a wide wicker chair on the gallery, was quiet, her brow furrowed as if she were considering his most generous offer. Then she looked up from the document and smiled at him, blushing so prettily he itched to caress her.

When her sparkling eyes teased, luring him, he should have been warned.

"If I sleep with you, for old times' sake, would you let me stay?" Her voice was soft and husky, shaking a little, yet her invitation flowed through him like music, causing something vital and true, something ripe and raw, in him to leap toward her.

"What?" he growled, his gaze lowering to her breasts despite his best intentions, because he was truly tempted by her outrageous offer. Which she, no doubt, knew.

Damn her silky hide.

She laughed at him. "Oh, dear, even your ears are turning red. Why is that, I wonder?"

Because he felt as hot as a volcano about to burst.

"Quit staring at my breasts like I'm offering them to you on a serving platter! I was just kidding. Okay? You looked so grim and uptight I thought a little levity would do us both good."

"Well, I wouldn't kid about something like that, if I were you," he snapped.

"Why? Because you're mad that you want to sleep with me too much?"

"I don't want to sleep with you." His voice sounded strange to his ears, maybe because he was speaking through gritted teeth.

"Good," she said in a teasing tone that said she didn't believe a single word. "Because I don't want you, either. So, we're both safe. In no sexual danger from each other. You have your pretty Alicia, aka Butler Shipyards, and I have my work in progress."

"No boyfriend?"

Why in hell had he asked that? He didn't give a damn whether she had a boyfriend or not.

"Would you care?"

"Stop it."

"I can ask a question if I want. You don't have the right to tell me what to say or do any more."

"I never told you any such thing. We weren't ever that important to each other."

"Thanks. They say it's good for one's character to be humbled once in a while."

"I want you off my land. If you don't agree to my terms, I'll have my lawyer contact you. Trust me. The fight over the legality of this lease will cost you far more than it's worth. If you're smart, you'll take my offer."

"I can tell you've grown used to pushing people around."

"Damn it."

"You know, I almost feel sorry for you. Nine years haven't taught you anything. Oh, sure, you're richer and colder, which means a lot of people probably think you're pretty successful. But I'll bet you're not nearly as happy and as satisfied with your life as you try to pretend, or you wouldn't be trying to bully me. You're living a lie, Logan Claiborne, and I'm one of the few people who knows it. That's why you want me to leave. You don't want to face the truth about who you really are and what you really feel. You're no elegant, refined gentleman. You use your money like a shield to fend off anything that's real…like me."

"Rip up that paper. Do the smart thing for once. Just say you'll take my money."

"Or you'll what?" When she licked her mouth, making her lower lip shine wetly, something that had been wound too tight for nine damn years snapped inside him, unleashing a force he would have denied with every breath in his body.

With a suddenness that startled them both, him most of all, he seized her slim shoulders. Jerking her to her feet, his hard arms circled hers, and then crushed her against him. "You shouldn't have come back here. You shouldn't have messed with me again."

"So, you do want me, a little," she whispered, her musical voice a husky taunt against his throat. "Is that why you're so afraid of me?"

"I'm not afraid. You have to go," he muttered furiously, too aware of her soft breasts mashed against his chest. "You know it. And I know it."

"Do I?" She paused. "Well, now I'm going to tell you something. I don't know it. You and I haven't been on the same page in ever so long, Mr. Claiborne. Lucky me."

"Damn you."

"I want to stay and I will—until I'm good and ready to go. And I will go, but only when I decide."

"If you're smart…"

"I'll what? I'll leave before I tempt you into my bed again?" She laughed.

A faint breeze swept the wide veranda, stirring gold tendrils against her temple. She was so damn sexy, and her body felt so warm, he lost his train of thought. How could he think with her in his arms? With her voluptuous breasts pressed against his chest? With her hair smelling sweetly of shampoo and her body of jasmine scented soap? With her half-open lips too close to his to resist? With her saying things to deliberately tempt him?

Yes, she was right. He wanted her naked and writhing and wet underneath him again.

On that thought his mouth came down on hers. If only she hadn't clung, maybe sanity would have returned. But she did, pressing herself against him, shuddering as violently as he did, causing him to gasp and kiss her again and then again. And with every kiss, his long-repressed hunger grew until it was a thunderous, pulsing fever. When she purred, melted and opened her delicious mouth wider so that his tongue could fill it, the world began to reel past him in a dizzying rush.

He had no idea how long he held her and devoured her mouth, or how he summoned the strength to finally push her away before it was too late to stop.

Panting hard, he stared down at her. He'd been seconds away from carrying her to the *garçonnière* where he would have taken her wildly and violently, not tenderly as he had on their first night. And once would never be enough. He felt as obsessed by her now as he had in the past.

As his guilty eyes held hers, he saw that she was burning up just like he was. Her cheeks were red, her mouth swollen, her eyes aflame, her tumult more than equal to his.

"I still hate you," she said, breathing so hard and fast, those beautiful breasts of hers were heaving, tempting him to new indiscretions.

"I hate you even more than Jake does. I hate you for

what you did in the past. For who you were back then. But most of all, I hate you for who you still are. And for what you just did. You take, but you don't give."

Then why was she running her tongue over her lips as if to taste him again?

"Good," he whispered, loathing himself even more than she and Jake ever could. "Concentrate on that, then, and maybe we'll get through this without tearing up our lives again."

"And I thought I was the only one who suffered," she whispered. "Was I wrong?"

Never in a thousand years would he admit that he'd suffered because of losing her, that he'd caused Noelle to suffer, and yet… The truth was that after he'd jilted Cici and had willed his overpowering attraction for her to die, so that he could marry Noelle and make her happy, his determination had failed him. Back then he'd thought if a man had enough willpower, he could make himself do anything. He'd believed he could create the life of his grandfather's dreams through sheer force of will. But instead his obsession with her had dominated him.

Through the years, she'd haunted him. Every time he'd come home to Belle Rose, even with Noelle, Cici had been there, memories of her sensuality and sweetness luring him.

Why wouldn't her power over him die?

Not daring to look at her a second longer for fear of losing the last fragile shreds of his control, Logan turned and vaulted down the stairs beside the ugly ramp she'd built. Striding around the back of the house as if ten demons were on his trail, he called to his grandfather.

Cici came running, her dark eyes wide, as a smiling Pierre held up a hand to stop the tour, so he could see what his grandson wanted.

"Is everything all right, Logan?" Pierre asked.

"It's time I left." He took his grandfather's hand and shook it gently, noting how weak the old man's clasp was.

"Then you're through with Cici and she's free to finish the tour with me?"

"Yes," Logan muttered. "I'm through with her."

"Wonderful. I'll be happy to finish the tour," Cici said, her lilting velvety voice so cheery behind him he was further infuriated although he continued to smile at his grandfather. No doubt she thought she'd won.

Not that he so much as glanced at Cici as she rushed up to join his grandfather. Logan didn't meet the gazes of any of the people clustered around his grandfather and Cici, either, but he could tell that they sensed some of the dramatic undercurrents because they were staring from him to Cici much too avidly.

He did manage to nod a final goodbye to his smiling grandfather even as he swore to himself that tomorrow morning, he'd tell Hayes Daniels, his CEO, to sic the full force of their legal department on the defiant Cici. The house, after all, which was open to the public, belonged to Claiborne Energy.

Logan smiled grimly. She wouldn't last long after such an assault. He would soon be rid of her.

Four

Logan, who had the headache from hell after a night of no sleep, had arrived at his office shortly after 6:00 a.m. Work on the last few details of the merger went smoothly for a couple of hours.

The first sign that Cici had launched a counter attack of her own before he'd even gotten his planes in the air occurred shortly before 9:00 a.m. Logan was just settling into a meeting with Hayes Daniels in Hayes's lavish office after a lengthy chat with their attorneys about Miss Bellefleur, her illegal lease of property on company land and a strategy to deal with her when his secretary called him.

"But this isn't just a phone call," Mrs. Dillings said,

her voice sharp with indignation after he'd dared to point out that he'd given her strict instructions that she was not supposed to interrupt him. "I thought you would want to know that your grandfather's here. Especially since you went down to check on him yesterday."

"Here? In New Orleans?"

"Here. In your office. And if I may say so, he hardly looks like the invalid you described. You'd never know he had a stroke except for that slight limp. But he does seem most anxious to talk to you. He said *immediately*. Oh, and you know how his jaw juts out the way yours does and how you both growl when you're not getting your way? Well…looks like a storm is brewing."

She would know. His grandfather had been her former boss. Obviously, Mrs. Dillings was very good at what she did and knew her value, or she would never have dared to comment like that. Maybe someday Logan should remind her that more people got fired for poor people skills than for being bad at their jobs.

"I'll be right there. See if he wants anything…a cup of coffee…a beignet…hell, order him a dozen beignets."

"He's with a most charming companion. A Miss Bellefleur."

At the mention of Cici's name, a pair of pert breasts stretching a hot pink, jersey top with a biker's nasty face on it arose in his mind's eye, causing his headache to worsen. The same restlessness that had hammered in Logan's blood all night long and had kept him awake began to pulse anew. He arose from his leather chair, walked stiffly to the door and then, stopping himself, began to pace.

"Miss Bellefleur's already asked for a whole tray of beignets. She likes them with extra powdered sugar."

Would she eat all that sugar with a spoon and then lick her fingertips?

He stared out the window at the city which was shrouded in murky mists. Unbidden came the memory of an eighteen-year-old Cici sitting across the table from him under the famous green-and-white canopy of the Café du Monde, licking powdered sugar off the curve of her thumb. How enchanted he'd been by everything she'd done that afternoon.

"Right. Indeed." Heat suffusing him, Logan said a stern goodbye to Mrs. Dillings. Continuing to pace, he directed his attention to Hayes, who was leaning back in his black leather chair, his long, muscular legs crossed, his tanned fingertips steepled in front of him.

"She's here," Logan said.

"Who?" Hayes said smiling, his black eyes mild as he studied him.

"Cici," Logan snapped as if such a question were ridiculous.

"Our infamous Miss Bellefleur." Hayes leaned forward. His black eyes became piercing, which was bothersome.

"Well, that didn't take our lawyers long. We barely hung up and now the villain's here to plead her case," Hayes said, his smile broadening.

"Obviously our attorneys failed to reach her. Because she's here and not at Belle Rose, where she belongs, so she could have answered the damn phone."

"I thought the point was that she *doesn't* belong there."

"Right. Exactly. Of course. *But my point now is that she jumped the gun. Again.*"

"Your Cici is beginning to sound like a handful."

Of course, any woman foolhardy enough to risk her neck in war zones, the long lens of her Leica camera her only shield against bullets, is bound to be a handful.

"She's not *my* Cici!" he yelled, he who never yelled.

"If you say so. All you've talked about is her. Nothing—ever—not even your wife has ever distracted you like this."

"Because she's using my grandfather to get to me."

"Dirty trick."

"She's full of them."

Hayes, his best friend, his former college roommate, his CEO, was tall and dark and tough as nails, way tougher than Logan. Which was why Logan had hired him. The trouble was, Hayes, who was nosy as hell, was observing him with far too much interest and probably far too much insight.

"I'd better go deal with her," Logan said.

"But you just brought in our legal team so you wouldn't have to be involved with her personally. Why not send Abe? You said you didn't want to get your hands dirty. You said this is a trivial, domestic matter."

"Right. That's what I said."

Suddenly, this whole matter with Cici felt way too personal to turn over to anybody else, even his ruthless lawyers, of which Abe was the head.

"Did I ever tell you how much I dislike being slammed with my own data?"

Hayes laughed out loud. "Don't we all? Keep me posted. I want to hear how round two comes out. Your Cici is much more interesting than any merger with Butler Shipyards. By the way, I'm beginning to wonder if Mitchell Butler has been entirely honest with us. At this point it's just a gut feeling…but…"

"Check it out," Logan said.

Logan's heart had been beating at a ferocious clip ever since he'd shut his door only to see Cici and his grandfather, their chairs pushed close together, enjoying a makeshift picnic of beignets and rich black coffee. Oblivious to the crumbs they'd scattered all over his coffee table, they were smiling at each other.

The old man looked happier than he had in years, and that would have been heartwarming if Logan trusted Cici. But how would his grandfather feel when Cici finished her book and returned to putting her life on the line in the fast lane just to take a few pictures? Cici was an adventuress, not a caregiver.

Sitting down at his desk, Logan punched a button on his intercom and told Mrs. Dillings to hold his calls. When he looked up his grandfather had moved his chair so that it faced Logan's desk.

When the old man frowned, Logan scrunched lower in his chair. Nobody could make Logan feel four years old again just by sticking out his jaw except this man who'd raised him. How many times had he stood in this very same office when it had belonged to his grandfather and waited for the old man to begin some lecture because he'd committed some minor, boyish infraction?

As he waited, Logan began to feel caged in his civilized office that was filled with leather and chrome and too many polished wooden surfaces. And he knew who to blame for his discomfiture.

Not that he was about to give the delectable Miss Bellefleur, who was, indeed, licking her fingertips with a grace any feline would envy, the satisfaction of looking at her.

Even so, all he saw was Cici. All he felt was her.

In her purple T-shirt and tight black jeans, with her childishly sticky fingers, fingers he wanted to lick clean, she was a garish splash of voluptuous color in his too elegant, beige suite.

Did she always have to dress in outfits that screamed, *look at me?* Did she even own a decent dress? Or a conservative suit? Or plain black pumps that might have concealed those livid, purple toenails, which, by the way, on *her,* were sexy as hell? At least, they matched her T-shirt.

He had memories about those half-naked feet. After sex, she used to climb on top of him and stretch out, placing the soles of her feet on top of his feet. God, he'd loved the feel of her on top of him as he'd wondered what she'd do next.

And her hair—it was wild this morning—springy curls tumbling to her shoulders. Big hair was not a look he liked on his woman…usually…except right after sex. Still, he was hard as a rock, and the view wasn't what was turning him on.

Ignoring Cici, Logan concentrated on his grandfather. "You seem upset, Grandpère. Why are you here?"

"Maybe because sitting around Belle Rose isn't doing me much good. I was always a man of action."

"Yes, you were."

"I'm here because I want to start by righting a few wrongs."

"Such as?"

"In the past, I was unfair to Cici. And so were you."

"At whose instigation?" Logan whispered.

"Mine. I take full responsibility. I was so furious at Bos and so discouraged by your father's failures and Jake's wildness, I didn't want Jake to be seduced by Cici and marry her. I didn't know what a niece of Bos's might do to our property if she married into our family. I didn't trust her. So, I asked you to intervene to save your brother, who was always more susceptible to temptation than you."

Little did he know.

"And because I did, Cici was hurt so badly she ran away and got into a dangerous, heartbreaking profession. She stayed away, until now."

"Is that what she told you?"

He nodded. "Last night we had a long talk."

Logan could well imagine that they had.

"She wants to come home," Pierre said. "She says she forgives me. She's persuaded Jake to come home, which is what I've wanted ever since I got sick. And for that, now you want to throw her out."

After such noble praise of Cici, Logan's gaze swung across the room to the young woman. Her fragile face framed by masses of gold curls looked tense and shadowed in the morning light. Beneath his scrutiny, she blushed and averted her eyes.

"Last I heard, Belle Rose isn't and never was her home," Logan said. "She should lease some other place. Grandpère, I don't think…she's the best influence on you…in your present state."

"Let me be the judge of that. I'm not the man I was, and Cici's never been the girl I thought she was."

Logan swallowed. He felt guiltier than he ever had for the past, so it didn't help when he noticed Cici's hands that were knotted in her lap were trembling.

Had she had trouble sleeping last night, too. Had she relived that damn kiss on the gallery again and again as he had, wanting more? Or did she hate his guts as she had every right to do?

"I want you to relent and let her stay…near me," his grandfather persisted.

For another long moment Logan's gaze lingered on Cici's pale, contrite face. Strangely, he felt touched by his grandfather's request and like his grandfather, ashamed of his own actions nine years ago.

Most of all he hurt. But he couldn't undo the past. Jake had left because he was furious at Logan for doing his grandfather's bidding by bedding Cici just so he couldn't have her. He'd said he was tired of the way the Claibornes always thought they could manipulate other peoples' lives.

Logan had tried to explain why he'd acted as he had to Jake at the time. "Grandpère said the family couldn't afford another marriage like our parents'. One of us had to do the smart thing. He knew you'd probably go the whole nine yards, including marriage if you slept with her, so he told me to make love to her. To save you, Jake," he'd said.

"What are you, his puppet? Cici doesn't deserve that. She's not like Mother. You're not like Daddy. Funny, I used to think that was a good thing. I used to admire you. You always worked so hard, made such good grades. Now, I just want out of this family."

Jake's fist had slammed into Logan's jaw on his way out. Logan hadn't seen him since.

Suddenly the wrenching pain of the past held Logan's heart in a death grip. He'd thrown Cici away, blindly, stupidly. He'd told himself he'd done it for Jake. For his grandfather. For the family. And for Cici even, because she would have been unhappy in his uptight conservative world. He'd convinced himself he'd done the right thing.

Damn it, he'd been so sure of himself back then.

But could he say he'd acted honorably toward all concerned? Toward Cici?

Logan shut his eyes. Then he pressed his eyelids and sucked in a long breath.

"I've always trusted you to do the right thing," his grandfather said. "You used to watch out for your brother. It was almost like you were older and wiser. Because I trusted you, when Jake ran out, I cut him off without a cent, and I gave you the reins of Claiborne Energy. And, yes, you made the family a fortune. I was proud of you, boy. Back then that was all I cared about."

"And now…"

"For nine years I've been estranged from Jake, and now Cici tells me he's doing well. She says that after he ran off, he went back to school, that he's done wonderful things in Florida and in New Orleans."

"I tried to tell you…"

"Before I got sick, I was a stubborn fool. I didn't want to hear about him, did I? Praise of him made me feel guilty. I know I tried to teach you to be exactly like me, but I was wrong about that, too. Don't be like me, boy. If I've learned anything in this last month when I've felt so weak and old and useless, it's that a grandson like Jake is worth more than any amount of money. I should never have set you on a collision course with your twin and then disinherited him for getting angry at us. And now…for Cici's help in talking Jake into coming to my birthday party, I want to repay her kindness by letting her live in the *garçonnière.*"

"Did you ever think that maybe the reason Jake's such a success now is because I saved him from Cici? From the way she's been playing you since her return, I'm beginning to think you had her figured right back then."

Uttering a soft, wounded cry, Cici sprang to her feet. In a halting voice she whispered, "I can't listen to this. I'll be right outside, Pierre. Don't wear yourself out defending me." Then on a whisper of wood trailing across carpet, the door closed behind her.

"It's my fault you think she's as trashy as Bos. But you're wrong. She's a very sensitive woman with a great heart, and she's made a success of her career…even if it hasn't been all that lucrative. I want to help her, to make up just a little for what I did in the past."

Had she been whining about money to his grandfather at a time when he'd been weak and needy? Was that what she wanted—money?

"Did it ever occur to you that maybe she's using you to get back at me? For sleeping with her? For jilting her?"

"Cici would never do that."

"Oh, wouldn't she?"

Abe stalked into the office before Logan, who wondered if he wasn't being set up, could say no more.

"If this is a bad moment…" Abe paused.

Pierre cleared his throat. "No. It's a wonderful moment."

After a few more seconds of silence so tense it nearly

hummed, the old man continued. "I'm glad you got here this fast, Abe. Things around here are about to change. I'm tired of rest and relaxation at home. It's time we moved forward. First, I'll be coming into the office twice a week—starting Monday. Second, I'll be moving into my old office. The young lady who's waiting for me outside has hired me a driver."

"Grandpère, do you really think you're strong enough? It's bad enough that Cici is using you to get back at me."

"Third," his stubborn grandfather continued with a frown, "I'll want you to write up an airtight lease. On the *garçonnière* behind Belle Rose for the little lady in the waiting room. Miss Bellefleur is a long-time family friend. Really, she's practically a granddaughter. She'll be wanting a twelve-month lease."

"Twelve months? You can't be serious, Grandpère."

Again his grandfather ignored him.

"You see, Abe, she's writing a book with the working title, *Lords of the Bayou.*"

Logan stared gloomily at his polished desk. No doubt she'd slam him as the environmentalist's worst nightmare. He'd have all the tree huggers picketing him again.

"The *garçonnière* is quiet," Pierre continued. "She says the setting is perfect for her research, especially since I'm there to help her. She's won all sorts of awards, so it'll be an honor to have her, not to mention a joy to work with her. I have a library full of history books on the subject, and I can put her in contact with all the right people."

Logan had the power to override his grandfather's decisions, but he loved and respected the old man too much to belittle him like that.

Fortunately, the tense meeting with his grandfather, who began to fade the moment Abe left, didn't last much longer. No sooner had Cici ushered the old man downstairs to her Miata than Hayes walked in, his excuse being a thick stack of legal documents on the Butler merger that needed his signature.

"From the look of your face, I'd say it's pretty clear who won round two. But cheer up. She's damn sure worked a miracle where your grandfather is concerned. The old man looked as fit as a bull when he was climbing into her sports car. Nothing like a young girl to get an old man's blood up, now is there?"

Suddenly, for no reason at all Logan wanted to punch Hayes's lights out.

"Hey, how come you didn't mention she was a knockout?"

"Don't...don't say another word. And as for her being a knockout, if you know what's good for you, you'll stay the hell away from her."

"I see. You sure had me fooled. Me and everybody else. We all thought you were serious about Alicia."

"You don't see a damn thing. I am serious about Alicia!" Logan thundered.

"Right." But Hayes's dark eyes were glinting, and the

corners of his lips were twitching with amusement, as he fought a losing battle not to smile.

"You said Mitchell Butler's story might have a few holes in it."

"So far it's only a hunch."

A sad, lost, homesick feeling swamped Cici as something vicious stung her above the elbow.

"Ouch!"

She quit knocking on her uncle's door long enough to slap at two giant mosquitoes on her arm.

Closing her eyes, she listened for a long moment. Not that she could hear anything from inside her uncle's cabin over the chorus of whistles and chirps coming from the swamp.

"Uncle Bos, why don't you open the door? I know you're in there. I know you left the bar because I've already been there and Tommy told me you're not feeling well. He sent me over with some of his spicy boudin, made just the way you like it. And Noonoon and I cooked up a big pot of gator gumbo. The roux came out real good. We threw in some cayenne pepper, onion, celery and bell pepper.

She drew a breath and stared at the huge stack of wire crawfish traps, gill nets and hoop nets leaning against the ten-foot pilings beneath her uncle's shack. "Uncle Bos, I'm beginning to feel stupid yelling at your door."

Her gaze wandered from the bayou with its dark, funereal vegetation, past the wreckage of his old rooster pens, to the ruined ponds behind their sagging fences where she used to help him raise thousands of little turtles that they'd marketed as pets to kids all over America. Other than the aluminum outboard tied at the end of his dock near the thick stand of tall rozo cane instead of her red pirogue, not much had changed.

Well, maybe the dark brown water had crept a little closer to the house, land being a vanishing commodity in Louisiana thanks to Logan and his kind.

"Okay. If you're going to be stubborn, I'll just leave the pots on your doorstep and come back for 'em later. When you're done, you can leave 'em outside for me to pick up."

Slowly she climbed down his stairs and walked past his motorcycle and then further out onto the dock to stare at the glimmering reflections in the bayou. Sagging posted No Trespassing signs were nailed to every cypress tree trunk. Her uncle, who'd always been something of a loner, wasn't the most welcoming type.

No wonder she'd never felt like she belonged. Uncle Bos certainly hadn't wanted her. She'd been eight when her parents had been washed away by a wall of water caused by a crevasse, or a break in a levee, when the Mississippi had run too high one spring. Luckily she'd clung to a board that had swept her to a tree where she'd held on to a branch for hours.

No, her uncle hadn't wanted to take in an orphaned niece, but he'd been her only relative. And he hadn't believed in public welfare. At least, not for any relative of his, even if she'd been a little sissy who didn't know the first thing about life in the wilderness.

He hadn't understood her reading or her fascination with pictures in magazines. He'd called her lazy for writing and extravagant for shooting so much film. He'd quit school after the sixth grade because in his view education was a waste of time. Real life was fishing and trapping and hunting and carving and drinking, and pitting one of his prized cocks against another's and laying bets. He'd made a small fortune cockfighting before it had been outlawed. Not that he was always a man to follow the law.

She and he had had nearly nothing, other than their mutual love of the swamp in common. Yes, she'd come to love the swamp, so mostly she'd tried to stay out of his way. Then, to make matters worse, there'd been the times when he'd vanished for days on end, maybe to attend illegal cockfights. Maybe to drink in the houseboat he kept in the swamp. Maybe to be with a woman. Who knew?

She'd hated being alone, but she hadn't told anybody because she'd been too afraid the authorities would take her away from him. Logan may have suspected her plight because often when her uncle disappeared, he'd sent Noonoon over or had come himself to check on her and bring her food.

Back then, before Uncle Bos had fallen out with the Claibornes over his bar and cockfights, he'd worked part-time as a gardener at Belle Rose. She'd loved going over to the plantation, loved following the Claiborne twins around, loved hearing about all the exciting things they were doing from Noonoon, who'd often let her inside to help in the kitchen.

Everything at Belle Rose had seemed beautiful and as magical as the places she'd read about in books. After the twins' parents' fatal car wreck, Pierre had welcomed them. He hadn't disappeared for weeks without telling them where he'd gone. He hadn't made them feel lost and left out or like they didn't belong. He'd taken them on wonderful vacations, too. When they returned, she'd pestered them into telling her everything they'd seen and done and into showing her their pictures.

How she'd longed for the stability she'd known with her parents, but that was a vanished world, one she only dimly remembered. Once her uncle had taken her to her old neighborhood. A new house had stood where her family's home had been. The place had seemed empty and utterly foreign to her. She'd felt alienated. It was as if she'd never lived there. As if her life with her parents had been completely erased. How she'd craved to feel some sense of belonging somewhere.

Over time Belle Rose had become a symbol for the kind of home and loving family life and stability she'd longed for but didn't think anyone like her could ever achieve again.

Cici leaned over and stared into the dark water. When she caught sight of her own reflection, she laughed out loud. Talk about a bad hair day!

Driving over to her uncle's with the top down hadn't

done her crazy, Princess Leia hairdo any good. She looked like she'd sprouted a pair of wild pompoms above each ear. With a smile she remembered watching part of an old Star Wars movie with Noonoon's granddaughter, who'd wanted to pretend she was Princess Leia after the film was over. Cici had fixed Latasha's hair and then her own.

She was still laughing at the memory when she heard the unmistakable sound of a big car on the gravel road. Turning, her smile dissolved the second she recognized the grim, broad-shouldered man in the silver Lexus pulling up beside her Miata.

What was *he* doing here? Logan Claiborne was the last person she felt like talking to after the horribly humiliating scene in his office yesterday. He wasn't welcome here, either. Her uncle held a long-standing grudge against all Claibornes.

Squaring her shoulders she headed toward the tall man in the three-piece black suit who was swinging himself out of his car while scowling at her.

Ignoring the acceleration of her heart and his forbidding expression, she said, "Didn't you see the signs? You're not exactly welcome here, you know. Tommy told me…"

Logan shot her a tight smile. "Tommy can go straight to hell." As always his narrowed, blue gaze lingered a little too long on her breasts.

She was wearing a tight black T-shirt today with big pink letters that said, *Pretty Woman*. Not that the T-shirt was anything a Princess Leia clone should be caught dead wearing.

"You're not too welcome here yourself from what I hear," he said.

"Your being here will make me even less popular, but that's none of your business. I've been reading up on the Butler-Claiborne merger on the Web. Don't you have big important rich guy stuff to be doing back in New Orleans? Or maybe you could drill up more of the wilderness we both used to love, digging your canals to get to your well heads and thus destroying the natural water flow, your machines throwing so much mud up on the banks, you smother all the vegetation and habitat for good."

His eyes climbed from her breasts up her throat to her face with such searing intensity she blushed. When he suddenly smiled, she wondered if it had anything to do with her crazy hairdo.

"Cici, why did you come home? What do you want? Why are you hanging out with my grandfather and pestering me?"

"I could argue as to who's pestering who. This is my home, too, you know."

"Is it? Did your uncle ever really want you?"

She took a deep, painful breath. "That tack won't win you any points. And as for Pierre, I like him. Ours is a friendship born of mutual need."

"I thought you ran away to get away from all this. This place must seem pretty tame to a woman who's lived like you have."

"No, I ran away from you. From how you made me feel, which was cheap and horrible, if that gives you any satisfaction. Talk about jumping from the frying pan into the fire. It didn't take me long to discover there are worse monsters than you. And by the way, you don't know anything about how I lived…although I imagine you think I lived wild and loose."

"What'll it take for you to go away again?"

"Maybe it's time you learned that I have as much right to be here as you do."

"Your uncle doesn't want you any more than he ever did. I don't see him opening his damn door. Not even for Noonoon's gumbo."

"He will. He's just being stubborn." Her lips curved. "Like a lot of other people…you," she taunted.

"He and I are nothing alike."

"You say you don't want me. I don't think you mean that any more than he does. I think I'm messing things up for you, maybe…maybe because you don't feel like you pretend—indifferent to me."

Logan's head jerked back as if she'd slapped him. "Shut up," he whispered even as he stepped thrillingly closer.

"Okay. Then why did you kiss me? And why are you looking at my lips like you want to do it again?"

"Stop it."

"No. Because maybe I can't stop what I feel any more than you can."

"I can stop it, all right."

"Right." She laughed. "You're the guy with all the

willpower. You probably skip lunch to jog. So, why'd you leave your fancy office and track me here?"

"I came here to work out a compromise."

"No. You didn't. You want what you want. The problem is maybe so do I. And maybe I've finally learned to go after what I want."

There was a startled cry from the swamp. They both turned as a blue heron flapped its wide, gray wings and took flight, skimming low just above the brown water.

"You know what I think, Logan," she said, turning back to him and finding his eyes glued to her face. "I think we've both caught the same fever. If you're so sure you're immune to me, kiss me again. Prove I'm wrong about you. About *us*."

"There is no *us*."

"So, prove it, big guy. Kiss me."

When he took a step backward, probably to seek the safety of his car, she reached out and grabbed his tie. Reeling him close, she stepped into his arms.

Stiffening, he stood up straighter. For a second, she was sure he'd push her away and barricade himself in that tank of a car. But he just stood there on the edge of surrender, his heart pounding so hard she could feel it.

She pulled him even closer. "Kiss me."

In the next instant his breath was hot and ragged against her forehead.

"I don't want to hurt you again," he whispered even as she tightened her hold on his tie. "I'm no good for you."

And with those words, which were better than an

apology somehow, the worst of her anger and hurt that she'd been harboring for so long melted a little.

Gently, she let go of his tie and touched his thick, dark hair, combing her fingers through it, mussing it a little further. Then she reached up and, framing his face with her hands, she placed her lips gently against his throat.

"I've always liked your hair," she said. "It's one thing about you that's always a mess."

He smiled. "You don't know the half of it."

In the next instant his hard mouth was on hers, tasting sweeter than honey and burning hotter than a flame, but then it always had, even if that was a cliché. His mouth sent fire dancing through her veins as she melted against him.

The kiss was unlike the last one because he wasn't fighting it, and neither was she. Their lips joined them. Every part of him belonged to her in that primeval man-woman way that felt wilder and more dangerous than the swamp.

His hungry mouth still locked on hers, he tightened his hold on her, pulling her even closer, his muscular arms binding her to him. Not that she had any desire to run from his kisses or the possession of his powerful embrace. No, like a fool, like before when she'd been a naive kid, she wanted to stay in his arms forever and do all the naughty, forbidden things they'd done before. Was she a fool or what? Yes. Where Logan Claiborne was concerned, the answer was all too obvious.

Unfortunately, Uncle Bos must've been spying on them all along. Suspecting her of having less than wise instincts where Logan Claiborne was concerned, Bos banged his door open and hollered down to her.

"If you come by for a visit with me, girl, I'm up here waitin'. The door's wide open. But it won't be for long unless you get rid of him, yes. If you miss the chance, the next time you see me I might be laying up in my coffin."

"Well," she said, smiling triumphantly up at Logan. "See, he does too want me. And maybe, just maybe I'm right about you wanting me just a little bit, too, yes?"

Logan pulled her against him and held her close so that she was in no doubt about the hardness or size of his erection. "Maybe a little, but just like always, the old cuss's timing's lousy."

With a shaky laugh, she raised her hand and smoothed his sensual lips which were still hot with a gentle fingertip.

"See you," she promised huskily.

"Cici, I don't want to hurt you. This isn't going to work."

Why not, because I come from this hovel on stilts half sunk in rot and muck and you come from your beautiful, charmed Belle Rose? Will I never, ever be good enough?

Not that she spoke such truths aloud. She wasn't in the mood for a quarrel or a reality check. No, she had much more appealing ideas about how to spend her time with Logan Claiborne.

"You really do need to go," he chided. "I never considered your Uncle Bos a patient man."

She smiled, causing him to grin, too. "You have a beautiful mouth," she said. "Lots of straight, white teeth."

"The better to eat you with."

"Naughty boy."

His eyes glinted as they moved over her face and then down her T-shirt. Tipping her chin with a fingertip, he gently nicked her nose with his teeth. "Naughty girl."

"You do have a point." Fluffing her pompoms, she swished her hips, just to get his mind on her ass where it belonged. Turning, she left him.

Feeling his heated gaze burning into her spine, she put more swing into her hips and really began to strut.

Not once did she look back or say another word, not even a sultry goodbye.

He chuckled out loud.

It was amazing how well they could get along if they stopped talking.

The inside of her uncle's cabin was as dark and musty as ever, maybe mustier. Imagining all sorts of terrible molds, Cici itched to open all the windows and take a scrub brush soaked in chlorine or lemon juice and scour every surface.

"You knocking on Logan Claiborne's doors, too? Bringing him gumbo? Trying to win his heart since he be single and the most eligible bachelor in Louisiana again?" Uncle Bos demanded gloomily. "He's not for you, you know."

His expression surly, he was sitting at his rusty dinette set playing with a knife he'd carved out of a razor-sharp alligator tooth while she heated his gumbo over a single flame. His sleeves were rolled so high she could see the beginnings of his many tattoos, which were angry swirls of dragons, snakes and spiders.

"No, you might say he's been knocking on mine."

He slammed a beer bottle onto the table and violently yanked the top off another. "Well, it would be a mistake to trust him. I hear he's got a new rich girlfriend."

She swallowed against the painful thickening in her suddenly dry throat.

"Name of Alicia Butler. Her daddy owns a bunch of shipyards. Banks, too. I seen her with him on television."

Instead of meeting her uncle's eyes that were much too watchful, she stared at his crucifix earring. "I know. He told me about her already."

He slammed his beer down. "I hear she's as beautiful and sweet and high class as his first wife, Noelle, who sure was a pretty thing."

Glancing away, Cici swallowed and then took a quick breath. She felt trapped suddenly and wished she was anywhere but here.

"Not that his wife ever smiled or looked happy the few times I seen her." He kicked back his chair so that he was now sprawled at a disrespectful angle.

"So, how have you been feeling, Uncle Bos?"

All four feet of his chair slammed the floor again. "I can't complain. A little tired since the chemo, but the doctors say they got it all. But then they probably always say that, the bastards."

"Maybe they're telling you the truth."

"Maybe," he agreed gloomily. "Tommy and Noonoon, they showed me all those pictures you took. I tacked a couple up in the front room."

"Yes, I saw them."

"I like the one where the vulture's about to eat those starving little girls in the desert."

"A lot of people like that one."

Everybody except her. She'd won an award for the picture, but it haunted her dreams even though she'd been able to save the girls afterwards. Still, the photo always reminded her that there were too many little girls who wouldn't be saved.

"I've quit taking pictures for a while."

"That's too bad," he said. "Why would you stop, when you're so good at it?"

Because life could get too scary.

She didn't feel like telling him that her hands shook every time she even looked at her camera case. "I needed a rest from it, that's all. It's called burnout."

"So, what did you come back here for?" he asked, a wealth of suspicion in his gravely tone.

Again, his narrow gaze was much too keen and hostile for her liking.

"I'm writing another book about Louisiana."

"That's not what I asked you, girl, and you know it. You'd be a fool if you came back because of him."

When she ignored that, too, he said, his tone caustic now, "How long you be staying?"

"It all depends."

"Not on Claiborne I hope. Don't you know that all he'll ever want from a girl with your background is to do what he did before, to get in your pants and then dump you?"

"People can change…sometimes…."

"Not so much. And not him. I know him and all his kin. And none of 'em have ever been our friend."

"Okay. We haven't so much as spoken in nine years. Can't we please…"

"You two aren't much different than you were back then. Oh, I know you think you're a professional and all because you write and took all them pictures that made you famous for a day or two. But you didn't go to college like he did. And he didn't just go to an ordinary college. He went *back East. Ivy League,*" he said sneeringly. "He's rich and powerful and conservative as hell. You're not. He lives by a set of rules that you could never cotton to, no."

"Gumbo's ready," she said, ignoring him still.

He studied her and then looked out the window in exasperation. "I don't blame you for not listenin'. There was too many times in the past, when I ignored you, too."

"I didn't come here to fight with you about Logan."

"Do you still love him?"

She swallowed tightly and didn't answer. But his eyes bored into her, and she was afraid that he saw the confusion she was determined to hide from him.

"Don't threaten him or hurt him to protect me from being a fool," she whispered.

"So that's how it is," he muttered. He spit toward a corner in disgust.

"You're wrong. I don't love him."

She bit her lips and was silent, and he made no promises to behave. But at least, he made no threats.

"After we eat some of this here gumbo, you want to take a spin with me in the swamp," he said at last. "Maybe you could help me with some traps I need to check before it gets dark."

For Uncle Bos that was as close as he was likely to come to offering to smoke the peace pipe.

"There's nothing I'd like more."

"Weird thoughts come to you when you get sick and find yourself stuck in a hospital bed," he said.

"Like what?"

"Regrets. I—I wasn't never much of an uncle to you."

"But you took me in. Where would I be if you hadn't? I wouldn't have anybody."

"Maybe you'd be better off. You wouldn't have known Claiborne."

"At least you've always been as hard on yourself as you were on me." She paused. "Just for the record, I'm glad you opened your door today."

"I resented you back then. I was through with females. I didn't think I needed any little girl messing around in my bachelor life, such that it was."

"I know."

"You'd be better off to leave this place, to leave me and Claiborne forever."

"Probably. But you and me—we don't always do what we should, now do we?"

Five

When Logan arrived at Belle Rose, and a valet parking attendant in a crisp white shirt jumped up from the steps and rushed to open Alicia's door, he wasn't surprised by the hordes. Nor was he surprised by the twinkling lights that turned the grounds into a magical fairy land or the least bit amazed when he entered the mansion with Alicia on his arm and found the house blazing with light and filled to the rafters with lively swamp pop, Cici's favorite brand of music.

All week Mrs. Dillings had been paying extravagant bills from caterers and florists and making healthy advances to various bands. If he'd raised the slightest objection to the cost of an item, his grandfather had called him, demanding that Cici, who was having the time of her life arranging everything, have her way.

Logan had done nothing but lose ground as far as Cici was concerned, and he still didn't know what she was up to. She just seemed to be moving in and taking command of his grandfather and Belle Rose, rewriting their past. In short, she was fast conquering territories that had long been his.

He was hoping tonight, somehow, that she'd do something so outrageous Grandpère would come to his senses and Logan would once again be able to assume control of his own grandfather and family again.

Logan ushered Alicia, who looked beautiful in a long backless, gold gown inside the mansion.

She stopped and glanced up at the swirling staircase and crystal chandeliers that were garlanded with fresh yellow roses. "Why, darling, your old home is even lovelier than I imagined."

Frowning because he had Cici to thank for Alicia's compliment, his gaze swept the tall vases on mantels and polished tables that overflowed with the same yellow roses as well.

"Yes. Thanks to Cici," he said.

"Talented woman."

No, dangerous.

"It reminds me of the parties my mother used to throw," Logan said. Ironically, in trying to prove her worth, his mother had destroyed it.

Those parties had stopped abruptly at his parents'

deaths when the Claibornes had found themselves mired in debt and on the brink of financial ruin due to his mother and father. Still, he remembered a younger Cici standing outside on the gallery, peeking through the windows, her round dark eyes awed and made hungry by the splendor of it all.

Grandpère was seated in the parlor holding court next to a big table stacked high with birthday presents. A dozen older women had pulled their chairs around him and were all vying for his attention. The old man appeared fit. He seemed to be having the time of his life when he looked up and saw Logan just beyond his admirers' blonde heads.

The corners of the old man's thin lips tilted upward in what appeared to be the beginnings of a smile.

Logan rushed Alicia over to meet his grandfather.

"Who is this beautiful lady?" Pierre demanded, his eyes sparkling at Alicia. When Logan introduced them, Pierre's smile warmed. A few more moments of conversation had him beaming.

"He's enjoying your company immensely. Since Grandmère died, I'm afraid the dear old fella's been lonely. And since his recent stroke, even lonelier," Logan whispered a little later. "Stay here and keep him happy a few minutes longer, while I get you something to drink, why don't you?"

"My pleasure," Alicia replied in a low voice. "I'm having fun, too. You favor him, you know."

"Chardonnay as usual?"

When she nodded in that agreeable way he found so calming, he released her elbow, nudging her a little closer to his grandfather.

Logan was on his way to the bar that had been set up in the main salon, when an uproar in the ballroom caught his attention and he turned.

At the sound of Cici's merry laughter coupled with the deeper notes of Jake's deep baritone, Logan abruptly pivoted, changing course. But when he saw Cici in a shimmering metallic sheath, her voluptuous body wrapped tightly in Jake's arms, Logan froze just outside the doorway. For a long moment Logan couldn't take his eyes off his tall, leanly muscular brother and Cici.

As the couple moved to the heavy beat of the music, he couldn't stop watching them.

Was he over-reacting or was she going after his brother now?

Whatever her motivation, Logan, who'd long regretted his past actions to both her and Jake and wanted reconciliation with his twin, suddenly felt like strangling him.

"That's some outfit." A man's voice from inside the ballroom said.

"Who are you kidding? You and every other man are looking at her legs," a woman said.

Logan clenched his fists.

"He's been gone nine years."

"The prodigal grandson. What made him come back?"

"Need you ask?" the man said. "She's hot."

"You should have seen how happy Pierre was when Jake showed up. The old man wept. So did Jake. It was so touching."

Hell.

Logan's angry gaze flicked from Cici to his dark, broad-shouldered brother, who looked too tough and strong to ever cry. Still, their grandfather's sentimentality must have affected him. Or maybe it was hard for Jake to see how much older and frailer Grandpère was.

Suddenly Logan wondered if Cici might be right in her handling of Grandpère. He was clearly thrilled about his party. Maybe the old man needed more independence and responsibility and activities rather than less. Logan had thought the old man required quiet and rest and more medical attention, but Grandpère acted like he was bored with quiet and rest. Instead of retiring to an assisted living facility, he seemed to want his active life back. He'd said he wanted to return to the office. Was that really what he should do?

"Has she interviewed you for her book?" the man standing in front of Logan asked his companion.

"Next week. We're having her to lunch. Oh, and she's bringing Pierre."

"He came with her when she interviewed me as well. She's loads of fun."

"The old man's crazy about her," the woman said. "And no wonder. She pays attention. She listens. And, yes, she's fun. It's horrible the way old people are so neglected. I don't think the poor fellow knew what to do with himself when his stroke forced him to retire. He said he got pretty gloomy until she showed up."

Jake pulled Cici close, and her laughing gaze swung to Logan. When their eyes met, Logan felt like he'd been sucker-punched.

He wasn't jealous.

Then the music stopped, and luckily he still had enough presence of mind to remember Alicia. He was turning to go after her wine, when a small, smooth hand with garish, red nails closed over his arm from behind him.

"You're late," Cici whispered against his ear, her breath as hot and soft as the satiny caresses of those searing fingertips. Her face was young and as open as it had been when she was a child.

"It was raining in New Orleans. We had trouble getting out of the city," he said.

"I missed you. So did Pierre."

"Not that that stopped you from burning up the dance floor with my brother."

"Jealous?"

"Of course not."

"You are," she whispered gently, her eyes seductively aglow. "You don't need to be."

"What?"

"It's your turn. To dance with me. But, hey, only if you want to." Again, her darkly sparkling eyes lured him.

"I have a date."

"Alicia? The merger girl?"

"That's not why I'm dating her."

"Of course."

"I left her entertaining Grandpère. I promised her a glass of wine. I'd better go."

"I'm sure your grandfather is enjoying her immensely, and she him. Jake can check on her."

"Cici, no…"

But she had already run over to Jake and was tugging at his long white sleeve. As his twin's dark head lowered over Cici's springy curls, his estranged brother looked up and then past her to Logan. Jake's eyes grew as hard and unforgiving as they'd been right before he'd slugged him and walked out. But when Cici finished talking to him, Jake turned and obediently headed out the other door, no doubt to avoid him on his way to find Alicia.

Cici returned and threaded her fingers through his.

"There's something wrong about this situation," Logan said. "I should check on Alicia myself."

"Trust me. This is a party. We're supposed to mingle a little. She came here to meet your family, didn't she? And your Alicia will love Jake. I promise. He's a do-gooder. She's a do-gooder."

"How the hell do you know so much about Alicia?"

"Research. I'm a journalist, remember."

She pulled him onto the dance floor. "Besides, what can one little dance hurt?"

Had the snake said to Eve, "What can one little apple hurt?"

Probably.

When the music resumed, he crushed Cici more tightly to him.

Even with the help of her heels, she barely came up to his shoulders. Maybe it was because she was so small and petite that her long-lashed eyes seemed so vulnerable.

He liked tall, elegant women, he reminded himself. Women who wore classy, backless gowns.

But Cici looked fresh and wholesome, and her eyes sparkled in such a way that she appeared young and playful.

He wasn't supposed to be thinking admiring thoughts about her he reminded himself. He was supposed to be trying to figure out how to get rid of her.

But it was hard to think when the effect of her body brushing against his was so electrifying. It became even harder after the music took over, and the pleasure of holding her and dancing with her stripped him of his last shred of his reason. When the first song ended, she didn't let go of him, so neither did he. One tune after another, they kept dancing. Pillars swirled past, as did the faces of those in the crowd watching them, for Cici and he were fast becoming the center of attention now.

Eyebrows were arched. Curious glances followed them. Not that Logan cared. At one point Jake even tried to cut in, but Logan ignored them all.

With each dance, Logan held Cici closer, bound her tighter, and slowly, irrevocably the voltage between them grew so strong it charged every atom in his body.

By the fourth song her eyes were closed, her cheek pressed against his shoulder, her body fused warmly to his.

When the music stopped, he was rock hard. Opening his eyes, he saw Alicia, who'd been watching them earlier, leaning on Jake's arm.

"I've got to go after Alicia," he murmured, but his husky voice lacked passion for the task.

"Yes, you really should," Cici agreed, curling a fingertip into his hair. Then another song started, and her body swayed against his. "One more dance?" she whispered as Jake turned and left the room, pulling Alicia with him.

"I'm sorry. I really do have to go to my date. I don't know what came over me. I really meant to…to stop after one dance."

"Me, too."

He bowed before leaving Cici in search of Alicia, who should have been easy to locate in her stunning, backless gown. Since she'd just left, she couldn't have had much of a head start.

But neither Alicia's slender back nor Jake's broad shoulders were anywhere to be seen.

Logan was standing at the front door about to ask the valet parkers if they'd seen his brother when his grandfather hobbled up, leaning heavily on his cane.

"Lost your date?"

"I was just about to ask the valet parkers if they'd seen her."

"Alicia wasn't feeling well, so Jake drove her home.

She told me to tell you not to worry about her, that it was just a headache."

"Thanks Grandpère."

"Is everything all right?"

Before Logan could answer, an older woman cried, "I see our birthday boy! Time to open your presents!" Then a bevy of women spilled out onto the gallery, encircled him and led him away.

When Logan dialed Alicia's cell phone, Alicia, who always picked up on the first ring, at least when he called her, didn't answer.

She had caller ID. His instinct told him she was deliberately avoiding his call. Not that he could blame her. He hadn't intended to dance with Cici more than once.

A mist was rising up from the swamp, its curling wisps threatening to envelop the grounds and soon the road with damp. If he was going after Alicia, and he was, he'd be smart to leave now before it was impossible to see. But suddenly, through the veils of mist, he thought he glimpsed a dim light come on in the top rooms of the *garçonnière*.

Had he driven Cici from the party, too, the party she'd been so excited about and had worked so hard on? Jolted from his original purpose, he took a step into the mist and then another toward the *garçonnière*.

He knew he really should go after Alicia and make sure she was all right, and he would, but first he'd tell Cici goodbye and encourage her to rejoin the party.

A waiter came up holding a tray of champagne flutes.

Logan took two. Slugging them, he smiled before replacing the flutes on the man's tray. Then, carefully, so that nobody saw him, he backed into the shadows and left the gallery.

Only when he was well away from the house and concealed by the mists, did he sprint across the thick lawn in the direction of the *garçonnière*. This time, when he reached the top of the stairs and was breathless from running, he knocked. When she didn't answer immediately, instead of barging inside as before, he forced himself to pace the landing.

When she still didn't answer, he beat his fist against the door again and yelled her name. "I know you're in there!"

"Coming," she said at last.

Still, it was several more minutes before she finally pushed her door open. Not that she even looked at him. Busy dressing, she bent her head and shrugged into a black T-shirt.

"Wonderful party," he said.

She wore the black T-shirt and dark jeans, but because she'd only lit a single lamp and the *garçonnière* was full of shadows and her body was back lit, revealing her slender shape which seemed so sexy, he sucked in a breath.

"I'm sorry I made trouble between you and your date," she said, turning away as she tucked the T-shirt into her jeans.

He inhaled sharply again. "That was my fault," he said, feeling awkward around her.

When he jerked his eyes from her body, he saw her dress on the floor where she'd tossed it, the garment sparkling up at him as if with wicked glee.

Cici, her slim back to him now, was squatting on her haunches—well-shaped haunches encased in tight black denim, too. Leaning over, exposing more of her delectably rounded butt, she began to dig through the chaos of her shoes that spilled out of her closet into her bedroom.

Heat engulfed him, which was ridiculous. He was thirty-five, not some lust-driven teenager. Still, his heart began to slam in slow, painful strokes.

Ignoring him, she shoved bare toes into a jogging shoe and then began rummaging for its mate.

"What do you think you're doing?" he demanded.

"I'm taking the pirogue out in the swamp."

"At this time of night? Are you crazy?"

"What does it look like?"

"You're supposed to be Grandpère's hostess."

"I'm supposed to be a lot of things." She was trembling as she threw her shoes about. "Thanks to you, I need some air. Some space. Lots of it."

So Alicia wasn't the only woman he'd upset. He stepped into her bedroom. "I don't want you out there. All alone. In danger."

"Since when is my putting myself in danger any of your business?"

"There's ground fog. You could get lost."

"Isn't that what you want? Me gone? So, big deal! I'm going!"

"Anything could happen."

"So? I'm a big girl. I can handle myself."

"Something might eat you." So, he was probably exaggerating. Still…

"Hey, there. If this scares you I won't tell you about the time I had a pilot drop me off at the Zambezi River on a dirt strip, and my contact didn't show up because he'd been gut shot and was on an operating table. The plane flew off, and I was all alone in a jungle and lions were roaring."

She laughed and then stopped. "Sorry." She paused. "If I'm feeling a little hysterical, it's because I'm a lot more scared of you than I could ever be of the swamp I practically grew up in. You were right. I shouldn't have come back. But now that I'm here, I've got to figure out how to deal with what I'm feeling. I think best in the swamp."

He swallowed. "Cici, the reason I followed you out here is because I don't want my actions to ruin the party for you."

"Oh, really? Is that why?" Again she laughed, but not gaily.

"I shouldn't have danced…"

"Do you think you can lie to yourself and to me forever? You want me. I could see it and feel it on the dance floor. I can feel it now, too. You're wondering if we're still as good together as we were in the past."

"Why do you always push?"

"Is it me pushing? Or is it something inside us?"

He turned away from her.

"Something like sex," she said. "Let's be honest. You're a man, so, naturally, you want sex, and you think you don't stand a chance tonight with your Alicia, who's probably mad as hell at both of us—and I don't blame her. You think it'll be easier to get it here from me than from her. Plus, it'll be of the no strings variety, 'cause you're who you are, and I'm who I am. And no strings and something strange is just the thing to tempt most men…especially hypocrites, like you, who can't even admit what they feel."

"No, listen…"

"No, *you* listen! Why don't you do us both a favor and go chase your tame Alicia, who's so perfect for you? I'm sure she's more than willing to believe any lie you choose to tell her."

"I don't care about Alicia," he whispered, shocked by the truth of that statement even as he said it. "I want you. Not her. There! I admitted it! Are you happy?"

"You'd say anything—"

"I want you! I've tried not to."

When Cici stood up, both shoes on now, he had to strain to see her expression in the dim light. "You tried not to? How do you think that makes me feel? We've done this before. We made a lot of people miserable, including ourselves."

"And I thought you liked living dangerously."

"Not tonight. Not with you. Sure, in the past I've taken a few risks. Mostly because I was too foolish and young to know what I was doing. Like that time I was telling you about in Zimbabwe. That happened just after…after you'd dumped me and…and I'd left."

The incredible pain in her eyes hit them hard. "But this is different. Maybe I've had my fill of my heart being broken. Maybe I just want to write for some local newspaper and settle down to a simple, predictable life with a nice boring guy who loves me and is sweet to me. Maybe I've finally realized that what I want, which is happily ever after with some boring guy, is impossible with you."

He leaned his shoulders back against the jamb of her door. She'd given him his out. He should take it.

"So, like I said, go. Do us both a favor, and spill your heart out to your pretty, proper, rich Alicia. Like I said, she'll forgive you."

When he said nothing, she took a step toward him. "Damn it, go!" When he didn't, she took a quick breath.

He stared at her, willing himself to do as she said and go. But he couldn't.

The tension built until the humming in his blood was so loud he was afraid she could hear it. Finally, he crossed the room and pulled her into his arms. The instant his hands wrapped her, she shivered, her heat and passion flowing through him like a contagion. Pulling her closer, he shuddered.

"Go," she whispered huskily even as her hands clung to him. "You're scaring me."

"You didn't used to be afraid of anything."

"Not even of hungry lions." She laughed weakly.

"Funny, I value my life so much now that I'm afraid to pick up my camera, afraid of you…afraid of feeling all this…"

She didn't look afraid. Her cheeks were flushed. Her eyes glowed. Every inch of her felt electric and silky and hot.

"I'm afraid of dying now…I think because I want to live so much," she said.

The mists were seeping into her wide-open windows, swirling around them. In the distance he could hear the mating cry of a wild bull alligator in the swamp.

"Kiss me," he said, his voice rougher, needier.

Then, too impatient to wait when she remained frozen, he claimed her mouth, driving his tongue deeply inside her with a violence that scared him even more than it frightened her. His hands slipped beneath her T-shirt and unhooked her bra.

"You taste delicious. Like champagne," she said.

He should slow it down, but he couldn't.

With a shudder, his arms wound tighter and he forced her closer.

"Two glasses. Couldn't resist," he said. "Not much really."

His breath was loud and harsh now. He wanted to possess her with every cell in his being, and he was fast losing control.

Besides pressuring her, what he was doing was probably wrong on a dozen levels. But when she began kissing him back, hesitantly at first, her lips were sweet and hot and quivering beneath his. Then when she gave him all she had, he was soon driven past all thought and reason.

As if shocked by the pleasure he gave her, she let out a startled cry.

His arms wound tighter. He had to have her. And it was more than a physical need.

To hell with right and wrong and sanity, he thought as his need blazed ever higher until it consumed him.

"Did you bring a condom this time?" she whispered, sounding as frantic with passion as he felt.

Six

Cici was being stupid, and she hated that because she always regretted being stupid later. Logan Claiborne was the one man she should never sleep with because he held the key to a part of herself she wanted to protect forever.

So why had she made sure he had plenty of condoms? So why was she lying naked on his bed with him sprawled heavily on top of her? They'd barely started making love, but already, with his every caress, with his every kiss, he was stripping her soul so bare that she felt like she was crashing and shattering and flying into a million jagged pieces.

After he was finished with her tonight, would she ever be able to feel whole again?

Logan's mouth traveled from her throat down her belly, across her scar, pausing there and kissing it so tenderly that she wept.

Her breath stopped and she began to quiver. In a flash she remembered holding their precious son in her arms that one time.

Their son. The only human being she'd ever loved half so much as that darling child was Logan.

Only when Logan's lips moved ever lower, and he found her softest, most secret flesh and began stroking her there, could she stop thinking about their lost baby and breathe again. But soon, too soon, he had her emotions in turmoil again and she was, clinging and shaking, but by then he was, too.

Wet and ready for him, even before he spread her legs and laved her long and deeply, she drove her finger through his hair and drew his head closer, moaning as his skillful mouth and deft tongue licked her and sent shiver after shiver hotly pulsing through her, evoking forbidden longings she hadn't felt in years.

Hadn't wanted to feel!

She bit her lips and tightened her fists in an attempt to fight her fierce pleasure. But it didn't work because what she felt was too powerful.

A younger, more naive Cici had imagined herself madly in love with him in this same room. She'd lost that happy, glowing feeling at immense cost to her soul, because he'd thrown her away. To save his brother, he'd claimed.

She did not want to be in love with him again. He was too cold and logical. Too cruel. He'd shown her once that he was a man who always did what was best for him or his family.

But what if she was no more in control of her easily bruised heart than she had ever been?

Maybe her fierce anger and the self-destructive hatred that had driven her to taunt death had been the dark side of her love for him. What if she was willing to risk anything to be his, willing to pay any price for another chance?

When his tongue found *the zone* and began licking small, satiny circles, a series of wild thrills such as she had never known rippled through her. Opening wider, she arched her pelvis against his mouth.

The *garçonnière* was an utterly dark cocoon. Nine years ago, in this same bed, she'd been a virgin. Again she reminded herself that he'd taken her and then had cruelly discarded her.

What would he do tomorrow? With these worries in her mind, the hotter her passion grew as Logan claimed her with his mouth and tongue, the more her emotions spiraled into fear.

She'd borne him a son with hair the exact dark shade of Logan's. When the doctors had told her that they'd lost her little boy, she'd asked to hold him. After his funeral, she'd locked her terrible secret in her heart, intending to keep it there forever.

Until tonight, when Logan had walked into the ballroom and looked at her, his gaze as lost and feverishly dark as her own broken soul, she'd believed herself incapable of ever loving him or ever sharing her profound loss with him. Now old emotions were reigniting.

He spread her legs wider. His tongue delved deeper, and she moaned as the throbbing excitement built, spreading like a ravaging flame that devoured every part of her until she burst in a final explosion and became completely his.

Breathing hard, she shut her eyes.

Do we choose those we love? Or are they a gift? Hadn't he always possessed her soul?

"For nine years I've wanted to do that again," he whispered, "to taste you, to hear you moan like that. To give you pleasure."

At his husky words and tender embrace, she held onto him tightly, not daring to let herself believe anything he said.

It was just sex. "Don't say things we'll both regret."

"The last thing I want is for you to regret anything about tonight," he murmured. Then he moved up to straddle her.

"No regrets. I promise. I'm a big girl now."

She wrapped her arms around his neck and drew his mouth to hers.

"I was a fool nine years ago," he said.

"So was I."

"You were only naive, but I was cruel. Can you ever forgive me?"

"That will depend on what you do next."

"I don't want to hurt you like that ever again."

Then don't, she thought as he put on a condom.

When he finished, she kissed his lips in a long, soul-shattering kiss. When she felt his sheathed manhood probe at the velvety folds of her secret entrance, she opened her legs, and he plunged—deep and true. For a long moment, he simply held her and was still, and she savored the sensation of being joined to him.

Oh, the pleasure, the immense pleasure that only being with him could give her.

"I promise not to hurt you," he whispered.

She nodded, not really believing him. After all, he'd promised such things before.

Slowly his hands began to caress her hair. Then his mouth brushed across her lips, her cheek, before moving down to her throat.

Bending over her, he began to move with her in such abandon, she was soon crying out.

Wrapping her arms around his shoulders, she arched her body higher and higher, meeting his every thrust. Their passion built, and she surrendered completely, exploding with him.

Afterward, she buried her face against his shoulder and held on to him for a long time, wishing, no, longing for so much more than a man like him could ever give a woman like her.

"What are you thinking?" he asked, his arms tightening around her as he brushed her hair out of her eyes.

The confused emotions in her heart made her suddenly shy. "Sex makes people, especially women who are fools like me, do and feel the craziest things. I could write a book on the subject."

"Please don't. Not if you're going to write about me."

She giggled. "You're a prude. You know that, don't you?"

"Conservative."

"Not in bed." She smoothed her fingers through his chocolate dark hair. When the thick lock fell back over his brow immediately, she pushed it back again and smiled. "Only afterwards, do you get uptight, when you fall back into being your true self."

"My true self? Who the hell is that? Do we ever know our true selves? For years I did what my grandfather taught me to think was best for the family."

"I found mine behind a camera."

"Lucky you."

"Or not. I saw too much pain. I can't even pick up a camera now."

"You didn't answer my original question," he said. "What were you thinking a while ago."

"I don't know. I've forgotten."

"Then I'll make love to you again, in the hope that you'll remember."

"Will that be your only reason?" she teased.

As soon as he began to kiss her, the moist warmth of his mouth and tongue had her shivering in newly heightened awareness of him, maybe because the first time they'd made love tonight, he'd broken down all the walls of her resistance and she was wide open to him now. As before he swept her on a dark tide of passion to the other side of the moon, to a wild place that was theirs alone, a place where she forgot herself and might have whispered desperate, foolish things against his ear, but fortunately in that last shuddering moment, she remembered all that divided them.

In the past he'd hurt her, and it had taken her years to get over it. Who was to say that although she was older and wiser, it couldn't happen again? No matter how close to loving him she felt, she could not let herself succumb.

"I never thought I'd feel like this again," he said afterward, triumphant that he'd taken her to such heights, maybe because his manhood was still embedded deep within her and she was clinging to him fiercely.

She couldn't think with him inside her. She felt too warm and snug, too safe, and such feelings were not to be trusted.

"I have a lot of making up to do for how I treated you, don't I?" he said.

"An entire lifetime wouldn't begin to suffice," she said. "So we agree then, that you owe me?"

He pulled her even closer if that were possible. "Big time. I will make it up to you. I swear. I don't care if it takes an entire lifetime."

Her heart caught as she eased herself out of his arms. Not that she was about to let herself hope for anything from him, for she had learned that hope, not fear, not grief, was the cruelest of emotions. And men like him would say anything in bed. The truth would come in the morning.

When he yanked the sheets around them and wrapped her in his arms again, she thought about the dark-haired little boy they'd lost, the little boy he didn't know about…yet.

Then, soon, because of Logan's body heat and his tenderness, the image dissolved. For the first time in years, she felt almost safe even though she knew she shouldn't, not with him, not ever with him.

Despite her misgivings, she fell into a deep, fathomless sleep.

Logan woke up first, wrapped in the warmth of a beautiful woman, the one woman he should not be with, their tangled sheets reeking of steamy sex. Alert, in the dazzling light of a new morning, he froze.

It was a helluva shock to find Cici's head resting so trustingly on his shoulder. Not that it should have been. What did last night mean?

Had he been lying to himself when he'd been so determined to send her packing? Remembering how tenderly she'd held him each time after they'd made love, he winced. She was sweet, as sweet as she'd been as a girl. What did she want? Need? Had he ever thought of that once?

Had he simply used her?

She deserved better.

Hell, any woman deserved better.

Even as the memory of her mouth all over his body stung him, he told himself she couldn't possibly fit into his life. Last night hadn't changed anything. And yet....

Slowly, trying not to wake her, he shifted his weight. Gently placing her head onto a pillow, he had eased himself almost to the edge of the bed before she stirred. Rolling over, she faced him. With a happy little sigh, she tenderly traced her fingertips down the length of his arm.

"Logan," she whispered dreamily.

"Right here," he murmured, trying to resist the instant high voltage coupled with the unaccountable tenderness he felt for her.

Long lashes fluttered again, revealing dark eyes glimmering with too much hope and affection. "I thought you'd be long gone."

Hell.

He should have been. He didn't know what to say. He only knew he didn't want to hurt her any more than he had to. "I'm where I want to be."

"Really?"

"Really!" It *had* been heaven lying in her arms. That part was undeniable. Determined to leave as fast as possible, he threw off the sheet and then couldn't help but admire her beautiful body. And her smile. She had an incredible smile. Then he frowned when he saw the vague, moon-shaped scar on her abdomen that he'd first noticed the afternoon he'd barged in on her. Without thinking, his hand lightly traced the white curve.

"What happened to you here?" he murmured, growing more concerned when she trembled.

Her eyes snapped open. Meeting his, they grew huge and confused, so painfully confused, and then tears, real tears filled them. Before he knew what had happened, she was turning away from him.

"What's wrong?" he demanded. "You've got to tell me." Gently, he placed his hands on her shoulders and felt her body trembling even harder.

Her face was pale. Her lips quivered when she turned toward him again. "It doesn't matter," she said. "At least, not right now, when you probably have a million things to do."

Alarm filling him because she was so passionately upset, seemingly for no reason, he pulled her closer. He felt guilty as hell, wondering if this fresh emotional turmoil could possibly be his fault.

"Tell me," he said, forgetting everything he needed to attend to in New Orleans and concentrating on her.

"I tried to tell you…once…"

But, as she was about to begin, his cell phone began ringing, interrupting her.

"Go on," he said, ignoring it.

But his ringing phone had her distracted. "Hadn't you better answer that first?" she said.

"It can wait."

"No. Go ahead. It doesn't really matter. You know how easily women become emotional. You have important things to do."

She turned away, and he reluctantly lunged for his phone.

No sooner had Logan said hello, than Mitchell Butler blasted him. "What the hell did you do to my daughter?"

"What's wrong with her?"

"She becomes very upset every time I ask her a question or mention your name."

"Okay," he said, feeling guilty as he waited for more.

"No! It's not okay, and until I find out what you did to her, the merger's off."

"I can explain." But could he?

"Then get your sorry ass back to town and do so." Mitchell hung up.

"What's wrong?" Cici asked. "Was that Alicia?"

"Her father. He's calling off the merger. I need to call Hayes."

She nodded, her expression cool, as he punched in Hayes's number.

Hayes answered on the first ring. Logan didn't bother to identify himself. "Butler just called. He wants a meeting."

"I know. This afternoon. At one sharp. He says the merger's off. Mind if I ask what the hell's going on?"

"I can be in New Orleans in an hour or so. I'll explain everything then."

"Must have been some party. Did Miss Bellefleur throw you another one of her curve balls? Did you strike out or hit a home run?"

"Don't hold your breath until you get the update." Logan flipped his phone shut and whirled on Cici.

"Sorry about all that," he muttered, feeling bad about how he'd treated Alicia. Suddenly he was too aware that their lives were on opposite tracks. "I guess I'd better get back to New Orleans and start putting out all the fires I've started."

"Sure," Cici whispered, but her voice caught. And her face was paper white. "I'll make you some coffee and toast, so you won't have to stop for breakfast on your way home."

"You were telling me what happened to you," he said as he grabbed his slacks off the floor.

"Not now, when your world's in pieces because of me and you're in such a hurry," she whispered, her voice sounding sad and lost as she turned away.

"But I want to know happened to you," he said.

"It doesn't matter. Like I said, it's obvious you have truly important concerns this morning."

"Cici…"

Ignoring him, she opened a can of coffee.

"Well, if she wouldn't tell him, she wouldn't tell him. He had to respect her reasons and let it go, at least, for now.

He dressed hurriedly. Not that he didn't look a mess with both his shirt and slacks so wrinkled they looked like he'd slept on them. Hell, he probably had.

"Last night was great," he said.

"Right," she said, popping two pieces of bread into her toaster.

"Incredible," he persisted.

"I'm glad you feel that way…if you do."

"What the hell is that supposed to mean?"

"It means whatever happened last night, this morning…these phone calls are your reality."

"Hell."

"Then tell me I'm wrong."

He couldn't even look at her, much less lie to her, so he stared out the window for a long minute while that telltale nerve in his jaw jumped painfully. "Look, I do have to get back to New Orleans as fast as possible."

"Of course. I know." Her teeth chattering, she wrapped her red robe more tightly around herself and concentrated on her toaster. Frowning, she began to tap her nails on the counter. "Damn it, why are appliances always so slow?"

Hoping to dispel the distinct chill in the morning air, he smiled and said, "It's because you're watching it."

She didn't look up from her toaster. He could tell she was in an even bigger hurry than he was for him to be gone.

"Hey, would you quit worrying about my toast? I can eat on the road."

"I'm not…worrying…about your stupid toast. Or you. I'm thinking about my looming deadline. I need to work. You're not the only one with a life, you know. I need to get some writing done. No more procrastinating. The last thing I need is *this* distraction."

"So, that's all I am now to you, a distraction?"

"I can always hope, can't I?" she said quietly.

"Me, too."

When his toast popped out, she jumped. Then clenching her fists at her sides, she took a deep, determined breath before plucking the two pieces out and tossing them onto a plate.

"So, the sooner I leave, the happier you'll be?" he said.

"What do you want me to say? What other choice do I have here?" Her tone and gaze were bleak. "You have your world of mergers and wealth. I have mine. Nine years ago I didn't fully understand such realities. I do now. Last night was great. But it's over. So, go. You're free. No strings attached."

The woman who'd writhed in his arms with total abandon, his Cici with the sparkling eyes, was gone. In her place was a woman with a bad case of bed hair, an ashen complexion and dull, swollen eyes. He'd made her unhappy—again.

Obviously, she was right about their situation, but for some harebrained, illogical reason, this thought didn't make him happy at all. He hated upsetting her.

"Eat," she commanded gently. "Then go. For both our sakes. Oh, and lock the door on your way out."

"So, you're saying last night was a mistake?"

She was padding toward the bathroom, but at his question, she stopped and turned. "You didn't look all that happy when I woke up, so for you…I think it was. So, I'm saying don't ever knock on my door again… Not unless…"

"Unless what?"

Her warm eyes fixed on his face and held his gaze for a long, intense moment.

"You're smart. You figure it out."

He wanted to rush across the room and pull her close. He wanted to crush her to him and never let her go. He wanted to stay and drink coffee and talk to her for hours. Which was ridiculous.

Instead, he swallowed. She was right. They'd had sex. Nothing more. Shrugging, he turned. Then bracing himself, he walked out the door.

But with every purposeful step he took away from her, his feet felt heavier. And so did his heart. He wanted to hear about everything she'd done when she'd been away.

The merger he'd worked so hard on was going up in flames, and all he could think about was Cici's wounded feelings and his own leaden emotion as he faced his life without her. What the hell was wrong with him?

Seven

A front was sweeping in from Texas. The gloomy morning matched Logan's mood as he stood at the front door of one of Jake's new houses, talking to Jake's real estate agent.

Cici. As Logan had driven to New Orleans, he'd kept seeing her in her red robe with her messy hair tumbling about her face in those crazy tufts, with her brilliant blue eyes lit by despair and hope. Even then, she'd seemed utterly beautiful.

And once away from her, his body had reacted viscerally to her absence. With every mile, the lump in his throat had grown and his chest had tightened until his heart had seemed squeezed by a vise. He hated the way they'd parted.

More than anything he'd wanted to turn back and floor the gas pedal. How could it feel so insane to be leaving her, when what was really insane was his tense longing to be with her? Why couldn't he focus on the merger?

"Thanks for your help," Logan said aloud, trying to sound normal, as he handed Jake's real estate broker his card. "So, if you see my brother, you'll be sure to tell him to call any of these numbers. Mr. Mitchell Butler wants to make sure his daughter's all right, and we think Jake was the last person with her."

"Then she's safe and sound," the man said reassuringly. "Jake's the most trustworthy guy in the whole world. But you should know that—you're his twin."

"Right." Logan nodded. Then the door slammed, and Logan found himself standing alone on the porch of one of the newly built houses Jake and his investors were constructing in the Lower Ninth Ward.

With solar panels on the roof as well as an escape hatch in case of another flood, the home was sleek and modern. The first floor topped the required eight feet above sea level by at least a foot or two.

Logan leaned against the railing. He had thirty minutes to get to the emergency meeting Mitchell Butler had called in Hayes's office, and he didn't have anything new to give to Mitchell.

Still, Logan took a second or two to study the rest of the half dozen new houses his brother had under construction. Jake had certainly made something of himself. He wasn't just rich; he was making a difference. Like the house Logan was standing on, all Jake's houses were modern, affordable, green, and well-designed and well-built, too.

Other than Jake's project and a few others like it, not nearly enough progress had been made rebuilding neighborhoods like this since the hurricanes. Vast empty fields and broken roads and a few trailers were all that was left of the once vital community that had been flooded when the nearby levee had been breached several years ago.

Logan forced his mind to Alicia. He didn't blame her for not answering her phone, but if he couldn't reach her, how could he appease Mitchell before their meeting about the merger?

Earlier Logan had dropped by the building in the Quarter where Alicia lived. Her doorman had been only too happy to inform him that she'd come home early this morning with a man who looked a whole lot like Logan, that she'd packed a bag, and that the two of them had left almost immediately.

"He had his arm around her. He seemed to be comforting her. Until you showed up, I thought he was you."

So, where were they?

Logan punched in Alicia's cell phone number, but as it rang, a vision of Cici naked in bed beneath him last night sprang into his mind. God, she'd felt so deliciously hot he couldn't stop thinking about her.

All morning as he'd searched for Alicia and Jake, Cici had been on his mind. He kept remembering her taste and the thrill of her soft, wet lips when she'd gone down on her knees to pleasure him. He got hard every time he thought about it, which was all the time, damn it.

Last night had been wonderful. Everything had been great after they'd started making love until he'd awakened to sobering reality this morning. Even so, he hadn't been gone from her five minutes before he'd wanted to turn his Lexus around and drive right back and reassure her.

He had his own life, even if it was a mess at present. He couldn't let himself care about Cici Bellefleur. But suppose he did care.

As Logan raced down the steps to his Lexus, he dialed Alicia's cell phone. When her voice mail picked up again, he snapped his phone shut. Clearly, she wasn't ready to be found. At least not by him.

Who could blame her?

He was jamming his key in the ignition, when his own phone rang. Finally, he thought, sure it was Alicia.

Hayes spoke instead. "Mitch just walked in. You'd better get the hell over here."

"He's early. It's only twelve-thirty. Our meeting isn't until one."

"He's here. He says you're late. He says the meeting's supposed to start now."

"He always thinks all meetings should start whenever he shows up. He's being unreasonable—as usual."

"I don't think he likes you very much this morning, either. Would somebody please tell me what the hell is going on?"

"Mitch thinks I hurt Alicia."

"Well, did you?"

"Not on purpose. Alicia won't talk to me, so I don't know exactly what is wrong with her."

"Is Miss Bellefleur involved in any of this?"

"I don't want to talk about her."

"Okay. So, sounds like she's involved. Not good." He paused. "Mitchell just told me he has another offer—a very attractive offer from J.L. Brown. So, where does this leave our merger?"

"You'd better ask Mitchell."

The door of the dress shop closed behind Cici with a tinkle of merry, silvery bells. Her emotions had been in such turmoil ever since Logan had left, she'd been unable to think, much less focus on her book. So, she'd driven into town on an errand for Noonoon and to check a book out of the library for Pierre. And, now after seeing the blue dress in the shop window, she was shopping to distract herself.

Besides, she'd been desperate to get away from the telephone because despite everything she'd said to the contrary to Logan, she'd longed for him to call. If everybody else on the planet hadn't phoned to say how much he or she had loved the party, maybe she wouldn't have noticed Logan's neglect quite as much. But every time the phone had rung, she'd driven herself crazy wishing it was him.

If only she could stop thinking about him, stop wishing he'd acted differently this morning.

Stupid. She knew what kind of man he was.

The elderly saleslady at the cash register looked up and smiled. "May I help you?"

"That dress in the window. It caught my eye. The blue one with the full skirt."

"The sweet little sundress?"

"I was wondering if you had it in my size."

"You're a four, aren't you, dear?"

"How did you know?"

Cici's gaze was then drawn to a red lace bra and matching thong.

"Sexy, aren't they? Just the things to win a man." The saleslady smiled at her dreamily. "I used to be a four…and wear naughty underthings…but that was many, many years ago."

Maybe so, but her step was as light as a girl's as she hurried to the rack in the back and found the blue dress Cici liked in a four.

In no time Cici had the dress on and was staring at herself in a long, gilt-edged mirror lit by spring sunshine.

Twirling, she imagined the warmth in Logan's eyes when he saw her in this dress. Would he approve? Was it demure enough?

Forget him. He's in New Orleans with rich, perfect Alicia.

You don't know that. Not for sure.

For almost sure. She's beautiful. She has a fortune. Then there's a merger in jeopardy. You can't begin to compete with her. Or his real life.

The bodice clung to Cici's breasts and made her waist look tiny. The blue skirt floated, swirling around her legs and hips every time she took a step.

He hadn't gone after Alicia last night.

The dress was sexy, but classy, conservative, too. Not really her at all. *Well, at least it was sexy.*

"Cinderella," the saleslady said. "You're Cinderella in that dress. Minus the glass slippers."

A sign?

Cinderella *had* married her prince.

"I'll take it," Cici said. "Next I want to try on that red bra and thong."

"I have a couple of other dresses that you'd be equally stunning in. Would you like to see them, too?"

Later that afternoon at the *garçonnière*, Cici, who was three demure dresses richer, removed her bright nail polish and pulled her hair neatly back, tying it at the nape with a blue ribbon. She put on her new blue dress and turned around, eyeing herself in her mirror.

Satisfied with her maidenly appearance, if only because she believed it to be more to Logan's taste, she picked up her briefcase and her computer. Then she walked over to Belle Rose and let herself into the library where she intended to do research for her book.

A dress and a hairdo won't make any difference, her little voice taunted. *You're still who you are. Swamp Girl.*

Ignoring the voice, she went to Pierre's shelves and began pulling books down that had to do with her subject. Not that she really wanted to read them. Noonoon told Pierre she'd come over, and he came downstairs and took the book she'd gotten for him and began to read on the couch.

While she forced herself to work, he intermittently napped and read. She took a break, and they had tea and crackers together. But all the while, her mind was only half on her work because she was secretly waiting for her phone to ring and for Logan to say he was missing her as much as she missed him.

Crazy. They'd had sex. Meaningless sex.

The first time her cell rang, she jumped for it. But it was only her Uncle Bos calling to say he was having a bad day, which meant he was having a very bad day since he wasn't a whiner and never called her, and would she stop over later and maybe tend bar if he was still too tired. Of course, she said yes.

Cici stood up and went to the window. Looking out at the gray wet, she told herself that she had to quit thinking about last night, about how wonderful she'd felt in Logan's arms.

Clearly it was over. Clearly last night hadn't meant anything to him. Therefore, it couldn't mean anything to her.

An hour later she was hard at work, taking notes feverishly in an attempt not to think about Logan when the phone rang again. This time it was her agent.

"How would you like to do a feature story on the bombings in Egypt near the pyramids? You always said you wanted to see the pyramids. This would be just the thing…and a *feature*…a *feature*…that is, if you're ready to pick up your camera again."

Part of her wanted to run away from last night, from what she'd done, from what she was afraid she felt for Logan. A monthlong shoot hiding behind her camera far, far away, focusing on other people's misery would be just the thing to take her mind off her own recklessly foolish behavior here at home.

"I have a deadline," she said because, of course, like any self-destructive, infatuated idiot, she was too fixed on the object of her torment to consider leaving him.

"What if I could get you an extension? I think this project would be worth your while." Her agent named the generous fee the feature would pay. "Can you afford to pass it up?"

Not really. This is your career. Logan's probably with Alicia right now. So, for once, do the smart thing. Pick up your camera again. Leave him. Run. Don't risk this getting out of hand.

Cici remembered the night she'd held their little son in that sterile hospital room. His skin had felt so thin and papery, and yet soft, too. He'd seemed so fragile and broken. And she'd felt like the loneliest human being in the universe when she'd finally kissed his cool brow goodbye.

She really should run. Because if she wasn't careful, she had no doubt Logan would hurt her again, maybe even worse than the first time.

* * *

Exhausted, Logan sat hunched behind his desk, which was littered with dozens of documents that would never be signed by Mitchell or himself. Even after hours of negotiation today, the merger was dead.

A year of work, hopes and dreams were down the drain. His future with Alicia was over as well. So, what?

Logan ran his hands through his hair. Curiously, he was too tired to care. Maybe tomorrow, the loss of it all would hit him. but then maybe not. All day he'd felt different, curiously free of his seething ambition. Things that always mattered to him more than anything, hadn't gripped him.

Someone knocked on the door of his outer office, and he heard Mrs. Dillings greet whomever it was much too cheerfully for it to be so late in the day. And on a Sunday.

She was amazing. She'd come in early. Did she never tire?

Then his own intercom buzzed. "It's your brother," she said in a calm tone, as if Jake's reappearance at Claiborne Energy at such a disastrous moment on a Sunday evening after an absence of nine years was a matter of course.

Forgetting the merger, Logan sprang to his feet, dashed to the door and threw it open just as Jake was striding toward it. When his twin's hard gaze met his, Logan stiffened, but only for a second.

Relaxing, Logan grinned. "You're not going to hit me this time, are you?"

Jake smiled as he thrust his big hand toward him. Without hesitation Logan shook it heartily.

"Welcome home. It's been too long," he said.

"Much too long. What can I say? We Claibornes are a stubborn bunch. Unforgiving to a fault."

"It's genetic," Logan said. "I was high-handed and completely out of line."

"To say the least. Still, I stayed away too long. I guess we both take after the old man."

"In any case, I'm sorry for manipulating your life. And Cici's."

"Hey, I guess I should have been used to it. But what about Cici?" Jake's smile died. "After the way you two danced together, I can't help wondering if she's forgiven you, too?"

"Not yet, but maybe I'm working on it." Logan paused. "Care to sit down?"

"Another time. This will just take a moment." Jake was smiling, but he seemed tense.

Logan shut the door.

"The reason I came by," Jake said, "or one of the reasons is that I know you've been calling Alicia last night and again today." He hesitated. "Because I was with her when you did, you see. So, I know she hasn't returned your calls."

"Is she okay?"

"She's fine. But she says it's over between you two, or rather that it never was. And I wanted to know if that is true."

Logan inhaled. "If she says so."

"What about you? Would you care if she started seeing someone else?"

"Meaning you, I suppose."

"She wants nothing to do with me. She says it's too soon. And that I'm the last man she'd ever date because I remind her too much of you."

"Sorry. I'm afraid I behaved badly toward her at the party."

"I explained about you and Cici."

"I should have explained things myself, but I was in the middle of them and didn't understand them too well myself."

"You never did. You loved Cici, you know. You were just too damn stubborn or arrogant to admit it."

"Well, I wish Alicia every happiness. You will tell her that if you see her or talk to her before I do, won't you?"

"Right now, she's not taking my calls."

Jake soon turned their conversation to a safer topic, their grandfather's health, and the next ten minutes were spent pleasantly. When they parted, they shook hands again and wished each other well.

It would take a while to mend the rift of years and renew their former emotional closeness, Logan thought as he turned off the lights so he could leave, too. But, at least they'd made a small start.

Cici was eating a sandwich for supper at her kitchen counter while she watched the news on her television.

The breakup of the merger between Butler Shipyards and Claiborne Energy was such big news, it was on every channel.

She was grabbing her purse on her way out to T-Bos's Bar when her cell rang.

"I want to see you," Logan said, his voice so deep and dark, the energy in it charged her.

"I saw the news about the merger. Sounds like you had a rough day. I'm sorry."

"Are you busy tonight?"

"What am I? Your consolation prize."

"Hell, I don't know."

"What kind of answer is that?"

"What kind of question is that?"

All day she'd thought about his kisses and lovemaking until she'd felt he'd branded her as his own. And he didn't even know why he was calling her.

"I was on my way out when you called," she said.

"I can't quit thinking about you."

She couldn't, either. "So what? Bad habits are hard to break."

"Cici…"

"So, how's Alicia?"

"I haven't spoken to her."

"Why?"

"Because she won't talk to me, that's why. But you might say she sent a message to me through a friend. It's over between us."

"Oh, you're feeling lonely and vulnerable as a result.

Which is why you're calling me. And like a stupid sap I answer. So, you think maybe I'll make myself available to you again?"

"No. That's not it."

"Of course, you won't admit it. You're a man. Last night turned you on. If this is about sex…you wanting it…thinking you can get it from me…and not being able to get it from your fancy girlfriend…and nothing else…"

"Cici, I do want to see you. Forget Alicia. Like I said—that's over."

"Look, you didn't call me all day. So, it's a little late now, okay?"

"I thought about you all day…all the damn day. Does that count?"

"Why should I care?"

"I thought about you until I'm sick of thinking about you! I couldn't call because I was dealing with Mitchell Butler and his unreasonable demands. Which were many. Then I was stuck in meetings with the board doing damage control after he trashed our merger."

"Poor little rich multimillionaire. Or is it billionaire? Well, I can't see you. Okay? Not tonight. Because I've made other plans. My uncle's sick, and I promised to help him out."

"Tomorrow, then?"

"Not tomorrow, either."

"Why?"

"I have a life, you know, and so do you as you clearly demonstrated this morning. Oh, and there's my deadline.

You should thank me. I'm letting you off the hook. I'm trying to be smart and logical for a change. And that's not easy for me."

"Cici…"

"Goodbye!"

She hung up on him. When her phone rang again, and she saw it was him, she leaned against her counter with clenched fists. She felt all mixed up, wild to see him on the one hand, but scared to death where it would lead.

All day she'd felt almost sick with longing for him, and then he'd finally called. But what was different between them? He wanted her for sex, and she was afraid she was already too involved to resist him.

Better to stop now, if she still could.

A least ten minutes passed before she got herself together enough to walk into her bathroom and splash cold water onto her hot face. After bemoaning the fact she looked absolutely awful whenever she was this upset, she carefully touched up her makeup. Then with a swish of her blue skirts, she marched down her stairs with her head held high.

Nobody at T-Bos's could know that her heart was breaking tonight. Not for Logan Claiborne. They'd think her a fool, which she probably was.

Eight

Logan pulled up beside Cici's Miata which was of course parked squarely in the middle of at least thirty or more big black motorcycles. His gaze drifting over cobras and rattlesnakes and angry streaks of red flames painted on the various bikes, Logan cut his engine. Not that he was eager to get out of his Lexus and face these bikers from hell.

Logan swung himself out of his car and took the stairs two at a time. Then he pushed the rough, unpainted door open. Hard rock music slammed him. Just as he was about to step inside, the meaty claw of a biker's fist shot toward him through thick waves of cigarette smoke.

"Not so fast," Tommy snarled.

Logan smiled. "Hello, Tommy. Is Cici around?"

"What's it to you if she is?" he bellowed. "What in the devil makes you think you've got the right to set foot in here, Claiborne?"

Logan stared into the bloodshot blue eyes of T-Bos's bouncer. A dozen members of Tommy's little gang, all squatting around their dirty tables or leaning against the bar slammed their longnecks down and scowled at him.

Not that Logan recognized any of the hulking figures through the haze of smoke. Except for the neon beer signs, strings of colored lights decorating the bar, television sets mounted in every corner of the building and the flickering strobe lights, T-Bos's Bar was dimly lit. This was probably a good thing.

"Where's Cici?" Logan repeated.

Two bikers kicked their chairs over and stood up, stretching their brawny arms before crossing them menacingly over their wide chests and beer bellies.

"What business you got with Bos's Cici?" Tommy demanded.

"I called Bos, and Bos told me she was here."

"You talked to Bos?" Tommy relaxed visibly.

"He sent me."

"He damn sure didn't tell me."

"So call him, why don't you? Ask him."

"Bos don't like me botherin' him when he don't feel good, that's why."

When cockfighting had been legal, Logan's grandfather had pressured T-Bos to close his bar and his cockfighting establishment. Ever since the pit had been closed by new legislation, the Claibornes hadn't been the most popular people with Bos and his biker clientele.

"Cici's out back," Tommy finally said through gritted, yellow teeth. "You better not be lying about Bos sending you." Then with a meaningful shrug, Tommy disappeared. As his biker buddies crashed back in their chairs, even as their gazes pinned him, Logan heard him yelling for Cici.

A new song began to play that was even louder than the one before. Strobe lights began flashing to its beat.

In less than a minute Cici waltzed in looking like an angel in a pretty blue dress, the like of which Logan had never seen her wear before. Ablaze in the white light, she held a tray of glittering amber beer bottles high over her head.

Logan shoved a chair aside and loped through the throng of angry bikers to her. He felt embarrassed, nervous with so many tense gazes tracking him. When her shining eyes fixed on his face, she lowered her tray.

"You're crazy…coming here," she said. "Tommy's not too crazy about you."

"I had to see you. It doesn't make sense, but there it is. *I had to see you.* Ever since you came back, nothing in my life makes sense anymore."

She smiled, but tentatively. "You—being here—makes zero sense."

"I missed you today," he said.

"You said that on the phone. Why should I believe you?"

Her smile softened her expression, and something in her eyes welcomed him at least a little. Did she look dazzled? Or was it just the strobe lights? Well, a man could hope, couldn't he…maybe, just maybe it was him that had made her face go so soft and radiant.

Desire for her and some other emotion raced along his veins, lighting his nerves. The bikers' sharp gazes were drilling holes in his back. He should have been embarrassed or maybe scared to death. But suddenly he didn't care what any of them thought.

He caught her hand, pulled her nearer. It was simply too good to see her again after the long hours apart. Everything else he'd done today, Mitchell, Hayes, Alicia, the merger, Jake, seemed so unimportant. Which was crazy.

Although it was dark, he could detect her cheeks flush just as he felt himself washed with similar heat. Gently, he intertwined his fingers with hers and brought her hand to his lips. Then he gripped her fingers tightly and just held them against his cheek for a minute or two. It felt good, and so damn right, just to be with her.

"When do you get off work?" he asked finally, letting her go.

"Two hours."

"What can I do to help? I can wash glasses. Wait tables."

"No. You're to stay away from these guys. Pull up a stool behind the bar and just stay out of trouble. No conversation. Don't even look their way."

"You're letting me off too easy."

"If we get out of here without you getting into a fight, I'm happy. You're not too popular around here, you know."

"As long as you're glad I'm here…."

"I'm not making you any promises, Claiborne."

"Fair enough," he said.

When Cici left the bar on Logan's hard arm, her heart beat thunderously at the base of her neck.

"What do you want to do now?" she asked when they stood before their cars.

"First we kiss. Just once."

"Here? No way. We need to beat it."

"Here," he whispered sharply.

His tanned face lowered toward hers. His blue eyes flamed. Then his mouth touched hers as tenderly and innocently as he'd kissed her that first time, so many years ago when he'd made her realize it was him she wanted, not Jake. His body barely brushed hers. Even so, she felt his heat and wanted more.

Afterward, when he pulled away, he gazed down at her for a long moment. "Can we go somewhere and talk?" he asked.

It was harder for her to concentrate after his kiss. He was standing so close, and he felt so deliciously warm. Yet she couldn't let herself trust him.

"We could drive to Belle Rose. Make a pot of coffee and then drive into New Orleans," he said.

"Look, it's been a long day. I'll bet you're every bit as tired as I am. I think you should spend the night at Belle Rose. Not with me. In the big house across the hall from your grandfather. You should have breakfast with him. Pay attention to him."

"Okay, if I follow you home tonight, so I can make sure you don't have a breakdown?" he said.

She nodded. "I suppose that's allowed."

He opened her car door for her, and she slid inside.

"I'm glad you came tonight. I wanted to see you again. You know me—the wild swamp girl with the self-destructive streak."

"Cici, I want it to be different this time."

"I'm not sure I want…a this time," she replied. "I'm not sure I could ever trust you again."

"I don't blame you for feeling that way. All I can say is that ever since last night… I'm not myself."

"Right, you lost the merger and your girlfriend. So, you're feeling a little vulnerable."

He was about to argue, but she pressed a fingertip against his warm lips. "Cheer up. This too shall pass. You'll be your old killer, ambitious self in no time. I promise."

"Maybe that's not enough for me anymore."

"One night of sex with me and you're a changed man? Forgive me if I can't quite buy into the new, reformed Logan Claiborne. I know I'm good, but that would take a miracle worker." With a laugh she turned her key in the ignition and revved her engine. "Better hop in your car. You're going to have to drive pretty fast to catch me."

As she roared out of the parking lot, the last thing she saw was his headlights flash on and leap forward through the darkness after her.

The scent of freshly brewed coffee and cooked toast filled the high-ceilinged kitchen that had been used as the prep room in the olden days. Back then the large brick ovens in the real kitchen had been outside.

Through the open double doors, Cici could see the lovely dining room as she leaned against a long table, munching toast and sipping coffee. And for a moment, the room with its glittering crystal and silver seemed as fantastic as it had when she'd been a child, standing outside peering through the windows.

"Belle Rose was always a magical place to me," she said. "I used to love helping Noonoon cook. But most of all I loved hearing her stories about you and Jake."

"You were so infatuated with Jake back then."

"I did have a crush on him for years and years. He was so reckless and wild. Always doing something like chasing gators to get a girl's attention. You were so serious."

"You mean dull."

"No."

"Yes. I was dull because Grandpère was always throwing my father and mother up to me. Besides, one twin had to pay attention to business. I was ten minutes older and, therefore, the older, more responsible brother."

She laughed.

He opened the refrigerator. "There's leftover crawfish étouffée, dirty rice, yams and some gumbo. Are you hungry for more than toast?"

"I'm okay."

"It was wrong of me to come between you and Jake that last summer," he murmured, his voice growing darker as he shut the door. "Wrong to justify my actions by saying I was saving Jake from you. Wrong to give in to my grandfather's grudge against you."

"Are you finally apologizing?"

"For what it's worth, yes. But saying I'm sorry can't undo the past."

"You're right about that. But we wouldn't be here now, if you hadn't wooed me then." She faltered, not wanting to say more.

"And we wouldn't have had last night," he said.

"What are you saying?"

"I'm saying I'm not sorry about last night."

"Not even if it cost you the merger…and Alicia?"

"No. I'm not sorry."

She took a deep breath. "That's saying a lot, then."

"But do you believe me?"

"It's too early to tell. But I'll keep you posted."

"Cici…"

"What?"

"Nothing. Eat your toast."

He flushed darkly as if he suddenly felt shy around her. She laughed. "Tongue-tied?"

"What's with the new, subdued look?" he asked. "The hair…brushed and tied back so neatly? The demure dress?"

"Maybe last night changed me, too. Although not as profoundly as you claim to be changed. But I'll be honest enough to admit that I was thinking about you when I bought this dress, thinking maybe I should try to tone my image down."

"Cici, I'm not asking you to change. You can even go with the Princess Leia look if you wish."

"Who said I was changing just to please you?"

"Nobody, but I do like the dress. Not that it matters."

Smiling, she set her empty coffee cup in the sink. "I guess I'll go out to the *garçonnière* now. Catch up on my beauty rest…"

"Would you like to go dancing first?" he asked. "Maybe at Rousseau's. That's not so far. And we wouldn't have to stay long."

He was smiling, and his eyes were sparkling. She was tired; she should be wary. But being wary was not in her nature.

"Maybe I wouldn't mind a little dancing," she said archly. "But only if we go in my car…and you let me drive…with the top down."

"I like a woman who likes to be in charge once in a while," he whispered.

"Well, don't you dare try to be a backseat driver."

His white teeth flashed as he put his arm around her and led her outside onto the gallery and then down to her Miata. Then he stopped and quickly wrote his grandfather a note telling him he'd found Cici and that they were driving to the well-known dance hall. After placing the note in the kitchen, they raced out to her car.

She put the top down and said, "Buckle your seat belt."

Once behind the wheel, she drove fast, maybe to scare him a little or maybe because that's the way she always drove. Not that he acted the least bit scared.

As the humid darkness flew by, he talked about how for years his life had been nothing but business. He told her that running Claiborne Energy was so challenging he often worked seventy-hour weeks, sometimes even more.

"I guess I thought I had to work like that because my father let Grandpère down, and maybe because Jake had walked out because of me. I think I thought I had a lot to make up for."

"Or maybe you were simply ambitious."

"Maybe."

Petrochemical plants along the river lit up the darkness from time to time, their smokestacks belching noxious fumes, but other stretches beside the levee were edged thickly with trees. They rushed past a stand of willows that streamed eerily in the breeze.

The moon was high and golden, but she paid it no attention. She was too busy watching the road and listening to him. When she saw the sign for Rousseau's, the wildly popular dance hall since the 1930s that was located on a tiny piece of sinking land beside the bayou, she pulled over.

"You were married," she said, after they found a picnic table on the plywood porch outside the dance hall, because his marriage interested her more than his work did. "Surely, even someone as ambitious as you didn't work all the time."

"But I did. I was never home."

"I'm sure she understood," Cici lied, hoping for more as she nibbled a cracker and watched a pair of elderly dancers through the windows as they slowly glided past them.

When Logan ordered beer and crawfish tails and andouille, a spicy, smoked sausage, she wondered how a man could eat so much and remain in such good shape.

"I guess I told myself she did…at the time," he said.

"I have to confess I've read about you and Noelle through the years. I poured over every glossy picture of you and her in front of your Italianate mansion in the Garden District I could find. Even when I was overseas I kept up on the Internet. I was still curious to know how the glamorous Claibornes lived. About how you lived."

"Magazine articles are as airbrushed as those photographs on their covers. They leave out a lot."

"Your life with Noelle sounded like a fairy tale," she said, turning the conversation back to what she was curious about.

"Yes. It was supposed to. We were much admired."

His deep voice sounded full of pain. "Image was important to me then."

"But no longer—after last night in my bed," she said.

"I think you've made that point before." His eyes met hers. "Don't sell yourself short. "Still, I've always had a knack for getting what I want, and back then, I was greedy for success." He hesitated. "But, be careful what you wish for, as they say. Even success can be dangerous."

She could tell him a thing or two about danger. Like tonight. What was she doing here with him? Listening to him? Believing him? Almost forgiving him?

She shifted on her seat. "So why did you come looking for me tonight?"

"You mean besides the fact that you are a sexual goddess."

She laughed.

"You are, you know?"

"Right."

"You're spectacular. And not just in bed." His hand reached across the table and folded hers inside his fingers, causing a trill of warm sensation to flood her.

"Cici, I received many calls today, thanking me for the wonderful party I threw my grandfather. Apparently, he had the time of his life all because of you. Thank you for making him so happy."

"I can't take all the credit. You paid for everything. You've been letting him come into the office."

"You showed me that I was neglecting him…just like I neglected Noelle. And he's actually proved himself useful at the office. He knows so much about the company's past, and he's very wise. Hopefully, because of you, I'll be more attentive to him in the future."

"Like having breakfast with him in the morning?"

"Like that."

She smiled. "He loves you so much."

"I love him, too. I owe him everything."

"Funny, how easy it is to forget those we love sometimes."

"Not so funny." He pressed her hand tightly and then brought it to his lips. He kissed her fingertips warmly. "I've run roughshod over the people I've loved," he whispered. "It's time I stopped."

"You know what they say about good intentions, Claiborne."

"If you can wear that demure blue dress, maybe I can change a feather or two of my plumage."

"It's not so easy, you know."

"You forget how determined I can be when I want something."

Their food and beer came, and he withdrew his hand. She ordered more crackers. For a while their food and drink proved so distracting, they didn't talk. Then he asked her to dance, and being held in his arms was even more distracting than chatting or holding hands or eating had been.

He pulled her close, his voice in her ear as they swirled faster than the elderly dancers. Tonight there was no one to stop them from dancing with each other as long as they liked, so they remained on the dance floor for nearly an hour. She was breathless when he led her back to their table.

"It's late, and I'm very tired," she said. "Would you drive me home?"

"You trust me to drive?"

"Yes, but that's all I trust you to do."

"For now," he said in a husky tone.

Nine

It was a balmy spring morning with water splashing in the nearby fountain and bees buzzing in the azalea blossoms.

Logan was being the perfect gentleman, not that he was to be trusted, Cici reminded herself. Still, she was enjoying his company as well as Pierre's way more than she wanted to as she sipped steaming chicory coffee and nibbled at her scrambled eggs and spicy Chaurice sausage on the wide veranda.

A swamp girl could get used to the high life. Yes, she felt totally at ease with them and their elegant sur-roundings as the old man proceeded to extract each detail concerning the failed merger from his grandson.

"This is a temporary setback," Pierre said. "A challenge. Mitchell will come around."

"I don't think so, and frankly…I'm not sure…" Logan's sudden grin revealed a flash of straight white teeth.

Underneath the tablecloth, his leg was nudging Cici's much too flirtatiously, causing her to gasp.

"You'll see. If you ask me, Mitchell was a bit too happy to sink the deal," Pierre murmured before turning to include Cici. "But we're boring you."

The warm heat of Logan's calf grazing hers had her blushing now.

"Not at all," she murmured, scooting further away from Logan.

Pierre patted her hand. "Nevertheless, I insist we talk about the wonderful party you gave me. I had the time of my life—seeing friends I hadn't seen in months."

"I'm glad," she said.

"Me, too," Logan agreed.

When breakfast was over, Logan walked her to the library before he had to leave for the city.

"You make him happy," he said. "I like that. Still, I'd like to be selfish and borrow you so I could enjoy you myself for a while. I do have a library in New Orleans, every bit as good as this one."

"I'd love to see it sometime," she murmured carelessly as she lifted a book off a table.

Gently he took the book from her and closed it. Setting it down, he said, "Why not today? Cici, I think we've wasted enough time…and all because I was such a fool."

"You were far worse than that."

"You're right. And I am sorry. And I know I'm probably rushing you, but like I said, I'm selfish. I'd really like for you to follow me back this morning. I lay awake all night thinking about this. We need to get to know each other better."

"I grew up here, remember. I've known you most of my life."

"I mean…know each other as adults. I have a huge house. You could stay in it…write in my library. I'd be away all day, but in the evening we could go out together. We could talk, dance… We could see where this thing between us is going."

"I don't think so. My uncle is here. I'm set up here…"

"Why not? Just for a day or two, then. What if I promise not to touch you?"

"That would be dull indeed."

"Don't tease me. What I'm suggesting is an old-fashioned courtship."

"Forgive me if I'm missing something, but I don't think old-fashioned courtships have ever consisted of young women who've already spent the night in a young man's arms moving in with him."

"Well, then it'll be an old-fashioned courtship with a modern twist. What do you say, Cici?"

"You probably think this is just the sort of proposition that would appeal to a swamp girl like me."

"I beg you not to tease me."

"That's harder than you think, you know."

"Will you come?"

"I shouldn't."

It was nearly noon when Cici followed Logan's Lexus up his narrow driveway in the Garden District. Looking up, she saw his double-galleried, three-story, Italianate mansion lit softly by golden sunshine filtering through the trees.

Grinning at her for gaping at his mansion, he got out of his Lexus and swung her car door open. "Well, what do you think?"

"Your city home is every bit as impressive and magical as Belle Rose."

"I hoped you'd like it. And, remember, I'm not bringing you here for sex."

"Oh, really?" she teased, lifting her eyebrows with a pretense of schoolteacher primness. "But would a man who clearly wants to impress a girl with his wealth turn it down if *she* offered it?"

"Such a girl shouldn't push her luck. Not with a man whose character has been less than perfect in the past. There are six bedrooms in this house. You can have any of them."

"Even yours?"

"That one, too. I repeat: your choice. But I thought maybe we should slow it down."

"What a shame." With a smile she followed him up the stairs onto the lower gallery of his fabulous mansion.

After a night of passion, he had come after her, saying he was a changed man. He had brought her here to his home, saying he wanted to formally court her. Nonsense...probably...even thought he did seem boyishly sincere.

His mansion was as formal and classical inside as the outside.

"Oh, how lovely it all is, but then I knew it would be," she said. "But then I already said that, didn't I?"

"My mother restored this home as well as Belle Rose. She had impeccable taste and spared no expense. It would have been a marvel simply to restore both houses, but, no, leave it to her to acquire original furniture, portraits, and then mix them with antiques she carefully chose."

"So, do you have time to give me a tour of this wonderful house before you go to the office?"

"All right. For starters, the house was built in 1860, right before the Civil War. I'm sure Noonoon told you that our family were royals who left France with nothing but the clothes on their backs and their jewels sewed into their pockets during the French revolution. Because of their title, their children married into the wealthier families in Louisiana. So, marrying well has always been part of the family culture."

"No wonder your grandfather didn't want a girl like me for one of his grandsons," Cici said.

"Times change. But back then our ambitious family

bought plantations with their jewels. By marrying well, too, they prospered. Then one of my most enchanting Creole ancestors, Francoise, married Able Claiborne, an extremely rich American, and he gave her this house for a wedding present."

"Lucky girl."

"What if I told you he kept the quadroon mistress he'd been in love with before his marriage?"

"Right. Back then a man could marry well and maintain the woman he really loved on the side."

"Sometimes. In any case, Francoise didn't get to enjoy her honeymoon here long. The Yankees occupied the house during the war. When she got it back, she was horrified to find her furniture burned for firewood and hoof prints from the Yankees' horses on the ballroom floor and stairs. Of course, now these very same hoof prints are much prized."

Cici laughed. "And I thought that was a cliché."

"It is."

He led her to the staircase and showed her the hoof marks. Then she looked up as he explained that the staircase coiled upward past large windows and double doors that opened onto a back piazza. The ceiling above the graceful stairs had magnificent plasterwork and a stained glass oculus in its center.

Once upstairs, he showed her all six bedrooms, the last and most splendid being his large master bedroom where an immense four-poster bed dwarfed the other furnishings.

"So, which bed will you choose as yours?" he asked, catching her off guard while she stared at his red satin spread.

Startled, she whirled. In the confined space of his bedroom, his height and wide shoulders made him seem huge. Or was it his teasing reckless grin that made her feel so vulnerable?

"Why…why…maybe that last one at the end of the hall," she said too quickly.

"The one that is as far from mine as possible?"

"Exactly! You did say you wanted an old-fashioned courtship."

His grin broadened.

She caught her breath.

"Relax. I'll bring your bags up before I go to the office. The kitchen downstairs is well stocked. If you need anything you can't find, anything at all, don't hesitate to call me." He pulled out a business card that contained all his phone numbers and circled his cell number. Then he leaned down and planted a chaste kiss on her cheek.

"You didn't show me the library," she whispered even as her heart drummed violently in reaction to his lips.

"Oh, that," he said, his breath warm against her skin.

"After all, it was your library that tempted me to accept your invitation."

"Not me?"

"No, definitely, it was your library."

"I warned you about teasing me," he murmured in a

husky undertone. "Now I really must prove you wrong." He caught her hand and pulled her nearer.

"What are you doing?"

"Taking you up on your challenge." Catching her shoulders he pulled her into his arms. She let out a little cry before his mouth came down on hers.

His kiss was so tenderly reverent, she imagined in its sweet heat promises he'd never made before, promises she didn't dare let herself believe. And suddenly all the joy she'd hoped to find in his loving her when she'd been a naive eighteen-year-old girl filled her heart anew, and she surrendered to his exploring tongue for a few delicious moments without the slightest reservation.

Her arms came around his neck, and she clung with far too much relish. But slowly sanity returned and she remembered that a woman her age had to be smart about wealthy, sophisticated men like him. Sucking in a sharp breath, she pushed against his chest.

Reluctantly he released her. "I'll get your bags." Then he turned, and she heard his footsteps loping down the stairs.

In his beautiful bedroom, she stared after him and longed for another taste of him, longed for all the things that had been rudely ripped from her when she was eight…and then ripped from her again by him later…love…security…family…the sense of belonging to someone, somewhere, forever.

Before she knew it, she heard him downstairs again, returning with her bags. The last thing she needed was for him to discover her in his bedroom so shaken from his kiss she was harboring all sorts of wildly romantic fantasies.

Determined to get to work and get her mind off him, she dashed down the stairs to explore his library while he carried her luggage up to her room.

Knowing that Cici was at his house and would be waiting for him, made it more difficult for Logan to concentrate than usual. He called her twice. When she said he was interrupting her, he called her back and then teased her for answering when she chided him again.

He hung up. Almost immediately he picked up the phone and called a florist to order flowers for her.

Five minutes later he was on the verge of calling her back when Hayes strode inside his office without knocking.

"Good news," Hayes said, his black eyes as sharp as his voice. "At least, it could be good for us. There's rather more to Mitchell Butler's asbestos problem than he led us to believe. Not only that, he's just lost that big government contract to build more patrol boats for the U.S. Coast Guard. He's carrying a boatload of foreign debt. I think he's in trouble with the Feds."

Hayes went to Logan's computer and pulled up a Web page.

"Wow, this is bad," Logan said. "He's been bilking the company like a bandit. Looks like you need to give him a call and make a new offer."

"What exactly do you have in mind?"

When Logan gave him a rock bottom number, Hayes let out a low whistle. "You certainly haven't lost your killer instinct. Yesterday you were so down…"

"Save the compliments. Just make the offer. See what he says. Then get back to me."

"Enjoying your crispy quail salad?" Logan said.

"Oh, my goodness, yes!" Setting her fork down, Cici glanced up at him. "Excuse me. Yes." She dabbed her lip with her napkin. "It's delicious."

"So delicious, you haven't said a word to me in at least five minutes. I never thought I'd be jealous of a quail salad."

She laughed. "Then order one for yourself."

"Did you get anything done on your book?"

"Your library was too fantastic. You might say I bogged down in my research."

Their restaurant was located in the heart of the French Quarter. He'd told her it was world famous, and she could see why. It's soft lighting, slow but attentive service and excellent food made for the most romantic dining experience, at least, when a girl wasn't gorging on her quail salad.

"I didn't mean for you to stop eating," he said. Then he frowned as he glanced to his right at a couple who'd just walked in and were being seated at a table against the far wall.

"Oh, no," he murmured when the brunette, who'd

been about to take her chair, saw him, stood up again and fled.

"Alicia?" Cici hadn't seen much of the woman other than her stricken expression and slim back, so she wasn't sure who it was.

"I'm afraid so."

Her companion, an older man with a tanned face and thick, silver hair, stood up and turned toward Logan. Instead of following his dinner companion, the man threw down his napkin and strode over to their table. When Logan thrust out his hand, the man stared at it so coldly, Logan let it fall to his side.

"Your CEO called me today, Claiborne."

"Sorry to hear about your recent…er…troubles," Logan said. "Still, you weren't completely honest."

"So, you're moving in for the kill." Mitchell's expression darkened as he turned vengefully to Cici. "I'd watch him, if I were you, young lady. He's not just some nice, tame guy who takes pretty girls to expensive restaurants. He eats people alive."

"That's uncalled for, Butler."

"Is it?"

"You were the one who lied. I'm merely exposing the lie and offering to bail you out." Logan pushed his chair back, but not before Mitchell had begun backing away from the table.

"Go to hell."

"If you're smart, you'll consider my offer." Logan turned back to Cici. "Sorry about that," he added. "I hope he didn't ruin your quail salad. He and I have some unfinished business. I'm afraid he wasn't entirely forthcoming about his shipyard. Or his other affairs."

"Nothing could spoil my salad," she whispered.

But strangely, as it turned out, she couldn't eat another bite. She kept remembering Alicia's stricken look and Mitchell's warning to her about Logan. Of course, the man was bitter about the merger and Logan's new offer, so his words could mean nothing. Still, it was nearly half an hour before she could resume her participation in the light banter they'd been enjoying before Mitchell Butler had so rudely interrupted them.

Who better than she should know that Logan was not a nice, tame guy?

He eats people alive.

Was that true? If so, did that still include the people he loved?

Ten

In silence Logan walked Cici up the stairs and down to her bedroom where they stood together in the long shadows sweeping the hall, holding hands.

"I'm sorry about Mitchell," Logan repeated, pressing her fingers.

She licked her lips. "You wanted me to come here so we could get to know one another better. You're a business man, and he's part of your world. Maybe it's for the best that I met him and realized some people see you as a hard, ambitious businessman."

"Maybe. But I would have preferred different circumstances for our first night out together."

"And what would they have been?"

"I was dining with you. I didn't feel like being surprised, at least, not by Mitchell. He's not a particularly nice guy." He paused. "Well, I guess I'll say good night."

When he leaned down to kiss her, she stood on her tiptoes, eager for his lips, surrendering the instant his mouth claimed hers. She wanted more than a goodnight kiss. Yes, what she wanted was to acquiesce to the passion she felt for him again, as she had that night in the *garçonnière*.

Still, she couldn't let herself fall under his spell. If it didn't work out, she would be getting in too deep, too fast again. He was right about the need to slow it down.

"It feels warm all of a sudden," he said.

Because of his kisses, heat blazed through her, too, and made her tremble.

He undid the ribbon in her hair, so that untidy masses of springy gold flowed silkily over her shoulders. A shiver rippled through her. Feeling herself on the brink of surrender, she caught her breath. Then, making a huge effort to behave wisely and heed Mitchell Butler's warning, she clenched her hands against her sides, and determined to fight the awakening desires in her body.

Their night together in the *garçonnière* had made her know too well, exactly how much she wanted him. When he hadn't called all day, she'd felt rejected all over again. How much trust could she place in him?

Reading her transparent face, he sighed and took a

long step backward. "Maybe Mitchell's right. Maybe you should doubt me," he said.

An acute feeling of empathy swept her. "I hope not."

"Sleep well, Cici. You'll find everything you need in your bedroom. Oversized T-shirts or regular nightgowns to sleep in…whatever you prefer…a new toothbrush. The bathroom's in the corner…"

"I know. You're very generous."

"I wouldn't argue that point with Mitchell."

She didn't smile at his attempt at humor.

She longed for another kiss, longed for it so much she feared it. Determined to be strong, she turned away, walked inside her room and shut her door.

As if a piece of wood between them could make her heart stop racing or her blood cool. She closed her eyes and leaned against the thick door for many minutes, counting backward from one hundred until she felt calmer. When she reached the number twenty, she padded over to the bed and pulled back the heavy covers, determining that tonight, as he'd promised, they would sleep apart.

Choosing a scarlet nightgown instead of a long white T-shirt, Cici showered and dressed for bed in Logan's perfectly-appointed, pink marble guest bathroom. As she slipped the cool, red silk gown over her shoulders and let it slide down her body, Cici couldn't help but wonder how many women Logan had brought here before her.

Turning away from the mirror she returned to her

bedroom. Had Alicia slept in this same room? Worn this nightgown?

Probably not. Feeling cherished, Alicia had no doubt lain naked in Logan's arms in the master bedroom.

Frowning, not wanting to dwell on Alicia, who'd run at the sight of Logan tonight, Cici climbed into her bed and squeezed her eyes shut.

No matter what Mitchell had said, she was here tonight, tucked between Logan's crisp, sweet-smelling sheets. He'd been sweet to her, attentive, protective even. He'd said he wanted to be with her. And not just for sex. But was he trustworthy?

Wanting desperately to believe him, she shut off her light. But the darkness made her feel strange and lonely in Logan's big, unfamiliar guest bed, and she couldn't stop thinking about him being at the end of the hall in his own big red bed. At the thought of his long, tanned body beneath his equally crisp sheets, the pulse in her throat began to jump erratically. Her skin started to burn, and soon she was so hot she threw off her covers. Was he as wide-awake as she was?

Slowly she arose from her bed. Stretching and then sighing, she walked restlessly to the door inside her bedroom that opened out onto the gallery. Stars lit the black sky. Maybe fresh air would make her relax and feel sleepy.

Pulling the drapes back and unlocking the door, she would have stepped outside, but a four-alarm siren began to scream through the house.

Putting her hands over her ears, she swallowed. She'd probably awakened everybody in the neighborhood. Not to mention, Logan.

In the next minute, the siren stopped, and Logan began knocking loudly on her hall door.

"Come in."

He stepped inside, holding a cordless phone. Clad only in a pair of black pajama bottoms, her heart sped up at the sight of his wide, dusky shoulders and cut abdomen.

"Are you all right?" he asked.

"I couldn't sleep," she said. "I'm sorry."

The phone rang, and he told his security company that a guest had opened a door but that everything was fine. He gave them his code and hung up.

"You can open your door now," he said. "I should have told you about the alarm. This is New Orleans. Our crime rate is not the best in the country."

"I know that, of course. I should have thought. But then since I camped out in so many war zones, I probably don't worry about crime the same way normal people do...even in New Orleans."

"Don't remind me of how you lived...because of my actions."

"Don't blame yourself entirely. I was an adult."

"You were a young, vulnerable woman, whose heart was broken."

"Don't…"

He said no more on the subject. When she stepped outside onto the gallery, he joined her. She slid into the moonlight while he kept in the deep shadows, his feral eyes gleaming in the dark as he watched her every movement.

"I couldn't sleep...for thinking about you," she admitted, her gaze drifting over his muscular brown chest and hard arms again.

A light breeze caused her silk gown to ripple and cling to her swollen nipples as well as to the lush curves of her hips and legs.

"Funny, I'm having the same problem," he said, his deep voice husky. "I shouldn't have followed you out here."

Her senses catapulted in alarm. Sexual chemistry seemed to ignite the air between them. To hide her nervousness she slid her hand back and forth along the slick black railing and laughed softly. "I forget. Why exactly are we sleeping apart tonight?"

"Old-fashioned courtship. So that I can prove I don't want you just for sex."

"Oh, right." *So, why were his warm, gleaming eyes glued so hungrily to her breasts?*

"Now we know why old-fashioned courtships didn't sanction sleepovers," she said. "Hey, maybe I've always been too open to risk. Maybe I don't have to know you're perfect and will treat me perfectly forever and ever."

"You're sure about that when I still don't know how I see this thing between us long-term," he said.

"Maybe I want to lie cuddled in your arms all night too much to resist sharing your bed."

He sighed. "I wouldn't say no. But then, be honest.

Ask yourself, once you're in my bed, do you really think you can trust me to stop at cuddling."

"Or me? I just said cuddling to make myself sound ladylike…and…er…demure."

His gaze seared her. Even though she felt his swift movement toward her through the darkness, she hissed in a breath when his big hands wrapped her close, his heat instantly warming every sensual cell in her body.

Fool. Fool.

She couldn't help herself. She felt small and feminine and very desirable in his arms. Like a marshmallow over a fire, she burned on the outside and turned to mush on the inside.

His lips eager, he kissed her brow, her mouth. When he finally let her go, her heart was thudding furiously in her throat, and her entire being was ablaze.

"Cici, I don't know what I felt nine years ago, but whatever it was, it damn sure knocked me off course. I'd been dating Noelle when I came down to Belle Rose to see Grandpère and Jake that summer. I'd even decided to marry her. Not that I'd asked her or that I was even seeing her exclusively. Still, I'd made up my mind."

"You were good at that. Stubborn to the core once you set your course."

"So, when I saw you in your pirogue that first day and realized you were all grown up, I never imagined that you and I could ever be seriously involved…even after Grandpère convinced me I had to save Jake from you." He broke off.

"I understand. There was no place for me in your life."

"I was slightly angry that you weren't that cute little bratty girl who followed me around in the swamp anymore, but there you were with the sunlight in your hair. A sex goddess of the swamp. Irresistible."

"Little girls do have a way of growing up."

"Yes. Do they ever. I couldn't take my eyes off you. When Grandpère convinced me to save Jake, I soon became so obsessed with you myself, I no longer knew what I was doing. Not that I could admit it."

Logan bent his head and kissed her softly. "After we made love, I was wild to have you again. And again. Then you told me you were in love with me, and I realized maybe I'd gone too far."

"Because I was naive."

"I…I was so determined to go out and conquer the world. My grandfather was convinced I had to have someone like Noelle at my side. He had my life all planned out. Since the family was in trouble, I went along with whatever he said. I didn't think I had the freedom to choose."

"And you had Noelle waiting in the wings."

"I was stupid where she was concerned. She was never more than an illusion. I should have behaved more responsibly toward both of you."

Logan was caressing her with both hands, slowly running his callused fingers down her arms and hips, causing her to shiver.

"Do we have to rehash all this…when it feel so good just to be together?"

"I want you to know how it was with me…and Noelle. I married her on the rebound. I was still crazy about you. Maybe I told myself in the beginning that I seduced you to keep Jake from having you, but that couldn't have been all there was to it. Because of my feelings for you, I was messed up for years, maybe until I saw you naked in the *garçonnière* and wanted you so fiercely. I never felt a tenth for her what I felt for you that day. I sure as hell never loved her. Looking back I see that I worked all the time, probably to avoid being home alone with her and having to face the truth. As I told you before, I'm afraid I neglected her and made her very unhappy. She told me how miserable I'd made her shortly before she died. She tried so hard to be a good wife, too. She was a lovely woman. She didn't deserve to be slighted any more than you did. I'll always regret how I treated her. Not that it fixes anything. She's dead. There's no going back."

"Why are you telling me all this?"

"Who knows? As a little girl, you looked at our big house and at us, and you built the Claibornes up into lordly beings we aren't."

"Like my book title, *Lords of the Bayou*."

"Exactly. I want you to know who we are, at least, who I am, warts and all. I don't want to lead you on."

"Don't worry. How could I have illusions about you after how you treated me? But you thought you were doing what was best for your family. It's in the past."

"I was blind."

"So was I."

"I'm so sorry."

Then she pressed a single fingertip against his mouth. "I don't care about the past," she whispered.

Logan began to caress her with both hands, causing her to shiver.

"You're so soft and feminine," he said. "So beautiful. So sweet. How could I have ever thought you couldn't suit me?"

"Maybe because you were too used to thinking of me as a child who was constantly out to get your attention by doing all those silly things…like stealing your hat or hiding your fishing lures."

"Back then you were a part of my life, like the air I breathed. I took you for granted."

And now? What did he feel now? She pulled free of his embrace and ran the length of the hall to his bedroom, knowing he would follow. Maybe she shouldn't make love to him with so many unanswered questions, but she couldn't seem to stop herself.

"From the moment I heard you'd come back to Belle Rose, I've been like a man possessed."

Something inside her she'd thought long dead had instantly taken her over from the moment she'd seen him at the *garçonnière*. Ever since she'd made love to him, she'd been consumed by her feelings for him. She wanted him. And not just for a casual affair. He felt essential in ways she couldn't fathom.

Inside his bedroom, she whispered a single word. "Condom?"

"Right," he muttered, his own voice as rough as hers. "Almost forgot."

After he led her to the bed, she was vaguely aware of him opening a drawer and shredding a foil wrapper. Then he was like a man possessed as he kissed her lips and throat and breasts before savagely tearing off his clothes as she flung her own off onto the floor.

Sheathed, he pulled her under him on the bed. Then he lowered himself over her and drove himself inside her soft, wet depths with a single thrust. On a blissful sigh she locked her legs around his hips and held on tight. Not that he remained still long.

Suddenly there seemed no softness or tenderness in him. But she didn't care as he drove into her again and again. Tonight she wanted it fast and hard. She wanted to be claimed, possessed and dominated. No matter what the future held, she wanted to feel that she was his, solely his, if only for tonight.

Their mating was fierce and violent. It was almost as if they'd each been afraid she thought afterward as she lay trembling and spent in his hard, warm arms. But afraid of what? Surely not Butler's warning at dinner.

Logan made love to her again and again that night, and every time her hips surged to meet his, their bodies locked in the perfect rhythm of an ancient dance. Always as he slid inside her depths, into the hot sleek perfection of her womanhood, she would writhe and cling as her own pleasure engulfed her. But each time her excitement held that strange, desperate quality, even as it built past anything she had ever known.

When it was over, she knew she had to tell him about their son.

Eleven

Underlined

"Logan?"

"What is it, darling?" he murmured drowsily.

She pulled free of his arms. At the thought of the little boy they'd lost, misery made her tremble. "You asked about my scar. It's from a Cesarean operation. The reason I called you in the fall after that summer we were lovers…was…was to tell you…that…that I, that I was pregnant…with your child."

His body went rigid. Then she felt him slide away from her, leaving her wrapped in coldness.

"Oh, my God… I never once thought of that," he muttered.

Her eyes filled with tears, so his shadowy form on

the other side of the bed became a merciful blur. "I know. And before I could…say anything you…"

"I cut you off by telling you that I'd married Noelle," he said in a low, dead voice. "Always the bastard…"

"No…"

"Damn it, yes! I am. I had to get you off the phone because just talking to you made me know how much I still wanted you. And I was married. Did I think of how I was hurting you? Did I?" Finally, he said, "Tell me everything."

"I was so devastated I didn't care if I lived or died," she admitted, her voice thick with remembered pain.

He was silent for a long time. When he finally spoke again, his low tone had a faraway quality. "How did you manage alone without my help?"

"I don't know." She lay back against her pillow and stared up at the dark ceiling. "Somehow I just got through the days, one at a time. I guess I took care of myself…because of our precious baby." She paused. "Even so, he only lived a day. That was the worst part."

"He?"

"We had a son. He had dark hair like yours. I loved him so much…more than anything. I named him Logan."

"Oh, my God! So, that's why you cried when I kissed your scar in the *garçonnière,* why you're crying now," he said, his voice still strange and distant. "He died, and you had to face all that alone. It must have been unbearable. I can't believe I was so horribly cold to you…even before the worst had happened."

"You didn't know."

"As if that excuses my behavior. What did you do next?"

"I buried our baby and my pain. I tried to forget him and you as well, by hiding behind my camera. For years, I preferred to be a witness to other people's pain."

"No wonder."

Something in his voice and manner filled her with new apprehension.

"Even though I was running from my own heartbreak, I wanted my pictures to scream victims' stories, maybe because my own pain was locked so tightly in my heart."

"You threw yourself in danger because of what I did to you and our son. You could have died, and I would never have known how deeply I had wronged you. I would never have known about our little boy. I would have gone on living my silly, stupid, self-serving life. Mitchell Butler is right about me."

He sounded so utterly stricken, she lifted her gaze to his and found his eyes cloudy with dark emotion.

"It wasn't *all* your fault," she said gently. "Maybe I should have been stronger. Or maybe I was too bold. I did sort of throw myself at you that summer."

"As many young girls do, who don't know the power of their sexuality and where it can lead. No, I was older. I should have faced the reality of what I did, of what happened…that I cared about you…*deeply.* I knew you loved me, and I was stupid and cruel and set on an idiotic course because of outdated ideas about duty and family. Damn." Guilt and shame filled his broken tone.

She leaned across the bed to touch him, to comfort him, but the moment her fingertips slid against the hot, hard flesh of his shoulder, he jerked away from her.

"No. I don't deserve you. Not after this."

"Logan, it was a long time ago."

"Do you think that matters?" he demanded icily. "I should have thought about the possibility of a baby. I should have listened when you called me. Cici, oh, God, Cici, I'll never forgive myself for making you go through that alone. I can't even begin to imagine how terrible it all must have been for you."

When he stood up and began to dress, her heart began to slam in slow, painful beats. "I didn't tell you about our son to make you unhappier or guiltier. I think I forgave you a long time ago. Tonight, I just wanted to share his short life and my love for him with you. That's all. I wanted you to know that we had this precious, darling son together."

"Well, I'm glad you told me," he said coldly. "Now I'm going out. I have to be alone."

"But Logan...I need you..."

"No, you don't. When have I ever satisfied any of your real needs? Tomorrow I think you should leave."

"What? You're sending me away?"

"It's for your own good."

"You're really serious?"

"Someday you'll thank me," he said savagely.

"No. I won't. Don't I have any rights in this relationship?"

"Like I said, you'll be better off!"

"But what if I don't see it that way? You have no right to make this decision for me."

"I have news for you. The decision has been made." He stalked toward the door.

"You're as high-handed and arrogant and hateful as you always were!" she shouted.

"Finally, you understand me as well as Mitchell Butler does—only he's got an advantage—because he's exactly like me. I eat people alive!" He opened the door, banged it shut and was gone.

She heard his footsteps slamming down the stairs. The front door opened and closed. She heard his car start. Then tires squealed down the drive.

After that, except for the pulse that knocked painfully in her throat, his empty house was silent and still.

Eight hours later the gray afternoon sky threatened rain as Logan knelt before Noelle's white marble, above-ground tomb in Lafayette Cemetery No. 1.

Carefully he laid a single red rose on the gleaming white step before the marble angel that bore a profound likeness to Noelle.

"I'm sorry I made you so unhappy," he whispered, hoping she could hear him. "I wanted to marry you so much. I was so sure I was doing the right thing. But I lied to you. And to myself. And I hurt you…just as much as I hurt Cici and our son. Just as much."

There was a low sigh, and he started. Looking up, he saw it was only the wind in the trees.

How could he have been so horribly wrong about everything when he'd been so sure he was right? He'd hurt so many people he'd thought he'd loved.

Last night when Cici had told him about their son, the pain in her voice had pierced his heart like a knife. If he'd helped her back then, maybe their son would be alive.

He'd driven around all morning, thinking about Cici and all that he'd put her through. He loved her, but after the torment he'd caused her, he knew he didn't deserve her.

He loved her. Maybe he'd always loved her. Too bad he hadn't known it until it was too late.

He had to let her go. For once in his life he wouldn't go after what he selfishly wanted, just because he wanted it.

He wasn't worthy of her. She was better off without him.

Slowly he arose, and as he walked out of the cemetery he thought of the bleak, empty years ahead and wondered how he would ever find the courage to face a future that didn't include Cici Bellefleur. Would he ever be able to live with what he'd done to her?

Cici was wearing dark glasses to hide her red eyes as she stepped out of the elevator on Logan's floor late that afternoon just as Mitchell Butler rushed from the offices of Claiborne Energy.

"You!" he snapped, bristling upon seeing her.

"Good afternoon," she whispered as she tried to move past him.

He grabbed her arm and then realizing he shouldn't have done so, dropped it. "If you're smart, young lady, you'll stay away from him. He's marrying my daughter, Alicia."

"What?"

"Don't say I didn't try to warn you last night. He's buying my shipyard and marrying my daughter—to seal the bargain, so to speak. So if you think he wants to have anything to do with you, you're crazy."

"If you think I'll take your word for that, Mr. Butler, you're the one who's crazy! I know you probably feel pretty desperate about the merger. You'd do or say anything…"

Hatred and wrath seemed to spew from his eyes even as his jaw went slack. Not wishing to prolong their unpleasant exchange, Cici ran past him into Mrs. Dilling's outer office.

"Is your boss here?" she asked, turning to see if Mr. Butler had followed her and feeling relieved when she saw he hadn't.

"Sorry," the woman said as she looked up from her computer.

"Where is he?"

"Do you have an appointment…Miss Bellefleur, is it?"

Cici nodded. "When...when do you expect him?"

"Not until next week. Do you wish to make an appointment?"

Without bothering to answer her, Cici walked to Logan's door and threw it open. Like his house, his office was empty and felt cold and dead without him in it.

"He'll be back next week," Mrs. Dillings said from behind her. "I'd be happy to schedule—"

"That won't be necessary," Cici said in a dull, defeated tone. "He's made it very clear he doesn't really want to see me."

The next morning an article in the *Times-Picayune* caused quite a stir over breakfast at Belle Rose as the early morning sun slanted across the emerald-green lawn and turned the columns of Belle Rose to pillars of gold.

"Mitchell Butler says right here that Claiborne Energy is buying Butler Shipyard and that Logan's marrying his daughter," Pierre said. "I thought you and he...I mean I thought that you went to New Orleans to be with Logan."

Cici didn't trust Butler, so she wasn't so sure that Mitchell's account was entirely accurate. Still, since what he said upset Pierre, her hands tensed as she tried to frame an answer.

"I'm afraid that's all over," she said. "I'm going on assignment to Egypt. A feature story about..."

"But you can't leave," Pierre said from his wicker chair on the gallery. "What about our tours? And your book? Our research? Our interviews? Logan?"

Wincing because he'd been so enthusiastic about helping her when she'd first arrived and now, because now at the thought of her leaving, he looked so small and lost, Cici gently set her tea cup down.

Leaning toward him, she patted his hand. Its coolness and thinness along with the slight tremor she detected frightened her a little.

"You know you can give the tours without me. And…my agent got that extension she promised me, so I can put the book off for a while."

"But I just set up an interview with Eugene Thibodeaux. And I told you how busy he is."

"I'm sorry, but I'm afraid I must ask you to cancel it."

"Because of Logan?"

"I do have a life of my own you know," she said.

Pierre's hands had begun to shake. The color had drained from his face. He looked too white, too thin, and very old.

Damn Mitchell Butler.

All lives, but especially those of the very young and the elderly are so fragile. Because of Butler, Pierre, who didn't need to be upset, was in real emotional pain.

"I'm truly sorry, Pierre," Cici said softly. "But I'm afraid this can't be helped."

Her uncle chose that moment to call her on her mobile and say he'd read the article.

"Not now," she whispered. "I'm trying to explain the situation to Pierre."

"As if anything needs explaining," he said. "Call me back when you get the chance." He hung up.

"It's my fault," Pierre said. "I was too imperious and intolerant back in the old days. And I insisted Logan follow suit. Together we've made you think you don't really belong and can never be happy here."

At the thought of losing the chance at happiness she'd longed for only yesterday, her voice caught. "You've made me happy while I've been here this time."

"Not happy enough apparently."

As he lifted his coffee cup, she wondered if Pierre had heard anything she'd said other than that she was leaving. His face was pinched and set, and he was squinting as he stared unseeingly into the sun in the direction of the swamp and her uncle's land beyond.

He'd adjust, just as she would. He just needed time. Anybody who'd lived as long as he had knew changes and losses were inevitable.

"I'll go and make an airplane reservation," she said.

He looked so ashen and lost as she arose, she wondered if she should call Logan and warn him she was worried about him. After all, he'd give her all his phone numbers.

No, he'd made it clear he couldn't deal with the past or his guilt or her.

She wouldn't talk to him; she would tell Noonoon to call him instead.

Twelve

Logan's bedroom television was blaring. Not that he was concentrating on it even though the story was about Mitchell's deluded lies. The man's empire was built on hype and debt. He'd gone off his rocker after Hayes had pitched Mitchell his offer.

Not that Logan was thinking about Mitchell. He'd asked Hayes to deal with Mitchell.

All Logan could think of was Cici. Did she believe Mitchell about Alicia? If she did, maybe it was for the best. She would hate him more and forget him sooner.

Logan's gaze drifted to his bed. In this room, on that bed, he'd made love to her for the last time, a mere twenty-four hours ago. He'd been the happiest man in the world until she'd told him about their son and he'd realized how utterly unforgivable his behavior to her had been. In some ways he was exactly like Mitchell Butler.

Noonoon had told Logan Cici would be leaving for Egypt soon. He regretted driving her away, and it saddened him he might not see her again for years. But it was for the best. How could he ever look at her again without remembering what he'd done?

She'd accused him of being high-handed and arrogant. Why couldn't she understand that unlike the last time he'd left her, he was leaving her for her own good this time?

When his phone rang, he was sprawled in his easy chair thinking about her because he was unable to focus on his business journal or the television. Thankful for any diversion, he grabbed the receiver.

"Mr. Pierre, he be gone," Noonoon said in a worried tone.

"What?" He grabbed his remote and punched Mute.

"I tried to get you earlier, only I got a message saying you had your phone turned off."

"Sorry about that. I've been doing some thinking. What about Grandpère?"

"Mr. Pierre, he been in bad mood ever since he read the paper and had breakfast with Miss Cici. She told him she would be going away. After that nobody could console him. Not even me. So, he be gone. Mr. Jake, he come as soon as I called him."

Why in the hell had he turned his phone off?

"Mr. Jake and Miss Cici and Mr. Bos, they be in the swamp in Mr. Bos's boat looking for him."

"I'll be there as fast as I can," Logan said. Slamming the phone down, he jumped to his feet.

Dressing hurriedly he tore out of his bedroom, down the stairs, taking them two at a time. Then he was outside his mansion, storming blindly to his Lexus.

A cool, cloaking mist was seeping up from the swamp, shrouding everything. There was no wind, no movement of any kind.

Cici felt cramped, hemmed in.

"Pierre?" she called, her heart hammering as the swirls of fog wiped out familiar landmarks.

She hated the damp this evening, hated the way everything was so still and gave off the dank odor of rotting vegetation. Uneasiness swept her. Pierre wasn't strong. She was no longer sure where she was on the plantation, so how could she possibly help Pierre? Would he venture this far into the swamp?

The last of the sunlight was almost gone, but, at least, the evening was still fairly warm. So, maybe he wouldn't be too cold despite the damp. Still, the thought of him walking in this mist, especially after it grew dark, filled her with dread.

Their search party had split up hours ago, so Cici was alone as she picked her way through the dense forest made up of blooming dogwood and tupelo gum as well as cypress and oak at the northern edge of the Claiborne property.

"Pierre?" Her voice sounded soft and fearful even to her own ears, muffled as it was by the mist.

Off to the right she heard a twig pop as if stepped on by a heavy boot, and she jumped.

"Pierre?" Her voice cracked. "Is that you?" Please, God, let it be Pierre.

There was a long silence. Then another twig broke, this one nearer than the first.

"Pierre!" she cried.

"No, it's me, Cici," Logan said, his voice deep and cold.

"Logan…" Relief swamped her.

She almost ran to him before she remembered he'd deliberately rejected her, just like he had before. Freezing, she stood her ground even though the mere sound of his hard, strained voice made her feel as if chains that had bound her heart ever since he'd walked out on her were falling away.

"Where are you?" she said.

"Stay where you are," he commanded. She heard crunching footsteps. Then he stepped out of the fog, but no joy of recognition or love lit his tense, blue eyes.

She drew a deep breath in an attempt to fortify herself.

"I'm sorry about Pierre," she whispered. "This is all my fault. He hasn't been the same since I told him I was leaving."

"I tried to call you."

"But my phone was turned off." His bleak eyes held

no light as he stared through her. "Like always. I'm never there when you need me."

She felt the final death of something in his low tone and couldn't bring herself to reply.

"We'll find him," Logan said but in a heavy, dull voice that didn't cheer her. "This isn't the first time he's pulled a stunt like this. He always just reappears, almost as if by magic, from his wanderings. Usually…he turns up…right before dark. I think the old fellow has a healthy respect for the dark, or maybe he's being considerate of us. He's not that far gone that he doesn't know exactly what he's doing."

"He wants his way, and I can't blame him."

"Still, it's one of the reasons I wanted to move him to New Orleans. His little disappearances always scare everybody half to death—me included."

She swallowed. "I'm sorry that I didn't consider this possibility. Noonoon had told me about the other times."

"When will you leave?"

"In a week."

"So, you have plenty of time to prepare and pack," he said indifferently. Then he turned. "Maybe we should head back to the house just to make sure he hasn't come home already. Like I said, he doesn't like being out after dark much."

Sure enough, everybody, including Pierre and Jake, was on the porch drinking hot tea and laughing when they returned.

"Can I pour you a cup, Mr. Logan, yes?" Noonoon

asked, a smile in her voice now that the crisis was over, and she saw Logan with Cici.

"I'm afraid I have to get back to New Orleans," Logan said curtly as he shook his head. Turning on his heel, he strode off into the darkness in the direction of his car.

Everybody began chattering anew, and Pierre seemed very happy to be home safely and to find himself the center of attention after his misadventure.

All Cici could hear were Logan's footsteps dying away on the gravel path.

"Stubborn, high-handed idiot," Jake muttered, slamming his teacup down. "Some things never change."

She'd told Jake about her misunderstanding with Logan earlier, and he'd told her that Butler had, at least, been lying when he'd said Logan intended to marry his daughter.

When she could no longer hear even Logan's footsteps, pain clogged her throat. He was still stubbornly set against her.

He'd said he was walking out on her for her sake, but to her it felt like history was repeating itself. He was leaving her, and she couldn't bear it. And he didn't care.

Jake leaned toward her. "What are you waiting for? It's obvious you're both miserable. Go after him. He loves you. He's always loved you."

"And you know this how? You've barely spoken these past nine years."

"I still know," he said. "He thinks he's protecting

you. He's hell on wheels when he's protecting one of us. I should be the one to know. Don't let him drive you away, the way I did."

As suddenly as she had when she'd been a child and had seen Logan disappearing into the woods or swamp, she gave a little cry and began to run after him, slowly at first and then more swiftly.

"Logan!"

He didn't answer.

"Logan, wait!"

His legs were longer than hers and he'd had a head start, so he had already reached his Lexus by the time she caught up to him.

"Logan. I love you. Don't leave me, or you'll hurt me more than anything you've ever done before. I love you and I'll be miserable forever if you walk out on me."

He was about to open his door, but when she said his name and then said she loved him in such a breathless rush, he paused.

"You couldn't possibly love me."

"Do you love me?"

"Yes. I love you."

"So, why are you hell-bent on breaking both our hearts?"

"I thought it was for the best."

"For whom? What gives you the right to always make decisions for both of us? Being a couple means you listen to each other and make a decision together that's best for the couple as a unit."

Suddenly she couldn't trust herself to go on. What if he remained dead set against her?

Biting her bottom lip, she felt like her life hung in the balance as she stood there, waiting, hoping that he would change his mind about their future.

"I do love you," he said. "So much…that what I did seems unforgivable."

"Love can forgive anything."

"Can it?"

"In this case. It's my heart. I should be the one to know."

"But I don't deserve you."

"Don't…say that ever again…" She went up to him and silenced his lips with a fingertip. "Kiss me," she said. "Hold me. These last few hours without you have been such hell."

"What about Egypt?"

"I was running away for your sake more than mine this time. Now…there's no reason to go…and every reason…I think…to stay."

"I love you. You do belong in my life. You've always belonged. I was just too blind to see it."

"And you were blinding yourself again to how much I love you and have always loved you."

"My love," he said.

"After I saw your ravaged face in that newspaper photograph after Noelle's death…from that moment I think I wanted to come home. You've suffered enough."

"Hopefully I've finally learned something in the process."

She smiled. "I'm sure of it." But in the next breath she was in his arms, clinging to him tightly, feeling renewed faith in tomorrow and in the day after tomorrow.

Tears of happiness and relief overflowed in her eyes. Once more the future was bright with shared dreams and goals and in the dazzle of all the mutually shared adventures they would have.

"I thought you deserved a better man than me," he said.

"And you always do what's best for those you love on your own, don't you?"

"I try. But this time I didn't know how I'd live without you. I really didn't."

"Me, either. It's scary to think that if Pierre hadn't disappeared, we were both so stubborn set on our path, we might have never had another chance together."

"So I owe him even more than I already did." He looked down at her, his face wide open, his blue eyes filled with love and yet with pain and fear too that he'd come so close to losing her again.

Logan bent his head and buried his face in her hair. She felt the warmth of his lips on her scalp as he wrapped his arms around her and hung on to her as if she meant everything to him.

"You're going to have to be careful about protecting the family from now on," she teased.

"So my best trait…is my worst trait."

"Only sometimes."

"Oh, Cici," he whispered. "My darling…"

"Logan," she murmured in a tone that was equally

passionate. "Logan, I've never been this happy, not even when we began, not even when you first said you loved me. I love you. I love you so much."

He caught her hand, laced his fingers through hers. "Then marry me," he whispered against her ear. "Tomorrow. Or at least as fast as possible. We've wasted way too much time already."

Instead of answering him with words, she reached up and kissed his lips which were hot and hard as they hungrily devoured hers, demanding everything and more that she had to give. Her heart was pounding as he crushed her closer.

Wrapping his arms around her, he began to lead her to the *garçonnière.*

"Shouldn't we tell everybody that we've made up?" she asked.

"All in good time," he said. "I've put you through hell again, so, first, I have to make it up to you."

Cici's warm body lay mashed beneath Logan's on the same bed in the *garçonnière* where they'd first made love. His manhood was deeply embedded inside her. This time he wore no condom because she'd said, "I want another child."

Spirals of her wiry gold hair fanned out on his pillow.

How he loved lying like this with her, body to body, the two of them locked together as if they were one being. He loved the softness of her skin, her velvet voice, her smell. In a lifetime, he would never get enough of her.

For as long as Logan could remember she was all he'd ever wanted; the wild hair, her dark eyes alight with sexual mischief, the slim voluptuous body and even the legs wrapped so tightly around his waist.

Her womb quivered, causing his heart to race even faster. What if she was already carrying his baby?

"Well, go on. What are you waiting for?" she teased in a low whisper.

"You didn't say whether or not you'd marry me."

"Oh, that," she said playfully even as her warm, sparkling eyes made more than enough promises to make his heart overflow with bright, shining hope.

"If I want your baby, marriage definitely goes with the territory."

Epilogue

Everybody from the bad news bikers with their tats and piercings from T-Bos's Bar to the richest and most elegant lords of the bayou in the county came to the Claiborne wedding ceremony which was held at Belle Rose under a big white tent set up at the edge of the swamp. Alicia clung to Jake's arm and watched an unsmiling Bos give his niece, Cici, away to the grandson of his ancient enemy.

Hayes Daniels was the best man, and Noonoon was the matron of honor.

Maybe the guests all came because nobody believed Logan Claiborne would really stand up to his side of the bargain and marry Cici Bellefleur.

But marry her he did, and with such a hot look on his tanned face that every man there knew the groom couldn't wait for the formalities to be over and for his honeymoon to begin.

No, nobody, not even Pierre missed the love and passion in the bride and groom's eyes when the wedding march began in earnest.

Nor did anybody fail to note that the brightly smiling Cici, with demure white roses in her hair, wore a shockingly short white mini skirt and five-inch stilettos as she joined Logan at the altar. What kind of wife would she make such a man, some wondered.

Then the ceremony was over far too quickly, and the groom kissed his bride far too long and much too passionately, because the rest of the world, even his wedding guests, had ceased to exist and did not matter to him at all.

2 FREE BOOKS
AND A SURPRISE GIFT

We would like to take this opportunity to thank you for reading this Mills & Boon® book by offering you the chance to take TWO more specially selected books from the Desire™ 2-in-1 series absolutely FREE! We're also making this offer to introduce you to the benefits of the Mills & Boon® Book Club™—

- **FREE home delivery**
- **FREE gifts and competitions**
- **FREE monthly Newsletter**
- **Exclusive Mills & Boon Book Club offers**
- **Books available before they're in the shops**

Accepting these FREE books and gift places you under no obligation to buy, you may cancel at any time, even after receiving your free books. Simply complete your details below and return the entire page to the address below. You don't even need a stamp!

YES Please send me 2 free Desire stories in a 2-in-1 volume and a surprise gift. I understand that unless you hear from me, I will receive 2 superb new 2-in-1 books every month for just £5.25 each, postage and packing free. I am under no obligation to purchase any books and may cancel my subscription at any time. The free books and gift will be mine to keep in any case.

Ms/Mrs/Miss/Mr _____ Initials _____

Surname _____

Address _____

_____

_____ Postcode _____

E-mail_____

Send this whole page to: Mills & Boon Book Club, Free Book Offer, FREEPOST NAT 10298, Richmond, TW9 1BR